PLAYED

The Games of the 1936 Berlin Olympics

A Novel

Glenn Allen • Richard Kaufman

WordServe Publishing
Denver, Colorado

WordServe Publishing
An Imprint of Valor Press
A division of WordServe Literary Group
700 Colorado Blvd. #318
Denver, CO 80206
admin@wordserveliterary.com

Cover Design: Kiryl Lysenka

Interior Book Design: Greg Johnson

ISBN: 978-1-7331707-5-8

First Printing, January 2024

Printed in the United States of America

Dedications

Richard Kaufman
to The Kaufman's, The Pohly's, and The Esberg's,
who suffered under the horrors of the Nazi regime,
yet persevered to keep our families strong.

Glenn Allen
to my team, Diane, Glenn, James, Ashley, and Roberta,
and to Mom, who first inspired me to be a writer.

To The Reader

"Would the Holocaust have happened had the US boycotted the 1936 Berlin Olympics?"

It's a question that can't be answered . . . but it's fair to ask it. Of course, we can't go back in time and change history insomuch as we can change the outcome of a sporting event. But we're obligated to study history because it teaches us how to move forward. At least we hope it does.

The world witnessed the horrors of the 1972 Olympic Games in Munich. Decades later, a bribery case scandalized the International Olympic Committee (IOC) during the 2002 Winter Olympics in Salt Lake City. Just months before the opening ceremony of the 2014 Sochi Olympics, Russian President Vladimir Putin signed what became known as the "gay propaganda law." Scandals like these are not always relegated to Olympic Games, but they are magnified by the mystique of the Olympic "ideals."

Sports and politics (two of our country's favorite topics) often converge to teach us lessons. We've been researching and uncovering these incredible stories of everyone involved in the 1936 Berlin Olympics for over twenty-five years, to tell the *complete* story of these Games. And by doing this, one can see how truly great the achievements of the athletes were.

This, in turn, becomes part of an even bigger story, that of WWII and the Holocaust. To this day, people wonder, how could this have happened? Others say, "something like that could never happen today!" To the reader, we ask, is it so impossible? To quote the philosopher George Santayana, "Those who cannot remember the past are condemned to repeat it."

This is our fictionalized account of the insanity and hysteria that ensued in Germany, the US, and all around the world from 1931-1936.

-Rick and Glenn

The Players

Americans

The Politicians:

Avery Brundage, *Head of the American Olympic Committee (AOC)*
Ernest Jahncke, *International Olympic Committee (IOC) Member*
Judge Jeremiah Mahoney, *President, Amateur Athletic Union (AAU)*
William Dodd, *US Ambassador to Germany*
Mattie Dodd, *his wife*
Martha Dodd, *their daughter*
Bill Dodd Jr., *their son*
Mildred Fish Harnack, *educator, spy*
Franklin D. Roosevelt, *N.Y. Governor, US President*

The Athletes:

Jesse Owens, *100m, 200m, long jump, 4x100 relay*
Archie Williams, *400 meters*
Marty Glickman, *4x100 relay*
Ralph Metcalfe, *200m, 4x100 relay*
Louis Zamperini, *5,000 meters*
Foy Draper, *4x100 relay*
John Woodruff, *800 meters*
Sam Stoller, *4x100 relay*
Mack Robinson, *200 meters*
Frank Wycoff, *4x100 relay*
Glenn Morris, *decathlon*
Eleanor Holm, *swimmer*
Marjorie Gestring, *diver*
Katherine Rawls, *diver*
Dorothy Poynton-Hill, *diver*

Bob Moch, *rowing*
Don Hume, *rowing*

The Press:

Alan Gould, *Associated Press (AP) Sports Editor*
John Kieran, *N.Y. Times Reporter*

Germans

The Politicians:

Adolf Hitler, *Chancellor of Germany*
Joseph Goebbels, *Propaganda Minister*
Hermann Goering, *Head of the Luftwaffe*
Rudi Diels, *Head of the Gestapo*
Hans von Tschammer und Osten, *Reichssportsfuhrer*
Karl Ritter von Halt, *German IOC Representative*
Carl Diem, *German IOC Representative*
Theodor Lewald, *German IOC Representative*
Captain Wolfgang Fürstner, *Deputy Kommandant, Olympic Village*
Eva Braun, *Hitler's mistress*
Putzi Hanfstaengl, *Hitler's right-hand man*

The Athletes:

Luz Long, *long jump*
Gretel Bergmann, *high jump*
Dora Ratjen, *high jump*
Helene Mayer, *fencing*

<u>The Press:</u>

Leni Riefenstahl, *Director of "Olympia"*
Hans Ertl, *her cinematographer*

Introduction

*"The Olympic Games help connect countries
in the spirit of peace."
-Adolf Hitler, 1936*

On *Flatow Allee Straße*, German citizens stood shoulder-to-shoulder, one hundred deep, waving little Nazi flags in the air, chanting and cheering. Nazi soldiers, neatly uniformed, stood on every street corner. Towering over the throng of Germans were government buildings covered with humungous banners bearing swastikas. It was a sea of red, white, and black.

The most excited people among them were the young and the middle-aged. There were very few elderlies, and those who were there participated with less enthusiasm. But this wasn't their Germany. This was the new Germany.

Suddenly, the crowd started to notice something down the street. Children squeezed through their parents' legs to get a better look. It was a wave of outstretched necks, and people jostling to get a better position. Some were pointing as the cheering got louder, more excited. And then it came.

A blond-haired, blue-eyed young man adorned in a modified Greek toga, complete with a crown made of twigs and fig leaves jogged steadily through the streets of Berlin carrying a ceremonial torch. The flames rose and fell with each step of the runner. As he ran past the adoring crowd, they cheered him on, yelling epithets for their beloved Germany. The runner endowed every embodiment of the Aryan race--a perfect specimen of the Third Reich.

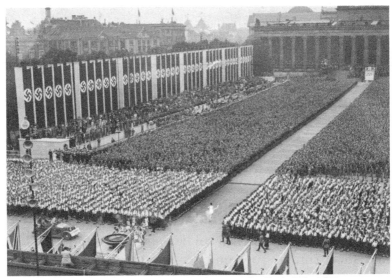

The inaugural Olympic torch run enters Berlin in July 1936.

Some of the crowd stood out more than others. They were not waving Nazi flags or cheering or chanting. They were Germany's Jews who had come to see the spectacle, but there was a serious tone about them. They were less interested with the runner than they were with the nationalistic tone of the crowd that surrounded them. As the chanting grew more fevered, they disappeared away from the masses.

The largest crowds were assembled near the entrance of the Romanesque *Olympiastadion.* It was a colossal construct decorated with flags of every participating country, although the Nazi flags were, by far, the largest, and flew the highest. This was a crowning achievement for the increasingly wealthy German government. An enormous zeppelin flew overhead, bearing a large swastika on its tail.

At the far entrance of the stadium, Adolf Hitler, Josef Goebbels, and Olympic organizers, along with a few of Hitler's main generals and bodyguards, got in position to enter the festivities. Eva Braun, Hitler's lover, was forced to stand behind him (and everyone else, much to her dismay) and was accompanied by two young German girls dressed in Bavarian outfits. When the time came for the group to enter the field, Hitler walked forward with great pride. The crowd went insane as their beloved leader strode toward a young girl walking toward him carrying flowers. He smiled as 100,000 plus people chanted *"Heil Hitler."* He leaned down and accepted the flowers and a brief hug, and then continued his way to his seat with Goebbels close behind him.

AOC President Avery Brundage was already at his seat waiting for his German friends in Hitler's box. He felt so proud this day had finally arrived and he had personally guided the US team here over such adversity. When the entourage finally arrived, Brundage shook the hands of all the German Olympic organizers, and then was introduced to Hitler and an extremely unimpressed Goebbels. But Brundage didn't notice the Propaganda Minister's disgust; he was meeting the greatest leader of the times. Hitler was to Brundage a modern-day Caesar, a leader who had guided his country from the brink of devastation to a modern, thriving, and global powerhouse. He shivered at the man's mere presence.

"Not too shabby, huh Avery?" one of the organizers said to him.

"Not too shabby at all," Brundage replied, looking around the stadium and up at the Hindenburg floating overhead.

Moments later, on the field, the famous composer Richard Strauss raised his hands and cued up the Berlin Philharmonic Orchestra and a chorus of one thousand singers all dressed in white. They commenced with Strauss' *Olympische Hymne*, written especially for these Games. From the Press Box, Associated Press Editor in Chief, Alan Gould, and his friend New York Times correspondent, John Kieran, took it all in. The music filled the stadium, and every German spectator beamed with pride. Gould was a bit intimidated by all the glory for Hitler, but once the "parade of nations" began, it was all he or anyone else could keep their eyes on.

The Greek team entered first, commemorating the birthplace of the original Olympics. They all saluted Hitler with their arms outstretched as they passed his box in the center of the stadium. He proudly returned the salute. The teams followed in alphabetical order, each donning a unique uniform; *Afghanistan, Argentina, Australia, Austria, Belgium . . .*

From a tunnel near the entrance to the field, the American team watched as each country's athletes gave the Nazi salute to Hitler. In another show of subservience, the flag bearers at the head of each team lowered their flags in deference to Germany. The Americans couldn't believe it.

Egypt, Finland, France . . .

Gould watched as famous German filmmaker; Leni Riefenstahl leaned on her cameraman's shoulder. Their cameras spun relentlessly, capturing everything from multiple positions around the stadium. The cheering crowd, the music, the flags, the *Hindenburg* flying overhead--it was all very cinematic.

Poland, Sweden, Switzerland . . .

Next it was the United States' turn. As they passed Hitler's box, the athletes did not give him the Nazi salute. Instead, they held their hands over their hearts with flagrant disobedience. Hitler's eyes narrowed as he tried to maintain a dignified posture. What made things worse for him was that the American flag was not lowered--instead it was raised proudly, even a little bit higher than when they entered the stadium. This brought a smile to both Gould and Kieran.

Finally, the German team entered the stadium last as the host of the Games, and the crowd resumed cheering wildly as they saluted their Führer. After all the fifty-three nations settled into their places in the center of the stadium, Strauss conducted his orchestra, and they held a single, sustained note. The crowd stood in anticipation.

A bell rang and the orchestra launched into its Olympic Hymn as the torch-wielding runner burst through the opening gates and entered the arena. The 100-thousand spectators erupted in applause. He circled the track towards the far end of the stadium and climbed a canopy of stairs to a giant raised cylinder, which was the Olympic torch. He reached up and tipped his torch into it to ignite it, sending the crowd into a frenzy. In unison, they gave the Nazi salute with a hearty *"Heil Hitler."*

PRELUDE
1931

Inside a quaint bakery in the heart of Berlin, workers were frantically carrying trays loaded with loaves of bread toward the store's entrance. Outside, hundreds of people waited for the next batch to be handed out.

"Sir, they're threatening to smash the windows down with stones if we don't hand over the reserve bread!" the nervous steward said to the owner of the bakery.

The owner shot back, "The Republic only paid for two hundred loaves! No more!"

"But there's 500 hungry women out there! Maybe more. And they're not just hungry, they're angry."

"*I'm* angry!" Just then a rock came smashing through the window sending shards of glass everywhere. The owner raced to the gaping hole in the window, but before he could utter a word, another rock flew through the hole and hit him in the neck. It had a razor-sharp edge, and blood began squirting from his Adam's apple.

"Boss!" the steward screamed, as the owner fell to the ground clutching his neck, blood oozing between his fingers.

Outside the shop, roughly 700 women were rioting in the streets. Stones were flying in every direction, stores were being looted, a male passerby was assaulted.

It was mayhem in the streets of Berlin.

That was, until the popping of gunfire echoed loudly amongst the crowd. A handful of German police officers were racing onto the scene firing their pistols in the air. One officer, fearing for his own life, aimed into the crowd and fired. His bullet found purchase--in the eye socket of a thirty-year-old woman.

Clutching her face with both hands, unable to see, she stumbled into the arms of another young woman. She too fell victim to the police when a bullet exploded between her eyes. They both crumbled to the curb--a chilling sight to the other women who witnessed it as they ran for cover.

On a side street approaching the riot, two men, both carrying luggage and dressed in neat business suits, walked hurriedly toward the fracas. THEODOR LEWALD, in his sixties, and his protégé, CARL DIEM, thirties, turned the corner and stood frozen in shock at the scene.

"The Weimar sponsored this to calm the people!" said Lewald.

"It didn't work!" Diem responded and looked around, "Over loaves of bread! This is madness!"

"Keep moving!" Lewald yelled.

Theodor Lewald and Carl Diem were the Heads of the German Olympic Committee, although Lewald clearly was the mentor and held seniority, obvious by his demeanor, not to mention the graying hair near his temples. And Carl Diem didn't mind. In fact, he appreciated and respected Lewald, and was honored to be the heir to his friend's post.

They maneuvered through the panicked crowd, bumping and jostling past women who were running for their lives. Up ahead was the Berlin Train Station, and they picked up their pace, leaving the crowd behind them. As they neared the track, Lewald waved his tickets at the stationmaster, who yelled, "Last call for the express to Barcelona!"

Lewald and Diem crashed through the turnstiles and sprinted down the platform with their suitcases. The train whistle was deafening. The steam engine began puffing as they jumped onto a rail car.

The train began its departure and they stumbled into a coach cabin, sweating and out of breath. They found an empty compartment where Lewald stowed their suitcases. Both collapsed onto a bench across from one another and smiled. Diem took a deep breath and leaned over to pull the window's curtain aside. What they saw turned their victory of making the train into a stark return to reality: beggars with outstretched arms were swarming them as they exited the station. Beyond them were poor homeless citizens digging for food out of garbage dumpsters. Children were running in and out of dilapidated buildings.

Diem turned to his friend Lewald. "Is Germany even prepared for an Olympics?"

"Of course," Lewald replied. "Clearly we need the revenue. Who else are they going to give it to? Spain can't even choose a government let alone plan an Olympic Games."

"And the Weimar is any better?" Diem pointed out the window. "Look around, Theodor. If the Nazis take control-- pardon me, *when* the Nazis take control, will they even care about the 1936 Olympics? The Bohemian Corporal doesn't seem like much of a sports fanatic."

Lewald looked at him earnestly. "Carl, we can't worry about the future." He reached into his coat pocket and produced a silver flask. He opened it, took a swig and offered it to Diem, who gladly accepted, before saying, "To Barcelona."

"To Barcelona."

The train gained speed as it snaked through the city. Beyond the billowing smoke of the steam engine sat a sad version of Berlin; the capital city of a country mired in a deep depression.

Theodor Lewald and Carl Diem stared out the window, both knowing that Germany needed a catalyst for change. But neither of them could ever imagine how important this train ride would be to Germany and the Third Reich.

*   *   *

In the main meeting hall, International Olympic Committee (IOC) President, HENRI BAILLET-LATOUR, sat calmly in the center of a raised rostrum surrounded by other IOC officials from various countries. Facing them were the representatives of the National Olympic Committees; each identified by its country's flag. Every member wore a headset that was linked to language interpreters so that they were all in full understanding of the day's unfolding event - the voting and announcement of which country would host the 1936 Olympics.

Sitting behind the American flag was the grizzled Assistant Secretary of the Navy, ERNEST LEE JAHNCKE. He was the United States IOC representative, and by looking at him one knew that he took his post very seriously. Jahncke looked down at his ballot card. At the top it read "1936 Olympic Games" with two countries below in bold: **BARCELONA** and **BERLIN**. With his pen, he scribbled a check next to Barcelona, folded his ballot, and placed his secret vote in the concealed ballot box.

Outside the hall in a nearby anteroom, Carl Diem paced nervously. "What's taking them? Isn't Berlin the obvious choice?"

Theodor Lewald, sitting on a bench at the other end of the room, calmly checked his watch. He looked at Diem and smiled. "I've been waiting for this moment since 1916."

At that moment, a man burst into the room. "The voting has been completed!"

Lewald got up from the bench, adjusted his suit jacket, and stepped in front of Diem, who was about to run into the main hall. "You ready?"

"I think I'm going to piss myself." Diem said.

Inside the meeting hall, Diem and Lewald found their way to their places next to the two Barcelona representatives. At the front of the hall, President Latour adjusted his microphone.

"Gentlemen, the vote of the 29th session of the IOC, the allocation of the Eleventh Olympiad, goes as follows: 16 votes for

Barcelona, Spain and 43 votes for Berlin, Germany."

With the announcement, Diem bear-hugged Lewald, who gave a sigh of relief as Latour continued, "Representatives of Germany, you have the right of priority under Article Six of the Olympic Charter to choose a location for the Winter Games to be held in the same calendar year as the Berlin Summer Games, or pass."

As Lewald began to walk toward the microphone, Diem, like an overexcited child on Christmas Day, barreled him over and grabbed the microphone. "We choose to select the Bavarian village of Garmisch-Partenkirchen to host the Winter Games, Monsieur Latour."

"And so it is done," Latour replied. "Let us welcome back into the Olympic fold our friends from Germany after too long an absence. May this be the beginning of a renewed global spirit of peace and goodwill."

The crowd of international representatives stood and applauded. Carl Diem and Theodor Lewald stood gleaming. It was a great victory for Germany, and a personal victory for both of them.

On the opposite side of the room, United States IOC representative Ernest Lee Jahncke gave a courteous, but callous, applause.

*   *   *

The office of AP Sports Editor, ALAN GOULD, was dense with cigar and cigarette smoke as he and his intrepid band of reporters deliberated over the 1931 AP Sports Man and Woman of the Year. Square-jawed and almost always bow-tied, Gould, who originated the awards, had his men throw pictures of their candidates on his desk as he listened to their pitches and smoked his cheap cigar.

"I think King Vidor should get it. 'The Champ' was a perfect sports film," said golf reporter Joey Glenn.

"Are you drunk?" Gould inquired.

"It was a good boxing film, Boss" pugilist reporter Baker chimed in.

"Someone say something with some sense, please," Gould pleaded. Baker redeemed himself when he threw swimmer Helene Madison's picture down. The men were unanimous with their approval. She had dominated the woman's circuit and was destined to sweep her races in the upcoming Los Angeles Olympics. Sports*man*, however, remained a daunting choice. Gould stressed it wasn't just about the numbers, but what the athlete brought to his team or sport. Knute Rockne, who had just perished in a plane crash, was the sentimental choice. Gehrig, Schmeling . . . all worthy candidates as well, but Gould was not impressed.

It was Tank, baseball reporter extraordinaire, that nailed it down. "Pepper Martin, The Wild Horse of the Osage, hit .300 during the season and was impossible to get out during the Series. He batted .500 with twelve hits, including four doubles and a homer."

Gould interjected, "It's not just about the num--"

Tank interrupted, "But above all, he was the team's catalyst all year. And on a team of superstars, Martin single-handedly led the Cardinals to a Series crown, and all in his rookie season." Gould was pleased. That was the angle he was looking for and always had--an athlete that could rise above the rest.

Gould was a Philly boy raised in Western New York who loved all kinds of sports. He was not as big as his athletic classmates, so he didn't play, but he wrote about it in the school newspapers. His keen eye, dry humor, and passion showed, even at an early age, his capacity to evaluate talent and write with maturity. His hunger and grasp of sports journalism was so intense during his high school years, that newspaper magnate Frank Gannett hired him before he even graduated. This was the beginning of a life-long commitment.

By the time he got to the AP sports desk in 1922 at the tender age of 24, he was being groomed as the great Walter Camp's replacement for Executive Sports Editor. And three years later, when Camp died suddenly in his sleep at 65, that is exactly what happened. At 27, Alan Gould had become one of the most important men in American sports journalism. And he wasted no time making the job his own. He created the College Football AP All-America Team, which unlike Camp's more subjective poll, which barely recognized any West Coast Colleges or their players, was a combination of views from 100 coaches and 100 critics from around the country. Gould understood inclusion was a necessity for sports to thrive, and that included the press. He got to know as many American athletes personally as possible, which kept him working all the time.

Alan Gould (left), AP Sports Editor, sits in his NYC office with Mississippi State Football Coach, Major Ralph Sasse, in 1935.

His wedding and the birth of his two children were the only days he had taken off since becoming Editor, and the latter, only because his wife Mary would've killed him. His high school sweetheart and subsequent bride, Mary Denton, kept him grounded and humble. She was the only woman he had ever loved, and she was quick not to let him forget it. Her brutal honesty, rapid-fire wit, and good looks were sharp and kept him on his toes, and along with the kids, who were just as keen as both their parents, transforming into a family man had made him a more honest, patient, humble, and judicious journalist. And Alan Gould was at the top of his game. The only thing that eluded him was a Pulitzer, but that was more of a joke amongst him and his colleagues than an actual desire.

He reminded his gang of colorful correspondents that 1932 was going to be a big year for sports, including an American Winter and Summer Olympics. Though he wasn't quite sure how American Olympic Committee President Avery Brundage was going to pull them off during a Depression, Gould did know Brundage well enough to realize the man would do just about anything to get his way.

*   *   *

In another part of Manhattan, AVERY BRUNDAGE walked the hallways of the American Olympic offices. Mid-forties and muscular with a silvery, balding scalp, Brundage walked with a vigorous gait. By the way he whizzed past the neat rows of action photos from Olympic Games past, one could say he resembled the athletes that hung from the walls. In fact, he was one of them. Brundage competed in the pentathlon and decathlon in the Stockholm Olympic Games of 1912. Once a promising amateur champion, he competed well but was overshadowed in every event by the legendary Jim Thorpe. He never won an Olympic medal. While Thorpe went on to play professional baseball, Avery turned his attention to handball. Forever an athlete, at age forty-three he routinely beat the US national champion, Angelo Trulio.

Avery Brundage was a wealthy man from his construction business and vast collection of art. He never accepted a single dollar for his involvement in sports administration. But he was a tenacious competitor and his Olympic failures gnawed at his soul.

Avery Brundage (middle), Head of the AOC, shakes hands with Judge Jeremiah Mahoney, Head of the AAU, his main adversary in the vote on whether or not the US attends the 1936 Berlin Games.

Aside from taking out his frustrations on the handball court, he took them out on his secretary, MARGARET. In her late thirties, Margaret was a wiry, pretty brunette clinging to her prime and always clinging to Avery's hip. She hugged a stack of newspapers and struggled to keep pace.

Avery spoke to her as if she were invisible. "I have sponsors and countries backing out of the Summer Games like explosive diarrhea and all the IOC keeps harping on is how the transportation problems at Lake Placid are going."

Margaret assured him they were going terribly. She had pleaded with Governor Roosevelt for assistance to no avail. Roosevelt believed in the American tradition of politics not interfering with the Olympics. She had also reached out to local businesses and the rest of the small skiing community for aid, but the response was slow.

This incensed Brundage to no end. New York would reap the financial benefits brought in by the international tourists, but the state wouldn't lift a finger for development or management. And Roosevelt's attitude was putting the much larger Summer Los Angeles Games in jeopardy, which would then put the sponsors for Berlin in 1936 in jeopardy, and this, Brundage could not, and would not have.

He told Margaret to book two tickets to Lake Placid so they could see firsthand what everyone was "bitching" about. He would also appeal to Roosevelt himself. "Maybe if I ask him to open the Games with a speech, he'll see it as a good campaign opportunity and remember the American team in thirty-six when we go to Berlin after he's elected . . ." he paused and held back a mock puke, ". . . the fucking President."

Margaret turned her head as she sashayed away toward her desk, "The Republican era is dead, Avery. Hoover and his cronies made sure of that."

PART I

RETURN TO GLORY

1932

DODD

It was an unusually warm January afternoon as Professor WILLIAM DODD, a tall, lean man in his early sixties, walked towards the famous D.C. landmark. Otherwise known as the "Grande Dame of Washington," the enormous Mayflower Hotel was a sight to behold, and as he approached it, Dodd was consumed with the thought of how such an establishment could look so magnificent from the outside but be completely broken down on the inside--the Mayflower had declared bankruptcy just a few months earlier, amidst fraud charges against its owners, American Bond & Mortgage.

The irony was not lost on him.

He centered his thoughts on the task at hand and entered the lobby with some trepidation. He had just taken a much-needed sabbatical from his professorship at the University of Chicago. He also desperately wanted to work on, and hopefully finish, his book about America's Deep South. But Franklin Delano Roosevelt, the New York Governor, Presidential candidate, and most likely soon to be President-elect, had summoned him to the swamp on the Potomac, so Dodd caught the first train out of Chicago.

He was escorted to a private garden in the back of the hotel where Roosevelt's right-hand man, Louis Howe, stood waiting, lighting one cigarette with another. Howe crushed the dying butt out with his shoe and extended his hand, "Bill, it's damned good of you to come on such short notice." Dodd smiled and shook the shorter man's hand.

"My curiosity demanded it," Dodd said.

The two men strolled through the snow-covered garden and Howe got right to the point. He told Dodd that Roosevelt, when elected, wanted to offer him the position of Ambassador to Germany. This was not such a wild notion; Dodd had written

Thomas Jefferson's biography in German, and it had become wildly popular when published in the Fatherland.

Dodd expressed his pleasure as Howe lit yet another cigarette. "Well, I'd be lying if I told you I haven't thought about a diplomatic career. The University has become draining, and I'd like to finish my book on the history of the Southern states." But Dodd knew there was something more to this probable appointment. He also knew he couldn't have been the first choice, which made him even more suspicious. "Okay Louis, but you must tell me the Governor's agenda beyond speaking fluent German to a group of politicians in Berlin."

Howe appreciated Dodd's intuition and got serious; he spoke of Roosevelt wanting to end Germany's delinquency on their World War I reparation payments. American lenders were patient and willing to reduce interest, but payments *must* resume. But the astute professor figured there was even more to it. "What else, Louis?" Dodd asked. Howe smirked and took a letter from his breast pocket and handed it to Dodd. It was a letter from Roosevelt himself.

"Our intelligence suggests that the Nazis are formulating unethical doctrines. It's getting some religious groups very rattled here in the States. There's nothing our ambassador can do politically, but he must protect American citizens in Germany should there be any troubling developments. Dodd is the perfect man for the job."

Dodd needed no more prodding. He was curious to see where Germany was headed once the inevitable transfer of power shifted to the Nazis. "Tell the Governor he can count on me." Howe smiled and took a deep drag off his cigarette.

"We are very pleased, Bill. And it should be a great adventure for your family."

BRUNDAGE

Five hundred miles to the north in Lake Placid, N.Y., Avery Brundage and Margaret stood by the bobsled course next to Godfrey Dewey, the local millionaire who was financing most of the 1932 Winter Games that were now two weeks away. Dewey smiled as the course engineers rushed by on a practice run. "Pretty exciting, huh Ms. Bailey?"

Margaret smiled like a kid who had just seen her first Mickey Mouse cartoon. "Just awesome."

"You've done a fine job here, Godfrey. I can't tell you how much the AOC is indebted to you," Brundage added.

"I can tell you exactly how indebted," Dewey fired back. The 45-year-old doctor, and son of Melvil Dewey, the inventor of the Dewey decimal system, was not happy with Brundage and he let it be known. In Rome at the IOC meeting five years prior, the US was granted the Olympic bid, and Dewey was instrumental in landing the Games. Brundage assured him and American IOC member Ernest Jahncke that the AOC would help in the endeavor at all costs. And so far, Brundage had done bupkis.

"It's a global pandemic," Brundage cried. But Dewey was not hearing any of it. Brundage had shaken the two men's hands and promised. And Dewey was a man of his word.

"Fix the transportation problem, Avery. You've treated the Winter Games like a red-headed stepchild and now you better put up or shut up." Dewey then turned to Margaret. "Ma'am, it was a pleasure. If you are ever interested in working for honest professionals, give me a call." He shook her hand and walked away toward the course workers, leaving Brundage stewing in his two-tone Spectator loafers.

Brundage had to act swiftly. As his mind raced to figure out a solution to the transportation fiasco, he caught a glimpse of

Margaret lighting a cigarette - something she usually saved for their post-sex ritual. *That's it,* he thought.

"You need to do something for me. That guy you dated, the one who works at the Port Authority . . . You need to call him. I want two dozen buses here by Friday."

"I'm not calling him," Margaret protested. "All he ever wants from me is my body."

"Then give it to him," Avery demanded without missing a beat. "Take a bullet for the team."

"More like a pin prick," she shot back.

He smiled, "Then it won't be too demanding for you."

GRETEL

On a crisp February afternoon, forty-something year old PAULA BERGMANN walked through the second floor of her modest home in the friendly little burg of Laupheim in Southern Germany, looking for the culprit or culprits that had made a mess of her newly cleaned bedrooms. She weaved through the house and found each room uniform in a disheveled state - every mattress had been stolen from its frame. "MAX!" She yelled out for her husband, while running downstairs and exploding through the back door.

There she saw what she had supposed; her eldest, 18-year-old GRETEL BERGMANN, pretty and athletic, had gathered the mattresses and piled them on top of each other to have a safe landing spot for her high jump practice. A tree branch acted as a horizontal bar. To add insult to injury, her youngest children, 14-year-old Ernst and 10-year-old Hannah, were using the makeshift landing area as a trampoline between jumps. "Again, with my bedding?!" She yelled toward her husband.

MAX, Gretel's father, turned toward Paula, "Until the new sports club is complete, this is the best we can do. It's only a few more months," he promised his weary wife.

Gretel Bergmann, World Champion Woman's High Jumper, poses in her local sports club outfit in Laupheim, Germany, circa 1932.

"They'll catch cold!" Paula yelled.

"Please, Paula!" Max waved her off and continued to coach his eager daughter. "Now I'm going to raise the bar another half meter and this time, try launching a step later and see if you can make it," he advised Gretel.

She laughed, "Poppa, I've never made that height. I've only jumped that height in my dreams!"

"Then you've already done it. Trust me," he said. Gretel nodded, took a deep breath, and sprinted towards the jump. She launched herself and cleared the bar with the grace of a gazelle. Her brother and sister cheered.

Paula shook her head in frustration as her younger children resumed jumping on their new trampoline. "I give up", she conceded, "You can all cramp inside one room on a cot for what it's worth." She went back inside the house.

Max turned to Gretel. "Don't let your mother discourage you. If you keep your eyes on your goal, nothing can stop you."

"Do you think that's really true, father?" Gretel responded.

"Yes, I do," Max said.

Gretel trusted her father more than anyone. He had convinced her to try out for the Ulmer FV club when she was a lanky 16-year-old. She easily made the team. A year after that, in 1931, she won her first high-jumping title in the South German Championships. Her goal now was to prove that she was not only the best high jumper in Germany, but the best in the entire world. When her father spoke to her with such conviction, she felt invincible.

Practices like this went on week after week, even when the weather didn't cooperate. Max would shovel a running path for Gretel and clear every flake of snow from her launching point. Gretel was in awe of her father's dedication and used it as fuel for her own efforts. She never had to be persuaded to practice and approached each jump with the same mindset. She always remembered the day, as a young girl attempting her first jump in competition, when Max told her, "Remove the word 'difficult' from your vocabulary and replace it with 'challenging'." She had used that advice ever since.

As for the stolen mattresses, after practice each night Gretel, Ernst, and Hannah would drag them back into the house, stiff and wet from the winter's bite. This increasingly infuriated Paula until about three weeks in, when she saw Max and Gretel practicing in the freezing rain one morning. If they were willing to practice under those conditions, nothing could stop them, she thought. After practice she would toss Gretel a warm towel and say, "You certainly are your father's daughter."

*   *   *

Winter shifted to a short spring, and when summer finally came, it was time to retire the mattresses. Max and Gretel Bergmann approached the spanking new Ulmer FV Club sports facility with great anticipation. Finally, young athletes from their region would have a fitting landscape to hone their specific concentration. Max saw his daughter's eyes sparkle as she stopped and stared at the facility's entrance.

"It will be my home away from home," Gretel mused as she transferred her heavy gym bag from one shoulder to the other. This was the catalyst she needed to get to the top of her game. Coaches had told her for more than two years now that she could be the best in the world at woman's high jump if she had the proper training. And now nothing was going to stop her ascent to the top. "Let's go inside, Papa," she said excitedly.

Immediately, a hulking yet smiling club official named Bruno met the two. "Ms. Bergmann, we've been expecting you. Let me take that for you." Gretel handed him her bag. "You'll have your own private locker, of course." He then pointed beyond a set of

- 23 -

double doors, "Over there is the cafeteria, and trainer's room to the left. Mr. Bergmann, there's also a coach's- slash-parent's lounge for your enjoyment on the second floor overlooking the practice field."

Max swallowed hard and fought off tears. He only wanted the very best for his children and now his oldest, and favorite, was the happiest he had ever seen her. *No more jumping over tree branches and landing on mattresses for my daughter,* he thought. He had never pushed her or any of his children in one direction or another, but if they showed more than a passing interest in something, he would strongly encourage it. The only exception being when Gretel wanted to fight for Germany in The Great War; he had to explain to the crying, adamant child that the Army didn't take girls, and certainly not 5-year-old girls. He was pleased when she turned her patriotic attention to national sports shortly after.

Gretel kissed her father's cheek and disappeared towards the woman's locker room. Max waited a beat, took one last look around the beautiful facility, smiled widely, and proudly walked back toward the exit.

Gretel entered the women's locker room and was stunned. The place was not only enormous, but everything was brand new; the lockers, benches, training tables . . . It was a fleeting moment. After she caught her breath, she quickly felt at ease. The other female athletes were either getting dressed or stretching, and they all stopped what they were doing and turned their heads. They all knew who Gretel was. Some of the girls greeted her warmly; they had competed or trained together at various amateur meets over the years. Others were in awe. They had heard of her accomplishments and record-setting jumps, but to see her in person was something else. She was striking and confident as she strolled to her locker. Her name was etched on top.

She put down her gym bags and surveyed the room, confident and determined. She would not take this for granted. To her, it was one step closer to showing the world what she could do. The other girls looked away sheepishly. Gretel smiled. The tall, young champion from the south had arrived.

GOULD

That same summer, Alan Gould tagged along with Baker to Paris, France on his assignment covering the Middleweight Championship of the World. France's own Marcel Thil was taking on the reigning champion, Gorilla Jones. Jones, a ferocious American fighter, was defending his title for the second time. But you would have never known it from the placards in the jam-packed stadium. Photos of both fighters facing each other, fists raised, read:

"Noir American, Gorilla Jones vs. posseder du France, Marcil Thil - pour la Poids Moyen Championnat de la Monde"

Jones was just another black American fighter to the French promoters, and this did not sit well with Gould. Jones was an exceptional young talent and a champion, who rose from the ashes of poverty in the Deep South. And he was a perfect gentleman, whom Gould had befriended early in the boxer's career.

Baker wanted to rush to their press seats ringside, but Gould had a secret to tell his overly eager reporter. "Baker, I waited to tell you until we got here, but we are sitting next to Mae West tonight."

Baker gasped, "Oh my God! Are the rumors of her and Jones true?"

Gould looked at him deadpan, "None of your business. And if you know what's good for you, you won't ask her."

The fight was a good one with constant action throughout. By the tenth round it was anyone's fight.

"It's one helluva battle, huh boys?" Mae West yelled to them over the crowd.

"I've got Thil up by two, but Jones looked really good that last round," Baker added. Gould wasn't listening. He was transfixed on referee Juan Casanovas huddling off Thil's corner with the judges and French officials.

"What's going on over there, I wonder?" he asked aloud.

But before West or Baker could look over, Casanovas ran back into the ring for Round Eleven. Jones came out crackling like a roaring fire, landing two body-to-head combinations that made Thil's knees buckle. The crowd erupted and Mae West jumped up like a cougar, "End it here, baby!!"

But it wasn't Jones who ended the fight--it was Casanovas. On Jones' next exchange, the referee quickly cut in waving his arms, disqualifying Jones on a mysterious technicality. The crowd went wild.

"What the fuck just happened? Was it a low blow?" Baker inquired.

"A French farce is what just happened here!" West said in disgust.

"Poor kid." Gould added.

Casanovas and the judges exited near them, and Baker could not help himself, "This is an outrage! *Tricheurs* !" The offenders, now under police escort, picked up their pace. Jones and his coaches then approached the press area.

"Ain't no respect anywhere in this world for the black man, no matter how hard we fight, Mr. Gould!" Jones expressed with a slowly swelling face.

"The New York Boxing Commission is not going to let this stand, William," Gould assured the dejected fighter.

"Ain't nothin' gonna change," Jones said then turned to West, "You comin' baby?"

"Oh Billy, honey!" She hugged his sweaty broken body. "Thanks for the company, boys," West said to Gould and Baker with a sad smile.

Gould watched as they exited the chaotic scene. In the ring Thil was parading around, arms in the air like he had earned the win. Gould did everything he could not to puke on the spot.

BRUNDAGE

At a poolside cocktail table at The Roosevelt Hotel in Hollywood, Carl Diem and Theodor Lewald sipped strawberry daiquiris, basking in the sunlight and the warm air. It was August and the Los Angeles Olympics of 1932 were underway. A few of the athletes milled about; many relaxing in the pool.

Avery Brundage and another member of the German International Olympic Committee, KARL RITTER VON HALT, walked towards them holding drinks of their own. Von Halt stood 6' 3" with broad shoulders, blond hair, and a nasty scowl that wouldn't go away even when he smiled. He had challenged Brundage in the pentathlon and decathlon events in the Stockholm Games back in 1912, but by their demeanor, they were no longer competitors, but very good friends. They put their drinks down on the table and sat next to Diem and Lewald.

"Avery, you pulled off Lake Placid, and these Summer Games seem to be going very smoothly. The IOC is pleased," Diem said.

"Thank you," Brundage responded with a broad smile.

"And the addition of the victory podium is a very nice touch," Diem added.

"I thought it would be."

Lewald piped in. "Was it your idea for the Olympic Village?"

"Everything you see, Theodor, was my idea," Brundage said confidently.

"Why just the men then?" Theodor asked.

"I wasn't going to put our limited funds into accommodating one hundred twenty-six pains in the asses: they're just fine at the Chapman. I'll tell you, I'm not so sure the Greeks weren't onto something when they didn't allow women to participate in the ancient Games." Brundage replied. Von Halt nodded and laughed in agreement.

Lewald was stunned. "They're hugely popular however, which means more revenue. Interesting how quickly you would dismiss this."

"It's just too bad, that's all I'm saying," Brundage said.

Diem chimed in, "Well, all I know is we have a hard act to follow. I only hope we can put on a show half as good in Berlin in '36."

"You should hope more teams can afford to come. Every athlete on the Brazilian team was given coffee beans to sell to pay their port fees. Most of them didn't sell enough to afford to disembark the damned boat." Brundage informed them.

"If you knew that was going to be the case, then why didn't you make it easier for them?" Lewald kept hammering at Brundage, who finally looked back at him completely exasperated. Von Halt picked up on this immediately. He raised his glass to break the tension.

"To better times ahead and hopes that in four years nobody has to sell coffee like a filthy Brazilian to get to Berlin."

They all raised their glasses. Brundage toasted, "Here, here! To Berlin in '36 and to the boys of Stockholm 1912!" All the men smiled, clinked their glasses, and drank, but deep down Brundage seethed with resentment toward Lewald. He respected him for his contribution to sport and that he was an IOC member but hated that the old Jew showed him no respect in return. Brundage didn't have the money the Nazis were going to throw toward the Berlin Games; this made successfully pulling off Los Angeles very difficult. He also didn't like being questioned by a man who was going to be handed the keys to a kingdom that didn't even want his kind around. Brundage could only manage a crooked grin as Lewald droned on and on about his plans and vision for an even grander Olympic spectacle in Berlin. Brundage predicted that Lewald would take this opportunity to indirectly point out the deficiencies here at the Los Angeles games. But there were plenty of things about Lewald that he didn't know.

Theodor Lewald was not always a practicing Jew and rarely acknowledged his heritage. His wife Elisabeth was moderately better. She at least socialized in Jewish circles and went to Synagogue once a month. Theodor blamed it on his work, his "obsession" Elisabeth would say. But every once in a while, she would persuade him to put down his pen and paper and blueprints and join her on an evening with their Jewish friends. And it was on one of these rare occasions, just before going to LA, that Theodor Lewald came to a beautiful, historic, and lasting revelation.

It started with a few drinks at the home of Rabbi Josef Wulffstein and his family. Some light banter was exchanged. Politics was ignored, much to Lewald's satisfaction, and conversations ranged from the weather to the upcoming American Summer Olympics in Los Angeles. Lewald was more than happy to speak of that. The German National Team looked strong, and Lewald wanted nothing more than to be there when his team embarrassed his old friend Avery Brundage's American Nationals on their own turf. He knew Brundage was pulling out all the stops for these Games including a new attraction - the 'Olympic Village'.

Lewald and Diem had been looking for something to elevate the Berlin '36 Games past what was expected in Los Angeles, but other than a more advanced Village, they were coming up short. Even the new grand stadium constructions weren't enough for Lewald. He was looking for something more profound. And that's just what he found at the dinner table shortly after.

"Blessed are You, Lord our God, Ruler of the Universe, who has sanctified us with commandments, and commanded us to light Shabbat candles . . ."

While Josef continued the prayers before dinner, his family began to pass a lit candle around the table. The light shimmied and swerved but never faded off. And when the prayer was complete, the candle had made its way completely around the table with Lewald the last in line. Josef encouraged him to make a wish and with that candle, light the main candle on the table.

It was as if a lighthouse flashed on over Lewald's head. He hurriedly lit the center candle on the table, handed the original one to Elisabeth who was sitting next to him and abruptly excused himself. The guests stared at him in bewilderment as he ran to the parlor and grabbed the telephone.

Carl Diem was eating his own dinner when Lewald called him in an excitable state.

"The scripture says that the reason we light candles is to 'illuminate our eyes' . . . to see the truth . . ." Lewald began.

"What are you talking about, Theodor?" Diem mumbled between bites of schnitzel.

"I just witnessed something very interesting. It was a ceremony where everyone passed a candle around the table before a larger, main candle was lit by the original."

Diem was still confused why he was getting a play-by-play of Lewald's dinner events, "And?"

"I felt... a connection to everyone," Lewald expressed, and then continued, "What if we could connect the whole world in a candle lighting ceremony?"

That's the exact moment the same lighthouse went on above Diem's head, "Go on," he said excitedly.

"Hear me out," Lewald laid out his plan, "We start with a runner in a distant country. He's carrying a torch . . ."

GOULD

A day later, inside the Los Angeles Olympic Aquatic Center, a very beautiful face stared ahead--focused and completely concentrated on the goal at hand. This was the stunning nineteen-year-old ELEANOR HOLM, who stood on a platform at the edge of the pool. At the sound of a gunshot, Holm leaped backwards into a pool along with seven other women as they competed in the finals of the backstroke. The pace was furious. It was a tight race as they pushed themselves to their limits.

The cheering crowd urged the women on. Alan Gould, one of Holm's biggest fans, sat in the front row near the finish line. At the turn Holm took the lead and never relinquished it. She touched the finish line and popped up to look at the results. Smiling widely, she jumped out of the pool and was mobbed by her coach and teammates. She dried off and was escorted to the eager press where she immediately approached Gould with a proud look on her face. "I did it, Gould."

"You sure did, kid. How's it feel to take the Gold?"

"Satisfying," she replied.

"Good. Take it easy with the celebrating tonight, okay?"

She looked at him confidently. "I've got three screen tests at three different studios tomorrow morning, so, it'll be an early night no matter what happens."

Gould smiled. "Break a leg."

Other journalists swept in and surrounded her, throwing

microphones and lights in her face. She peered over them to get a last word into Gould. "Hey Gould!" she yelled. He stretched out to see her. "Thanks for the AP's constant support . . . and *your* support!"

American Sweetheart, Eleanor Holm, smiles after her Woman's Backstroke Gold Medal performance in the Los Angeles Olympics in 1932.

Gould smiled. "You bet, kid. You're a star!" She smiled back at him, and then turned her attention to the mobbing press. Gould watched as she handled them with charm and ease. "She's a star," he said to himself.

Eleanor was one of his favorite athletes. He had met her when she was a junior high phenom and then followed her through her entire AAU existence. She was troubled and wild and seemingly morality free, but damned if she wasn't the best swimmer he had ever seen. And around him she was a complete sweetheart. She was also more honest and open with him than even her own coaches or parents. He had never quite met anyone like Eleanor and though every other person in the country saw her as a sports goddess and sex symbol, he saw her as an older daughter-type. Though he was pretty sure she was quite the handful for her own father.

*   *   *

A month after the 1932 Los Angeles Summer Olympics ended, a forty-foot sailboat cut through the choppy waters in the middle of Lake Borgne, just to the east of New Orleans. At the helm was Gould's friend, Ernest Jahncke. Though he was six months shy of retiring as Asst. Secretary to the Navy, he never passed up a chance to take the helm. Being the American IOC representative kept him from his passion most of the year, but New Orleans and these lakes and estuaries were his home. His family had built the seawall from West End to Spanish Fort, so there wasn't an area unfamiliar to him.

As he sailed through a narrow channel towards the Gulf, he couldn't stop thinking of the Olympic vote from the year before. Germany was becoming something very different since then, and he truly felt the IOC was heading into murky waters. Jahncke was the kind of man who couldn't fathom the type of hate building throughout Europe. He was too pragmatic to comprehend something like anti-Semitism, and even though he was born and bred in Deep South New Orleans, he certainly couldn't stomach racial intolerance. Prejudice in all its forms was an evil spawn of ignorance and it made his blood boil. And if given the opportunity, Jahncke wasn't shy about showing his displeasure. He passed these upstanding ideals to his family.

His teenage son Stanton sat next to him. Stanton was the spitting image of his father. The boy wiped ocean spray off his face and looked up at him. "Pop, after you're done with the Navy are you gonna come home?"

"I like being part of the IOC and now I'll be able to concentrate on it more," Jahncke said.

"When you and Grandpa built the levees, you came home every night. That was nice," the boy replied.

"Well, yes, but that engineering job led to a political appointment, which led to the IOC. And that's nice too. How many kids you know from New Orleans visit their folks in places like Washington, or Paris, or get to go to the Olympic Games?"

Stanton racked his brain, not realizing it was a rhetorical question.

"None." Jahncke suddenly pointed to the sky. "Look at the sky in the east, Stanton." A cloud mass seemed to be exploding like a terrifying bomb, expanding menacingly.

"What's happening, Pop?"

Jahncke said, "Those puffy cumulus clouds I showed you when we first got out are now rising vertically."

"Is that bad?"

"It means they are turning into cumulonimbus and a storm is coming."

"And you sure it's headed our way?"

"Look . . . the tops of the clouds are pointing in our direction. And now you feel that wind picking up?" The boat suddenly rose and fell a little steeper in the waves.

"Should we head back to the Rigolets then?" Stanton asked and steadied himself.

"Yes. We need to stay ahead of this storm. It's gonna be a big one," Jahncke said as he steered the boat back towards land, dark clouds looming ominously behind them.

1933

At a raised podium, ADOLF HITLER addressed the supporting crowd of thousands of proud German citizens. Behind him his closest advisors gleamed. There was the enormous ERNST "PUTZI" HANFSTAENGL, the svelte, debonair HERMANN GOERING, and the steely-eyed, perpetually grimacing JOSEPH GOEBBELS. Next to him was the obese, round-faced ERNST ROHM. This was Hitler and his Nazi Party's crowning moment; from the time of the Armistice, Hitler had vowed revenge on Germany's enemies, and now the failed soldier and artist had orated and bullied his way to Chancellor, second in command to President Hindenburg. "With profound distress, millions of the best German men and women from all walks of life have seen the unity of the nation vanishing away, dissolving in a confusion of political and personal opinions, economic interests, and ideological differences."

In a similar fashion in America that same year, FRANKLIN DELANO ROOSEVELT gave his inaugural address. "In the field of world policy, I would dedicate this nation to the policy of the good neighbor--the neighbor who resolutely respects himself and, because he does so, respects the rights of others - the neighbor who respects his obligations and respects the sanctity of his agreements in and with a world of neighbors." He was supported by his wife Eleanor, their children, and his staunchest political allies, including Louis Howe, who sat next to the First Lady, and his soon-to-be Secretary of State, Cordell Hull.

Hitler shouted to the crowd, in a way, answering the American President's speech, "Regarding our foreign policy, the National Government considers its highest mission to be the securing of the right to live and the restoration of freedom to our nation. Its determination to bring to an end the chaotic state of affairs in

Germany will assist in restoring to the community of nations a State of equal value and, above all, a State which must have equal rights!" Hitler slammed his fist on the podium and the crowd roared. His advisors behind him jumped to their feet and applauded. He turned to them and smiled like a fox just let in a hen house.

GRETEL

Carrying her gym bag while chatting with two friends, Gretel Bergmann entered the Ulmer FV Sports Club sports club and casually walked past the front desk as she had done every day for months. The usually affable club official, Bruno, approached the young women with another man, a short, menacing, SS officer dressed in black leather from head to toe and confronted the girls. "Stop there, Gretel Bergman. I'm afraid I'm going to have to ask you to return your membership card and leave immediately," the short one said.

Gretel looked at her friends and smiled, then turned to face the men. "Bruno, what's all this?" She pointed to the SS officer with mockery and outright disdain, "Is this a joke?"

The SS officer took umbrage and stepped towards Gretel, who stood tall. Bruno put his arm out and held the man back. He then looked sharply at Gretel, "This is no joke. Hand over your card or we shall take it by force and remove you in the same fashion."

"I don't understand. What have I done?" Gretel pleaded as her eyes began to well up with tears.

"You were born a Jew," the short one said. "And under the new laws of our Chancellor and the Nazi party, it is illegal for you to continue your membership."

Gretel's friend responded, "This is absurd. She's the world record holder in the women's high jump for God's sake!" Bruno approached her and Gretel's other friend.

"The two of you will go practice this instant." Thoroughly intimidated, they quickly walked away from the situation. Bruno then turned and advanced toward Gretel with equal menace. This time Gretel took a step back in fear. The sudden change in his demeanor was alarming. "Your membership card, *fräulein*. Now!" Gretel battled back her tears and begrudgingly handed over her membership card. "Remove yourself!"

Gretel stared in Bruno's eyes with contempt then turned and walked out of the sports club.

As she walked home, Laupheim suddenly appeared a much darker place. On almost every corner there was a Nazi guard, the cafés were filled with men wearing some kind of military uniform or another, and outside every Jewish owned shop, random mobs would pop up and hurl insults at any customer going in or out. These hate-mongers were some of the same people she knew growing up; her neighbors, parents of kids she went to school with, and sadly some of her very own schoolmates.

At home that evening, she sat with her head in her hands crying at the dining room table. Paula sat beside her trying to console her. In the background their dog Fritz played with Ernst and Hannah.

Max was pacing back and forth. "We have no alternative, Paula. When I go to London, I'm taking her with me and I'm registering her at the London Polytechnic. Gretel, you can study there and participate in the school's athletic programs."

Gretel sobbed, "And leave you and Momma, Father? I think we should all go to London."

"Don't be ridiculous," he said. "This insanity is not going to last."

Paula intervened. "We'll be fine, Gretel. Your father is very respected in the business community. The Nazis won't bother us."

"They already have, Momma! My God!"

Max walked over and put his hand on Gretel's shoulder. "*Liebchen*, my concern is my children first. You go to London and excel. You can show the rest of the world what you can achieve." He looked over with a sense of worry at his other two children. "And if God forbid, we have to, we will all join you. But first things first, in three weeks you are off on your adventure."

Young Hannah rose excitedly, "I want Gretel's room when she leaves!"

Ernst responded, "You wish! I'll be the eldest child now; therefore I get the bigger room."

Gretel smiled as she wiped away her tears. "I guess I can't leave fast enough. Such loving siblings I have."

Hannah ran over to Gretel and hugged her. "I'll miss you more, so therefore *I* should get the room, right?"

Gretel laughed. "That's hard to argue. She is very cute. Ernst?"

"Father is a reasonable man, I'm sure he will make the most judicious decision. Right, Father?" Ernst asked.

Max said, "It stays Gretel's room until she's married, final word." The two children were suddenly deflated. Gretel smiled warmly at her father, who smiled right back.

DODD

The newly appointed Ambassador William Dodd and his energetic wife MATTIE were assisting movers as they unpacked a truck in front of a beautiful mid-town Berlin mansion. Dodd watched his wife and smiled as she directed the men with a bulldog's tenacity. "Mattie, all the boxes are clearly marked which room they go into. Let them do their jobs."

Mattie replied, "This is just so exciting. I get to decorate a European mansion. Why don't you walk to your new office and get the lay of the land?"

Just then, their twenty-six-year-old son BILL, JR., and stunningly attractive twenty-three-year-old daughter MARTHA ran out of the house excitedly.

"Oh, Poppa, it's just so keen," Martha said. "My room is triple the size of the house in Chicago."

Dodd nodded and turned to Bill. "Everything up to your severe code of acceptability?"

Bill responded in his best German, " *Wunderschön, Vater.*"

"Good. I'm walking over to work. Would anyone like to join me?"

"Are you going to meet Herr Hitler?" Martha asked.

"No, Martha. Though I'm sure he is as anxious to meet as I am, I don't start the job until Monday. That's when I will schedule that meeting."

Disappointed, Martha said, "Oh, how dreadfully boring then. Well, have fun. I'm going shopping."

"Not alone you're not. Bill, drive your sister and don't let her out of your sight." Her overly protective father declared.

"Jeez, Poppa. I'm not a child," she said.

Dodd shot back, "I don't care. You are not running about all alone until I know exactly the kind of city we've moved into."

At that moment, something inside the house smashed loudly. Mattie quickly turned to run inside. As Dodd followed her, he turned back to his son Bill. "Drive your sister and stay with her!"

Inside the mansion, Dodd and Mattie saw that the movers had smashed a vase accidentally. Glass was strewn all over the floor. Mattie picked up a piece and said to her husband, "This isn't one of ours."

Just then, a middle-aged Maid and Butler ran into the room nervously. The Maid saw the vase and gasped. They both looked extremely upset and ran over to the mess, quickly gathering the pieces. Dodd and Mattie watched the peculiar couple, then Dodd knelt to help clean. "Let me lend a hand," he said.

The Maid responded in broken English, "No, I shall get it, Mr. Ambassador." She carefully gathered the pieces in her apron. The Butler put his arm around her to console her.

"William, what's going on?" Mattie asked.

Dodd stood up, assessing the situation. "I believe we may be carpetbaggers, dear." They all stood in an uncomfortable silence for a moment.

"Well, this won't do at all. We can't stay here." Mattie turned to the Maid. "Miss, my husband will find us alternate lodgings."

The Butler interrupted. "No, please, you must stay here. We are quite comfortable on the top floor, and we do not want to make trouble."

"It's no trouble. My husband will find us something." Mattie said, not quite fully understanding the situation. "William?"

The Butler pleaded. "Please Mr. Dodd, do not. You will be comfortable here. We will make it comfortable for you here."

The Dodd Family (L-R, Bill Jr, Martha, William, Mattie) share a rare moment all together in their backyard in Berlin.

Dodd had come to the realization that the Jewish couple were being forced to give up their home. He understood the situation and replied, "Okay. We will stay as your guests then. Fair?"

The 'Maid' and 'Butler' smiled in relief. "God bless you, sir." They picked up the last of the broken vase and walked off arm in arm. Dodd and Mattie looked at each other with great concern.

HITLER

In the center of Berlin, Carl Diem and Theodor Lewald walked quickly down a street bustling with pedestrians. Diem carried a briefcase and Lewald awkwardly clutched a bunch of rolled up blueprints.

Lewald said, "Do you think Hitler will be there?"

"I don't know. We are meeting in his office. Goebbels will be there for sure." Diem said, as they turned a corner, then both stopped dead in their tracks. They looked up in awe. Nazi banners now adorned the entire length and height of the newly designated Sports Reich Office building. The men shared a concerned look and continued towards the entrance.

Inside the sport building's, *Amt des Obersten Bundeskanzlers von Deutschland* (Office of Supreme Chancellor of Germany) Hitler sat, quietly impressed at the presentation unfolding in front of him. Most of his key players for the '36 Games had assembled to review preliminary plans; Nazi Propaganda Minister Joseph Goebbels, Director of the German Sports Office HANS VON TSCHAMMER UND OSTEN, and IOC member Karl Ritter von Halt stood around a diorama of the Berlin Olympic layout with Diem and Lewald and HAUPTMANN WOLFGANG FURSTNER, the designer and developer of the Olympic Village. The detailed grounds looked magnificent to Hitler.

Everything was falling into place for Adolf; he was now Chancellor, the impotent obese President Hindenburg was finally about to drop dead, and by the time the Games rolled around, Hitler would be the *Führer* and *Reichskanzler*. He and his Nazi party would answer to no one, and the Berlin Olympics, as Goebbels reminded him ad nauseum, would be a grand stage to show the rest of the world the Nazis had arrived.

Hauptmann Wolfgang Furstner (kneeling) shows his colleagues, including Carl Diem (in the hat), his plans for the Olympic Village.

Diem used a long pointer to help his presentation. "And this is where the athletes' village will be. Men's *and* women's quarters on either side of an oblong practice field. They will share the field and a commissary which we feel will create a healthy camaraderie."

Goebbels beamed. "*Fantastisch. Uber fantastisch.* Gentlemen, this is fine work." He pointed to Lewald. "You . . . the idea of a torch run from Athens to Berlin to open the Games brings all the countries together and also harks on the glory of the ancient Olympics. I am glad you took my advice and added this." Lewald looked to Diem, his mouth agape. Goebbels was taking full credit, and this was the first he had ever heard of it. "This will be a crowning achievement for Germany," Goebbels continued. "The other nations will see our country at its best."

Defiantly, Lewald interjected, "Is the rest of the world even going to come?" Hitler shot up and glared at Lewald. Diem dropped his head, embarrassed at his partner's sudden outburst.

Goebbels, who sensed his boss' anger without even a glance, tried quickly to diffuse the situation. He shouted, "Don't be so dramatic. Of course, they're going to come! It will be a great display!" He snatched the pointer from Diem, "And just look how Berlin will be transformed. Nothing will stop us." He aimed at the diorama as Hitler looked on momentarily placated.

While the meeting was taking place, on one of those very streets Goebbels pointed toward, a Stormtrooper parade was in progress, and Lewald's fears would soon become a tangible concern.

One hundred SA Military cadets (known as the "Brown-Shirts") marched in unison. Some rode along slowly in cars. Trombone and trumpet players dressed in uniforms resembling an Army marching band, walked alongside the torch-bearing military trainees. German citizens lined the streets and cheered on the group.

Martha Dodd, holding shopping bags full of new clothes, stopped to watch the parade. What a spectacle, she thought. As the music came to a stop, the Brown-Shirts gave the *"Heil Hitler"* salute in unison. The crowd of onlookers, including Martha, cheerfully returned the salute to the cadets.

A young Man and Woman, hand in hand, walked through the crowd, ignoring the loud exhibition. A young Brown-Shirt, sitting atop a float, noticed the couple who seemed oblivious and were not saluting. He jumped off the float and tore through the crowd towards the couple. When he reached them, he grabbed the young man's shirt and spun him around, demanding a salute. *"Heil Hitler!"* he shouted.

The surprised young man responded, "Okay. Heil to your damned Hitler." They attempted to walk past the brute, but he blocked their path. Other people in the crowd noticed the growing confrontation and gathered around.

The bully demanded, "Salute! *Heil Hitler!*"

"We're Americans, it's okay."

"It's not okay! Salute!"

"We're fine. My father --"

With that the Brown-Shirt smashed the American in the face with a hard right cross and his fellow cadets laughed. He punched the American again sending him to the pavement. The young woman screamed and was held back by the attacker's friends.

Martha Dodd watched in shock and the shopping bags dropped from her hands. Other SA cadets started kicking the American man in the gut and head, and he was beginning to lose consciousness. The American woman freed herself to try to interrupt the onslaught, but another random thug suddenly struck her.

Martha ran to a Policeman who was standing on the corner, looking the other way. "Do something!" she pleaded. He turned and walked away, completely ignoring the vicious beating. When she turned back towards the American couple, not exactly sure what she was going to do, she saw a cadet lift a large rock from the road and heave it at the American woman. It ricocheted off the woman's head, sending her to the ground moaning in pain.

Like a pack of wolves, a group of them then descended on the American couple and savagely punched and kicked them over and over. Martha watched helplessly, and slowly backed away from the scene.

*   *   *

Hitler could not have imagined in his worst nightmares the backlash this incident would ignite. Ernest Jahncke, who had distrusted the Germans from the beginning was furious. "How other countries are not outraged by what is happening, is beyond me. It's beyond all comprehension!" He screamed, while he and his assistant half-ran to the formal IOC meeting being held in Vienna a few weeks later to determine the host of the 1940 Games.

"Unbelievable, sir. It's like the rest of the world is complicit," the trusted young man added.

"Well, I'm not going to sit idly by as this insanity grows." Jahncke started to tremble, "Barbarians! I knew Berlin was a goddamned mistake!"

In the conference hall, IOC President Latour once again presided over the meeting. The representatives of Tokyo and Rome were taking the stage for their presentations when Jahncke interrupted the proceedings. "Mr. President, I would like to address the members before we continue with any presentations," he began.

"If there are no objections," Latour followed. And no one raised any hands, but Von Halt, Lewald, Diem, and the other German IOC representatives shifted uncomfortably in their seats. "What's on your mind, Secretary Jahncke?" Latour inquired.

Jahncke spoke with a controlled anger, "I would like to discuss the new Nazi Doctrine versus the Olympic Ideals. It is my opinion that these unjust laws against humanity that the new German government has passed, and no doubt will continue to pass, counteract every belief the Olympics stand for."

Von Halt jumped to his feet, "Who are you to decide another nation's political policies? Look at your own biased country, sir. We could have protested with a very similar argument when we voted for Los Angeles."

Jahncke erupted, "We don't sterilize people over their color or corral them in work camps because of their religion, Von Halt!

- 45 -

And we do not assault innocent tourists! If the IOC does not take action, I will make sure the United States of America does!"

Von Halt laughed, "Oh please. Save us your histrionics. Your President doesn't care about the Olympics, and knowing Avery Brundage as well as I do, he isn't going to jeopardize any future status he may have with this committee."

Jahncke hated Brundage and knew Von Halt was right. So, he cleverly appealed to the Nazis reliance on propaganda. "I happen to have very close ties to the American press, Mr. Von Halt, and the majority sides with me and are appalled at your new politics. So, when I explain to them as an eyewitness what is going on firsthand in Germany, the voice of your old crony Avery Brundage won't matter one damned bit!"

Von Halt bit his lip; he needed the support of the American press, or Goebbels and worse, Hitler, would have a fit. Lewald just put his face in his hands. The dream he had fought so hard to re-attain after losing the Games of 1916, was now beginning to crumble, yet again, because of German aggression.

GOULD

The Oak Room at the Plaza Hotel in mid-town New York City was at capacity. Alan Gould and his good friend and professional competitor, NY Times writer JOHN KIERAN, stood at a lounge table drinking manhattans, while watching the lively crowd, all dressed for the newly arrived fall weather, decompress after a long week of work. Suddenly, Kieran's eyes lit up, "Don't look now, but Charlie Chaplin just entered the place."

Gould couldn't help himself and snapped around. Patrons began to applaud and cheer for the actor as he made his way to the two reporters. "Shit, he's coming this way," Gould said with surprise.

Chaplin took it all in and thanked everyone with a Tramp-esque walk and tip of the cap. He headed straight over to a familiar face. "John, thank you so much for your kind review of *City Lights* and sorry it's taken me so long to say that."

"Of course, Charlie, it was a beautiful film." He then pulled Gould closer, "Charles Chaplin, this is my very good friend and inferior competitor at the AP, Alan Gould."

The two men shook hands, "I am more than honored, sir. My wife and I see everything you do," Gould said, star struck.

Chaplin was just as enamored, "The honor is mine. I read everything you write. I especially enjoyed your work on the L.A. Olympic Games. You made celebrities of those athletes. Eleanor Holm should pay you for the free publicity you threw her way."

Gould was embarrassed, "Pay? Oh no I could never . . ."

"He was kidding, Alan," Kieran informed him.

Chaplin continued, "The next Games are shaping up to be something very interesting, aren't they?" Gould and Kieran agreed wholeheartedly. Kieran, a jack-of-all-trades at the Times, would, along with Gould, travel to Berlin to cover the Games.

"We shall see it firsthand, whatever spectacle it may turn out to be," Kieran exclaimed. "What's next for you Charlie?"

Without missing a beat Chaplin quipped back, "Well, I was going to do a modern social satire, but who knows, if Germany keeps it up there might be enough material for a real knee-slapping comedy. I mean, the little bastard stole my look anyway."

The men smiled as the *maître d'* approached them. "Mr. Gould, you have a phone call." Gould and Kieran looked at each other, surprised.

"Sport never sleeps. I'll let you get to your call. It was a real pleasure Mr. Gould," Chaplin remarked.

"Oh, all mine, Mr. Chaplin." Gould was a bit in shock. Charlie Chaplin's praise, and a personal phone call at the Oak Room all in a mere ten-minute period. He felt like a Warner Brother. After Charlie and Kieran said their goodbyes, the *maître d'* brought over a house phone and handed it to Gould.

"Hello . . ." Gould listened to the other line intently, and then frantically grabbed his pockets for a pen and paper. He was ill prepared; Kieran smirked as he handed his friend the necessary tools from his own breast pocket. Gould took a few notes, made a few facial expressions that his competitor tried to distinguish, and thanked the other end, "Of course, Mr. Secretary. Thank you very much for the call. I'll expect a follow up soon." Gould then hung up the phone and looked at Kieran stone-faced.

"Should I even ask?" Kieran probed.

"Just a former Department official getting back to me," he responded matter-of-factly and handed the pen back to Kieran.

Kieran dug further, "Covering politics now, Alan?"

"Actually, not quite sure how to categorize this story, John. I just know it's shaping out to be a doozy," he said as he downed the rest of his manhattan. "I gotta fly. Mary is making dinner."

Later that evening Gould stood in his kitchen drying dishes while his pragmatic and pretty wife, Mary, prepared dinner. Their two young children, Mary Anne and Alan Jr., played the board game *SORRY!* in the adjoining dining room. Once again Mary was ribbing her husband on his undying belief that sport was truly newsworthy. "It's sports. No matter how much passion you and other fanatics have for them, a knockout, a home run, a touchdown, is not comparable to famine, loss of life, or unemployment, no matter where it takes place."

He thought about the injustice he saw at the fight in Paris and the dire warnings from the phone call from Jahncke earlier that evening regarding Berlin. "I disagree. Sport is growing beyond mere competition. And Germany is a powder keg. The Berlin Olympics stands to be a huge story." He grabbed her close to him.

"I may even win a Pulitzer." A prize that had, as of yet, alluded him.

"Ha! You wish." She pecked him on the cheek and continued her task. "Hitler and the Nazis won't even be around in three years. No one outside of Germany is going to take him seriously. And certainly the US government is not going to let his behavior continue. He's a clown. He looks like an angry ugly version of the Little Tramp."

Gould smiled and grabbed his wife again. He had not told her about his meeting Charlie Chaplin earlier in the evening, "You have the mind of a cinematic genius, darling."

"I'm not sure what that means, but I'll accept it."

"It's very sexy. Maybe we should skip dinner, put the kids to bed, then go to bed ourselves," he said with a Cheshire-cat grin.

"SORRY!" Mary Anne screamed at her brother in the dining room. "You lose!" It was the same sentiment her mother gave her father in the kitchen.

LENI

Hauptmann Wolfgang Furstner was a devoted husband, father, and soldier, who served under three separate German regimes. The Empire, for his bravery in World War I, had decorated him, and he would not even consider leaving the service after being seriously wounded. Though his battlefield days were done, under the Weimar he would become an Army architect and land developer; a trade he had learned from his father. The brawny, stern, but affable 37-year-old then easily transitioned to the Nazi Army. Furstner enjoyed its structure and passion for a greater Germany, all traits he found admirable. There never walked a prouder German, and his stride showed it. When called upon by the Reich, by Goebbels himself, to develop a glorious Olympic

Village, his pride swelled even larger. Furstner jumped into the assignment with such intensity and commitment and sheer joy, even his Nazi superiors were a little surprised. But they shouldn't have been. He approached all facets of his life in this manner. He was that type of soldier, that type of man.

And on a cool day at the construction site of his 'baby' - the Olympic Village, Furstner walked with two of his many superiors, Carl Diem and Theodor Lewald. The difference in these two gentlemen, as opposed to his military bosses, was that these two men understood land development and management. And he could talk to them without the interference of Army protocol, which Furstner found to be refreshing.

Diem explained to him that they expected everything to be operational at least two weeks before the athlete's arrival in late July of '36. Furstner assured them that would not be a problem. The only real challenges he believed he would face were the plumbing and getting gas and running water to the kitchen in the commissary. He was sure this would not cause delays.

Lewald reminded him that the American Avery Brundage was coming for an inspection late '35, and that Osten was adamant that all Olympic construction be in their latter stages. Diem added that Hitler himself had commissioned the workhouses to make the pillows and mattresses for the dormitories, so construction on those had to be a priority.

"I will oversee everything. I'm very excited to be an integral part of this, gentlemen. This will make the Los Angeles Olympic village look like a ghetto. It just makes my . . ." He stopped dead in his tracks when he noticed a small film crew shooting the workers and machinery. "Hey! You there! What's the meaning of this?" He yelled toward the cameraman and his tall and very striking female associate. They looked over toward the three approaching men un-phased and kept rolling.

When Diem, Lewald, and a somewhat exasperated Furstner reached them, the woman addressed them immediately, "I am filmmaker LENI RIEFENSTAHL."

"Who?! I don't care if you are Brünnhilde, you are not authorized to be here!" Furstner shot back. But Leni wasn't backing down.

Leni Riefenstahl and her cinematographer, Hans Ertl, set a shot in Berlin's Olympic Stadium in preparation of her epic documentary of the Games, OLYMPIA.

"That's where you're wrong, soldier boy. I am most definitely authorized to be here. Herr Hitler has commissioned me himself to document these Games. He has given me carte blanche to go anywhere and shoot anywhere I deem important for the production. Is this understood?" The three men stared at her dumbfounded. "And this is one place I deem absolutely necessary. It is the future nexus of the sports universe, as integral as Olympic Stadium itself. I am looking forward to your complete cooperation in what I am sure will be one of the cinema's greatest achievements. And one that will make your Chancellor beam with pride. Now, no more talking, I need the ambient sound." She then turned her attention back to her camera operator.

Diem, Lewald, and Furstner stood quietly and obeyed like three helpless dogs.

ELEANOR

Eleanor Holm had taken a day from practice to visit her parents in Brooklyn. Though she rarely got back these days, the house brought back such sweet memories, and especially during the holidays when her parents had never spared an expense for decorations. It had become quite the friendly competition in the close-knit neighborhood and every house on the block was more festive than the next one.

Inside, she bee-lined past the Christmas tree and straight to her room. It was exactly like she had left it after graduating Erasmus Hall High School two years before, all her ribbons and trophies still lining the bookshelves. Hours and hours of swimming, since as early as she could talk, would exhaust her, but this room was her fortress. It was the one place she could decompress, whether having a good cry after a disappointing loss, or a rock-solid sleep after a long day of laps, her room was all her own.

She sat and smiled into her mirror. The same mirror she grew up play acting into and turning into her idols Mary Pickford and Janet Gaynor. She playfully blew herself a kiss while catching a faint smell of dried flowers emanating from around her vanity. This sent her back to her junior prom. Her date was Art Jarrett, a good-looking guy who hung around the musician groups at Erasmus. Eleanor wondered if Jarrett still came around the old haunts. She had heard from her mother, whom she suspected of trying to get them together, that he was performing at the Cocoanut Grove. But she hadn't been there for some time.

"Hi Princess," her father said, surprising her out of her thoughts. He was decked out in full fireman regalia, like a knight back from a day at the Crusades.

"Hi Daddy!" She jumped up and into his arms. "Gosh I've missed you."

"Back at you. Let me get cleaned up and we can have some lunch, okay?" He turned to walk away, "You need to eat, Princess."

"Okay, Daddy," she said and rolled her eyes. Eating was not a past time for Eleanor; it was a necessity she found very little interest in. Her coaches forced the required calories into her before and after practices. She was a modern-day athlete, one that wanted to achieve but look fabulous doing it. And eating created a bulge of fat around the waist, which then would create drag in the water, thusly creating slower times, and worse, any hope of being a Hollywood movie star would go the way of the Dodo. Glamorous movie stars had no fat. If she couldn't win Gold and look fabulous in a gown, what would make life worth living?

Her mother served fresh chilled roasted chicken with snap peas and boiled baby potatoes with a dab of butter melting on top. And as soon as the plates were on the table, a knock came at Holm's door. Her mother jumped to answer. "It's for you, Eleanor," she yelled from the front door.

"It's probably reporters," she said to her father who waited patiently to eat. But when she got there, she smiled widely. It wasn't a reporter at all. Art Jarrett, hair slicked back and impeccably dressed, stood across from the threshold and grinned. "Well, I guess we should let you inside, wouldn't want the neighbors to think we associate with entertainer types," Eleanor said.

Art, of course, joined them for lunch. Mrs. Holm had orchestrated the whole event with the smoothness of Glenn Miller, but Eleanor was enjoying the moment. Art was grown up now, a real man, with a great job and lots of confidence. She kept catching herself staring at him and she knew he caught her more than once. But she was catching him doing it as well and it all felt very good to Eleanor. She felt giddy and devoured her lunch and two glasses of wine like a lioness. She then accepted a date from Jarrett for later that week in the City, kissed her Mom and Dad, and went back up to her bedroom, falling quickly into a deep peaceful nap as soon as her head hit her old, trusted, and self-made feather pillow.

The rest of her week was swimming and reading over lines for audition pieces. And these two things were all encompassing. Eleanor found the swimming, even with all its physical exertion, easy compared to acting. She could be herself in the pool, but acting she had to become someone else; it may have come easy to her as a kid in front of her vanity mirror, but in real life, in front of producers and directors, it was nerve-wracking. And Eleanor just couldn't get past her thick Brooklyn accent. Since winning Gold, the studios who found interest in her had all suggested voice and articulation classes, but Eleanor couldn't find the time and the few she had taken were disastrous. There was just no taking the Flatbush out of this girl.

When Friday night arrived, however, Eleanor's thoughts were all about Art Jarret. She stood in front of her full-length mirror admiring her athletic naked body and smiled wryly. Any man would beg, borrow, and steal to lie next to a female figure like this no matter what voice came out of it, and Jarret would be no exception. Eleanor was as sexually confident as most 1930's woman and she was not afraid to play it up.

After trying on several outfits, she settled on a tight turtleneck dress that a smitten Italian designer had sent her after watching her Gold medal swim in Los Angeles. It had form, she looked devastating in it, and function, it was the warmest cocktail clothes she owned, and this December evening in New York City was freezing.

Jarret picked her up in a cab and when she shed her coat, after sitting next to him in the backseat, she could see his eyes light up. He offered her a swig of his flask, which she accepted and gave back. "I thought we could swing by the Grove for a few drinks before dinner. Is that okay?"

"Of course. Tonight, you lead, I follow. Unless, of course, it's someplace dreadful." She smiled at him, and he laughed.

"Dreadful wasn't in my plans." He took a draw from his flask. "I'm gonna sweep you off your feet, Ms. Holm." He said with the confidence of a real-life Prince Charming.

"Oh, really." She snatched back the flask and took a big sip, "We shall see about that."

But indeed, he did. At the Coconut Grove they were treated like celebrities, with endless glasses of champagne and tins of caviar at the club's best table. Even though Jarret had taken the night off, he gladly conducted a rousing rendition of *For Me and My Gal*, while smiling at Eleanor the whole time. From there he whisked her off to Keen's for muttonchops, escalloped potatoes, creamed spinach, and two bottles of red wine, and then to Pete's Tavern for a warm toddy, before ending the night arm and arm staring up at the glimmering colors of the Rockefeller Center Christmas Tree.

He made sure she got back to her apartment safely and as he kissed her goodbye he whispered, "You are going to be my wife, Ms. Eleanor Holm. Rest assured." She didn't respond, but she had a feeling he wasn't wrong.

DODD

The Dodd's first official ambassador dinner was the social event of the season; replete with a limitless smorgasbord, multiple cocktail bars, an army of servers carrying champagne and appetizers, and a 6-piece orchestra. The winter-themed gala was to raise awareness for the Artistic Competitions of the 1936 Olympic Games. German Art was displayed throughout the house. It was also an extremely glamorous and well-attended *soirée*.

Mattie Dodd glowed as she weaved through the guests smiling and greeting everyone. At one point she took her son's arm and led him over to two of her friends. "Bill, darling, let me introduce you to two of Chicago's finest international correspondents. This is William Shirer and Sigrid Schultz."

"A pleasure. Berlin must be a plethora of good material for reporters these days," Bill remarked. They agreed but getting their stories out of Germany had become a major problem. Censorship ran rampant under the Nazis, and this infuriated the free press from around the world. This surprised Bill. He had thought that kind of behavior was targeted solely for the "Communist rags".

"That was our understanding as well, but communiqués seem to be in a constant state of misplacement and wire services, conveniently run by the Nazi Party, cannot, for some mysterious reason, figure out why so many reports are getting lost... Getting the truth out of here these days is as impossible as deciphering Herodotus," added the sardonic Shirer.

Mattie quickly slipped away. She had made a promise to herself to stay away from political talk. There is nothing more distasteful than a hostess on a soapbox, she had always believed.

She continued her rounds, and as soon as she entered the sitting room, a familiar voice rang out.

"Mattie, darling, such a sumptuous *soirée!*" It was Bella Fromme, 40-year-old buxom German-Jewish reporter who was a titan in her field. Fromme had covered German politics and diplomacy since before the Weimar Republic and knew everyone who was anyone in Berlin. She was also a decorated WWI Red Cross volunteer and though a liberal Jew, she had very powerful friends in the Nazi cabinet. 'All Germany, all the time, warts and all' was her motto. "Come over here, Mattie. I want you to meet one of our artists."

The obliging hostess bee-lined over to them, "Mr. Heartfield and I have already met, Bella." She leaned in for a hug and peck on the cheek, first from Bella, then from Heartfield. "John, don't say anything you may regret, this one is ruthless."

"I applaud his artistic attack on the current political situation. His photomontages are both scathing and hysterical," Bella said between puffs from her elongated cigarette holder.

"Yes, well let's just say Herr Osten doesn't feel quite the same way. I don't suppose he will be choosing me to represent Germany in any of the Artistic Competitions in '36," Heartfield said as he looked over into the adjacent room where Sports Director Osten stood next to other Nazi officials. They examined his artwork: a photomontage of Hitler's face on an x-rayed body; his heart a Nazi symbol, the background a collection of artist's tools. The men did not look pleased. "I have gotten death threats, Bella. I believe I'm taking my show on the road to Prague."

Bella was shocked, "No! All this over art?! This is becoming absurd." Once again Mattie excused herself from a political discussion. She grabbed two flutes of champagne and headed toward her husband who was in the middle of a conversation with German Filmmakers Fritz Lang and Billy Wilder.

"Mr. Lang, I thought *Dr. Mabuse* was a terrific and frightening film," Dodd said as he took a glass from his wife.

"Thank you but I believe some of your more political guests did not approve," Lang responded as Osten joined the conversation.

"In America, filmmakers don't have to worry about government interference," Mattie exclaimed, breaking her own rule on political grandstanding.

Osten coldly replied, "German filmmakers wouldn't either if they followed the law."

But the outspoken and biting tongue of Wilder did not hold back, "A law that stifles creativity. That's not a law, that's suppression. Smart Nazi like you should know the diff --. Oh wait, 'smart Nazi'--such an oxymoron."

"Smart enough to know that's dangerous talk even for someone planning to leave the country in two weeks," Osten reminded him.

"Freedom of expression is encouraged in this household, Mr. Osten," Dodd fired back then continued, "I think Hollywood's censorship board is even ridiculous. I always say if a film offends just don't watch it. It's as simple as that."

"I don't see it as simple as that. Subversion is not healthy. But let's agree to disagree," Osten acquiesced then excused himself from the conversation.

"How does the largest cacophony of sadists and sycophants ever assembled, gain control over civilized people?" Lang inquired, as he watched Osten walk away.

"Civilized? You give our people too much credit," Wilder remarked.

Once again Mattie was on the move, and once again she was apprehended. This time just outside the kitchen by her good friend MILDRED FISH-HARNACK. If Mattie had any illusion of steering clear of politics, it was certainly going to be shattered by

Mildred. Fish-Harnack was an outspoken radical American academic. And the woman never feared voicing her opinion, on anything.

"Come outside and join me for a smoke. I have something simply fabulous to tell you," Mildred prompted the hostess.

"Okay but I can't let William see me. He gets so upset," Mattie said and scurried off toward the back porch with her friend.

"He's one to talk with his stinky pipe," Mildred reminded her as they walked out into the chilling night air. She lit them both a cigarette and started right in on her story, "Mattie, I've been in constant contact with some of the heads of Berlin's National Socialist Party." Mattie was instantly appalled, and Mildred defended herself, "They are intent on solving the poverty and starvation problems here in Germany, unlike the Nazis who do absolutely nothing."

"You're going to get into trouble. Look who is standing right inside!" They peered through the bay window into the main room, "The head of the Gestapo!" Mattie warned her. But Mattie noticed something quite disturbing while trying to make her point, that very head of the Gestapo, RUDY DIELS, was speaking very closely to her daughter Martha.

Martha was having the time of her life. Finally, her stodgy father had agreed to a blowout. And she was going to make the most of it. Men were standing in line to speak with her and when they did, they were extremely complimentary, which put Martha at her flirtatious best. She was resplendent in her blue gown and Diels would not leave her side once his turn came.

"Martha, you are the most refreshing young lady to ever enter Berlin," the intense young man gushed, "You are like an early spring." Martha liked that, but Rudy nearly ruined it when the Maid began to refresh his glass of champagne. "I'll pour my own, filthy dog," he barked and snatched the bottle from her hand. The poor woman ran off on the brink of tears.

"You can remove yourself from my presence immediately," Martha pronounced much to the young man's dismay. "I will not tolerate that behavior."

"But she's a Jew," he said innocently.

"That doesn't bother me, and if you want to spend any amount of time with me, it shouldn't matter to you," she scolded him then walked away leaving the two-fisted Nazi in shame.

About an hour later the orchestra filled the dance floor in the main room with the German Waltz. Dancers rhythmically and frequently exchanged partners, and it seemed every guest present was twirling in delight. Martha began the dance with a humbled Rudy Diels; Dodd with his wife; Bill Dodd, Jr. with a young pretty lady, and most of the other guests had paired off as well. As the dance progressed, Mattie became paired with Osten. He bowed courteously and took her hand, then maneuvered the floor with unusual dexterity. Mattie smiled widely.

Martha was then thrust into the arms of Adolf Hitler's current closest advisor, the hulking Ernst "Putzi" Hanfstaengle. She was immediately taken with the older man's muscular physique. As they danced their waltz, a sexual attraction became quite apparent, and they leaned into kiss... But Dodd grabbed Putzi's arm and dragged him from the dance floor with subtle expertise before the act transpired.

"I am mortified Ambassador. Your daughter is just so appealing," Putzi said defensively in perfect English.

"Keep it to yourself, Putzi. Let's take a walk and have a chat." Dodd, still holding the larger man's arm, led him away. "Your boss has been dodging me for almost two years." Dodd got rather pointed, "The time is now for Herr Hitler to acquiesce and face me. If that doesn't happen, you can tell him I will take it as a personal insult. I will then announce this provocation to the American Olympic Officials."

The half-American, half-German assured the Ambassador, "I will personally relay the message."

Dodd and Putzi now stood at the front door, "Tonight." Dodd announced.

Putzi looked at him confused. "Pardon me?"

"You're leaving. And you're going to 'personally relay' that message to your Führer right now. I expect a reply, with a solid date and time, by the end of this party. You want to see my daughter again this evening, you get that done promptly," Dodd explained, then opened the door and motioned for the man to leave. Putzi could do nothing but oblige. He thanked the man for his hospitality and walked out into the Berlin night.

Dodd rejoined Mattie at the party. He peered over toward Martha who was now getting kissed on the hand by Diels. They locked eyes and he shot her a stern look. Martha looked back at her father with defiant innocence before leading Diels back to the dance floor.

*   *   *

As Dodd waited in Berlin to meet with Hitler, down in New York City's lower East Side, a burgeoning ally, JUDGE JEREMIAH MAHONEY, President of the US Amateur Athletic Union (AAU), walked past huddled homeless people on a cold winter morning. Mahoney was an imposing 56-year-old man who had spent his whole life on these tough downtown streets. Though poor growing up, he was a standout all-around high school athlete and that led to a college scholarship at City College. From there, the determined Mahoney paid his own way to a master's degree at St. Francis Xavier, and then a law degree at NYU. Within a few years he was appointed a New York Supreme Court Justice and quickly became known for his vehement opposition to any type of discrimination and intolerance. This angered Governor Al Smith and his Tammany Hall political thugs who put Mahoney on the seat, but the Judge was unwavering. He wouldn't play political games when it came to human rights and quit six years into his term. He promptly opened his own law firm and then took over the AAU.

He walked tall with a newspaper in one hand and a cigar in the other and as he turned onto Mott St., two orphans ran up to him and begged for change. He reached into his pocket and pulled out a couple of shiny silver dollars. Before he handed over the coins he said, "If I give this to you, you boys gotta promise me something. Tomorrow, the Amateur Athletic Union is sponsoring a free basketball clinic at the 'Y'. You gotta be there, okay?"

"Sure thing, Judge!" they said, accepting the coins and running off.

Mahoney watched the boys run off and continued his journey to a gym where his amateur athletes trained. Upon entering he saw Avery Brundage waiting for him. Brundage was not pleased with the unprofessional surroundings for a business meeting. Mahoney saw Brundage's discomfort and laughed.

"Sorry Avery. Wherever the athletes are is where I take my meetings," he said. Behind him there were boxers and wrestlers training on mats and heavy bags. The sound of tattering speed bags filled the room.

"You wanted to see me," Brundage said dryly.

"Avery, I'm leaning towards a boycott of Berlin. Secretary Jahncke and Ambassador Dodd have been giving me updates on the situation in Germany and it sounds like a fucking nightmare."

Brundage was quick to cut him off. "Let's hold off on that talk until my inspection later next year, okay? I'll have a better assessment when I see things firsthand."

"But Dodd and Jahncke are seeing things firsthand right now. An American couple vacationing in Berlin was savagely beaten for not saluting the Nazis while walking by a parade. Beaten in broad daylight in front of police and not one person raised a finger to help!"

"Why didn't they salute?" Brundage asked.

Mahoney looked at him like he was crazy. "They are Americans, Avery! Why the hell would they do that?"

"Out of respect! Hitler has restored prosperity and order to that country! If we had any balls, we would learn a thing or two from the Germans instead of loafing around like we do."

Mahoney stared at him. "Are you oblivious, or just totally apathetic? There are real problems, violent problems, and I don't feel comfortable sending our team - even if it does ruin your dreams of running the IOC."

Brundage stood up. "It's always such a pleasure. Just keep the athletes preparing. I'll take care of the Nazis."

"All by yourself, huh? Ambassador Dodd is meeting with Hitler next week. If things continue to get worse before next year, your visit may be in vain."

"I'll take that into consideration," said Brundage, as he walked away. Mahoney shook his head and turned his attention back to his athletes.

*   *   *

Back in Berlin, in what turned out to be two months later, Ambassador Dodd had finally gotten his moment. He was escorted by a young man dressed in full SS garb down a long marble-columned hallway. They turned a corner, which presented another long corridor. In the year of impatiently waiting for this meeting, Dodd anticipated a dozen different scenarios. Would the Chancellor be confrontational? Would he be dismissive? Or gracious? He thought he was starting to get a good sense of the man just by living in this country and by observing the behavior of his subordinates. But they were unpredictable, and Dodd always believed that such conduct started at the top.

They proceeded to a room at the hallway's end. Through a glass door, Adolf Hitler waited patiently, arms behind his back, staring at Dodd the entire time as he approached. The escort opened the door and immediately saluted. "Heil Hitler!"

Hitler saluted back. "Heil. You may go." He turned to Ambassador Dodd with a smile and a handshake. Dodd returned the handshake but not the smile. "Please sit down, Mr. Ambassador," Hitler said in a heavy German accent. He gestured towards a chair in front of his desk. Dodd sat but Hitler remained standing.

"Herr Hitler, with all due respect, we were supposed to meet two hours ago." Dodd said, then quickly added, "actually, this meeting was scheduled to happen *many months* ago."

"My humblest apologies. There are pressing matters at hand, as I'm sure you can appreciate. So, let's get right to the point. You called this meeting to discuss that unfortunate incident with the American tourists."

"For starters, yes. That boy happened to be the son of a Standard Oil executive. And I believe you and that company continue to have a nice little deal going, correct?"

Hitler didn't flinch. "That is correct."

"Well, they are still livid and are second guessing their decision to continue to do business. They want the person who did this to be brought to justice."

Hitler quickly replied, "Immediately!"

Dodd was surprised. He had grown suspicious of Hitler after all these months, but Hitler's agreeable conviction caught him off guard. Dodd cleared his throat and said, "I'd also like to discuss the Olympics."

"What about them?" Hitler replied, pulling up a chair and sitting next to the American.

"There are prominent officials in my country who are

considering a boycott if this violence continues."

"You have my absolute word, Ambassador Dodd, that the growing SA problem will be brought under control. The Olympics will not be jeopardized by a few radicals; I assure you that."

Dodd rose, reluctant but somewhat relieved. "Very good. Well then sir, I bid you a good night. And thank you for finally taking this meeting."

"My apologies again. Please feel free to call on me anytime, Ambassador. My door is always open," Hitler said.

Dodd headed to the door. "You will keep my office informed on the fate of the attacker?"

"As soon as it happens." The men shook hands and Hitler watched Dodd walk away down the long hallway.

As Dodd made his way through the maze of marble corridors, he had a sudden sensation of being in a dream. The meeting transpired without incident or confrontation. He left the building to find a black car waiting for him. The driver held the door open, perfectly timed for his arrival. He wondered for a moment if the timing was a little too perfect. Dodd also wondered how long it would take Hitler to deal with the SA attack, if indeed he was going to deal with it at all?

*   *   *

Later that night, in a dark alley, Putzi walked with purpose behind an apartment complex. He scanned each of the lit windows as if he was counting them. When he got to number six, he stopped and put on a pair of black leather gloves. Sneaking under a fire escape, Putzi entered the basement door and quietly walked up a flight of stairs. He paused at a landing when he heard a young couple giggling in the alley. He braced himself against a wall until the couple was out of sight. He looked around to see if anyone may have seen him, and then cautiously snaked

- 65 -

up to the top floor.

In a modest apartment kitchen, the young Brown-Shirt who began the assault on the American Couple at the SA parade, stirred a boiling pot of soup on a small kitchen stove. There was a knock on the door.

"Yeah?" the young man called. After there was no reply, he walked to the door and opened it. Putzi jumped in.

"Get on your fucking knees," Putzi ordered.

"Wha—?" Putzi destroyed the young unsuspecting cadet with a punch to the stomach and he dropped to the floor, gasping for air.

"That's better." Putzi looked around the apartment while the man struggled to breathe. "Who gave you the authority to assault an American citizen in broad daylight?"

The Brown-Shirt, gasping, said, "Rohm!"

"Rohm? The Chief of Staff?"

"Yes!"

Putzi calmly walked to the stove and took a sip of the soup from a ladle. "So . . . Rohm thinks his SA cadets can do what they please when they please?"

The young man, putting on a brave front, slowly and proudly rose to his feet, still gasping for air. "We can, and we will. There are three million of us ready to stand behind Rohm and the SA –"

Suddenly, with one swift move, Putzi threw the pot of boiling stew at him. The cadet screamed and covered his scalded face. Putzi then took the pot and smashed it over his head, over and over until he fell. Blood and brain matter smeared the kitchen floor and dripped down the wall until his body unconsciously started convulsing, moments from certain death.

Hitler's henchman watched the Brown-Shirt's last breath as purple liquid leaked profusely from his head wounds. He calmly returned the pot to the stove, looked around the room for a moment, then smiled and walked out.

As he strolled back to his apartment, Putzi felt gratified about the quiet efficiency of his task. But even more gratifying, he knew the outcome would indirectly please Ambassador Dodd, which, in turn, would make Martha Dodd happy. And Putzi would do anything to make the Ambassador's daughter happy.

These were feelings that did not please the Ambassador; directly, indirectly, or otherwise.

1934

It was late Spring, and the whole world seemed to be in upheaval. Mother Nature and mankind were creating havoc. A massive fire destroyed the city of Hakodate, Japan, killing thousands. A devastating earthquake hit the quiet but densely populated country of Nepal leaving only ruins in the wake of Mount Everest. Dust storms rolled over the entire US Mid-West creating a landscape unfit to farm and sending folks by the thousands due West. And John Dillinger and "Pretty Boy" Floyd went on a robbing and killing spree that would end in their own bloody demise.

Geo-politically, it was just as tempestuous. Communism was taking hold in China. Fascism overtook all facets of Italian culture. Assassinations in Nicaragua and Austria weakened the regions, and in the case of Austria, created a dictatorship that would become the first step in the country's eventual *Anschluss*.

But back in Chicago, Elizabeth Brundage, graceful, middle-aged, and content, sat at her breakfast table across from her devoted, but distant, husband Avery. She sipped coffee from her fine white China and studied him as he focused on the sports section of the *Chicago Tribune*. She wondered how someone could be so consumed--obsessed--with the results of men in tights running around chasing balls. Then it occurred to her that Avery was one of them in his youth, and men never really grow up after all. Avery was like her father in that way; he was a wealthy Chicago banker who secured loans to real estate developers during the day but played with his model trains late into the night.

She walked to the other side of the table and reached into Avery's newspaper, pulling out the Society section. Avery pretended not to notice. It was a subversive act, but only to gain a little of his attention. It seemed as if his every waking moment was focused on the Olympic Committee and sports in general, even more than when they were first married. The radio suddenly played *Happy Days are Here Again* and Elizabeth turned up the volume. As a trained soprano, she belted out the tune in perfect pitch.

"Can you please stop, Liz? That song is driving me crazy." While Avery admired her singing talent, he didn't share her appreciation of music. (At a performance of Wagner's *Die Walküre*, he said, "It started at 7 o'clock and I glanced at my watch at 10 o'clock, only to find it was 8 o'clock!")

She popped up from the table to oblige. "Oh Avery, only you would dislike the most popular tune in the land." She lowered the radio and the volume of her voice but kept on singing. Avery suddenly slammed down the paper.

"Mussolini thinks he can gain support by fixing the World Cup!" he exclaimed.

"World Cup?"

"Soccer! The World Cup is being held in Italy and FIFA is as greasy as a vat of olive oil. The glare from Mussolini's bald melon must be blinding everyone. Not me. When I'm on the IOC, no politician's going to tell me what to do." Avery shook his head.

"Why don't we take a break and drive down to Oak Street Beach today?" she asked.

"I'm leaving to go back to New York this afternoon. I may not be back for the rest of the year," he said, glaring back at the sports pages.

"Sometimes I think you enjoy being so far away from me," she joked. But she wasn't at all far from the truth. Brundage didn't dislike Elizabeth; they got along fine, and he appreciated the way she cooked and cared for him. He just wasn't in love with her anymore.

"Don't be ridiculous. I'll miss you terribly," he lied, straight-faced.

GOULD

It had only been five short months since Art Jarrett had shown up at the Holm's doorstep, but the impulsive Jarrett asked Eleanor's dad for her hand, nonetheless. Her father reluctantly gave his blessing, but the imposing fireman did explain to the young man that his blessing meant nothing. It would all depend on his daughter. If she didn't accept, there would be nothing he could say or do to change her mind.

Eleanor mulled it over for a few days, weighing the pros and cons, before judiciously accepting the proposal of marriage. By marrying Jarret, she would have a high-profile performing job at the Cocoanut Grove and still have time to practice swimming. It was advantageous for both her acting aspirations as well as her possible return to the Olympic stage.

So, on a beautiful Spring afternoon in her parent's backyard, the golden girl of American sports and the up-and-coming band leader at one of New York City's hottest night spots, married in a quiet ceremony of intimate family and friends. The only press invited was Alan Gould and though he was honored to be there, he wasn't too pleased the gathering was taking place. He thought it a huge mistake by Eleanor. He kept it to himself, however, as he walked down the line and congratulated the parents, then the groom, and finally the bride. Eleanor smiled at him and leaned in to give him a peck on the cheek.

"Love the new bowtie. Meet me out front in five minutes," she whispered in his ear.

"What is the meaning of this clandestine rendezvous, Mrs. Jarrett?" Gould asked as he lit his pipe, while he and Eleanor sat next to each other on the front steps.

"I can't tell you how much it means to me that you're here," Eleanor began as she lit a cigarette. She looked up at him with child-like guilt. "Don't tell my parents." Gould just rolled his eyes as she continued. "You've always been very good to me. Other than my dad, most men who are nice to me just want sex," she said bluntly. "But not you. You've always been supportive and kind, but straight up. And I can tell you want to say something right now but you're holding back. Is that true?"

Gould thought very hard how best to word his answer without offending the new bride. "Eleanor, even when you won Gold in '32, I still saw you as that same little girl who tore up the competition in AAU meets. But now you are a woman and decisions you make will affect every aspect of your life; professionally, athletically, and most of all, personally. And if you make wrong decisions in any one of them, hasty decisions, it could lead to a domino effect, and anything good you've ever done prior, won't mean a hill of sugar in a rainstorm."

Eleanor looked at the man hard. "I love him, Gould," she paused, "at least for now."

"You're a free soul. It's what's most appealing about you. And it's what gives you that edge. That freedom offers you the opportunity to compete on the highest level. And you have the talent to match. I would hate to see that be lost in you, Eleanor."

She smiled back at him. "Marriage will help me settle down and focus. I won't be such a party girl."

"Do you expect me to believe that? Gould said incredulously. "You'll be working at a nightclub in New York City."

She laughed, "True, very true."

"Look, I don't want to bring you down on your wedding day. Just don't lose focus on swimming while you are still young enough to dominate." He stared hard into her eyes, "Promise me that."

She grabbed both his hands, "I promise. And thank you so much for your generous wedding present."

"Save it for the annulment," he said with a wry smile. Eleanor couldn't help but laugh.

*   *   *

A few days later in the cramped offices of the Jewish American Federation, Judge Mahoney met with Jewish American leaders over their take on the situation in Germany. Many of them had relatives still in the Fatherland and communication had become minimal.

"My brother escaped to Holland in the middle of the night. Nazis were literally hunting him in his own neighborhood with dogs and rifles," one of the men told Mahoney. "Like a wild animal!"

Mahoney listened to story after story from the men, all a similar nature. Their stories coincided with the reports he was getting from both Jahncke and Dodd. Germany was beginning to go insane, and Mahoney knew sending a team was just too dangerous. The other men urged him to propose a boycott. But he didn't need their pleas; he knew it was the right thing to do. He would reach out to AAU members and the AOC immediately and strongly suggest cancelling US participation in Berlin. Brundage would be difficult, very difficult, but Mahoney had heard enough from too many. The first person he would reach out to, an ally he could count on, was his good friend at the AP, Alan Gould.

*   *   *

The Judge approached Gould at Roosevelt Stadium, the beautiful new outdoor track and field stadium along the East River. Both men watched as Olympic hopefuls trained and whose futures now lie in the hands of political machinations.

"So, the AP would back me on this one then, Alan?" Mahoney asked as the two men walked along the track.

"Secretary Jahncke has already reached out to me and described the situation. It sure is gonna be a shame with all the talent we have going into the Games. What's the vibe you're getting from the athletes?"

Mahoney pointed to a tall black runner sprinting on the other side of the field, a man faster than his size would suggest. "You see that man? His name is JOHN WOODRUFF." He then pointed to another black athlete, strong and stocky, taking his turn at the Broad Jump, "That boy's name is JESSE OWENS." Then he singled out a young white man, "And that boy, he is MARTY GLICKMAN, only 16 years old. They know what's happening to people of their ilk in Germany, and they want to stick it right to that little dictator. I don't want to crush their dreams, but I don't see a viable alternative." He put his hands in his pockets feeling dejected.

Gould put his hand on the older man's shoulder, "The AP has your back, Judge. I'll start planting the seeds for a boycott in my next column. Maybe the rest of the world will finally take notice."

Gould had to support Mahoney and his cause. But the deep-rooted sports fan in him wanted to see the athletes compete. To Gould, there was nothing in the world that compared to feats of greatness on the sports field. He wanted to see what Jesse Owens could do against the world's best. And if the kid Glickman could stick it to Hitler? Not only would it make a great story, but he would be there to witness it. Gould turned away from the athletes, shaking off his selfish speculations, and remembered that he was supposed to be a reporter first; a fan second.

GRETEL

On that same day, fifty-five hundred kilometers across the Atlantic Ocean, Max Bergmann approached the gleaming twin towers of Wembley Stadium with his insides ripping apart. His daughter, Gretel, one of Germany's greatest athletes, forced to compete in another country. He was as proud as a father could be, but his resentments quelled those emotions every time he approached a venue where Gretel was competing. This was Max's third trip across the English Channel to see her jump, and this would be his last. He would explain to her the reasons why, but only after the competition.

After he took his seat, he gazed around the magnificent stadium. He could hardly believe it had been a year since he decided to send Gretel to England. For weeks after she left, he lay awake in bed every night wondering if it was the right decision. As the weeks and months passed, discrimination and persecution of German Jews became unimaginable, and soon it became clear that he had made not the right decision, but the *only* decision. Today, as his anger reached a boil, he saw the athletes emerge from the bowels of the stadium, and he saw Gretel. His pride swelled, obliterating any other maleficent thoughts, and for a moment he felt like a father again.

Gretel entered the stadium and immediately searched for Max. After waving him a kiss, she turned her attention to the task at hand, as she had done the entire year away from home. After having been exiled from her homeland and stripped of all previous accomplishments including two world records, last year was now behind her. Though she had made many friends at the Polytechnic, and acclimated well to the English lifestyle, this was the first time she had felt like a true British national and not just a German-Jewish refugee. She began her warmup routine as Max taught her, gathering focus and control. Her event was the first of the day, and soon it was time.

Gretel peered forward with fiery intensity. Her focus was a thin, slightly pliable, cross bar thirteen feet away that stood 1.55 meters high. And nothing, not even the cheering crowd of thousands, interrupted her thoughts of clearing it. She was vying for the British National Championship, and this was the jump that would secure it. It was also a world record attempt. She nodded as the starter raised his flag. After a deep breath, she began her diagonal approach increasing her speed as she ran. The whole stadium was a blur, a current of colors flying by her as she neared the jump point. At the perfect moment she thrust her body violently upward and into a Western roll.

As she soared over the bar, she knew right away she was going to clear it. When she landed, the stadium erupted. Her fellow female athletes ran toward her and congratulated her with hugs and slaps on the back. Gretel was delirious. Once again, she was at the top of her sport. She raised her arms in triumph. The crowd cheered even harder.

Max Bergmann watched her from the stands as she received her Gold Medal. He wished Paula, Ernst, and Hannah could be there. The family missed her terribly, but it was obvious Gretel was thriving. And though he was ecstatic that she had won here in England, he couldn't suppress his anger. He would have to calm down before meeting Gretel after the ceremony.

*   *   *

Outside the stadium, Gretel greeted him with a bear hug and Max was a little surprised by how strong she had become. She must have been training non-stop, he thought, and for a moment he was jealous of those who were there to witness it. On top of that, Gretel seemed to be at home in London, pointing out her favorite restaurants and shops as they walked. It made it even harder to say what he was about to tell her.

"*Liebchen*, this will be my last trip here. Travel is becoming too difficult," he said to her as they sat al fresco at a café near the stadium. But in fact, travel had become impossible for him. The German government had frozen his papers and for him to even get the proper authorization for this trip it had cost him a pretty penny, which of course went straight into the pockets of Laupheim's local Nazi official.

"So now it has come to that?" She said through gritted teeth. Gretel was not pleased her father had put the family through this. His own obstinacy had kept them in Germany even after she begged them to come to London, and now there was no getting out. Even the students at the Polytechnic could recognize what was going on over there, and every day Gretel lived with the fear her family would cease to continue. "Poppa, the American Helen Keller once said, 'the only thing worse than being blind is having sight with no vision'. I would have rather you been blind."

Gretel had never challenged him before. But there was nothing he could say in his defense. Whether it was his pride or his ego or both, he ignored all the warnings and kept the majority of his family in harm's way. And now he had to answer for it to the one person he had been smart enough to relocate. He tried to appease her, "This too shall pass, Gretel." But she was not impressed and just shook her head in disgust.

"I'm going to move to the United States after graduation. I suggest very strongly you think about packing up *my* family and somehow joining me before something awful happens." Max was taken aback, not only at her brashness but this was the first he had ever heard she was considering such a big move. To him, America wasn't only halfway around the world. It was a nice experiment that wouldn't and couldn't last if greed and capitalism remained the rule of law in the young democracy. And their motto, "all men are created equal" certainly didn't ring true. It was a hypocritical and unrealistic fairyland.

"America? This is so far away. And that is not the utopia it seems. They have quite a few of their own racial and ethnic problems."

THE ATHLETES

In the heart of America, Columbus, Ohio, the spring semester was coming to a close inside Haggerty Hall, on the campus of Ohio State University. The Business Ethics students buzzed around like honeybees in preparation for their final class before exams. The professor entered the room and asked them to take their seats. He knew they were prepared for the material he would include on their tests, so he began this day with much different intentions. He wanted to figure out what kind of values these young people possessed. He asked one young man to rise.

"You are the CEO of a large American oil company, and a Fascist government has asked for a business alliance with you offering more than a handsome sum with a lengthy contract. Go!" The young man's heart stopped, and he looked around confused. After a beat he began.

"Well, if there are no government sanctions, I don't see how I could refuse. The purpose of the CEO is to make the investors as much money as possible, and a country with great wealth is a prime business associate." The class pondered this for a moment. The professor threw him a more direct question.

"So, if Adolf Hitler said, 'let's partner up', you would have no problem?" he asked.

"Why would I?" responded the young man. This triggered an open debate amongst the students. Some shook their heads negatively, saying things like, "Their credit may not last," or "Other countries may give you trouble." Others nodded in agreement. "Could be a great deal," and "It could further relations and influence future policy."

But the professor wanted someone else to answer the question. "Mr. Owens, what would you do?" He saw Jesse had been contemplating in silence.

Jesse Owens rose to his feet and spoke softly. "Being that this is a business ethics class, and Mr. Hitler's behavior is extremely unethical, I would pass. But I wouldn't expect anyone else in this country to understand. Racism is an accepted way of life here. It's condoned. Segregation is just another form of sterilization. I don't see much difference, and its business as usual here." Owens looked around at his classmates for a challenge, but none came; they only looked at him stunned. It was the most loquacious the student athlete had been the whole semester. And this pleased the professor greatly.

"So, would you vote for a boycott of the '36 Games, knowing the revenue from an Olympics will go into the Nazis coffers?" the professor challenged him.

"I know I want to win Gold and show not just Germany, but the whole world, what a black man is capable of. But when you put it that way, I'm not sure." He smiled, "It would be sweet to defeat the Aryan race, though."

A bell rang, signaling the end of class. Jesse packed his books and waited for his white classmates to exit the room, then followed them towards the door. The professor gave him a nod and Jesse smiled back. He walked down the hallway, surrounded by other students, and made his way outside to a courtyard.

The open courtyard was filled with students coming and going to class, sitting on the grass, smoking cigarettes, and chatting away in small cliques. The sun was bright and warm, hinting that summer was near. Jesse soaked it in. He took a deep breath and exhaled. He was proud of himself for speaking up in class. Although he was very popular because of his athletic achievements, he hardly said a word all semester, never taking the bait that his professors threw at him. He had learned to stay quiet as a young boy. As the youngest of ten children, his voice was the smallest, and in the midst of the Owens clan, not many people listened anyway.

At the age of nine, his family moved from Alabama to Ohio during the Great Migration, when 1.5 million African Americans left the segregated South for job opportunities in the urban and industrial North. Jesse's new teacher at school didn't even listen to him. When she asked his name, he said, "J.C." (James Cleveland). She thought he said, "Jesse". The name stuck, and he didn't speak up about it.

He had lots of thoughts and lots to say, but he was careful not to vocalize them when it came to racism. This day, though, he thought that maybe some of his white classmates were listening. For a moment, he was heard. His remarks in class were minimal, but it felt like a great victory.

While he basked in the sun's glow, he turned to see a few of his Business Ethics classmates walking by. He began to approach them to start up a conversation, but they headed straight to the water fountain in the center of the courtyard. *Whites only.* The *colored* fountain stood next to it. He saw one of his male classmates drink from the *white* fountain, then spit directly into the empty *colored* fountain. He halted his approach, turned, and walked towards his next class. It occurred to Jesse that maybe the only reason they listened to him was because he was a track star.

*   *   *

In the heart of Germany on that same spring day, another track star basked under the sun in the city of Leipzig. LUZ LONG was a tall, handsome, blonde, blue-eyed favorite of the Reich. He was the two-time German Broad Jump champion and was eyeing another in '35 and Gold on his home turf in '36. But fame did not come without a price; Nazi expectations and pressure to succeed were overwhelming and this put quite a lot of mental strain on the 21-year-old. It also meant he spent every waking hour on the practice field when he wasn't studying at the University. The one caveat, his father Jorgen, a WWI flying ace, was his coach, and Luz loved and admired him unconditionally, despite his militaristic approach to coaching.

"Focus, Luz! Hit the mark exactly!" Jorgen yelled as his son ran down the runway and then jumped. It was an incredible attempt and Luz came up cheering. "You scratched. The jump was meaningless," his father informed him, deflating the young man's enthusiasm. "This sport is like flying a plane." Luz had heard it many times before.

"Yes, father. A safe take-off, control in the air, and a perfect landing."

"If you fail in any of these, total disaster! You basically slid off the runway and killed everyone on board."

Luz rolled his eyes. "Okay, let's don't get crazy."

"Take off a split second earlier and establish a rhythm, then you can work from there." Jorgen took his son's hands and looked at him closely, "Luz, the Nazis will not put you in the Army if you continue to excel athletically. It is great that you are getting a law degree but I'm living proof that they will draft a lawyer. Athletes, however, look at Schmeling, he doesn't even have to join the Party! That's what I want for you. You are too nice of a young man to be a part of that behavior."

And indeed, Luz was. This was a person who still helped old people cross the street, stood when a woman entered the room, tutored other students who were struggling in their law classes, and befriended every opponent, appreciating the common interest they both shared in their sport. Though a champion, his father would question his 'killer instinct.'

"My objective is always to win, father. I just don't have to be an ass about it," was Luz' standard response.

Jorgen smiled. "And you will win. You'll see."

After the practice session, Luz walked the streets of Leipzig and headed for the intersection of *Via Regia* and *Via Imperil*, the center of two very important medieval trade routes, where he would find his favorite bakery and munch down his post-workout snack - a salty pretzel-stick and a *Kristallweizen* beer. Before he could reach his destination, he heard a buzzing sound from above. He paused and looked around for the strange noise. Other pedestrians were also frozen in the streets, looking up at the sky.

Suddenly, the buzzing grew louder, and Luz looked up to see a bomber escorted by a squadron of fighter planes. The crowd gasped at the sight, as if witnessing a solar eclipse for the first time. "I've never seen anything like it!" One person exclaimed. Another said, "It's a training mission." As the planes flew into the distance, the crowd spontaneously started to cheer. Luz thought that was an odd reaction. He walked past the clapping pedestrians who were still straining to get a glimpse of the distant squadron and headed for the bakery. He just wanted to get his pretzel and beer and go home.

*   *   *

Back in America, in Seattle, Washington, the Puget Sound was uncomfortably quiet. The University of Washington's 8-man rowing team, the mighty Huskies, had performed well below expectations during the 1934 season. Coxswain BOB MOCH took a lot of the blame for their mediocre season and vowed to roar back his junior year. He demanded the team practice all summer. Most of them were local boys and would be taking part time jobs in town until school started back up in September. So, every morning, Monday through Friday at five, the team took to Puget Sound and worked on rhythm, pace, speed, and endurance.

"Catch, press, swing it through!" Moch urged as the men cut their paddles through the still waters. "Bring it to your chest. Pick it up, one! Come on!" Moch knew the University's long-time coach Al Ulbrickson had three teams he could choose from to head the following year's slate of competitions, and Moch was intent on their team being the coach's number one. In fact, the coming year of 1935 was going to be one of the most competitive in the school's history and a half-hearted effort by any team would mean their certain doom. "Focus on the person in front of you and breathe!" he screamed as the crew panted and struggled.

Bob Moch (kneeling) and the rest of his University of Washington rowing Team, 1934

When the boys finally got back to the dock, Ulbrickson was there waiting. "That was pathetic," he yelled to them. "I've seen better rowing by a child in a bathtub! Pick it up boys, or any dreams of going to Berlin your senior year will go to the JV!" He then turned and walked away, embarrassed by his team.

After the berating, most of the guys rushed off to get to work. Moch was bar-backing at a local dive in Belltown, so his day didn't get restarted until 4pm. DON HUME, the stroke oar for this bunch of hooligans, and Moch's closest pal on the team, stopped him before he left to go back home to sleep.

"Sorry I was lagging a bit, Bob. Couldn't get it going there this morning."

"You set the stroke, Don. When you lag, we might as well be trolling," he said with a half grin. "Coming by the bar tonight?"

"I don't know if I should," but quickly followed that up, "Who am I kidding? I'll see you at five. I'll bring a couple of the guys," Don said, then noticed the time. "I'm late. Gotta run." He turned and was off like a cannon. Moch grinned as his friend had suddenly found his second wind. With a few hours to kill, he decided to grab a bite to eat, then stop by his parent's jewelry shop before heading to his bar-backing shift.

Bob's parents, Gaston and Fleeta Moch, had emigrated from Switzerland just before the outbreak of World War I. They sought opportunity on the west coast of America. Gaston had a keen business sense and good timing, and on the heels of the dwindled California gold rush, found an opportunity to sell jewelry and watches to the burgeoning population. It was a small shop, and that was perfectly fine. Gaston and Fleeta never expected to find a gold mine; they just wanted to raise a family far away from the increasing pressures of a changing Europe. In 1907, Switzerland had just organized the Swiss Army and their swift military expansion was alarming. By 1911, nearly a half-million men served in Switzerland's armed forces, even though they would remain neutral as the escalating hostilities simmered on its borders. So, the Moch's settled in the small town of Montesano, thirty miles inland from the Washington coast.

From outside the storefront window, Bob bit into a sandwich

and gazed in as his father meticulously repaired a pocket watch, needling it like a surgeon with his fine tools and magnifying glasses. He was proud of his parents, but never wanted to wind up stuck in a small town like this for the rest of his life. He thought that if he ever got the chance to leave, he would jump at it. He took the last bite of his sandwich and entered the shop to say hello and to deliver Gaston and Fleeta a couple of bowls of soup he had bought at the grocery store.

DODD

Dodd was beside himself as he waited on the phone for an operator to connect him to the US State Department. None of his dispatches were being answered, not even the ones he knew were getting out of Berlin unscathed. He had begun to personally drop them off at the last leg of their journey before being loaded on the plane to the US. There was no way the Nazis could get to them from there, and they certainly wouldn't dare keep mail from coming back into the Embassy, an open act of aggression. Open and read it, yes, withhold it, no. Yet, somehow, Dodd still received no responses.

"Yes, operator. Yes, the office of Cordell Hull, Washington DC." Dodd became even more anxious as he waited for what seemed like an eternity, until finally the call went through. "Mr. Secretary, it's good to hear your voice, sir. I know you're very busy so let me get straight to the point. I'm rather surprised, and somewhat disappointed I might add, about the Department's reluctance and/or desire to identify the gravity of the present situation here in Germany. I mean not even one response from your office. I'm not sure how to take that, Cordell."

Secretary Hull, a staunch long-time Southern Democrat and over all decent man, was shocked. "Now hold on. I'm a little in the dark here, William. Not even one of these 'more dire' reports from your office has gotten to my desk. I would have certainly replied at the very least. Are you sure they've even been getting out of Berlin?"

"Positive."

"Well, that's the darndest thing," he said half to himself, half to Dodd. "I'll try to find out what the snafu is."

"Please do sir. The situation here is getting untenable. It's all in my letters."

Unbeknownst to Hull, when the posts would arrive from Dodd's office, officials below the Secretary were opening them. These mostly Ivy League snobs were determining on their own that Dodd's warnings were the cries of a man 'unsuited to do his job' and who, 'coming from the University of Illinois, lacked any credible background for a diplomatic appointment'. So, they read the letters, laughed amongst themselves at 'the drama', and then filed them away. Hull was oblivious.

*   *   *

Dodd's daughter Martha had settled quite cozily into German life. It had been almost a year now that the Dodd's had been in Berlin and Martha had gained herself quite a reputation as THE American social butterfly. She had also begun dating Putzi and Rudy Diels simultaneously, which made neither Nazi very happy. Not intending to stop there, she also began a correspondence with SS Captain Willi Lehmann, who she had just happened to find out, under the covers and without much prodding, that he was spying for the Soviets. Hitler's right-hand man, the head of the SS, and a Soviet spy parading as an SS official; Martha couldn't have been more pleased with herself. There was not a more important woman in Germany since Marlene Dietrich. But it was all just a romantic game to her, and she loved to make the three of them jealous.

"Putzi, you know Rudy takes me to the opera. You take me on walks in the park," she said with mock disappointment as they strolled in Berlin's most central park, Tiergarten. But Putzi never did anything without an ulterior motive.

"A walk is refreshing and good for the lungs," he said. But he was leading them to a particular area. Hitler had found out Ernst Rohm was leading a rally of his Brown Shirts there and he wanted Putzi to listen in. "Why would you want me to do the same things with you as Diels? Isn't that your whole reason for not committing, so you can have a variety?" Martha smirked; she knew she had been called out.

When they reached the rally, both were taken aback, not only at the size of the crowd but the size of the man who was leading it. Ernst Rohm had the shape of a zeppelin but the charisma of a Hollywood movie star. The crowd roared as he rallied them around his SA 'Stormtroopers'.

"The SA is the true defender of peace and real German culture. Do not be mistaken, our numbers are strong, and our misguided *Führer* has made a grave error by not appointing me and other SA officials to the Defense Ministry. We will not be overlooked! One way or another," Rohm grabbed his side arm like a bloated cowboy, "we will show our importance and our muscle to the rest of the Nazi Party!"

Putzi took in every word as Martha driveled on and on about Diels and Lehmann. He was especially interested in Rohm's last comment.

"Have you heard a word I've been saying, Putzi?" Martha fumed.

"I've definitely heard quite enough," he answered menacingly, "And I'll give you some words of advice." He turned to her with fire in his eyes, "Watch the company you keep. Now let's go. I'm driving you home." Martha stared at him in shock.

He dropped her back off after a thoroughly silent drive and sped away without even a hint of a goodbye. She watched exasperated before storming through the front door.

Inside the house her mother was having tea with Mildred. Mildred seemed to stop in mid-sentence when Martha entered, and both women looked up at her like they had seen an apparition.

"What trouble are you two brewing over there?" Martha inquired rhetorically, eyeing them suspiciously on her way upstairs to her room.

"That was a close one," Mildred continued. "I'm telling you Mattie; the Communists are going to overthrow this man before the end of the year. And now I have their trust to help them with their fight." She leaned in and whispered, "I've asked them to give me an assignment."

Mattie put her hand on her heart, "Oh my God, Mildred. What in the hell are you thinking? Why don't you just stick to teaching? You are going to end up way over your head and in deep trouble."

"I'm done preaching to spoiled brats." Just then the Maid walked in to refresh their tea and Mildred couldn't resist. "You wouldn't be very upset if Herr Hitler suddenly lost his position, and all his power would you dear?" The older woman looked at her frightened.

"I'm sorry. I cannot speak of such things. My husband forbids it," she replied respectfully.

"You're amongst the American ladies, darling. Don't be shy. No one here is going to suppress you." But the woman just brushed it off, poured tea, and left quietly.

"That's why I'm getting involved Goddammit! Ordinary German citizens are scared to even voice their fucking opinions!" She screamed at Mattie.

"Mildred please, your language. The children are home,"

Mattie said out of habit.

"Are you kidding, dear? Have you met your daughter? I don't think there's a definition of that word she doesn't know."

Mattie glared at her, but Martha's inhibitions were becoming a problem. And the last thing in the world her delicate-stomached husband needed was unnecessary anxiety. His job was becoming difficult enough. So much for his much-needed sabbatical and extra time to finish his book, she thought. His job was becoming an all-encompassing beast.

*   *   *

Just a few miles from the Dodd residence, in the blaze of the next morning's summer sun, Theodor Lewald and Wolfgang Furstner walked past a group of construction workers where a foreman was guiding a crane hoisting steel beams towards the roof of a half-finished building. Bulldozers and tractors dotted the grounds. Other workers were hammering away on the rooftops of brand-new dormitories. The Olympic Village was starting to take shape.

Furstner was beaming. "I put the commissary at the center of the village, right between the dorms. I want it to be a place where everyone feels welcome," he said. "And right there will be a courtyard." He looked at Lewald, who didn't seem to notice. He grabbed Lewald's arm and faced him. "What's wrong, Theodor? Are you not happy with something? Is it the layout?" he asked.

"It's all fine, Wolfgang. The problem I have has nothing to do with your designs," Lewald said. "It's just . . . I'm not so sure you and I are going to be here when the Games finally begin?"

"What are you talking about?"

"You must see what's happening all around us?" Lewald asked.

Furstner shook his head. "My grandfather was a Christian

convert. That officially makes me a Christian," he said matter-of-factly.

"I wouldn't be so sure about that. People are talking about this becoming a formality... it's possible that anyone of Jewish ancestry could be compromised, convert or not," Lewald warned.

"Theodor, please. I'm a decorated Captain. I served in the war. I led a hundred men in battle for Germany! And you... you've devoted your life to the Fatherland. Don't be so dramatic." He patted Lewald's back. "C'mon, let me show you the Conference Hall. You'll love it." Furstner led Lewald towards a two-story building that would serve as a meeting hall for the worldwide media to organize special "press conferences" of athletes and coaches. Lewald, trying his best to be cordial, followed Furstner as he continued to rant and rave about his facilities still under construction, but Lewald, like Dodd, saw quite clearly the gravity of the situation unfolding before them.

BRUNDAGE

In the penthouse suite of the St. Regis Hotel in New York City, Avery Brundage looked up at Margaret as she straddled him on the bed, thrusting her hips, on the verge of climaxing. At that moment, and every time Margaret was about to finish herself off, Avery thought of his wife Elizabeth and how she regarded sex as a duty - a once a month affair if he was lucky. Then, at that magical moment, he returned his focus on Margaret and was on the verge of climaxing himself when there was a knock at the door.

"Paper!" a muffled voice shouted.

"Fuck off!" Avery yelled. Margaret laughed and rolled off Avery and onto her back next to him.

"Dammit! Every morning with the paper!" he said.

"Go and get it before you lose your focus," Margaret said. Avery kissed her, pulled up his shorts and got out of bed. He went to the door and peered out of the peephole. He opened the door and picked up the newspaper, staring at the headline as he shut the door and backed up towards the bed:

"BOYCOTT OF 1936 OLYMPIC GAMES BUILDING" by Alan Gould

"Son of a bitch," he said, tossing the paper onto Margaret's lap. "Get dressed. We gotta go."

They hopped into the first taxi they could find, and Brundage buried his nose in the newspaper, reading every word of Gould's article. Margaret looked over his shoulder and flinched every time Brundage angrily flipped to the next page.

At the AP offices, Alan Gould sat at his desk reviewing the next day's press release, when suddenly his door flew wide open. Margaret barged in, "Cancel your appointments. Avery Brundage is here." At that moment Brundage, newspaper in hand, edged past her and snaked into Gould's office. Margaret quickly left and shut the door behind her.

"Avery. How nice to see you," Gould said dryly. "For what do I owe this surprising and hopefully pleasant visit?" he asked as if he didn't know.

"Spare me the civilities. You could have requested a fucking interview," Brundage said.

"From whom, you?!" Gould laughed. "I don't want propaganda or general bullshit; I want the truth. I have reliable sources and they are telling me the AAU is considering this move. It's a reality." Gould said. "Sorry it doesn't fit neatly into your plans, but you're going to have to face it sooner or later. And let me just add, the AP supports the AAU, and would be a hundred percent behind not going to Berlin if that's what they decide."

Brundage tried to collect himself. He folded his hands behind his back and walked around the office. Framed photos hung on the walls with signatures and handwritten notes scribbled to Gould:

'Tackle you soon!' -*Bronco Nagurski*
'I'll save you seats in October' -*Dizzy Dean*
'Your pal, Jimmy' -*Jim Thorpe*

Brundage stared at the Thorpe photo for a moment, then turned and glared at Gould. "The self-described 'sports authority' thinks he can tell me what the pulse of the American athletic community is, huh? Well, you and your sources can suck my ass!" He lifted the paper and slammed it down on Gould's desk.

Gould never flinched or lost his composure, "If you have a problem with what I wrote, take it to the people I quoted--you know most of them quite well. And Avery . . ." He straightened his bowtie a little, "I'm covering every aspect of these Games, so be prepared for anything--including the hard truths."

"Then get this one straight!" Avery shot back. "There isn't going to be any fucking boycott on my watch. We're going to Berlin, as is our duty!" Brundage stormed out red-faced, slamming the door behind him.

Gould stared at the door, "Well, that wasn't a pleasant visit at all," he said matter-of-factly. He lit his cigar and smiled; it was becoming crystal clear to him that Mary was way off-base. If this sports story wasn't newsworthy, he didn't know what was.

Brundage flew down the AP corridors and out of the building. He could see that this was going to be a contest and with the same wily confidence he had on the playing field, he began to size up the competition.

*   *   *

A day later, IOC President Henri Latour sat behind a desk in a conference room at the Reich Sports Office in the heart of Berlin. IOC members Karl Ritter von Halt and Ernest Jahncke were at each other's throats again. Carl Diem sat uncomfortably in a far corner of the room.

Von Halt stood in front of Latour pointing at Jahncke. "Sir, this man continues to encourage the United States to boycott the Games in '36!" Von Halt belted out. "If that happens, what do you think the other countries will do? And let me remind you that Mr. Jahncke wanted a boycott since the day Berlin won the vote three years ago! As a member of this organization, I have to say that this behavior goes against the very nature of the Olympic spirit!" Von Halt exhaled loudly and sat down.

Jahncke sat in his chair with a calm demeanor. On most occasions, he and President Latour had agreed on Olympic Committee policy, but Latour's response stunned him. "I agree with you, Von Halt. Ernest, this talk of boycotting is very dangerous. It must stop immediately. Do you understand, Mr. Jahncke?" He turned to Von Halt. "And let me be clear to you, Mr. von Halt - you cannot keep any worthy athletes off of the German national team. Understood?"

Carl Diem rose up. "We will put our best athletes on the field, sir."

Jahncke and Von Halt avoided eye contact as they responded to Latour, "Understood." But Jahncke knew Von Halt would not honor such a proposal. He decided to turn to Mahoney and Gould to further the cause publicly.

ELEANOR

Inside a newly built sound stage on the studio lot of Paramount Pictures, Eleanor Holm was standing next to Gary Cooper. They were facing each other, both holding scripts, rehearsing.

From a darkened area someone yelled, "Let's do it again. Eleanor this time let's try something different, okay?"

She took a second to formulate, then nodded that she was ready.

"Okay, Action!"

Eleanor looked up at the ruggedly handsome Cooper and read her lines. "But you just can't go, Buck. Don't leave me like this." It wasn't a terrible delivery, but with her thick Brooklyn accent, it rang hollow.

"Cut!" someone yelled from the dark.

Two men, producers Barney Balaban and Sam Katz, stood behind a camera in the dark recess of the stage. Barney was positioning himself to become the head of Paramount Studios while Sam Katz was angling to oversee Paramount's operation in New York.

Barney turned and whispered to Sam. "Why the fuck are we wasting Gary's time? This broad couldn't do a voice over in a Popeye the Sailor cartoon."

On the stage, Eleanor turned to Cooper. "What's wrong? Why do they keep stopping us?"

"Don't worry, doll. This happens all the time," he said politely.

From the dark, Sam yelled, "Gary, can we have a word in private?"

"Be right back," Gary said, leaving Eleanor alone under the lights on the stage.

Moments later Sam Katz emerged from the darkness. "Listen, kid. I'm not sure you're getting this. We've been reading these lines for the past thirty minutes and --"

Eleanor interrupted, "Sam, I should've told you this, but I've decided to play in the '36 Games. Most of my time is going to be spent training, and I'm not sure I can dedicate myself to a production that's so big, with Gary and everything."

"Eleanor, you have loads of potential. Maybe down the road

we can work something out."

"Thanks, Sam." Eleanor said as she shook his hand and walked to the exit door at the back of the stage. Outside, Art Jarrett was anxiously waiting.

"How'd it go?"

Eleanor stared at him with a fiery contempt, "I'm going back to New York to swim. I want more Gold."

*   *   *

A few weeks later, Gould and Kieran were back at their usual table at the Oak Room in NYC drinking Manhattans, when Eleanor burst inside the place like a ray of sun. Heads turned as the ever-fashionable Olympian sashayed her sheer sundress through the lounge with the ease of a runway model. Both men smiled widely as she radiated their way.

"Oh, those look tasty," she said pointing to the men's drinks. "I'll take two."

Gould quickly caught the eye of the waiter and motioned for one more. "Let's start with one and see where that leads us." He said to her as she rolled her eyes.

"The ever-protective, Papa Bear." She turned to Kieran, "Johnny, you'll order me another straight away, won't you, dear?"

"I'm not crossing Papa Bear. He's paying tonight."

The waiter brought her drink almost immediately. Eleanor took a gulp and then announced to the two reporters she had returned to train for a spot in Berlin. She wasn't aware both men had already been alerted that her Hollywood auditions had gone terribly awry, and neither let on. Gould was just happy she had come to her senses and returned to what she did best.

"I think you've made the right decision. If you stay focused, another Gold is in the bag." He said, as she polished off her drink in two more big gulps, and then quickly ordered another. He shook his head, "You're supposed to sip a Manhattan, Eleanor."

"Are you going to continue working at the Cocoanut Grove?" Kieran inquired.

"Hell, no." She insisted. "I'm taking this more seriously than the L.A. Games. I want to swim the backstroke leg in the relay as well. Two Golds this time, baby boys!" Both reporters looked at her impressed. "I'm going to train every day. Ain't nothin' or nobody gonna stand in this girl's way," she professed, as she gulped down her second Manhattan.

*   *   *

A month later in the hallowed halls of the Women's Swimming Association of New York, just on the Brooklyn side of the East River, eight women thrashed the backstroke in a regulation Olympic-sized pool. Although it was a practice run, the pace was furious, and the team's coach let them know how serious it was. "Push it! Come on ladies!" She yelled at each swimmer in their lane.

One swimmer stood out from the rest and took a commanding lead – it was Eleanor, whose stroke was as smooth and powerful as it was two years before. Clearly, she was still a world-class athlete, and she was relentless, even though the next best swimmer was ten yards behind, Eleanor kept charging forward. She didn't even wait for the other women to finish before she climbed out of the pool, took off her swimming cap, and walked towards the coach as a group of photographers snapped pictures of her.

"Nice stroke, Eleanor. Keep it up," said a reporter.

"Thanks, but I'm still not where I should be," she said, and smiled politely as the photographers kept flashing. Her coach was not impressed and tried to shield her from the cameras.

"Take a break. You have a guest in reception. Take a towel with you," said the coach, who tossed one to her.

"I can talk to them after I'm finished training," Eleanor said.

"It's not a reporter. Go deal with it before you cool down too much," her coach said as she watched Eleanor walk away from the training area. She looked at the crowd of photographers who seemed obsessed with the swimmer, and she wondered what effect they were having on her prized athlete.

Eleanor walked through a corridor and opened the door to a reception room. Avery Brundage was waiting. He put out a cigarette and smiled at her. "Ms. Holm."

"Hi, Mr. Brundage. What a surprise."

"A pleasant one I hope."

"I'm not sure . . . you tell me."

Avery stepped towards her. "I just came by to tell you how pleased I am that you are considering returning for the Games in Berlin. You made quite an impression in Los Angeles, and I think that will carry over in thirty-six. You're very popular."

"Gold medals help with popularity."

"I don't know . . . I think it helps that you are very beautiful."

"Oh, thank you. That's very kind, but not so much in this ugly suit and I'm dripping wet," she said nervously.

"On the contrary – I can't resist a woman who is dripping wet."

Eleanor awkwardly covered herself in her towel and took a step back. Avery moved in slowly.

"I'm hoping we can work very closely together this time around. It would be my pleasure," he said.

Eleanor was desperate to diffuse the encounter. "Well, come by the pool and watch. We're going to have a terrific team."

"Because of you. Maybe we can have a drink sometime soon and discuss the Olympic experience. As you may or may not know, I was an Olympian as well. It would be my pleasure to regale you with my stories of Stockholm from the summer of 1912."

"Regale me?" she mocked. "That's very nice of you, Mr. Brundage --"

"It's Avery. Call me Avery."

"Yes, Mr. Brundage, but I have to concentrate on my time trials to get to Berlin. My schedule is all about swimming . . . and the occasional screen test."

"I heard you were pursuing that. Maybe I can help."

"I'm hoping another Gold medal or two will be all the help I need. I apologize, but I must go before I cool down too much. Thank you for your visit, it was . . . illuminating." She shook Avery's hand and backed out of the office as he stood gazing at her. Eleanor was no stranger to men looking her way; by now it was easy to brush off lustful stares, but there was something creepy about Avery and the way he looked at her. She clutched her towel and ran back towards the training pool.

HITLER

Hans von Tschammer und Osten was born into a family of "landed gentry," receiving an upper-class education due to his family's lofty social status. His father and grandfather were both Lords of their Manors during the days of feudal societies in central Europe. But his way of life ended abruptly at the outbreak of the Great War. Early in the war, Osten found himself dodging bullets in the muddy trenches of the Western Front. Although woefully unprepared, Osten proved to be a brave and worthy fighter and his superiors took notice, quickly promoting him to Colonel. After the Great War, he worked his way up the ranks of German sports administration, ultimately landing the post of Director of German Sports. But it wasn't just his sports acumen that impressed the Nazis. He was an adept strategist off the field as well.

"We simply can't have Jews on the team," Reich Minister of Propaganda Joseph Goebbels said as he and Osten walked side by side through the corridors of the Reich's Sports Office. "It's important that we excel in '36 for the morale and productivity of all German citizens."

Osten replied, "Sir, if I may . . . we must give the *appearance* of having German Jews participate. If we don't, even Brundage won't be able to stop a boycott."

Goebbels thought for a moment, and then nodded, "Agreed. See to it then." Osten exited the building and Goebbels headed for a scheduled meeting with Hitler.

*   *   *

"Heil Hitler." Goebbels shouted as he entered the Führer's office. Hitler rubbed his temples.

"For God's sake, Josef, tone it down, it's 8 o'clock in the fucking morning." Hitler said, then grabbed a few pills and a glass of water and drank them down. "My stomach had me up all night and now I have a splitting headache. I hope to hell you have good news."

Goebbels proceeded to lay out the plan he and Osten had devised. Though Hitler was skeptical, he gave his thumbs up. "And, Mein Führer, don't forget that I am going to Warsaw next week to speak at the University about the virtues of our Party."

"Yes, the same week Putzi is going back to Harvard for his graduation reunion and the same week I have to go to Italy and meet that fat sweaty bastard. The two of you!" He threw his hands up in disgust. "You would think I would get a little support. Instead, both of you are walking into places that hate our guts right now. The Polacks openly spit at us, and look what Roosevelt caused when he boycotted our goods. The Woolworth's right here in Berlin was destroyed by an angry riot. Eva and I love shopping there. Now, poof, all gone."

"You ordered that riot, Mein Führer. It was a smashing success." Hitler smiled at Goebbels pun. "Why don't you take Goering to Italy? He loves all that pomp and circumstance."

"Good God, no. Goering and Mussolini together? There isn't a space big enough to fit their inflated bodies or egos. I will go alone. Hopefully it will be quiet and uneventful, and that greasy Guinea will come to his senses that Austria will be German and not stay independent. Before you leave, however," Hitler continued, "Find out about a speech Vice-Chancellor Papen is giving in Marburg. Sources tell me President Hindenburg is behind it and it isn't very complimentary of our cause, and," he added, "see why Röhm is taking a leave of absence. Not that I care, the SA are becoming a nuisance, but I want to know what he is up to." Goebbels nodded.

"I don't trust any of them." Goebbels shot back. And he had good reason; the Marburg speech was incendiary. The Nazi opponents were becoming extremely vocal. And as hard as Goebbels tried to suppress the speech in the German press before going to Warsaw, the contents leaked out all over the international papers. It was quite the blow to the Nazi fervor. If Hitler and Goebbels thought Poland and the US were bad, the Marburg speech, with its talk of dissention and Nazi fanatical rule, added to the list of country's that would now cease trading goods and services with Germany. Goebbels would not broach the subject in his own speech in Warsaw, even when prompted by angry student's questions, "I have no comment," he responded. But deep down he had a lot to say. And the next meeting he had planned with Hitler, soon after they both returned, he would be a bit more direct about his feelings towards these, 'Filthy dissenters'.

*   *   *

Hitler's trip to Italy did not go off as quiet and peaceful as he had hoped. And it all started as soon as he got off the train in the pouring rain of Venice. He had imagined being greeted by Benito and a few of his men at the station, then being whisked off in a limousine to his hotel room before their formal meeting. The weather was so bad in Germany when he left, and he had been informed the weather wasn't any better in Venice, that he had thrown on ordinary traveling clothes and a beat-up raincoat for the ride and arrival. But Benito Mussolini had much grander plans.

Hitler was quietly enraged when he stepped off the train to a media circus, and Mussolini in full military regalia. Hitler looked like a traveling salesman from Wolfenbüttel compared to the gaudy Italian dictator. But Hitler just smiled at the press, shook everyone's hands cordially, and posed for the cameras next to Benito. Though inside he was volcanic, he never let on at the station. Nor did he let on in the limousine nor the soaking wet gondola ride, both while he sat uncomfortably between Mussolini and one of his (large) henchman who served as interpreter. Hitler didn't say a word as the Italian dictator droned on and on about his national football team's World Cup championship over the Czech Republic the week before.

After he was dropped off at his hotel and given the news the formal meeting would take place the following morning, Hitler erupted in his suite. Anything that could be picked up and thrown, was. He did such devastation to the room he demanded a different suite. When the hotel agreed to oblige, he made sure there was nothing left to break in the first one, including the bay windows overlooking the Grand Canal.

After a decent night's sleep, and a mercifully drier morning, Hitler was escorted by foot to the historic Metropole Hotel. A horseshoe arrangement of tables and chairs were setup in the Main Ballroom and Hitler joined Fascist Party politicians, who were ushered in before the two leaders. Of course, Mussolini made a grand entrance as the last to arrive. Hitler could hardly contain his puke at the rehearsed nature of the whole spectacle. And it was he who initiated the start of the action. "Enough theatrics let's get down to business, please. I plan on catching the last train today off this God-forsaken Island." Mussolini stopped dead in his tracks.

"Of course, Herr Hitler. I am sorry for any inconveniences." Hitler rolled his eyes. "Let us begin at once." Benito took his seat next to Adolf's and the two leaders began an extremely animated yet fruitless discussion about the course of their partnership. Mussolini wouldn't budge about Austria which exasperated Hitler. But Benito felt he was the elder statesman, and Hitler still had President Hindenburg to answer to. Il Duce was Italy's sole emperor. He had the upper hand in any negotiations with the Führer, and he would not relent.

Hitler wanted to strangle the fat bastard, and if Putzi hadn't taken a 'vacation' to fucking Boston, he would've ordered Putzi to kill the Italian right then and there. Hitler changed the conversation to racial issues, but again, Mussolini wanted nothing to do with it. At the time he did not approve of Nazi xenophobia, and he certainly did not approve of a world run by an Aryan race.

"And Jews are of no concern to us here in Italy. Your fascination with them confuses us." Mussolini said without hesitation. This set Hitler off on a tirade. Mussolini and his men sat and listened to the German for the next three hours as he spewed racial epitaphs and half-truths his Party had constructed. After he was done, Hitler stormed out of the ballroom, leaving the Italians bewildered.

"The man is a mad clown," Mussolini said to his men, shocked at the temper tantrum he had just witnessed. "Unhinged, and his politics are affected by this dementia." But Benito, and all of Italy, would be singing a much different tune at the two leaders' next encounter.

*   *   *

Hitler stood in front of a large window at his vacation home overlooking the fog-capped mountains of Bavaria. The Berghof, in Obersalzberg, was his oasis retreat, and after the meeting with Mussolini, he needed one. He wished his mother Klara could have lived to see such a view. She died of breast cancer when Adolf was just nineteen. And he loved Klara dearly. He imagined she would've been amazed at the spectacular scenery and would have thanked him. Then, as usual, his thoughts turned to his father Alois, who routinely beat him when he was a child. Almost every day he would be whipped unmercifully for the simplest of wrongdoings. After the beatings he would kick around a football in the yard, hoping to entice his father to play. But Alois would always ignore him and tend to his beekeeping. It was a hobby Adolf never quite understood. He spent many restless nights imagining ways to destroy his father's bee cages.

Adolf turned from the window and walked to a table where dozens of photos of various Nazi officials were spread. He studied the photos, picking up one after another and placing them back down. "This is excellent work. They're all very good, my dear," he said.

EVA BRAUN stood beside the table. She was a twenty-two-year-old model and actress, blonde and beautiful, and desperate to please Hitler with her display of photos on the table. "Thank you," she said. Then she stunned him with a calculating remark. "Adolf . . . you forgot my birthday."

"No, I didn't. I've made plans to go out to dinner tonight." He smiled at her.

"*Wulffie*, don't pretend," she said with a frown.

Hitler placed a photo back on the table and held her hand. "We'll have a wonderful birthday celebration this evening. What's the matter?"

Eva held his hand tight and said, "It's not just about my birthday. I'm terribly lonely here. I want to go back to Berlin."

Before Hitler could respond, the Butler shouted from another room, "Mr. Goebbels is here to see you."

Hitler and Eva Braun share a quiet intimate moment with their dogs at The Berghof, their country retreat in Bavaria.

"Of course," he said and watched Eva walk away, dejected. She was right; he had forgotten her birthday, but a month ago he had bought her a beautiful Edelweiss flower necklace which he saved for moments such as this. *The flower of purity*, he thought. He would surprise her with the gift at dinner.

Joseph Goebbels entered the room. "The renovations are looking fantastic."

"Thank you. Let's go outside," Hitler said as he led his devoted follower towards a fenced-in courtyard overlooking the mountains.

Inside, Eva secretly watched them. She wasn't jealous of Goebbels; frightened, maybe, but more than that, she was resentful over the amount of time these men demanded of her Wulffie. She wanted to be his *everything*, not a burden, or a forgotten sidenote he would attend to when he had the time.

Eva first met Hitler in Munich in 1929, at the studio of Heinrich Hoffman, the official photographer of the Nazi Party. There, she learned how to use a camera and develop photographs when she wasn't modeling. It was during one of her modeling sessions where she met the man who was twenty-three years her senior. Hoffman introduced him as "Herr Wolff." Hitler was immediately smitten, but she was a little intimidated by him at first. They started seeing each other more and more frequently, but never in public. It was usually at the studio, or at the apartment he shared with his half-niece, Geli Raubal. As they spent more and more time together, she became entranced by his charisma and proud of his lofty and patriotic aspirations. This was a man with a vision so clear, not even the best lens in Hoffman's studio could properly capture it. And intimately, he would satisfy her every need, like a man who knew exactly how to please her as if reading her mind. They christened every piece of furniture in the apartment when Geli wasn't home, including the sofa, reading chair, coffee table, radiator, wine cabinet, and even the staircase banister. *That was an interesting one.* It was a mutual infatuation; an addiction that was soothed whenever they laid eyes upon one another.

But as Hitler grew in stature, their time together waned. One day in 1931, Hitler came home to his apartment to find that Geli had killed herself with his pistol. Eva saw how affected he was by this, so a year later, to hoard his attention, she tried her own half-hearted suicide attempt with what amounted to a BB shot to the chest. It worked for a while; they grew even closer because of that incident, but now here she was again, pushed aside, less important to him than the constant gatherings and meetings with these self-important men of secrecy and politics.

She turned from the window and made her way to the walk-in closet to look for a dress to wear to dinner that evening. Something that would surely seize his attention.

Out on the patio, a German shepherd ran and greeted Hitler the minute he walked out of the house. "*Komm, Blondi*," Hitler urged, and petted his loyal dog. Goebbels leaned on the stone fence, waiting for Hitler's attention.

"*Mein Führer*, we must talk about the SA situation. I've learned that there are now three million Brown-shirts under the command of a certain friend of yours," Goebbels said.

Hitler turned away from Blondi. "So, you've been inquiring about Ernst Rohm."

"Yes."

Hitler picked up a stick, threw it, and Blondi chased after it. "Mr. Rohm and I used to be housemates back in our younger years. We would paint together. He used to paint portraits of me."

"He no longer wants to paint your portrait. He wants to replace it with his own," Goebbels informed him. "His Brown-Shirt cadets are running wild. We need support for the '36 Games, not speculation or doubt."

"Of course."

"There's also a disturbing rumor," Goebbels said, and paused, unsure if he should continue.

"What rumor?"

"That the French have offered Rohm a great sum of money in support."

"In support of what?" Hitler responded.

"A coup."

Blondi returned with the stick and dropped it at her master's feet. Hitler looked at her and smiled. He threw the stick again and

Blondi ran to fetch it. He then turned to Goebbels, steely-eyed, "I'll make arrangements to deal with Mr. Rohm."

LENI

Leni Riefensthal took photos of the street life of Berlin from a trolley car. On one corner there was a well-dressed woman with her children walking two little dogs. On another corner there was a heated exchange between two businessmen. As the trolley car came to a stop at an intersection, she saw an SS Officer holding a man at gunpoint in front of a shop. The man was painting a Star of David on his storefront window. After taking a few photos, she put her camera down in her lap and watched as people walked past the shop oblivious to what was unfolding.

Leni departed her bus in front of the Mezhrabpomfilm Studios. The German and Russian co-owned movie studio had produced over 600 films in the last twenty years. It was a successful experiment that was rumored to be shutting down soon.

A receptionist looked up at her as she approached the desk.

"I'm looking for a crew member named Hans Ertl. He's a camera operator."

The receptionist looked through some papers. "Stage One. And you are?" Leni ignored her question and walked past her, opening the door to Stage One.

Inside the studio a camera team was rehearsing an elaborate shot. There was a cameraman on a crane, thirty feet in the air, lining it up. Leni watched quietly, respectfully letting the crew do their work. A production assistant approached her. "Can I help you?" she said.

"Is that Ertl?" Leni asked, pointing up at the man up on the crane.

"That's him."

After the shot the crane lowered and HANS ERTL climbed down. Leni approached him. "I am Leni Riefenstahl."

Ertl studied her for a beat and smiled. "I know who you are. I appreciate your work immensely. For what do I owe this honor?"

"You come highly recommended," she said.

"Recommended for what exactly?"

"I have been commissioned by the Führer himself to document the Berlin Olympic Games, and I need a capable man to assist. I have chosen you as that man."

"I don't know exactly what to say. I'm not a Nazi, Fraulein Riefenstahl." Ertl said.

"Neither am I. But you will be paid handsomely by them if that's any incentive."

"I like 'handsomely'."

"Fine. We will begin work at once. You will abandon this job immediately and report to my office in Berlin on Monday." Leni said and walked away leaving Ertl dumbfounded.

It was a move that Leni had perfected in professional circles. Everyone in the business of moving pictures knew who she was, and she took full advantage of it when she wanted something. Outside of the business, it was another story altogether. In her personal affairs, to those who didn't know she was a filmmaking genius, she was just an ordinary woman. So, she clung to the role. It was uncomfortable to feel like an ordinary woman, mostly because when she wasn't behind the camera or ordering a film crew around, she was ordinary, and alone.

*   *   *

At a car dealership on the outskirts of Denver, Colorado, a middle-aged woman named Deborah Wallach revved the engine of a sporty Triumph Dolomite while staring at her dealer through the windshield. He was GLENN MORRIS. At 22 years old, Glenn was ruggedly handsome and built like Tarzan. He had a freakish strength due to his lifelong work on his family's farm. He was an exceptional athlete in football and wrestling during his high school years and earned All-American honors in track his senior year.

He waved a contract at her. "You're good to go, Ms. Wallach."

"That was fast," she said.

"So are you behind this machine," he said.

"I could show you how fast..."

Glenn blushed, "I don't think Mr. Wallach would appreciate that."

"There *is* no Mr. Wallach," she said.

"Four o'clock tomorrow," he said. She put the car in gear and drove away. He walked back towards the shop whistling a random tune when his boss stopped him.

"Nice goin', Morris. Keep it to a six-pack tonight, okay?"

"Six beers and six women to go along with it, Spank!" he said as he jogged back towards the dealership.

Later that day, Glenn's pickup truck kicked up a trail of dust as he sped towards a track near Colorado State University. His father EDGAR was waiting for him at the starting block. He checked his watch as Glenn stumbled towards him while tying his running shoes.

"Sorry I'm late, Dad. Closed a big deal today."

"Good. Cause you're gonna need that job when you get back."

"I'm not coming home without a medal, Dad. Then . . . fame!"

"Easy, Hollywood. Make the decathlon team first, then worry about a medal, okay?" Edgar set his stopwatch as Glenn prepared his starting point on the track.

"Ready? Go!" Edgar yelled and Glenn ran towards the hurdles that were lined up along the track. He knocked down the first hurdle and kept going, knocking down every remaining hurdle on the track. Edgar shook his head. "Fame . . . right."

JUNE 30, 1934
NIGHT OF THE LONG KNIVES

Two fencers dueled on a platform inside the USC Gymnasium. One was clearly the aggressor and after a series of deft maneuvers she lunged forward and stabbed perfectly at her opponent's chest target for the victory. HELENE MAYER, a slender, athletic blonde woman, took off her mask and shook her opponent's hand. Her coach jotted down a note. "That's enough for today, Helene," she said.

"Thanks Coach. See you tomorrow." She turned to her defeated opponent, "Good match," she said and unzipped her suit. She threw open the doors of the gym with swagger, still pumped full of adrenaline from her practice victory, and walked towards the women's locker room. She turned a corner and suddenly noticed someone menacing at the far end of the hallway. It was Putzi. He began walking towards her. Helene stopped at a water fountain and took a sip as the mysterious man approached.

"Can I help you?" she asked guardedly.

Putzi removed his fedora and smiled at her. "Ms. Mayer, I am a representative of the Reich Sports Office in Berlin. I'm here to talk to you about competing in the 1936 Olympics. You see, as a citizen of Germany you qualify to compete for the German national team, and we would very much like it if you returned to your homeland for the upcoming Games."

Helene regarded Putzi with a degree of uncertainty, but her confidence moved her to confront him.

"That's a very nice offer, but there's a reason I came to this country. I didn't want to leave Germany, but the circumstances offered me no choice. And to think, I'm only half Jewish, a practicing Lutheran, and a champion! And I'm still not wanted in the country I was born in."

"You're wanted very badly, Ms. Mayer. I can assure you that no harm will come to you or your family. The Führer has personally chosen me to meet with you directly." He stepped a little closer and said, "Let me put it another way . . . you've already won Gold for Germany back in '32 and you're a celebrity in the homeland."

"I could win another Gold and be a celebrity here in America," she said.

"And be a drop of water in a sea of celebrities," he responded. Helene nonchalantly took another sip of water. Putzi inched closer. "Beat the Americans and win Gold for Germany, and you'll be a legend . . . all over the world."

Helene was impressed by Putzi and flattered that the Führer would send someone across the Atlantic to make the offer. "I'll think about it," she said, and Putzi offered his hand. She shook it, and Putzi didn't let go for an unusually long time.

"Thank you for your time, Ms. Mayer. I very much admire your skills. Good day," he said and put his fedora back on and turned to leave.

Helene watched Putzi exit the gym. She turned away and as she walked towards the women's locker room her head was flush with conflicting emotions. While a bit shaken by the sudden encounter with the hulking stranger, she felt incredibly proud and excited by the idea of being a legend in Germany.

She undressed and walked to the showers. The idea of winning a Gold medal for Germany made her think of her paternal grandmother. She remembered the stories she told of growing up as a young girl in the German countryside. She thought of her accent and how funny it sounded when she told a joke. And the meals she cooked on late Sunday afternoons. Currywurst, and especially her famous Black Forest Gateau. As she entered the steaming shower, she began singing an old folk song "Oma" sang to her when she was a child . . .

A dark cloud of despair surrounds your heart,
Disillusion with life your face imparts.
You are wandering in a world of confusion,
Reality is hidden behind the web of illusion . . .

*   *   *

A different tune was playing in the pre-dawn darkness of a Chicago back alley. The muffled horns of Benny Goodman's Orchestra bled "Ain't-Cha Glad" from behind a heavy wooden door at the basement of a Speakeasy.

Ain't cha glad, we were made for each other,
Ain't cha glad, that we waited for each other,
We agree, constantly . . .

Avery Brundage casually looked behind him. The streets were empty. He walked down the concrete staircase and knocked on the unmarked door. After a few seconds, a rectangular grille slid open, and a pair of eyes checked him out. The grille slammed shut and the door opened. A hulking Italian man with a crooked face let him in with a smile. He waved his hand towards a table where three men, each with a girl on his lap and a cigar in hand, rose and fixed their ties.

It may have been an intimidating scene for some; dark men huddled in corners, scantily clad women on their arms, whiskey bottles on every table, money secretively exchanging hands... but Avery felt right at home. He waited for the men to come to him, and they did, greeting him with large smiles and a large martini. One of them put his arm around Avery and they disappeared into the smoke-filled room.

*   *   *

Alan Gould was on his knees wielding a stickball bat in the middle of a street lined with brownstone apartment buildings. Mary sat on the top step in front of their building, cheering on her two boys and the neighboring kids who filled out the defense. Chalk lines marked the baselines and the pitcher's mound. John Keiran, the umpire, stood behind Gould and the catcher, taking sips of his beer between every pitch.

"Strike two!" He yelled, after the pitcher hurled a low strike.

"Okay Dizzy Dean, bring me the hard cheese", Gould said, and the kids all got ready for the next pitch. With a mighty swing, he struck out and all the kids cheered.

Keiran shook his head, laughing. "You're out!"

*   *   *

The air was so thick in the boxing gym that one could barely see from one end to the other. Sweat from the athletes, and cigar smoke from trainers, permeated every corner of the gym. Olympic hopefuls fought their guts out inside the ring, while others trained on speed bags and heavy bags. Some shadow boxed in the corner next to others jumping rope. Judge Mahoney, dripping with sweat as if he'd sparred for ten rounds, had the best seat in the house. He sat on a round stool in the center of the room so he could quickly swivel and catch his favorite sound - the pounding of glove to flesh. To him it was the sound of effort, of competition, and he was alert to those boxers who satisfied his ears. They were the athletes that wanted it most and deserved to go to Berlin. He pondered the simplicity of what was happening inside the boxing ring. Man versus man, a fair fight, and to the victor belong the spoils. As it should be, he thought. He felt it his responsibility to see that these boys would get a fair shot to compete against the best in the world. At this moment, he liked their chances.

*   *   *

Adolf Hitler, in a long, dark overcoat, walked with purpose down a corridor of a Reich office building. He was flanked by three SS Officers. Without a word, they descended a staircase and exited the building where a black Mercedes-Benz waited, idling with its passenger doors open. Then men escorted Hitler inside the car first, then got in after him. The doors slammed shut and the car sped off.

*   *   *

Hans Ertl looked up from his lens and wiped the sweat from his brow. It had been the longest shooting day of his life. Leni demanded that they started before sunrise to make sure they were ready to roll film at the first hint of daylight. They were filming sections of the opening montage of Olympia, starting with naked men running, jumping, throwing javelins, and hurling the discus. Erlt manned the camera through countless takes and angles and by noon he was as exhausted as the athletes. Leni was tireless in directing the performers, even participating to demonstrate the action she desired to capture on film.

After a short lunch break, they resumed filming. This time it was the female athletes. Ertl wondered if Leni scheduled it that way to keep him focused for the remainder of the arduous day. If that was her intention, it worked. He was supremely focused and captured the female form like he never imagined. The chiseled women danced in front of stone monoliths, writhing in a free-form ballet with large brass rings, and weaved in and out of flowing drapes. But as the sun began its descent, Ertl's stamina was running short.

"Leni, we're losing light," he said, feigning a reason to wrap the day.

"Not yet," she said, looking through the viewfinder. She walked towards the female athletes who were exhausted themselves and positioned them in front of a backlit wall of foliage that provided a shimmering backdrop behind the silhouetted figures.

Ten minutes later, Ertl's patience had worn out. "When can we shoot, Leni?"

"When my eyes stop bleeding!" She yelled. Some of the crew laughed and she walked over to Ertl.

"I want them in full silhouette. See?" She waited a beat. "Now, we can shoot." Ertl looked through his viewfinder, and the light was perfect. He decided right then that he wouldn't let his fatigue inform a creative decision ever again.

*   *   *

In Colorado, a lone car bounced rhythmically in an empty parking lot. It was the brand new 1934 Triumph Dolomite that Glenn Morris sold to Ms. Wallach. Her legs dangled out of the window. Glenn was on top of her, thrusting with gusto.

*   *   *

In the choppy waters of the Puget Sound, Bob Moch led his Washington University Huskies in a training session. It was a stormy day, and they were warned about taking the boats out, but not one member of the team complained about it, or even mentioned it at all. To Moch, it was a sign that the team was coming together. He had been on teams where someone would be the first to complain about the conditions. That was the weak link that could bring down a whole team. He saw none on this team, and he kept testing them.

"Storm's comin!" he shouted and waited for a response. To his delight, he didn't get one.

*   *   *

Wolfgang Furstner, Deputy Kommandant of the Olympic Village, roamed the grounds of the site. It was night, but with massive cranes housing floodlights around the perimeter, it looked like mid-day. He saw a group of carpenters taking a cigarette break outside one of the dormitories and made his way over to them. He thought he'd share a cigarette and a word of encouragement. He knew these men volunteered for the night shift and were working hard for him. When the men spotted him, they immediately threw down their cigarettes and stood at attention.

"Kommandant!" One of them said.

"Relax, gentlemen. We have a long night ahead of us. I need you to pace yourselves, so you are focused and sharp. This site is going to revolutionize the sporting world. An Olympic Village like no one in the world could ever imagine. We are not building dog houses, after all."

Just then, an explosion rocked the ground and sent a fireball into the night sky that blinded them for a moment. At the foot of the explosion, a geyser of water sent a tractor on its side, gushing violently fifty feet in the air. Furstner screamed in horror and followed the men as they ran towards the calamity.

*   *   *

Jesse Owens thrust open the gate to the elevator and ushered in two well-dressed professors. His track shoes stuck out from under his uniform pants which were immediately noticed by the two professors.

Jesse's decision to attend Ohio State University was largely based on the position of elevator operator in the statehouse and a promise of a job for his father, which never materialized. He always wore his track gear under his elevator operator uniform because he didn't have time to travel back to his house, which was well off the campus grounds. The on-campus dormitory did not permit black athletes.

The professors gave him an odd glance as the elevator descended, then continued their discussion concerning a faculty matter that Jesse didn't understand and didn't care to. His mind was on track practice and his goal of breaking his personal best in the 200 meters.

At the 1st floor, the professors exited the elevator and Jesse's replacement was waiting, right on time. Jesse handed him a key ring and sprinted out of the statehouse towards "the Horseshoe" - the football stadium nicknamed for its shape. He peeled off his elevator operator's uniform as he ran, and by the time he got there, he was ready for practice. His black teammates greeted him warmly and he threw his gym bag towards the bench. The team gathered and began warming up and stretching until the coach's whistle signaled the start of training.

Jesse dug his toes into the cinder track next to four other members of the team. He loved the feel of the fine, porous stones that circled the grass field. At once, everyone turned to watch; groundskeepers, teammates, and even some of the football players who were getting in some extra practice time all stopped what they were doing to watch Jesse run. They weren't disappointed.

From his first thrust out of the starting blocks, Jesse was a stride faster than the nearest runner. By the time he reached the first turn he was ten meters ahead and gaining steam. His lead grew with each stride as the spectators watched in awe. For Jesse, he wasn't competing with anyone on the team. There was no point in measuring his speed by how far ahead he managed to get from his teammates. His opponent was the stopwatch.

He breezed into the final stretch, which elicited applause from the onlookers. As he crossed the finish line, his coach ran up to him displaying the stopwatch. Bent over with his hands on his knees, catching his breath, he looked at the stopwatch and smiled. Pretty good, he thought, but he'd try to beat that tomorrow.

*   *   *

Luz Long sat in a classroom at the University of Leipzig along with twenty-five other students. His law professor tapped a pointer on the chalkboard and read aloud what he had written.

"Regulations of the Reich President for Defense from Treacherous Attacks Against the Government of the National Uprising. This will soon become the Treachery Act of 1934, if it passes."

"*When* it passes," a student blurted out.

"Correct, *when* it passes. Until then, we will be discussing the range of sentences for such crimes . . ." the professor continued.

Luz was suddenly distracted by something outside on the grass quadrant in view of the classroom. There were about fifty young teenage boys, all in uniform, lined up in a formation resembling a military unit. They were marching to the instruction of an SA "Stormtrooper." Luz was aware of the Hitler Youth movement and its indoctrination of children into becoming race-conscious, self-sacrificing, obedient German citizens, but this was the first time he had seen a formal military operation involving such young boys.

"Long!" The professor bellowed. "Do you agree that the imprisonment of social outcasts is the proper sentence for such crimes."

- 117 -

"Yes, sir," Luz responded matter-of-factly.

"Why?"

"Eradicating opposition to the Nazi Party will allow the German economy to flourish," Luz said with little emotion.

"Excellent." The professor continued grilling other students, but Luz was too distracted by the military drills going on in the quad to pay much attention.

*   *   *

A stretch limousine pulled up to the entrance of the newly opened Tavern on the Green in Central Park, New York City. In the area of the park called Sheep Meadow, the converted pasture uprooted many African Americans once its location was decided.

Eleanor Holm exited the limo with Art Jarrett on her arm. A throng of photographers snapped pictures and citizens cheered as they walked towards the venue. There was a sign outside the door that read, "The Art Jarrett Band, with Eleanor Holm."

Eleanor received most of the attention and she soaked it all in. She was comfortable in the limelight. She sensed that Art might be getting a bit jealous of the outpouring of admiration. She grabbed his hand and raised it up in the air.

"The amazing Art Jarrett everyone!" She yelled, and everyone hollered and whistled. Art feigned modesty and took a bow and they both entered the brand-new gem of New York City nightlife.

*   *   *

At that moment, Ambassador Dodd, Mattie, and his daughter Martha were attending another banquet in Hamburg, Germany. It was an event to celebrate the formation of a pharmaceutical company founded by a man named Gregor Strasser, a chemist. Strasser was once a high-ranking member of the Nazi Reichstag who was forced to abandon his political post at Hitler's request. The reason for this was no secret - one of Strasser's brothers, Otto, was the editor of a newspaper called *The Nationaler Sozialist*--an opinionated publication and competitor of the Nazi newspapers in Berlin. Hitler suspected that Strasser still had ties to his brother despite having ample evidence to the contrary.

Dodd and his family were the special guests of Strasser. Since his departure from the Reichstag, Strasser and Dodd had become friends. Dodd enjoyed their discussions because they inevitably evolved from topics regarding the current climate in Germany to Strasser's personal conflicts with Hitler.

Dodd and Mattie mingled with some of the businessmen and investors of the company, all the while looking for Strasser and his wife, Elisabeth. But Strasser was nowhere to be found.

"Isn't it odd that the host isn't here?" Mattie asked.

"Maybe he's just late," Dodd said, but as the words came out of his mouth, he saw Elisabeth heading his way with a panicked look in her eyes. She walked right up to him.

"Something's wrong. Gregor was on his way here. He phoned me just as I was leaving home and said we'd arrive at the same time. It's been forty-five minutes. I just know there's something wrong." She cried.

"Hold on, Elizabeth. He'll be here. Something must have come up . . . he probably got detoured on his way, that's all." Dodd tried to assuage her.

"You know he didn't get detoured. He's always on time. I told him to stop meeting with Otto. I knew it would get him in trouble. I just knew it," she said, and was quickly ushered away by a young businessman in a fancy suit.

Mattie was stunned. "What do you think happened?"

"Nothing. She's overreacting. I'm sure he'll show up any minute." Dodd said. He scanned the banquet hall for Strasser, and his eyes rested on his daughter Martha, who was laughing and speaking to someone. He couldn't quite see who it was through the crowd. As he walked over to get a better look, he saw a soldier in a Nazi uniform hand Martha a drink, then kiss her on the cheek. He silently boiled inside but thought it would be best not to embarrass her at such a function. Instead, he decided to walk around the room to see if he could find Strasser.

He would later learn that Gregor Strasser was arrested that night as an enemy of the state. He was shot in the head with a Walther P38 from outside the bars of his prison cell. It took over an hour for Strasser to bleed to death.

*　　*　　*

Temporary stadium lights illuminated the practice pitch for the German soccer team. They were sprawled out on the grass, stretching in preparation for the night's training session. Carl Diem and Theodor Lewald watched from the sidelines.

"I stood up at the IOC meeting and assured them we would put our best athletes on the field," Diem said. "I understand there are no Jews on this team."

"They finished third at the World Cup. I think we can trust Coach Nerz that these are the best football players Germany has to offer. There he is," Lewald said, and with a wave, called over to Coach Otto Nerz, who walked onto the field carrying a bag of soccer balls. "Coach! If you finish as well as you did three weeks ago, that's at least a Bronze!"

Coach Nerz looked over with a deadpan stare. Lewald and Diem expected at least a smile and a wave from the good-natured schoolteacher-turned coach but didn't get either. A second later they found out why.

A column of Nazi soldiers walked through the gates of the field to watch the practice. In unison, the soccer players all sprung to their feet and gave them the Nazi salute, shouting, "Heil Hitler!"

Lewald turned to Diem, who was watching in disbelief. He shook his head and faced his friend with a look of great concern.

*   *   *

Ernst Jahncke sat at an outdoor café on Leipziger Street in Berlin. He had stopped by this café particularly, not only for an evening coffee, but because it was the only place in Berlin that carried American newspapers. As the waiter went to fetch them, Jahncke studied the busy Berlin streets. Automobiles swerved to avoid the electric trolleys, bicyclists swerved to avoid the cars, and pedestrian couples walked arm in arm down the avenue, seemingly without a care in the world. He wondered what they would think if they knew what was being discussed behind the closed doors of the IOC meetings. He hoped Gould and Mahoney would help open some eyes.

The waiter returned with a couple of newspapers and Jahncke thanked him. He sat back and opened the New York Times. The headline read: HITLER VOWS TO CONFRONT POLITICAL OPPOSITION WITHIN GERMANY. Without reading further, he put the paper down and finished the last of his coffee. He shook his head in disgust as people casually walked past the café.

*   *   *

Putzi, escorted by five SS thugs wielding machine guns, walked down a dark Berlin alley. He motioned for them to stop just beyond the lit windows of a building. Inside the smoky conference room, dozens of Brown Shirts gathered for a meeting. Putzi and his men crawled beneath the windows to avoid detection and stopped outside the door. He made a hand signal for them to wait and peered inside the window. The meeting was about to begin.

It was times like these when Putzi could feel his adrenaline start to spike. It felt better than any drug he had ever taken. Lately, though, the feeling led him to wonder where his lust for violence came from. Maybe it was the days of his youth, hunting deer with his father in the sprawling land beyond his family lot. Or maybe it was his fifteenth birthday. Walking home from school that day, he was thrashed senseless by a group of neighborhood bullies. Putzi was a scrawny teenager at the time. Soon after, a growth spurt gave him the confidence to exact revenge on the bullies. He did so, one by one, each increasing with violence, almost killing the last one with his bare hands.

At this moment, he decided to take a cleansing breath and put aside his curiosity about where it came from. Besides, it didn't matter; he had a job to do.

He peeked inside the window again. One of the organizers quieted the crowd and walked to the front of the room. Putzi nodded to his men and together, they smashed open the door. They flew into the room spraying the group with bullets, killing every single Brown Shirt in the room.

Ten minutes later, in central Berlin, Putzi and his men marched through a tavern where a group of Brown-Shirted Officers were drinking. One of the Officers stood up with a salute. Putzi whipped out a cutlass and sliced off the Officer's hand in one swift motion. Putzi's goons then unleashed long knives and slashed the throats of the other Brown-Shirts at the table. Blood sprayed everywhere as patrons screamed and fled the scene. Putzi and his men calmly exited the bar amongst the chaos.

*   *   *

Hitler and his Officers exited the Mercedes-Benz in front of a beautiful Berlin apartment building. He pulled a bullwhip from the pocket of his overcoat, and they walked up a flight of stairs inside the building. Hitler was focused and clutched his whip tightly.

Ernst Rohm, completely naked, was having sex with a perfectly chiseled blonde Aryan teenager in his apartment. Rohm would routinely lure young men to his apartment, but this was a special catch. As he was about to climax, the apartment door flew open. Hitler entered and was stunned by the scene; a look of shock and disgust overcame him. As his men followed him into the apartment, he took out his whip and began beating Rohm furiously, whipping every part of his obese body. The Aryan boy rolled off the bed and one of Hitler's Officers grabbed him by his hair and dragged him out of the room screaming as Hitler continued to whip Rohm into a bloody mess.

*   *   *

In their Laupheim home, Paula and Ernst Bergmann sat at the piano singing the same song Helene Mayer sang on her way to the shower back in California.

"So, my brothers, put your faith in the Above,
Say, "Hineni," I am ready to serve you with love."

Max and Hannah sat on the couch reading a children's book. Suddenly, the dog Fritz started barking uncontrollably.

"Let him outside, Max," Paula said. Max lifted Hannah off his lap and opened the door to the backyard. Fritz ran, barking like crazy.

"I'm sure it's nothing," Max said. At that moment, a gunshot echoed, and Fritz was silenced. Hannah screamed and they all turned and saw what seemed like a ghost - Hans von Tschammer und Osten was standing in the living room.

"Hans von Tschammer und Osten. Director of the Reich Sports Office." Osten offered a handshake to Max, who stood defiantly between Osten and his family.

"And that gives you the right to break into my home?"

"The door was open." Two Nazi guards entered the room.

Hannah ran to her mother. "What happened to Fritz, Mommy?"

"Fritz is okay, baby," Paula said.

Osten took off his gloves and looked around the room. "I understand your daughter Gretel is currently in London."

"That's right." Max said.

"I also understand that she has been asked to return to Berlin as a member of the Olympic high jump team . . . and has refused."

"I support her decision," Max said. "In fact, it was my idea. Now get the hell out of my house!"

Osten reached at his wristwatch and in one sudden move, pulled out a thin cord from the watch and lunged at Max, wrapping the cord around his neck. The family screamed and Osten's men held them back.

"Your daughter Gretel is a German citizen, is she not?"

Choking, Max replied, "Yes, she is!"

"Then surely she wants to win Gold for the Fatherland!" Osten let go of his grip and threw Max to the floor.

*   *   *

Twenty-four hours after The Night of the Long Knives, Gretel Bergmann finished her grocery shopping and left the London market. It was past ten o'clock, but Gretel was used to late night shopping after her long workouts. This night, though, the London streets seemed lonelier than others. She quickened her pace. As she turned a corner, a man confronted her.

"Guten Abend, Fraulein Bergmann." It was Putzi.

German-American Putzi Hafnstaengl, Hitler's right hand man and personal assassin, does his best to smile for the camera.

PART II

BEWARE OF WOLVES IN SHEEP'S CLOTHING

BRUNDAGE

Brundage stared at the now 4-year-old Bronze Tommy Trojan statue near Bovard Hall on the University of Southern California campus and read the inscription; Faithful, Scholarly, Skillful, Courageous, and Ambitious. He snickered at the thought of any of these spoiled college brats showing real Trojanesque attributes. He lit a cigarette, checked his watch, and then groaned with annoyance. "Where the fuck are you, Cromwell?" he asked himself out loud.

"Right here," a voice answered from the other side of the statue, scaring Brundage to death.

"Goddammit, what the fuck is a matter with you? How long have you been standing there?" At that moment a hulking 55-year-old came from around the corner laughing.

DEAN CROMWELL had been the head coach of the USC Track Team since 1909. He was a winner who had already guided USC to four national NCAA Championships, earning him the nickname 'Maker of Champions'. Most of the '36 track team would be coming from USC and that made Cromwell extremely satisfied. Politically, he was a staunch nationalist and a proud, racist, white man to boot. These three extremely Trojanesque qualities of athleticism, nationalism, and prejudice made him very attractive to Brundage, who was looking to hire a new assistant Olympic track coach.

Not that his current head track coach, the highly successful, very respected, well-liked, and unprejudiced Lawson Robertson knew anything about the appointment, but Brundage saw an ally in Cromwell. And he wanted Robertson out. The man was too soft with his athletes for Brundage's liking. "I want you to assist Robertson in Berlin." Brundage said abruptly, catching the man by surprise.

"I accept without hesitation." Cromwell fired back. "I hope this means that in '40 I'll finally be taking the reins from that nigger lovin' Scottsman."

Brundage smiled, "We'll see how it goes," he said and began walking away, "I'm off to Chicago. Just have your boys keep training for the trials."

*   *   *

And that was just what his boys were doing. FOY DRAPER raced down the track at the USC's training facility with a baton firmly in his grip. Draper was a short stocky speedster with a level head and ferocious desire to win. He was one of the only stand-out sophomores in 1934 on the Trojan track team and was priming himself at a chance to go to Berlin as a Senior. He was running with seasoned veterans though, who were also planning on making the trip, so any missteps were going to be glaring.

As he got closer to the finish line another relay runner, FRANK WYKOFF, began his turn. In perfect stride, Draper handed off his baton to Wykoff who accelerated into his sprint. Frank Wykoff had previously won Gold in the '28 Amsterdam Games and again in the 1932 Games in Los Angeles, both in the 4x100m relay and both in world record time. He was a role model young athlete, a winner who was just as smart as he was athletic. And as he studied for his master's degree, he trained for his third consecutive Olympic Gold in Berlin. He believed in, "Clean speech, clean sport, clean scholarship, clean life." He was a coach's dream athlete.

"Draper, c'mere!" yelled Cromwell, who had made his way back to the facility. The young man jogged over. "Son, if you make the Olympic team, you'd better not have Wykoff waiting like that. You made him two steps off stride. A two-time champion! He doesn't need a midget from Texas slowing him down."

"Why so suddenly worried about the Olympic team, Coach?

Robertson will take care of that." Draper said smugly. He hated his coach whom he found to be a mean and nasty son of a bitch whose offenses knew no boundaries.

"Because I just became Robertson's assistant, that's why." Cromwell shot back.

The young runner looked surprised. "Coach Robertson asked you to be his assistant?"

"Robertson had nothing to do with it. Avery Brundage himself assigned me. He probably figured I'd be taking over for Robertson soon enough anyway," Cromwell said and then walked away towards Frank Wykoff who was still catching his breath at the finish line.

Draper watched Cromwell leave and cringed at the thought of going overseas with him. He felt that his coach was the kind of person who demanded respect, not commanded it. During big meets Cromwell would berate his players instead of inspiring them, and Draper couldn't stomach that type of behavior. In the heat of battle, Draper thought, calmer heads prevail.

*   *   *

Brundage had always thought himself an internationalist, a well-travelled and seasoned man of the world. He was an accomplished businessman and former athlete, and currently head of one of the biggest sports committees in the United States. Which was one step away from his ultimate goal, membership and eventual Presidency of the IOC.

But Avery didn't control the AAU, that was Mahoney's, and if a vote to boycott Berlin was inevitable, it was going to come from members of that union. This was a war Brundage knew he couldn't win alone. And Avery did not like to lose. In his only Olympics he was embarrassed by "that fucking Injun" Jim Thorpe, and when the IOC stripped Thorpe of his medals under very speculative circumstances, Avery did nothing to help restore them after he took office at the AOC. So, with all his seasoned internationalism, Brundage's only hope in this fight was to turn to his old cronies back home in gangster-ridden Chicago. And one of those men was Tony "The Big Tuna" Accardo.

Accardo, also known as 'Joe Batters', dubbed by Capone himself after Accardo used a Louisville Slugger to bash in the heads of three Capone enemies at a dinner thrown by Capone in their honor, was a rising star in the mafia. He was owner of an unusually busy speakeasy during the Prohibition/Depression era of the times. It also happened to be one of Brundage's favorite haunts when he was back home. And Accardo always met him at the door with a martini.

"Avery, goddammit, it's good to see you back in the center of the universe," Accardo said and handed him a fresh martini. He turned to the striking blonde woman holding his arm. "Clarice Porter, this is my friend and one of the most important sports people in the world."

"Are you Lou Gehrig?" the all-American named woman asked in a deep Polish accent.

"No, honey, let me finish for God's sake. This is Avery Brundage. He is head of the American Olympic Committee." She stared blank-faced at him. "He's an important guy," he said defeated. He turned back to Avery, "Let's go sit down."

"Somewhere quiet Tony, if possible. This is also a business meeting."

Accardo looked at Brundage and his serious demeanor. "Well then let's take this right to my office, shall we?" Accardo turned to one of his henchmen, "Bring me our best scotch, or at least one of our less diluted."

In Accardo's office Brundage laid out the plan. He provided names and addresses of AAU members located in the Mid-West region. He didn't care how it was done but he needed votes in his favor. "These dumb-ass corn-pokes don't give two shits about the Jews. Hell, most couldn't tell the difference if there was one sitting right next to them, so it shouldn't take too much coercion I would think," said Avery.

"Well, are we talking broken legs here, or kidnapping children, or guns to the head? How far you willing to go Avery?"

"Jesus, try to avoid violence. I need them alive to vote, or at least I think I do. Be creative. And keep my name far away from anything."

"Okay. And I want my boys to get the cement contract for your new skyscraper. Kapisch?"

"Kapisch. I'll have my uncle draw up the contracts." The two men rose and shook hands.

"Don't worry. You'll get to Berlin, Avery."

GOULD

Gould and his reporters once again gathered around his desk at the AP. This time the discussion centered solely on the budding possibility of a vote for a Berlin boycott and the ripple effect it would have on the potential athletes. Deep down Gould was torn, he would absolutely support the AAU and knew a boycott was morally the right thing to do, but he also knew the athletes and their dreams and desires. The Olympics only came around once every four years, and the amateur athlete understood they only had one or two shots at glory. A boycott would crush a lot of dreams.

"I can't imagine any of the athletes are going to be pleased about this, Boss." Tank began and took a big swig of his coffee.

"That's exactly the angle we need to work. I want to know as many of the athlete's take on this as possible. Whether they are Negro, White, Jew, Catholic, Buddhist, male, female, it doesn't matter, I want to know if they want to go to Berlin or not and why," Gould pronounced. "Baker, I'm sending you to Barcelona."

"What did I do wrong? Spain's a tinderbox."

"You're gonna find out about the 'People's Olympiad'. I want to know if it appears a viable alternative to Berlin. Sit down with the organizers and pick their brains. I want to know if they have other countries onboard."

"Jeez Boss, what if a revolution or something breaks out when I'm there?"

"Then you'll have the exclusive." Gould took a puff from his cigar, "Joey, you handle the track and field athletes here. Go to Ohio State and talk to the Owens kid, and Michigan, definitely Michigan, and talk to Stoller, he's a Jewish runner that's as fast as Owens. I want to hear from him for sure. And go to USC and talk to Cromwell's boys." He turned to all of them, "Women, I want the female athlete's take on this whole thing. Tank, you take the pool."

"Even Holm?" He said with a sheepish grin.

"I'll talk to Eleanor, thank you very much." Gould replied bursting Tank's bubble. "You talk to the other swimmers, and Rawls and Poynton-Hill too. They are both former Olympians who I'm sure will have something to say. I'll continue handling the political side. Dealing with Brundage empowers me. Any questions?"

Nobody had any, and they emptied out of the office in a fog of cigar smoke, leaving only Gould, dirty coffee cups, and a bunch of half-eaten donuts in their midst. "Am I the only one who cleans up around here?" Gould asked aloud. He walked around with a garbage can and as he picked up the trash, he couldn't help but think what a mess a vote to boycott or not would create within the American sports world.

*   *   *

Across town Judge Mahoney sat at his cramped desk and looked over sheets and sheets of names and addresses of AAU voting members from around the country. He tried to wrap his head around what members may vote in favor of boycott or those who would side with Brundage. He had sent a preliminary questionnaire out as to gauge the temperature of voters, but results were slow to return. The ones that did come back were in favor of a boycott, but most of those were from the East and West Coast. The flag-waving voters in the middle of the country, he feared, did not care nor did they comprehend the situation in Nazi Germany. They just wanted to see Americans win medals, which in normal circumstances would be just fine, but these circumstances were far from normal.

Ambassador Dodd and IOC member Ernest Jahncke had given Mahoney graphic and vivid details about the bloodbath across Germany on the 'Night of the Long Knives'. This alone should have prompted IOC President Latour to change the host city for the '36 Games, but not a word from the IOC nor any of its members, except for Jahncke. Mahoney could not fathom the silence. He had never thought the IOC to be a credible institution to begin with, and now with all their talk of keeping politics out of the Olympics, it seemed preposterous. The IOC was comprised of the most corrupt band of self-serving politicians on earth. Mahoney knew Jahncke was one of only a few exceptions and he felt terrible that the man was basically standing alone in his fight to change the IOC's perceptions about Berlin.

*   *   *

Jahncke sat outside at a corner café in a popular square in Vienna and panned the passersby. Though he was looking for someone, he couldn't help but notice how very similar the

Viennese people dressed and looked like their German neighbors. It was probably just his imagination as he had also noticed the growing Nazi propaganda around the Austrian capital, and the subtle hold it was seizing over their usually level-headed populace. However, he couldn't shake the feeling he may as well be in Düsseldorf.

"Ernest, you look like you're in a trance. Is everything, okay?" Theodore Lewald asked as he sat across the small wicker table. A waiter came for his order before Jahncke could answer. "A cappuccino with light cream, please," the German ordered, then turned his attention back to the reflective American. "Though it is always a pleasure to spend some time with colleagues out of the office, I am curious why you asked to meet with me, Ernest."

Jahncke got right to the point. "Theodor, I have always valued your opinion on everything Olympic. You are a true example of the Olympic ideal." He thought hard about his next statement.

"I'm flattered. Why all the accolades?" Lewald interrupted. He looked at Jahncke hard. He knew where the American was going with this, but it was dangerous talk.

"Goddammit, Theodor," Jahncke couldn't hold back, "Even though you realize your very life is in danger, you go along with that idiot Von Halt. I understand you worked hard for this one. And I know it must be brutally difficult after the postponement of the '16 Games, but you must come clean about the reality of the situation. Tell Latour what is really going on in Berlin. Then, if you must, you and Elisabeth and the family can seek asylum in the US. I will sponsor you, for Christ's sake."

Lewald was moved by Jahncke's proposition. He, more than any other outsider Lewald knew, understood the writing on the wall. "I am flattered by your honest concern, Ernest. I truly am, but I have to believe deep in my heart that Germany will come around for the Games. I don't know what the future brings. I've never been much of a Nostradamus, but I, we," he implored, "must believe that an Olympics can bring a global peace through an understanding that all of us are not that different. That we all cheer our sports teams no matter what our language or color. That heartbreak is universal. That we feel the sting of defeat and the exaltation of victory the same. I truly believe the Olympics can save us from our political differences. I want the Games to happen despite the damned Nazis, Ernest. Von Halt is a puppet. I'm no fool."

Jahncke could not argue with any of this. The passion his friend and long-time IOC colleague conveyed was impermeable. But an incredible sadness overcame the hardened former Secretary of the Navy despite, and he looked softly at the German Jew, "Oh, Theodore." He grabbed the man's hand kindly, "I can only pray your idealistic dreams come true and I go down in history as an epic naysayer. Because the alternative, I fear, could be fatal." Lewald squeezed his hand and looked back at him with an uncomfortable grin.

"Pray hard, my friend."

*　　*　　*

Days later in New York City, on a crystal-clear summer afternoon, Alan Gould and Eleanor Holm walked the Central Park reservoir. Gould loved to escape there during lunch hours because of its remote peacefulness, and the fact it was always good for an interview. The surroundings put the respondent at ease and Gould could get them to speak freely.

The two of them made quite the pair as they strolled; Gould buttoned up with his bowtie and jacket and Eleanor in her pants, loose colorful blouse, and big floppy hat. "Tell me, Eleanor, what are you hearing in the AAU aquatic circles about a boycott? Are athletes in favor of it, or do they want to go to Berlin?" Gould asked. He knew if any athlete would give him the honest poop, it would be Eleanor.

"It's split as far as the swimmers and divers I've spoken with, but that's really only East Coast folks. If I had to bet, the Central and West Coast athletes are split as well. Don't get me wrong, everyone WANTS to go and compete, but the question of 'should we' is what people are grappling with."

"How about you?"

She smiled, "Oh, Alan, you know the answer to that already. Why even ask it?" He laughed out loud. He did know; she was dying to compete no matter what the situation was. "I could give a shit about politics. That's a job for asshole politicians. My job is to win Gold."

"What about the ethical side of things," he appealed to her conscience.

"You mean the Jewish situation?" She looked at him incredulously. "How is that any different from how we treat our black citizens in over half of this country? Would our politicians have changed policy if Germany didn't want to come to L.A.? I highly doubt it. The whole South would've said 'Tough shit. You don't like it, don't come'. Let's not both be naïve."

This was a response that took Gould by surprise. Yes, it seemed a cavalier attitude towards a growing crisis, but she did make a good point. Neither the US government nor the AOC would have changed a thing; a boycott of Berlin could appear embarrassingly hypocritical.

Eleanor continued, "The Olympics are about us, the athletes, no matter where we happened to come from. I'm pretty certain a champion like Gretel Bergmann doesn't care a lick about how the Nazi Party does business. She would've been just as happy to play under the British flag if Germany hadn't invited her back. Her mindset is on competing . . . and winning."

Gould wondered just how happy an athlete of Gretel's caliber, and religion, felt about playing under the Nazi flag. A question he would certainly have to ask her himself when they both got to the Games.

GRETEL

Gretel carried her bags into the sprawling German Olympic Training Facility swarming with athletes of every kind and walked with feelings of both giddiness and shock. She was pleased to be there, but the walls of every hallway were lined with murals of Hitler, Osten, and celebrated Nazi or Nazi endorsed athletes of recent past, such as Schmeling and the World Champion German Men's National Rowing Team. Red and black Nazi regalia also adorned every wall in some fashion or another.

This was not the Germany she remembered as a young girl. She was taken aback at how swiftly things had changed. It had been less than two years since she left for England, but now it felt like she had returned to another country altogether. She would never voluntarily be a part of the madness, but if it kept her family from harm, she would have to act like all the others. Aside from high jumping, hiding her fear would have to be one more thing to practice.

She approached a receptionist to get her room key and bedding. The receptionist smiled at her. "Bergmann?"

"Yes."

"We've been waiting for you," the receptionist said, then whispered closely, "It's good to have you back."

Gretel smiled politely and said, "Good to be back home."

The receptionist piled sheets, a blanket, and a pillow on the counter, and handed Gretel a key. Looking over her ledger, she said, "You're rooming with . . . Ratjen. Nice girl." she said, and pushed a clipboard in front of Gretel, who signed the papers and grabbed her bedding. They shared a smile, and while the receptionist seemed nice enough, Gretel couldn't help but be suspicious. She hid it well though, smiling back with a nod.

She walked through the corridors of the beautiful brand-new dormitory, reached her number, and knocked. "Come in," a voice called. Gretel entered. It was a quaint, but functional space with bunk beds in one corner and dressers in another. Aside from that, the room was empty. She put her things down on the top bed and turned to the bathroom where she heard running water.

Sitting on the sink shaving her legs was DORA RATJEN. Gretel thought the girl looked a bit odd but shrugged it off; the whole scene seemed rather odd but . . . "I'm Dora. Hope you don't mind. I'll make sure to clean up."

"I'm Gretel. Nice to meet you."

The sink was full of dark whiskers. Dora continued shaving. "Top or bottom," she said.

"Excuse me?"

"The bunk beds. Do you prefer the top or bottom?"

"Oh. I'll take the top if you don't mind," Gretel said.

"Not at all. I figured you like to be up in the air. British Champion, German record-holder . . . I know who you are. It's a real pleasure to room with you," Dora said as she wiped her leg off with a towel and hopped down off the sink.

Gretel smiled. "Likewise."

"Now, a toast!" Dora said as they walked back into the main room. "Just so you know, I don't make a habit of this." She opened her suitcase and pulled out a silver flask. She offered it to Gretel. "Schnapps?"

Gretel took the flask, opened it, and sniffed. "Oh, thank you. I think I'm going to like these living arrangements."

"To the room!" Dora shouted.

Gretel raised the flask. "To the room!" and took a swig. She handed it to Dora, who also took a sip and smiled.

After a fitting dinner in the commissary and hot showers, the female athletes retired back to their rooms. Ratjen fell asleep quickly and began snoring loudly. Gretel laughed. It was as loud as her father's. She stayed up and wrote a letter to her family. Afterwards she lay in her top bunk trying to put her head around such a dizzying day. Though she had her reservations, she couldn't have asked for a nicer complex to practice and get ready for the Olympic Games. She dozed off imagining how athletes from other countries were preparing.

THE ATHLETES

The 1st annual European Athletic Championships were held in Turin, Italy in 1934 and featured some of Europe's best athletes, but none more so than Germany's wildly popular, Luz Long. Luz had won his country's Long Jump Championship the last two years, and he was primed for an international competition victory. He was also the heavy favorite. With his father Jorgen by his side, Luz paced up and down the long jump path located in the field in the middle of the track of Stadio Benito Mussolini.

Jorgen noticed his son's mind was elsewhere. "You seemed pre-occupied, Luz. Or is it nerves?" Jorgen asked worriedly. The young man looked at his father dejected.

"They came for me last week, Poppa. They 'encouraged' me to join the Party." Jorgen immediately grabbed his son's arm.

"What did you tell them? Did they threaten you in anyway? *Schweinehunds!*"

"I told them I was concentrating on my sport and my law practice." Luz had just recently graduated with a law degree from Leipzig and was opening a firm in Hamburg. "They said I should continue to do that but as a proud Nazi. I reminded them

Schmeling, who was also a champion, had not become a Nazi and still boxed proudly for Germany." He looked down and sighed. "They told me they would revisit the subject with me after the Berlin Games. When I wouldn't be so focused on running and jumping." Jorgen raised his son's chin.

"We have two years to worry about this then. Let's for now focus on the task at hand." But Luz couldn't get his mind off it and when the competition was over, he placed a disappointing third with a final jump of 7.25. His lowest total in two years. His teammate Wilhelm Leichem took first at 7.45 meters and Otto Berg of Norway took 2nd at 7.31 meters.

After the competition father and son had dinner at a cozy place in the heart of the small Italian village. Luz was obviously dejected, not only for his third-place finish, but because he just wasn't into politics or the military or anything like that. He was 21 and handsome and strong and wanted only three things; his family's health, to win on the field, and many beautiful women. "Poppa, I'm not sure I can compete anymore knowing in the back of my head I'm just going to be used as cannon fodder after I'm done." He fought off tears. Jorgen looked back at him tenderly but spoke directly.

"Use it as motivation. Winning is the only way out. If you stay successful at home and begin winning internationally, you will be safe. You must believe that." Jorgen said, then took a swig of his Barolo. Luz looked at him skeptically. "Helene Mayer is another example. She is a champion coming back to play for Germany and she isn't being forced to join. Have faith. Just focus and then win." Luz smiled.

"Okay, Poppa. I'll take your word for it."

"Always listen to your Poppa." He pointed to his son's meal. "Now eat your veal before it needs a sweater."

*   *   *

Helene Mayer, the only German Jewish athlete other than Gretel asked to participate in Berlin, walked around the University of Southern California sports complex and mingled with some of the other athletes. Helene was eager to tell anyone who would listen that she had accepted the invitation of the German government to compete in '36. She walked over to runners LOUIS ZAMPERINI and Foy Draper. They were shocked she wanted to compete for Germany. Draper compared Coach Dean Cromwell to the Nazis.

"He is just as awful. And Brundage made him Robertson's assistant on the Olympic team. I heard Robertson was pissed," Draper said as he munched on a carrot stick. Zamperini shook his head in amazement and turned to Mayer.

"Helene, why would you decide this? You always told me the Nazis scared the shit out of you." She didn't even have to think about it.

"I am a Gold medal winner for my country. And despite recent political turmoil, which like all things shall pass, I am proud to be a German. Just as proud as you guys are of being American. You can't ever shake that out of your system. And I do believe things will get better. I mean, they finally came to their senses and realized I'm Methodist. That's a positive start."

"I don't know what to say, Mayer," Draper replied, "But I hope for your sake, you know what you're doing. I gotta fly. See you in Berlin."

Mayer turned to Zamperini whom she knew would have a strong reaction. He was a tough kid from the streets of Southern California, but he had a real soft spot for her, and she for him. They had recently begun an innocent, yet budding relationship and she could see that he was crushed. "I thought we would be able to hang out for the holidays. Was I even a consideration?" he asked.

"Yes Louis, and it certainly made my decision that much more difficult but . . . I want to do it."

Zamperini swallowed hard trying to hide his emotions, "Well how much time before you leave?"

"I'm not coming back after Thanksgiving break."

"Wow. Why even start the semester?" he said dejectedly. "Gosh, I hope we get to hang out?"

She touched his face with her hand, "Of course, and I do plan on seeing you in Berlin in a year and a half, Louis. So, you better make the damned team."

*   *   *

In Belltown, WA most of the summer of 1934 was gone, but Bob Moch was completely spent. His bar-backing job got him home at four in the morning; he had to meet the guys at the dock at five, row until eight, eat, and maybe catch four hours of sleep before the clock started over. The only saving grace was the bar was busy and he had no downtime. He had to eat while working, grabbing scraps from the chef when he could, or stealing the occasional French fry from a plate when he passed the expeditor station. Most nights a few guys from the team would come in for a cheap burger after they got off from their summer jobs and Don Hume was always one of them.

"You look like shit tonight, Bob," Don said to his friend with concern. Charles Day and Johnny White concurred.

"Real shit, Bobby," added White.

"I'm warmed by your sympathy," Moch shot back. "Hope you choke on your dinner."

Next to their table, four very white and very large longshoremen began to openly debate what they considered the University's growing problem of immigrants coming to Seattle to study. "Why the hell do I have to pass an Oriental on my street?

They can stay over there and study at their chop-suey colleges. What's next, Jews, then A-rabs? Jesus, could you just imagine?!" One of the men said then chugged his beer down.

"How about running into a fucking guy wearing a towel around his head right here in downtown Seattle? I couldn't believe he didn't get his ass kicked," another one added.

Moch and his teammates looked at each other hard. None of them felt this way, and they knew the recent talk of boycotting Berlin was due to this kind of rhetoric spreading throughout Europe.

"How can this country even stand looking at itself in the mirror?" Moch posed.

"And yet somehow we play the good guys," Don added.

The next morning pouring rain cancelled the boys' practice. Moch slept in a few extra hours, then ran to his parent's jewelry store to see if he could help in any way. When he arrived, he noticed his mother talking to a woman at the counter. They were comparing necklaces. When Fleeta saw her son approaching, she nonchalantly placed the necklace she was holding back into a locked drawer. The other woman stood holding a bright gold chain with a Star of David dangling on it. "Good morning, my dear." Fleeta began, "This is Mrs. Kirchenbaum. Judith, this is my son Bob."

"Good morning, ma'am. Your necklace is beautiful."

"Isn't he a sweet one," the woman said to Fleeta.

"He is going to be an Olympian in Berlin." Fleeta said with pride. Bob rolled his eyes embarrassed.

"Oh goodness. Berlin? I thank God every day I was able to get out of there. I couldn't imagine why anyone would want to enter that damned place." The older woman said.

"The Olympics," Bob replied dryly.

Judith Kirchenbaum put her necklace in her purse. "I'm not so sure it's a place for our kind to be visiting or participating in any sporting event. These are dangerous times." She warned, "Goodbye, Fleeta, and good luck young man." As she walked out, Moch shook his head.

"She thinks we're Jewish, Ma." He laughed, "She does know our last name is Moch, right?" Fleeta smiled at her son.

"Yes. She does."

*   *   *

A little over a thousand miles south, at the US Olympic Aquatic Center in Los Angeles, eleven-year-old MARJORIE GESTRING, a perky, all-American, all-California, little sweetheart sat with her mother and watched L.A. Olympic medalists, KATHERINE RAWLS and DOROTHY POYNTON-HILL, as they made perfect dive after perfect dive from the 3-meter springboard. Gestring smiled at her mother, who laughed. She knew her daughter too well. Marjorie was plotting. She wasn't awed by the two Gold Medal winners; she was sizing them up. For behind the facade of this blonde, blue eyed, Golden State native child, held the competitive heart of a champion.

When the veterans finished their practice, Marjorie's mom allowed her to approach them. "You two are really swell to watch." She extended her hand to Rawls who was closest, "My name is Marjorie. Marjorie Gestring." Rawls then Hill shook her small hand, both amused by the child's outgoing nature. "I'm a diver as well and I'm gonna win medals just like you!"

"Is that so?" Hill asked. "Well, you might want to beef up a little. It's hard to win when your built like a skinny chicken."

"That's just for now," she said confidently. "My Ma says I'm about to go through my changing period, so I'll be ready in two years for sure."

Rawls was taken aback. "You think you're gonna compete for the US in Berlin? You're a little girl, honey. It's okay to have

- 144 -

dreams but you gotta be realistic. It is okay to dream though," she said condescendingly, then patted Gestring on the head as she walked away.

"Good luck little chick-a-dee," Hill said and went off after Rawls towards the dressing room.

But Gestring didn't need much luck. Though a child in age and body, her abilities and drive were well ahead of their time. Unbeknownst to Rawls and Hill, she was the best diver in her age group in the whole US, unbeaten and unblemished, and just hours before had officially joined the woman's circuit. And young Marjorie Gestring was coming for them.

The young lady couldn't remember a time she didn't love the water and she had been diving since she was three years old. And not just for fun. Her first competition was at five, and even then, she was a ferocious bulldog. She had always gotten along great with all her opponents off the platform; polite smiles and small talk, but as soon as the battle began, she didn't even look their way, and not a word was spoken. Other divers knew to stay away from her. It wasn't that Marjorie was mean or playing mind games, it was all about her focus. She would let nothing else in but the dive ahead of her. That's what she saw in Rawls and Hill as well, and she knew that focus was the only way to achieve Gold.

*   *   *

Marty Glickman, more comfortable in his running attire than the dress clothes he was wearing, walked through the halls of James Madison High School in Brooklyn, NY. He was holding hands with a beautiful blond girl, Louise. It was the first month of his junior year, but Marty was already 'big man on campus'. His athletic ability far surpassed any senior at the school, and his charm and charisma were equally unmatched. Walking next to Louise, the sweetest and prettiest girl in school, didn't hurt matters much either.

They approached a classroom where a teacher was greeting students as they filed in. As Marty and Louise walked by, the teacher said, "Nice game last week, Marty. Two touchdowns against my alma mater. Impressive."

"Three," Marty said in passing, holding up three fingers.

Almost every student they passed said, "Hey Marty" or "Hi Lulu", or gave a wave or nod. They were obviously very popular amongst the students and teachers alike.

"Are your parents going to that boycott rally in Manhattan tonight?" Louise asked.

"Unfortunately. I begged them not to," he said.

"Why would you do that? I'm glad my parents are going. I would go myself if we didn't have school tomorrow," she said.

"I know, but I can't help but think of how great it would be to stick it to Hitler . . . if I could ever make the team."

"You'll make the team. You're the fastest kid in all of New York. But you have to graduate first, so get to class," she said, as they approached an intersection in the hallway. As they were about to go in opposite directions, Marty grabbed her.

"So, you'll have the house to yourself tonight?" he asked, smiling wryly.

"Yeah, come over around seven o'clock. We can study," she said flirtatiously as she backed away.

"Study." Marty waved and walked away with a hop in his step, trying, and failing, to hold back his wide smile.

As he turned a corner, he was accosted by a freshman student. "Marty! I need a headline for *The Moment*!" The Moment was the school paper, whose pages Marty frequented with his athletic achievements and compelling quotes.

"Class is starting," Marty said.

"Please? I'm desperate."

"Again? Why am I always telling you what to write? Don't you learn anything in journalism class?" Marty asked.

"I'm not a journalist--I'm an announcer. I'll be calling your games on the radio when you're playing for the Giants one day."

"Sure, you will. C'mere." Marty guided the young high school reporter to a secluded part of the hallway as the other students filed into classrooms. "Here's your headline." He fanned his arm out, scrolling in the air. "THE FASTEST KID ON THE BLOCK . . . and underneath, 'In a blaze of black and gold, Glickman runs wild for Jimmy Madison's Knights!'"

"Love it," the kid said while furiously jotting notes. Thanks, Marty. My deadline was ten minutes ago. You're a mensch!" the reporter gushed, and ran off to class, still writing in his pad.

Marty shrugged. "Nothing like waiting until the last minute," he said, and walked off to his class, indifferent to his tardiness. Another of Marty's greatest skills was his velvety voice. He was confident he could talk his way out of any problem, especially a late slip from his history teacher.

*   *   *

"Whoo-hoo!" Glenn Morris howled on a clear and crisp autumn night as he steered his speeding pick-up truck down an unlit road near his family's farm in Simla, CO. Two college-aged girls sat in the front cab to his right, drinking from bottles of cheap beer as the truck swerved along the rural highway. He grabbed a beer bottle from the girl to his right and took a swig.

As he handed the beer back, she decided to plant a kiss on him. He struggled to keep his eyes on the road. "If you're trying to distract me, honey, you're gonna have to do better than that!" he said. With that, the other girl whipped off her tank top, revealing her naked breasts.

"How's this?" she said.

Glenn took one look and said, "Holy sh—"

"Lookout!" the kisser screamed, and the pick-up swerved and jumped a curb, slamming into a mailbox and thrusting all three of them hard into the dashboard. When the truck came to a stop, Glenn saw that the mailbox was pinned against the windshield. He read the name on the mailbox.

"The Fenton's . . . fuck."

About an hour later, Glenn's father, Edgar Morris, entered the Simla police precinct office. He was not pleased. He approached a desk officer who nodded and addressed him in a familiar way. "Howdy, Ed," the officer said. "Follow me." He led Edgar through a hallway to a ten-by-ten jail cell where Glenn was slumped against a wall. "I know this wasn't necessary, but you know the routine," the officer said as he opened the gate to the cell. Glenn stood up and sluggishly walked out with his head down.

They drove home in Edgar's truck. Ed was a quiet man, but even Glenn, in his drunken state, knew that his father was hot. "You could've killed yourself! And those girls . . ."

"I know, Pops. I'm sorry. I messed up," Glenn said. "It won't happen again."

"Stop saying that! I've heard it before, goddammit!" Edgar shouted. "I'm taking away your keys. You're through driving that damned truck. You wanna drive something? Try the harvest tractor in field two. You'll start tomorrow at sunrise!"

They arrived home in pitch darkness. Glenn took the stairs up to his room. Edgar watched him go and walked to the telephone near the kitchen. He pulled a piece of paper from his wallet and dialed a number.

On the other end of the line, a voice grumbled, "Who is this?"

"Judge Mahoney?"

"Yes."

"This is Edgar Morris, father of Glenn Morris out in Colorado. You said I could call you any time."

"It's three in the morning," Mahoney said.

"I know, and I apologize. It's just . . . well, it's Glenn. If he has any chance to make the '36 team, he needs some help. He's a special athlete, but I'm afraid he's lost his way and I'm not sure I can help him anymore. He don't listen to me, but he might listen to you."

Mahoney didn't hesitate. He lived for his athletes, no matter how far away they were. "I understand. Let me find a time to fly out to come see the both of you. I'll talk to him then."

LENI

It was September of 1934 and Leni was hard at work. "Let the moment envelop you! You are the most beautiful men Germany has to offer, be proud of your nakedness. Jump into the lake like a stud overpowering his mare. Extend your bodies in the air so we see all of you when you thrust then penetrate the virgin waters!" Leni Riefenstahl directed a small army of naked men with a vision only she could understand. Ertl just rolled his eyes while rolling film. It had been three straight days of endless lines of naked men in and out of saunas and jumping into the lake. He wasn't sure if this was going to be a sports documentary or homosexual pornography.

Standing behind the elaborately lit and furnished set, behind Riefenstahl and Ertl and all the crew, was Adolf Hitler and Eva Braun. Eva was in a trance, mouth agape at the constant flow of penises large and small passing within feet of her. Hitler beamed with artistic fervor. Whatever it was Leni saw in the scene, Hitler saw it as well and his face was flushed with German pride. Riefenstahl was the best Germany had to offer, one of the finest filmmakers in the world, and one of the few that didn't emigrate. Hitler knew only she could do "Olympia" justice.

"Cut. Okay, take a break for ten minutes everyone. Stay fresh! No masturbation!" Leni screamed and then turned to Ertl. "Check the gate, I'll check on our guests." She walked over to the Führer and Eva. "Do you like what you see, Herr Hitler?" Leni Riefenstahl was the only person other than Eva, to address Hitler so cavalierly.

"It is magnificent Frau Riefenstahl, inspirational and profound. From what I've seen I can only expect a masterpiece. And I expect the same thing next week for our little shoot in Nuremberg." He turned, "Herr Ertl, come." Ertl reluctantly obliged. "Do not be afraid Herr Ertl, I do not bite. Maybe Eva a little, but not me."

"Oh Wulffie," Eva said, embarrassed.

"What can I do for you sir?" Ertl asked avoiding any eye contact.

"I want you to have the best equipment once at the stadiums. Do not hesitate to provide Osten with a comprehensive list of the top-quality tools and materials. *Verstehen?*"

"*Na sicher, danke.*" Ertl replied. Hitler gave him an awkward smile.

"You may leave now, Ertl." And he did without hesitation. Hitler turned back to Leni, "He's a little nervous, but seems competent enough."

"I would want no other by my side," she said. Hitler smiled at her loyalty. "Thank you for joining us today, Herr Hitler, but now I must go back to work. Will you be staying through lunch?"

"No, no. I think all this nakedness has been enough for Eva today." She shot him a cold look. "We are driving back to Berlin now, and from the look of things, I'm about to get an earful from my *Liebling*, so the sooner we are off, the better."

In the limousine, Hitler asked his chauffeur to close the automatic wall between the front seat and the backseat. The help didn't need to be subjected to the tongue-lashing he was about to get from Eva.

"Is it necessary for you to embarrass me, Adolf?!"

"*Poopsie*, I was only playing. Why must you always take things so personally?"

"I want that woman's respect. I am a photographer, and she is a great artist. Which leads me to an even bigger issue." Hitler braced for the worst. "*Wulffie*, I have decided that the Opening Day ceremonies of the Olympic Games will be my coming out party. It will be the moment you declare to the world I am your lover."

His eyes opened wide with surprise. "Won't that take away from the actual purpose of the event, Eva? It's about welcoming the athletes."

"And who better to welcome them then the new first lady of Germany?"

"Oh Eva, stop being so dramatic. You sound like Lady Macbeth. It doesn't suite you."

To his absolute surprise she grabbed his crotch with brave assertion. "Adolf, that day WILL be my coming out party. I do not ask for much." She gripped his crotch a little tighter making him squirm in an almost painful delight. "But you do, and I oblige without question. And now I want what I have earned and continue to earn."

"Okay, okay that's enough!" he screamed, and she relinquished her grip. They looked at each other and began laughing out loud. "I'll make it a grand party for you my dear," he conceded. "On that day you will become the Queen of Bavaria!"

She smiled at him. Little, timid, overlooked Eva Braun would finally get the respect she felt she so richly deserved.

*   *   *

Later that month, Leni peeked through her camera, capturing Hitler from behind as he waved to an adoring crowd of tens of thousands. Her tripod was planted behind Hitler's legs on a platform specifically built for the car ride into Nuremberg for a massive Nazi party rally, known to Germans as the "The 6th Party Congress." The streets were packed with citizens who all yelled "*Sieg Heil!*" and gave the Nazi salute as the car passed.

Leni turned to Ertl. "Roll out." Ertl removed the film magazine from the camera and loaded a fresh one. While he prepared the new magazine of film, Leni tapped Hitler on the shoulder. "I need you to wave again but hold your hand higher and turn your body to the right."

"Why would I turn to the right? I should be facing in the direction of where the car is going!" Hitler yelled.

"Your head is blocking your hand, and I can't move the camera," Leni replied.

"But it doesn't make sense! I'll look like a fool if you see the car going one way and me another --"

"The car is not in the shot! *Mein Gott*, you are impossible today!" she yelled back.

"I have a speech to write, so let's finish this nonsense so I can think straight!" he protested.

"This was your idea!"

"Regretfully!" he yelled and continued to smile at the crowd. Leni rolled her eyes.

Ertl looked through the lens and burned a few seconds of film. He turned to Leni and said, "Ready to roll."

"Thank you." Leni took a deep breath and returned to the lens. She shouted to Hitler, "Turn to the right for one take and we're done for today!" He finally took her direction and Leni got exactly the shot she wanted. "Good, we got it. Ertl, pack this up. That's a wrap for the car. Let's set up inside the Hall." Ertl started dismantling the camera and tripod as the car reached the entrance to Luitpold Hall.

Luitpold Hall was the massive outdoor stadium that was

newly renovated for the Nazi party's rallies. The outdoor hall featured seventy-six loudspeakers, forty-two spotlights, the largest pipe organ in Germany, and could fit well over a hundred thousand people.

Leni was in awe and even a bit frightened of the sheer number of people who flocked to Nuremberg. She had never seen a crowd this large and in such a frenzied state. It was said that a million people had come to the rally and to hear their Führer's speeches over the course of the five-day gathering. She would film it all.

Her crew consisted of 172 people, including ten technical staff, thirty-six cameramen and assistants, operating in sixteen teams with thirty cameras, nine aerial photographers, seventeen newsreel men, twelve newsreel crew, seventeen lighting men, two photographers, twenty-six drivers, thirty-seven security personnel, four labor service workers, and two personal assistants. Many of her cameramen also dressed in SS uniforms so they could blend into the crowds.

With a budget of over 280,000 Reichsmark ($120,000 US dollars in 1934), the production was the largest budgeted documentary in world history.

Later that night, Leni returned to the apartment she had rented for the duration of filming. It was spacious and fully furnished with a tasteful decor. It was apparent that Hitler was paying her handsomely. She put her bags down and collapsed on a couch. A moment later a gray cat jumped up onto her lap. Leni scratched the cat around the ears and said, "Let's eat."

A half-hour later, in a large kitchen, she prepared her dinner; Blutwurst (blood sausage), Spargel (white asparagus), and boiled potatoes. She tossed the potatoes into a pot of boiling water and sliced herself a piece of Gouda cheese from a cutting board, then turned the sausage over in a skillet. The cat followed her every move, rubbing against her legs as she cooked.

At the dining room table, it was a party of four. Her dinner guests consisted of a potted fern in the middle of the table, her typewriter, and of course, the gray cat. She poured herself a glass of wine, sat back, and admired the meal.

The room was silent. It was a much-needed respite from the chaotic day of shooting, and a sad and lonely scene that only a skilled filmmaker like her could embrace. She sliced a little piece of sausage from her plate and fed the cat from the palm of her hand.

Helene Bertha Amalie Riefenstahl had spent most of her childhood by herself. She was an only child for most of her youth and her imagination was her best friend. Her father Alfred, who owned a heating and ventilation company, wanted her to take over the family business. But even at the age of four, Leni wanted to be an artist and wanted nothing to do with heating and ventilation. Growing up, her father never supported her more artistic inclinations. Her mother Bertha enrolled the child in dance and poetry classes without his knowledge, and the young girl thrived. Her mother also recognized how athletic her daughter was, and as a preteen encouraged her to swim and perform gymnastics. Leni loved her mother for opening the world to her.

By the age of eighteen she was considered one of the top ballet dancers in Germany, but a foot injury that led to knee surgery derailed her future. It was this injury, however, that lead to her film career. While at a doctor's office, she saw a poster for a mountain film, a popular trend during the Weimar Republic. She was instantly hooked. She spent the next five years acting in this genre, and by 1932, at the age of 30, she began directing. Her star rose quickly; her first directed film, *The Blue Light*, won a Silver Medal in Venice. This got the attention of Hitler and the up-and-coming Nazi Party. It didn't take long for them to recognize Leni was the propaganda machine they were looking for, and they set up a meeting with her and the *Führer*. The filmmaker and Chancellor took to each other like bees and honey and within days she was directing the fifth Nuremberg Rally. The lonely child artist had found a cinematic home, and unlimited financial resources in the Nazi Party, and she envisioned grand things.

The one thing that had always eluded her however was a real love affair. She had had many lovers, but none she considered solid or intellectually or physically on par with herself. So, Leni found solace in the love of her cat. At least with a cat, she thought, you knew exactly where you stood.

*   *   *

Judge Mahoney and Glenn Morris walked past a chicken coup, then a pen crowded with feeding cows, and wound up at the edge of a field where a patch of vegetables grew in rows over a hundred yards long and wide. "What's that stuff?" Mahoney asked Glenn.

"Cabbage. Not much else grows this time of year," Glenn replied.

"I was promised steak and eggs if I came all this way to see you, not cabbage." Mahoney said.

Glenn laughed. "That's not why you came, though."

"No, it's not."

"Tough love?" Glenn asked.

"No, I think your father has that covered."

"What then?"

Mahoney turned and faced Glenn. "I've met a lot of folks like you over the years. They get into drunken barroom brawls, crash cars, stick up mom and pop stores, losers. And there are two types of athletes I've encountered. I just can't tell if you're the type who just doesn't give a shit and kicks ass, or the type that cares so much that they're *afraid* of succeeding."

"Afraid of success?" Glenn said.

"That's right, a fear of actually achieving greatness, a fear of challenging himself, and accepting the occasional failure. It's a very common thing." They walked for a bit in silence. "Your father says you train every day, rain or shine."

"I guess I'm not so sure how I'd do against those city kids. I ain't never been outside of Colorado," Glenn said as he looked out over the fields. "No one in my family has ever amounted to much beyond this farm."

"You have to convince yourself that's it's okay to be the best. It's okay to 'get the girl'. It's okay to be great. And you have greatness in you, understand?" Mahoney said.

"I think so," Glenn replied.

"I want you to show the world." Mahoney faced him. "And most importantly, I want you to believe that you deserve it."

Glenn smiled earnestly. "I'll try. I really will," he said.

"Good. Let's go eat." Mahoney slapped Glenn on the shoulder, as they turned back towards the farmhouse.

Edgar had a delicious meal prepared for the Judge's visit. Along with the promised steak and eggs, flapjacks with butter and honey, homemade biscuits smothered in sausage gravy, fresh berries with fresh cream, and thick cut bacon filled the dining room table. The three men dove in like wolves. Mahoney hadn't had a meal like this in, well, he couldn't remember ever having a breakfast like that. "Delicious, Edgar. Good thing your boy works out like he does, or he would be as big as a house eating like this every day."

"He burns it all off between his morning chores and the track and field. I can't feed him enough." Edgar replied.

"You think they will have good food in Germany, Judge Mahoney?" Glenn asked, as he shoved a whole flapjack in his mouth.

"Oh, yes. The food there is exceptional."

"Do you even think we're gonna go? Even out here in the middle of nowhere, we get the news about what's going on over there," Edgar inquired with a bit of worry.

"That is still up in the air. But all our athletes must keep practicing and be prepared," Mahoney replied, not wanting to let his true feelings be known.

"Would be a shame if I got a spot on the team and we ended up not going," Glenn added, then drank down a whole glass of milk.

"It sure would be nice to see my boy in Olympic competition," Edgar beamed as he looked at Glenn, "And a trip to Berlin would be a fine adventure for a young man. Who knows what surprises may be in store? You may even meet a real nice girl."

"Ah geez, let it rest, Pop." Glenn shook his head and looked at Mahoney embarrassed.

"Hey, you never know," Mahoney added with a smile.

THE DODDS

In a dimly lit French restaurant, Martha Dodd sat at a table with Rudolph Diels drinking champagne. As he read the menu, she stared at him. He looked up and said, "You're staring at my scars, aren't you?" Rudolph had two prominent scars, one along each cheek from his days fencing when he was a young boy in Austria. Fencing without masks was a ritual when he was a boy, an exercise to prove one's manhood. Martha smiled.

"It doesn't make you less handsome," she said. The modest, and certainly handsome Diels quickly changed the subject.

"Come with me to Cologne. I'm the new head of police," he said. "Let's get away from this madness."

"What are you talking about? You're going to Cologne?"

"What choice do I have? I'm lucky to be sitting here with you now. Two months ago, I was hiding in my grandparent's basement, waiting for Putzi to put a bullet in my head and Diels,

Diels, now everything is changing so fast."

"Just do what Goering says," Martha said. "Ask him to help you. He's the second most powerful man in Germany. Surely Hitler will listen to him."

Diels looked at Martha and smiled. "Whatever I choose to do, it's been a delight to be with you, Martha. And thank you for looking past the scars on my face."

"I try to look inside a person, Rudy, not the shell," Martha said. She was becoming bored with all of Rudy's pessimism and ordered another bottle of champagne.

At the end of the night, Martha stumbled back into her house as Rudy drove away. She hadn't seen him since what the press dubbed in Berlin, 'Night of the Long Knives' and he seemed anxious and twitchy; so, she just kept drinking glass after glass as the night went on until she was too drunk to listen to him babble anymore. As she passed her parents' room, they called for her through the open door.

"Yes, Mommy? Yes, Daddy?"

Dodd took a deep breath and began, "Martha, we are worried about your lifestyle here. We are considering sending you back home."

"That's ridiculous," she slurred and continued. "I'm a big girl now, a grown woman who has a very important place in Berlin society."

"You have no place in their society darling," Mattie interrupted. "You are nothing but a piece of flesh to them." Martha stared hard at her mom with no retort. Mattie continued, "Forget disrespecting the good name of this family, you are disrespecting yourself. And that is what I fear for my daughter the most." She began to cry.

Martha ran to her mother and hugged her, "Please don't cry. I'm just living my life. I'm just being me, expressing myself."

"Must you express so much of yourself, to so many people?"

Dodd asked through gritted teeth. He had lost his little girl and the woman she had become literally scared the shit out of him. His stomach was now in a daily wretched state.

Martha turned to her father, "I will try to be better. Tonight, I ended it with Rudy Diels if that helps," she lied.

"Certainly, it does," he proclaimed. She stumbled toward the door, ricocheting slightly off the wall. "Mattie, will you please put our grown-up daughter to bed." She grabbed Martha and led her out of the room toward her own. At that moment Bill Jr. poked his head into his parents' room.

"Anything I can do Pops?"

"Yes, from now on keep a hawk's eye on your sister. I want you to accompany her as much as possible, double date with her if you have to."

"I don't want to be associated with her crowd."

"Maybe if you're there, William, she'll stop associating with that crowd! Please?! Can at least one of my children understand my actions?" Dodd said.

"I got it Pop. I'll take care of it. Don't get yourself even more wound up."

"This whole experience is like some mad hypnotic dream." Dodd said, rubbing his temples as he collapsed in the armchair near the window.

*   *   *

It was a crisp October afternoon in Washington D.C. as Franklin Delano Roosevelt sat in his wheelchair in the Oval Office. The doors to the back garden were open as Roosevelt had always liked that cool, sharp, autumn breeze cutting through his old bones. "It keeps one feeling alive," he would tell Eleanor when she would come in and insist on closing the doors in fear of her husband catching pneumonia.

Across from the President that day sat Louis Howe and Ernest Lee Jahncke. Roosevelt had great respect for the IOC representative and former Assistant Secretary of the Navy, having served as the latter himself under President Woodrow Wilson.

"It's always good to see you, Ernest. How is life outside the Navy treating you?" The President began and adjusted the small blanket he had over his lap.

"For the most part fine, Mr. President. Thank you. How is your lovely wife?"

"Eleanor is doing . . . What is Eleanor doing today, Louis?" Howe crushed his cigarette out and leafed through his black book.

"She has a lunch with the Daughters of the Revolution at 11:30. Then tea with the British Embassy wives at three."

"Well, that's how she's doing. She's non-stop," FDR said to Jahncke with a smile. "Now, what can we do for you today, my old friend?"

Jahncke jumped right in, "I have seen firsthand what is happening in Germany. I'm in constant correspondence with Ambassador Dodd, who is living inside the growing chaos, and neither of us believe sending our Olympic athletes over there is a safe option. The President of the Amateur Athletic Union, the venerable Judge Mahoney, agrees with our assessment."

"Louis and I know the Judge quite well, a very fair man."

"Damned fair," Howe supported.

"So, if this is the opinion of everyone, don't send them. I don't see why the White House need get involved," the President remarked.

"It's got to be voted on by the AAU representatives and Avery Brundage is going to fight us tooth and nail on the AOC side. Mr. President, if you just set a mandate that the US government feels it too risky to send these young Americans, it will be uncontested."

"I just don't feel comfortable wielding power like that, Ernest. And to my knowledge, Ambassador Dodd has never sent a telegram to us that make it sound so dire there. Louis, get me Secretary Cordell." Howe jumped up and ran out of the office. "Let's see what the Secretary of State reports. You don't mind waiting do you, Ernest?" the President said.

"No. I appreciate any time you can put into this, sir."

"Hungry? Want a brisket sandwich? I have a cook downstairs. Her name is Lizzie McDuffie. She makes the most mouth-watering brisket sandwich. I can't tell the exact spice she uses - jicama maybe - she won't tell me, but it just tastes so Goddamned good!" Just then, Louis came back in with Secretary of State Cordell Hull. "Ah Cordell. Take a seat."

"Thank you, Mr. President." Cordell took a seat across from Jahncke.

"Cordell, this is Ernest Lee Jahncke. He's the American representative of the International Olympic Committee." Both men nodded and smiled. "Mr. Jahncke tells me he has been in constant contact with our Ambassador Dodd in Berlin and things appear dangerously dark over there. Has the Ambassador given you any indication of these feelings?"

"I spoke with him recently, just before Hitler took care of the SA situation. He seemed miffed that some of his letters were not getting responded to, but I tell you Mr. President, neither my boys in the diplomatic core nor myself were getting any of them. I asked everyone." Cordell said in his deep Southern accent still completely oblivious to his staff's chicanery.

FDR turned back to Jahncke, "I just don't know how we can help, Ernest. Even if those letters do exist, I don't feel Washington should get involved. It's just the way America has always approached it. When politics and sports begin to mix, things get very messy."

HITLER

Carl Diem paced outside the Reichsportsführer's office, checking his watch incessantly. "C'mon, Theodor," he said out loud, and took one last look out the window for his friend. With a sigh, he walked to the front door of the office, knocked, and was let in by Von Halt.

Osten sat behind his desk smoking a cigar. "Sit down, gentlemen," he said. Diem and Von Halt each took seats opposite the desk. Osten snuffed out his cigar and sat upright in his chair. He said with absolute clarity, "Your friend Mr. Brundage must understand no athlete will be disallowed to participate based on their religion. The Propaganda Minister is absolutely resolute on eliminating the United States' fears of discrimination in the Games." He chuckled, "The nerve of these people, will their gall never end? Ach, anyway, Brundage is here in less than two months. The practice facilities must be filled with smiling athletic-looking young Jews."

"Are they actually going to have an opportunity to try out?" said Von Halt in amazement.

"And why wouldn't they?" Diem challenged. "Some of them are the best in their field. They want to win Gold for Germany just like any other citizen." The other two men looked at him deadpan. He slowly sensed something rotten. He checked his watch again. "Theodor is running late. He should be here before we continue this conversation, Sportsführer Osten."

"Your esteemed colleague has been relieved of his duties." This remark shocked both Von Halt and Diem. "He has had mental fatigue and the Reich found it best to alleviate his burdens."

Diem was mortified. A great sorrow fell over him. "So, you fire one of Brundage's friends because he's a Jew, and you ask two others to lie to him and say we will allow Jewish athletes to participate? Isn't Avery going to be curious why Theodor isn't around?"

"You will tell him he's on permanent leave due to mental stress." Osten reiterated.

Diem shot up like a cannon ball. "Don't think for one second, I buy this bullshit story. This is supposed to be the Olympics. Fair play throughout the nations. Why are you fucking this whole thing up! I'm going to tell Brundage everything! How's Goebbels or the Führer going to feel about that?!"

"Sit down, Mr. Diem." Osten said calmly. Carl gathered himself and obliged. "Lewald is still on the IOC. There is nothing to get too worked up about. I would hate for you to say something you regret." Osten pointed to a cigarette holder on his desk, "Have a smoke, Carl. By the way, how are your in-laws doing these days?"

Diem stared at the man at first puzzled, and then came to a slow realization. "They are fine," he said.

Osten sat back in his chair. "I wonder if they've been rubbing off on you."

"I'm not sure what you mean, sir." Diem replied.

"I understand you quadrupled your salary. That's something a Jew would do, eh?" Osten looked at Von Halt and chuckled.

"The Führer's office approved the increase," Diem fired back defensively. "They've been very generous."

"You know what they call people with Jewish in-laws?" Osten asked.

"No, sir."

"White Jews," Osten said. "It's just a label. I don't put much stock in it. But just be careful you don't assimilate because of your close association with them. You are of German blood, Carl. Do you understand?"

"I understand, sir."

Osten stood up from his chair. "You will play by my rules," Osten threatened. "Get Brundage onboard and your wife's family will live peacefully, and blissfully unaware this conversation ever existed." He turned to Von Halt, "See to it that Brundage finds Berlin more attractive than fucking James Hilton's Shangri-La and I will give you sole responsibility over the Garmisch-Partenkirchen Games. He turned back to Diem. "The Berlin Games are yours for the taking Carl. The choice is completely up to you."

Diem nodded. "Thank you, sir." He stood and exited the office. As soon as the door shut, his thoughts turned to Lewald. He wondered how his friend reacted to the demotion after all their efforts. They had worked tirelessly for years to bring the Games to Berlin. Now that they delivered them, they were forced to give up any control or influence they might have deserved. He thought Lewald would take it hard. He was right.

*   *   *

Theodor Lewald walked with his wife Elisabeth along the banks of the Spree River. It was Elisabeth's idea to get out of the house and get some fresh air after Theodor received the devastating news. Years ago, when they were engaged to be married, they spent many afternoons strolling along the riverbank, watching the ferries and tugboats, or having a picnic, making small talk or big plans, depending on the day. Her idea was a wasted effort - he hadn't said a word in hours. His heart was completely shattered. All the time spent to perfect every nuance of these Games, *his Games*, wasted. With one swift stroke of his pen, Goebbels had transformed a lifetime of loyal service into one of silent futility. His wife tried to assuage him.

"You're still on the IOC," she said.

"With a voice no one will listen to. Like a ghost. What will I do now?" he replied.

"You can spend more time with me and your grandchildren." He looked back at her with little enthusiasm.

"I hope so badly the Americans do the right thing. And I hope Carl shows Avery exactly what Berlin is becoming."

"Do you think he will?"

"I think he would like to, but it's not likely. Carl, I'm sure, is being given very little choice in the matter, and knowing Avery Brundage, his ambition will not keep him away." Theodore looked across the river towards the Berlin streets and put his hands on his head. "What kind of world do we live in when peaceful people become an acceptable threat? Where is the logic?" He looked at his wife hard. "I feel it is too incomprehensible to accept the fact the whole world is going mad around us and no one else notices, so I've come to the conclusion it must be we are the one's going mad." His wife smiled sadly.

"At this point I wish that were the case," she said, and put her arm around him.

That was the moment he realized whatever life he had led, she had led as well. She had never left his side, and this made him even more melancholy. He touched her face. "You are a good woman, Elisabeth Lewald." And with that, Theodor Lewald took her hand, and they continued their walk along the river that divided Berlin in two. The architect of two successful bids for a Berlin Olympics, a faithful servant to three German governments, and a Jew by blood, strolled into the warm Berlin evening with a composed, yet silent futility.

*   *   *

On the outskirts of Berlin in Wustermark, Germany, two black Schwetzingen limousines pulled up to the entrance of the Olympic Village. Reichssportsführer Osten and Carl Diem exited the first car in silence. Hitler, Joseph Goebbels, and von Halt exited the second. The sounds of trucks and construction workers echoed from inside the complex. Hitler surveyed the surroundings.

"Peaceful town. Has there been complaints about the noise?" he asked.

"None whatsoever," Osten said.

"Good. Then they won't mind when we station some of our army here after the Games," Hitler said.

Carl Diem was taken aback. He imagined the Village would remain standing after the Games. Perhaps a training site for future Olympians or be converted to dormitories for a new university. It was the first time he heard of plans for the Village beyond the Games for military use.

Deputy Kommandant Wolfgang Furstner opened the front gate and smiled as he greeted the men. "Wonderful to see you! We're making great strides. I have so much to show you," he said. "Where would you like to start? We have the state-of-the-art dormitories, the main dining room, training facilities, the swimming pool . . ."

Furstner led the men through the main entrance of the compound as he rambled on about all there was to see. He pointed in the direction of each section of the compound. The grounds were teaming with engineers, plumbers, construction crews, and painters.

Goebbels interrupted him. "Show us the building where the press will gather."

"Ah! Yes! We call it the Hindenburg Haus. It's our main administration center, complete with a theater, and it's where the television exchange will be built. Right this way," Furstner said. He led the men down a path and pointed towards a large, curved, two-story building. As the group followed the path towards the building, Furstner let them walk ahead a bit, then grabbed Diem and pulled him behind a corner of a building. "Carl! You didn't tell me Theodor has been relieved of his duties. What's to become of me then?" he asked.

Carl looked downtrodden but tried to console Furstner. "Look at what you've done here. They're indebted to you. It's a grand legacy that can't be denied. Don't you see?"

"What I see is how they treated your partner Theodor," Furstner said. "He had a grand legacy, too, and they discarded him like a sack of garbage." He walked away from Diem to catch up to the group. When he reached them, von Halt confronted Furstner.

"I heard you've had some plumbing issues. There was an explosion not too long ago, no?" he asked.

"Minor setback. It's been taken care of without further incident," Furstner said.

Von Halt nodded. "The head of the American Olympic Committee, Mr. Avery Brundage, will be paying a visit in three weeks. This village needs to be in complete working order. Do you understand?"

"Completely, sir," Furstner said.

"No more plumbing issues, no more construction, and no fucking explosions!" von Halt exclaimed.

"Of course, sir," Furstner replied. He looked at Diem, who turned away.

*   *   *

Mildred walked down a lonely, deserted street in an industrial area on the outskirts of Berlin known as the Marzahn District. She had spent the evening with her best friend Mattie Dodd and was now bursting with anxiety over where she was headed. She approached a thick metal door at a brick warehouse. The door opened and a large bouncer greeted Mildred. He looked beyond her, checking out the empty street, and quickly pulled her inside.

The door slammed shut and the bouncer frisked her. "Go inside," he said, and pointed behind him. Mildred followed the dimly lit hallway which led to a large, warehouse loft. The walls were lined with odd-looking machines. She surmised that they were used to make nails as her boots crunched stray iron shards with every step. In the center of the room, a round table was set up where a dozen men studied papers and maps. A cloud of cigar and pipe smoke filled the room. These were the leaders of the Communist movement in Berlin. They were discussing plans as Mildred took an empty seat.

One of the leaders stood up and read from a newspaper. "The Anti-Communist Pact will be ratified in November. It states that, and I quote, 'the Communist Party in Germany not only endangers their internal peace and social well-being but is also a menace to the peace of the world.'"

A cigar-chomping man raised his voice. "That's the opinion of the Reichstag, not the rest of the world. I'm curious to know if we could garner support from the Americans."

Another man stood. "Gentlemen, this is Mildred. She is new to our group, and she is very close to Ambassador Dodd's family."

Mildred stood up and addressed the men. "I want you to know I am loyal to this cause, and I'm a very close friend with Ambassador Dodd's wife, Mattie. That being said, I will report back to you any important information that might be helpful, but I will not compromise my friendship with Mattie, at any cost."

The leader stood and nodded. "Thank you, Mildred. We see you as an integral part of this group. We appreciate your commitment, and we will consider your predicament very carefully." The other members of the group applauded, and Mildred beamed with pride.

GRETEL

Gretel Bergmann and Dora Ratjen sat in their bunk beds: Gretel on top and Dora underneath. Dora was scribbling a note on a piece of paper. Gretel looked down from her bunk. "Whom are you writing to?" she asked. "Let me guess, your boyfriend back home? What's he like? Tall, dark, and handsome?" she asked playfully.

Without looking, Dora pulled a blank sheet from her stack and offered it up to Gretel. "My father, he's always been worried sick about me."

Gretel grabbed the paper and said, "Yes, they do worry, don't they? Do you have a pencil?" As Dora handed her a pencil, there was a knock on the door. Gretel, in her long pajamas, jumped down from her bunk and opened it. A strapping young Nazi Youth standing at attention in full uniform stood at the door and held two envelopes in an outstretched arm.

"Good evening, Fraulein. The Director of the Reich Sports Office, Herr Osten, has sent me to inform you that you will both be competing in the Berlin Games in 1936. Congratulations." Gretel took the envelopes and the Nazi Youth strictly turned about-face and walked off. Gretel screamed and she and Dora hugged. They each opened their envelopes – the official letters of proof signed by Osten himself.

"Now I really need to write home!" Gretel said.

"And my father can stop worrying." Dora replied.

After leaving Gretel and Dora's room the Nazi Youth walked down the corridor past a few other dorm rooms. A couple of female athletes passed by and giggled flirtatiously. He tried to contain his smile but couldn't resist looking back at the pretty athletes. He turned a corner and got back into character. He pulled out another envelope from a satchel and knocked on a door.

"If that's you, Tilly --" yelled a voice. The door swung open, and Helene Mayer jokingly thrust forward her practice epee – until she noticed her uniformed visitor. She quickly retreated her sword behind her back. "So sorry, sir! Can I help you?"

After the Nazi Youth completed his announcement, Helene thanked him and closed the door. She threw her epee into the air and spun around and caught it in a perfect attack pose.

The Nazi Youth left the dormitory and walked across the courtyard to the central administration building. He walked down a corridor and knocked on a door. Inside, Osten sat at his desk with Carl Diem and Ritter von Halt across from him. They were looking over progress reports of the construction sites of the stadium as well as the dormitories. The Nazi Youth entered the office and saluted the men. "All of the women have been notified, Herr Osten." the boy said.

"You saw each of them personally? Even Gretel Bergmann?" Osten asked.

"Yes, sir. I handed her the announcement personally."

"Helene Mayer?"

"Yes, her also, sir."

"Thank you. You may go." Once the Nazi Youth left the room, Osten turned to Ritter von Halt. "Karl, it's your turn now. I trust that you will use these appointments, no matter how temporary, to your advantage when Avery Brundage comes to visit. I don't want him leaving Berlin with any doubt about Germany's inclusion of Jews in these Games."

Ritter von Halt nodded. "I'll make sure of it. We're preparing quite a visit for Mr. Brundage. Isn't that right, Carl?"

Carl Diem, wondering what his friend Theodor Lewald was doing at that moment, smiled, and nodded affirmatively. "Sure, that's right."

*   *   *

The next day, Gretel excelled in her afternoon workout, and she was proud. Her high jumps were still by far the best on the team. Her coach, Hans Waldmann, was thrilled with her effort and discipline. As soon as Gretel joined the team, Waldmann decided to adopt a policy of impartiality regarding Gretel and made a personal vow to judge her based purely on sportsmanship; a virtue that the coach took very seriously.

Drenched in sweat after finishing the grueling workout, Gretel headed to the clubhouse to take a shower. In the group stall, a few other athletes were already bathing; some partially hidden by the thick steam. They were Elfriede Kaun, Gretel's fellow high jumper, javelin throwers Tilly Fleischer and Luise Kruger, and the rather burly discus thrower Gisela Mauermayer. They were in a great mood, joking and laughing as if they had just polished off a bottle of wine after a hard day's work. Gretel stripped off her robe and entered the shower.

"Great day, Gretel," Elfriede said. "Your roommate's pretty good, too."

"Thanks Elf. I'd say we all have a chance at a medal," Gretel replied.

"Let's make it a sweep!" Elfriede said as she lathered herself up.

Gisela interrupted. "Where is Dora anyway? How come she never showers with us?"

Gretel had been wondering the same thing ever since training started but didn't want it to become a distraction. "I don't know. She's shy maybe."

"I think she's afraid to show us her tits. They're smaller than fried eggs," said Tilly, and they all laughed. "More like mosquito bites!"

"And yours are anything to be proud of?" Louise chimed in.

"Hey!" Tilly said. "What about you? Yours aren't exactly like Elfriede's over there. It's amazing she jumps more than a foot with those balloons."

Elfriede lifted her large breasts, one in each hand, and showed them off to the girls. "They give me momentum," she said and jumped up and down.

"They're going to give you a backache!" Gisela said and they girls howled. Gretel shook her head, but even she couldn't help but laugh with her teammates. She wished Dora could have been there to enjoy the camaraderie.

BRUNDAGE

It was just before Thanksgiving of 1934 when Alan Gould was summoned by Brundage to Chicago to meet and discuss the AOC President's upcoming trip to Berlin. Gould felt a little uncomfortable with the elegant décor of the Chicago Golf Club's outdoor dining porch, a lustrous exhibit of white linen tablecloths and napkins, sparkling silverware, and expensive china. The dining porch overlooked an impeccable golf course situated between the 9th green and 10th tee box. He sat at a table across from Brundage, pen and pad at the ready, and wondered if he could ever be a member of such a club. *Not a chance*, he thought. Although he did appreciate the game of golf.

"Oldest 18-hole course in North America, isn't that, right?" he asked Brundage.

"That's right. Built in 1892 for a whopping three-hundred dollars." Brundage replied.

"I hear it's almost impossible to become a member. How does one get in?"

"The only way is to be invited by another member," Brundage said, smiling. "It's a very exclusive club."

To Gould, that was loud and clear.

A waiter dressed in all white walked over and handed each of them a menu. Gould had a hard time reading the ornate calligraphy, apart from what was written in bold capital letters at the bottom of the menu next to the Chicago Golf Club seal. It read

NO JEWS ALLOWED. Gould turned the menu face down on the table, suddenly losing his appetite. "So, I'm curious . . . you hired Dean Cromwell to assist Coach Robertson for the Berlin Games. Robertson's coached the track team for the last three Olympics on his own. Why the change?"

Alan Gould and Avery Brundage share an uncomfortable lunch at the Chicago Country Club, an exclusive membership that includes Brundage, but advertises NO JEWS ALLOWED.

Without looking up from his menu Brundage said, "We expect to have many USC team members on this track team, and Cromwell has coached them all at the university. It's a perfect fit."

"So, it has nothing to do with Cromwell's support of the 'America First' movement? I understand you are a big proponent of this ideology," Gould said. 'America First' was a slogan used by William Randolph Hearst to sell his newspapers that flaunted headlines supporting the Nazi party's ideology.

Brundage shook his head. "Is this an interview or an

inquisition?"

"I think these are important questions, Avery, and seeing that you are going over to inspect the conditions in Berlin, I have to ask them. I mean, what's the point of this trip, really? I know you are close friends with Ritter von Halt. I'm sure he will take every precaution to give you ample evidence to bring back to America that all's well in Berlin."

Brundage rose from his seat calmly. "Get the fuck out. You don't come here, to this place, and insinuate that our decision to participate in these Games will be based on anything other than facts."

"Whose facts would those be, Avery?" Gould asked, as he rose, took a sip of water, and left without a handshake or even a glance at Brundage.

Brundage hated that bow-tied big-mouth hack. But all the negative press in the world wasn't going to stop him from winning that vote. And Brundage had Accardo pull out all the stops to make that a reality, starting that very night just up the road near Chicago's financial district.

*   *   *

Owen Van Camp was a nebbish. Throughout most of his life he was alone. As a child he played alone, and in high school and college his circle of friends was meager to none. But he had always relied on his keen ability to manage money, to meet people. As a child he would put every penny in his trusted "3 Little Pigs" piggy bank; of course, his was the brick laying smarter of the three. This unique ability had made him important friends and the title of Treasurer all throughout his academic career. As an adult it had raised this armchair sports enthusiast to Vice-President of the Central AAU and Chairman of its National Finance Committee. And after work every day, Owen would neatly organize his desk for the coming day's tasks, shut and lock his office door, and head for the local watering hole.

"Double bourbon, splash of cola with two ice cubes please," Owen ordered and took his usual seat at the bar. The evening was full of jacket-clad regulars from the surrounding financial district, except for the sexy blonde across the bar that was staring right at Owen. He smiled and the woman got up from her bar stool and walked over to him. It was Accardo's floozy, Clarice, dressed like Veronica Lake, and she made it very clear she was attracted to the "little funny man." The unsuspecting schmuck ate it up.

After more than a few cocktails, Owen took Clarice up to a room in the closest half-decent hotel. She coerced him into ordering a bottle of champagne from room service and proceeded to drug his first glass when he wasn't looking. He took a few sips, grabbed her tits, and then passed out with his shoes on.

The next morning poor Owen Van Camp awoke naked and disoriented. Clarice was gone and all that was left were photos scattered all about his bed of a blacked-out Van Camp with hookers shoving dildos in his ass. The panicked Van Camp jumped out of bed and found a note on the dresser that simply read, "Consider your Berlin Olympics vote very carefully."

THE DODDS

Around that same time, somewhere in the depths of Berlin's poorer section, Mattie Dodd's good friend Mildred Fish-Harnack sat opposite Nikolas in a dimly lit apartment. In the corner of the room, the glowing orange butt of Vladimir's cigarette was all she could see of him. For a second she wondered if it was possible to have a human connection to such a man. But she was not here to waste time thinking of Vladimir.

Nikolas unfolded a map of Berlin on the coffee table between them. "Under normal circumstances I would have one of my men carry out this important mission. But we're being watched, and there have been too many arrests. We need you to do this," he said.

"I'm grateful for this opportunity," Mildred said.

Nikolas pointed to a spot on the map. "You see this? It's an SS training camp for new recruits. It's just off the road at this busy intersection. But at night it's pitch dark at the breach."

"The breach?" she asked.

Nikolas motioned to Vladimir. "Bring it." Vladimir bent down and picked up a small suitcase and placed it on the coffee table. Mildred, nervous as hell, felt a rush of excitement sweep through her. Nikolas continued, "You'll see that the gate is well guarded at all times. You'll walk alongside the fence that runs to the left of the gate. Count off three hundred paces, and you'll find the breach in the fence. That's where you'll enter the camp."

Mildred looked at the suitcase and wondered what was inside. "How do I . . ."

"You don't need to detonate the device. Someone who will take care of that will be following you. You won't see this person. All you must do is enter the camp at the breach and place the package at the first structure you'll see; a long white dormitory with a Nazi flag at each end. Then you disappear. Quickly."

Mildred swallowed hard and smiled. "Thank you, Nikolas. And thank you, Vlad." Vladimir handed her a small envelope. "What's this?" she asked.

"A pill," Vladimir said.

Mildred looked at Nikolas, who said, "In case you get compromised."

*　　*　　*

On the other end of Berlin, Hitler sat at his desk and studied

- 176 -

his loyal servant Putzi, who paced back and forth in front of him and began to ramble. "Something's off about Rudy Diels... Did you know that those scars on his face are not from fighting in the Great War? He served, but he didn't fight at all. He sat behind a desk writing reports all day. Those scars are from fencing when he was a little kid," Putzi said with the utmost disdain. "Yet, he tells people he got those scars from hand-to-hand combat at the Somme. It's ridiculous, and people believe him. A man like that can't be trusted."

"He's Goering's boy," Hitler replied. "I've never had a reason to feel that way."

"And women say he's handsome. Martha Dodd says it all the time. He's hideous, if you ask me." Hitler rose from his seat and started to laugh. "What?" Putzi asked innocently.

Hitler approached him. "You've fallen for this girl." He laughed out loud again. "Maybe I should meet this Martha Dodd and see what all the fuss is about." He got right into Putzi's face and smiled, "No, you wouldn't like that very much at all would you?" He walked back to his desk. "Nevertheless, I want you to set something up for me and this mysterious beauty my soldiers seem to be fawning all over."

"Yes, *Mein Führer*," Putzi said, masking his disappointment.

"Good, now get out. And Putzi, beware of getting too close to any women, especially an American. Your allegiance is to the Nazi Party. I wouldn't want you to get all confused."

But it was too late. Putzi was intoxicated with Martha. He had been in love with her since the first time he laid eyes on her at her parents' Winter Gala almost a year before. He knew she didn't feel the same, but he thought with time she would. He understood she was tempestuous and flirtatious, but he could change her.

As he left Hitler's office, he walked down *Wilhelmstraße* and began to imagine he and Martha living blissfully together in a beautiful mansion in Berlin toting around two perfect Aryan children. His black heart raced; he had never been intimate with such a woman, and he did not want it to end. He considered killing Diels and burying his body in the cement of one of the Olympic stadiums going up, but that certainly wouldn't go over well with Goering, and then the Führer would most likely get involved; he wasn't sure it was worth the aggravation. And who even knew if Diels was the only other suitor he would have to kill. Knowing Martha, he may have to repeat his mass slaughter from Night of the Long Knives. In his position in the Party would that even be possible without getting in the least bit of trouble?

He shook his head to clear the cobwebs. Martha had softened him. In the past he wouldn't have thought twice about torturing or killing any of his rivals. He just would've gone out and done it. Putzi smiled with satisfaction and walked with a bit more confidence. Martha was really helping him grow as a person.

*　　*　　*

It was a glorious autumn morning as Martha Dodd and Rudy Diels drove through the Schorfheide Forest, the beautiful woods northeast of Berlin. They had been invited to Goering's country estate for an exclusive party and Martha was thrilled, not only for herself; she would be hobnobbing with the elite of the Nazi regime, but for Rudy whom she had pushed very hard to ingratiate himself even further into Goering's good graces. This was a very fine opportunity, and she would not let him pass it up.

"Why so quiet, Rudy? You should be excited. Every time Herr Goering asks for your attendance is one step closer to better positioning yourself."

"Yes. However, I'm not sure what we are about to walk into. And whatever happens, I do not want you to take offense," he said and turned his Mercedes onto a much less travelled country road.

"If you haven't noticed, I can handle myself. And stop being so dramatic, we are basically going to a picnic."

Rudy laughed. This was not going to be any kind of picnic Martha had ever seen.

They arrived at Goering's estate, *Carinhall*, and were met by two Nazi valets. One parked the car and the other led them inside to where the guests were.

Martha was immediately taken aback. The house was garish with a hunting lodge motif. Outside the back entrance a full orchestra was set up and played German classical music to the guests enjoying the large grounds. Exotic animals of all kinds roamed about, everything from peacocks, to zebra, to lions, to giraffes! Goering sat on the back lawn next to a large bronze statue of a resting elk. His attire was a white hunting outfit. Funny, Martha thought. In America no one would be caught dead in white after September 1st, and Goering wasn't even a hunter. Just the opposite even, he had recently pushed Nazi legislation that had given animals of all kinds rights that did not exist anywhere else in the world. They couldn't be used for scientific experimentation. They couldn't be hunted with dogs; wolves were protected, as were lobsters, crabs, and frogs. He was the furthest thing from any hunter she had ever seen back home.

After a while Rudy brought Martha over to greet him. "Minister Goering, this is Martha Dodd, daughter of Ambassador Dodd."

Goering, once slim and physically fit, had deteriorated to borderline obesity. His increased weight and size made him struggle to get up to properly meet the woman, and eventually he just gave up. He outstretched his sweaty hand, "A pleasure my dear girl. I've heard so much about you." She shook his hand and promptly wiped hers on Rudy's shoulder. Goering then turned to Rudy, "And I have someone for you to meet, Diels." He looked across the lawn to a pretty Fräulein who was petting a llama,

"Ilse, darling, come meet the man who will sweep you off your feet." He then turned back to Rudy and a now mortified Martha, "My niece, as I told you the other day, is perfect for you, Rudy."

Ilse ran over and greeted them. Without any consideration at all for Martha, Goering urged Ilse and Rudy to take a romantic walk to the lake. They quickly obliged and Rudy did not dare look in Martha's direction as he walked away with Goering's niece. Martha stood there in disbelief.

"I think they will make a beautiful couple," Goering exclaimed. Martha looked at him and half smiled. "Be a dear and help me get up, would you? I must change my outfit for lunch. I hope you are staying. It will be quite a feast." He outstretched his sweaty hand again, this time for help in getting up. Martha's eyes bored into him, and he retreated his hand. She turned and walked calmly away.

She returned to the valet area, retrieved Diels' Mercedes, and drove it home to Berlin. He could walk home from that madhouse for all she cared.

*   *   *

Close to midnight back in Berlin, Mildred Fish-Harnack walked on a dimly lit street alongside a chain link fence. She was carrying the briefcase loaded with explosives. She counted aloud her paces and when she neared three hundred, she saw the breach. Someone had cut a small hole in the fence, and she doubted she could fit through it. A young couple emerged from across the street, holding hands, giggling, but they didn't spot Mildred, who stood frozen in the darkness.

Confident that she was alone, Mildred squeezed through the opening in the fence and walked towards a long structure that was surely the barracks of the SS troops. On the other side of the camp, a hundred yards away, she saw a guard reading a newspaper. She approached the building and placed the briefcase down as instructed, then ran as fast as she could out of the compound.

She ran across the street and hid in the shadows of a townhouse. She looked around for the person responsible for detonating the bomb, never expecting to find him. There was total silence, and she was about to leave the scene when the case exploded. Flames engulfed one corner of the barracks, lighting up the night, and Mildred could hear high-pitched screams of men trapped in the inferno. She started to run away and looked back in pride as soldiers ran out of the barracks in flames.

THE ATHLETES

Madison Square Garden was packed with athletes and trainers from all over the country, buzzing with excitement for the Amateur Athletic Union's main event - the track and field competition that would crown the best athletes of the year. The winners would become the favorites to compete in the upcoming 1936 Berlin Games.

Spectators, many of whom were family and friends, jockeyed for the best seats close to the action on the floor. The 1936 Olympics Track and Field Coach, LAWSON ROBERTSON, looked over the athletes as they stretched and warmed up. To his left, runners John Woodruff and RALPH METCALFE were jogging together. To his right, SAM STOLLER from Michigan was stretching alongside his Big Ten rival, Jesse Owens. On a bench next to him, the young phenom, Marty Glickman, was having trouble un-tying a knot in his running shoes. Coach Robertson was about to approach him when USC Coach Dean Cromwell interrupted.

"My boys are here," he said, pointing to Frank Wykoff and Foy

Draper, his two promising USC runners. Robertson rolled his eyes. His attention was then guided towards Judge Mahoney, who was walking alongside the sturdy muscle-bound athlete, Glenn Morris. Robertson turned to Cromwell.

"Who is that with Mahoney?" he said.

"That's the kid from Colorado. Decent athlete, but he's small-time compared to my boys." Robertson nodded and watched Judge Mahoney walk over to a corner of the arena where he shook hands with Jahncke and Gould.

"I feel bad for these boys. But this shit just can't happen." Jahncke said to Mahoney.

"I'm going to make a motion to the AAU for a vote to boycott the Games," Mahoney said. "Brundage is going to do backflips to fight it, but . . ."

"Is this off the record, Judge?" Gould asked.

"Keep it under wraps until it's official."

In the stands, Avery Brundage peered at Mahoney, Jahncke, and Gould suspiciously. He turned to Margaret. "Did you book my passage to Berlin?"

"Yes, first class." she said.

"Look at them. Plotting, scheming . . ." Avery said.

"A good showing by the athletes will help win our case," Margaret said, eyeing the athletes warming up.

"They won't stop. The three stooges." he looked at Jahncke. "Our former Assistant Secretary to the Navy should go back to building levees in New Orleans. It amazes me how they obsess over politics while they're oblivious to the main point of all this, sending our best athletes to compete and win. Even a girl like you understands that."

She shook her head and blew off his comment. "Don't let it bother you, Avery. I'm sure all their talk won't amount to a hill of beans." Margaret said, snapping her chewing gum.

"I'm not bothered. I'm amused, actually." Avery smiled. "Make sure you pack enough warm clothes for our trip. Berlin is cold in December." But Avery had no real intention of bringing Margaret. If he didn't bring his wife on this one, there would be no dealing with her wrath.

*   *   *

Bob Moch was living a nightmare on the Bay in Northern California, and all he could do was scream for his team to row harder. In the cold damp weather, they were in the midst of getting trounced by the Golden Bears.

The team had worked so hard and felt so confident going into the race, but after falling behind from the start, they just couldn't catch up. It was a shocker to the whole team when the University of California team crossed the finish line a good four seconds ahead of them.

Coach Al Ulbrickson could not believe what he had just seen from his 'so-called' first team. Everyone from Shorty Hunt to McMillin to Hume seemed like they were rowing in slow motion, like they had all taken laudanum before the race. Worst of all, he saw them give up from the very beginning. He needed them to be strong and have the will to come back against talented international opponents. Maybe this wasn't the team he hoped for; maybe they just weren't the ones.

After the race, it was a long walk to the team bus for Moch and his boys. One by one they sauntered on, took their seats, and waited to begin the long ride back to Washington. Coach Ulbrickson stormed on board to address the team. "This was your last race before winter break and needless to say I'm highly disappointed," he began. "No one has a lock on being my number one team anymore. The effort out there today was close to humiliating." He became increasingly frustrated, "I just don't understand. You boys show signs of brilliance at times, but the rest of the time you row like chumps. It's confusing. How can I put a team out there that is more than willing to be embarrassed? You have the rare opportunity to compete against the best in the world. Why aren't you applying yourself and committing? The other teams in the Olympic trials will be. ALL the other athletes will be!" The boys looked at each other in absolute disappointment. "Think hard about all of this during Christmas break, boys. You just must get better, otherwise come spring; things are gonna change." Ulbrickson sat in a huff at the front, as the bus doors slammed shut.

On their journey home, while the team would normally sleep, or at least take a nap, everyone was restless. Moch decided it was time to speak up.

"Anybody sick and tired of losing?" he yelled from his seat.

A few of the boys shouted back, "Hell, yeah."

"You sick of these bus rides? Sick of Seattle, Washington?"

More responded with "Fuck, yes!" and "Damn straight!"

Moch rose from his seat. "Then let's go to Berlin! Let's go to Berlin!" The team cheered and soon the entire bus was chanting, "Let's go to Berlin!" which evolved into chants of "L-G-B! L-G-B! L-G-B!"

The bus rode into the night along the deserted highway. The bus driver could only laugh as he watched from his rear-view mirror as Moch led the rallying cry up and down the aisle, the team chanting in unison. Coach Ulbrickson pretended to be sleeping with his cap pulled over his face but couldn't hide his smile underneath it.

*   *   *

Marjorie Gestring did not want to be the kind of athlete she saw others becoming. She wasn't flashy or gaudy or brash. She didn't talk garbage to her competitors even though she knew quite well she was superior to them athletically. *Why throw it in someone's face*, she thought? It's cruel and didn't help give you any kind of edge. It just made you look like a 'meanie'.

No, Marjorie wanted only to be known as the best female diver in the world. She didn't care about movie contracts, sponsorship money, or appearing in fashion magazines . . . well the magazines maybe, but only because she'd be able to play dress up in stylish clothes. Above all, she, and her parents, wanted her to remain humble, and that was a virtue that came easily to her. She was one of the most popular kids in her middle school and got along well with every crowd. In fact, she was a bit of a celebrity because of her athletic success outside of the school, but she still never let it get to her head. And she had an innate ability to let things slide off her back, including losses, which rarely happened.

She had not, however, gotten over how her idols, Katherine Rawls and Dorothy Poynton-Hill, two of the biggest 'meanies' she had ever come across, patronized her when they had met the past summer. So, every day after school, Gestring would hit the diving board. And she would dive, one after another, for hours, until she was exhausted, and skin pruned like a raisin. Her coach would just watch in awe. Every single dive was near perfect, but never perfect enough for his young athlete. And so, he would sit there with her until she was satisfied. And then he would walk the exhausted little girl home.

Her twelfth birthday was no exception. She shuffled back home after a grueling practice session and couldn't even eat the special meal her mother had prepared. It was Marjorie's favorite, spaghetti and meatballs. She had a few forkfuls, kissed her mother and father goodnight, and immediately passed out. She didn't even notice her birthday cake.

Her mother checked on her later that night. As she stared at her little star athlete, she wondered if all the practice her daughter was putting herself through would even matter. She was concerned Marjorie's little heart would break if the US decided not to participate. She questioned whether her daughter should even be a part of the madness that was being written about in the papers. Germany seemed unreal. To a twelve-year-old from quiet California, it would seem like a nightmare.

GRETEL

One after another, the German women high jumpers took their turns at 1.53 meters, but only one was successful--Gretel Bergmann. Gretel was now the British and German record holder in the event and was the odds-on favorite to win the Gold for Germany in '36. Elfriede and Ratjen were right behind her, and the young women dreamed of a German sweep. The team took a seat on the grass, thinking they could take a break after a round of jumps, but Coach Waldmann vetoed that idea in a hurry.

"You think the Americans are sitting on their tuffs, sniffing daisies right now?" Waldmann bellowed. The girls grumbled a bit and Gretel was the first to get to her feet, offering a helping hand to the others. "Bergmann's the only one willing to put in the work, I see. Laps, now."

They began running, two by two, around the perimeter of the grounds. They didn't know how many laps to run; they only knew to keep running until Waldmann said, "Stop." Despite their grumbling, they liked Coach Waldmann and trusted his methods. And they wouldn't be outworked by the Americans or anyone else.

On this day, Osten and Von Halt sat in on their practice. Gretel noticed them as soon as they set foot on the grounds. She felt a chill--the same chill she felt that night back in July when that large man, Putzi, confronted her in London. She later learned that it was the same night Osten and his goons broke into her family's house and threatened them. Her father Max never told her what had happened. It was Hannah, her innocent little sister, who whispered it to her after Gretel read her a bedtime story during her first night back in Germany. Hannah didn't want Max to hear; she was protecting her father's pride. Gretel loved her for that.

"I never saw Papa cry before," Hannah said, almost in tears herself. She then told Gretel that she peeked out her bedroom window and watched the "soldier men" carry the limp body of their dog, Fritz, onto a truck and drive away. *Cowards*, Gretel thought.

Max would never tell her the details of that night, and Gretel would never tell him what Putzi said on that cold London street corner. "You will jump for the *Vaterland*, or no one, not you or anyone else, will ever see your family again."

Throughout practice, she had to pretend she didn't notice Osten, but that's all she thought about, each jump, each lap. She was glad to have Dora running by her side.

"Stop!" Coach Waldmann hollered. "Now you can sit. Three minutes. Stretch."

Gretel felt Osten's eyes watching her, so she turned around, surveying the area near Coach Waldmann and she was right - Osten was staring directly at her. *That chill again.*

Though Osten had to follow his and Goebbels' plan, he found it disgusting that Gretel was treated equally. And that she was the more exceptional athlete angered him even more. He called Coach Waldmann over.

"Hans, I know she is talented but is it completely necessary to treat her like the others?" Osten asked matter-of-factly.

The coach was appalled. "Have you been watching, *Sportsführer* Osten? She is far superior to the others. And still, I don't treat her or any of them any different from the other. And I don't intend to start." Waldmann was quite firm on this.

Osten and Von Halt looked at each other surprised. "If I

demand you to, that's exactly what you will do," Osten threatened.

Waldmann didn't budge. "I will not create animosity within my athletes. A healthy competitive spirit, yes, animosity, no. Morale will suffer, and performance will follow."

"Well God dammit at the very least train someone up to her potential, so she doesn't appear so high and mighty. What if she were to get hurt?" Osten shot back.

Waldmann glared at Osten, then turned to the women, "On your feet! Move the bar up to 1.55 meters and let Gretel go first!" He turned back to the two men, "This is world record height."

Gretel stretched, took a deep breath, and harnessed her rage. Keeping Osten in her peripheral vision, she sprinted towards the jump. Waldmann watched intently, praying she would help him make his point. And she cleared the bar with ease, jumping for joy after she landed. The other women ran and hugged her.

Waldmann looked over to Osten and Von Halt and smiled. "None of these women are up to her potential. And she is in better shape and healthier than anyone here. You treat her like a dog. I'm going to treat her as my Olympic Gold medal favorite." He then ran back onto the field and joined his athletes, leaving Osten and Von Halt stewing.

THE DODDS

The calendar had turned to December, but Putzi had been trying to get his boss and Martha to meet for months. "He needs a good woman, an American woman. And a beautiful lovely one like yourself, could change the whole destiny of Europe," he would say to her, even when they were making love. Martha just played it off as one of Putzi's many grand schemes. And though his intention was flattering, she couldn't help but thinking he was whoring her out.

Whatever the case, she was finally going to get an audience with the most mysterious head of state on Earth. And she was going to make the most of it, wearing a demure yet alluring dress. She found that is what most German men liked, their women pretty, not flashy, and without opinion. She would have to bite her tongue for the latter.

She and Putzi entered the famous Hotel Kaiserhof and bee-lined straight to the hotel's classic German dining room. There they sat with Polish singing sensation, Jan Kiepura, who was scheduled to perform onstage in the dining room later that evening. It was his last performance before returning to Warsaw after eight years of touring the capitals of Eastern Europe. Martha had seen him sing at the National Opera when they first got to Berlin, and she was a big fan.

They sat and had tea and Martha and Jan talked music. Putzi fidgeted more than usual, constantly looking over towards the room's entrance. At one point Martha had to send him outside because he was making her and Jan nervous. When he came back in, he was accompanied by a group of SS Officers and Gestapo. And in the middle of all of them was the Führer himself.

Hitler took a seat with some of his men at the table next to Martha's. Putzi came over and told Jan that Hitler requested his presence at his table. The singer excused himself and moved to the Nazis table. Putzi then told Martha as soon as she sees Jan get up; she is to approach the Führer. Martha did not like the ridiculous dance Putzi was creating and barked at him.

"What the hell, Putzi? I don't appreciate the musical chairs."

"I'm sorry *mein Schötz*, it will only be another minute. The Führer was very specific. But he is very much looking forward to your acquaintance."

And it became more and more obvious to Martha that Putzi was telling the truth. Hitler spent half his time looking her way.

Jan recognized immediately that Hitler wasn't paying any attention; but he couldn't just excuse himself from the situation without creating an international incident. So, he just kept talking. During one unusually long stare, Jan cleared his throat. Hitler either didn't pick up on it or didn't care. He just kept looking at Martha.

After a moment Hitler turned to Jan who was in mid-sentence, "Thank you for your time, Herr Kiepura. I've kept you too long. You must hurry and prepare for your performance." Two SS Officers immediately flanked the unsuspecting man and led him backstage, a mere four hours before the poor crooner's concert.

This was Martha's cue, and she played it as elegantly as a beautiful woman could. She sashayed over to Hitler with a smile as glowing and natural as the rising sun and presented her white-gloved hand. He kissed the back of her hand with a gentleness that surprised her. Then she waited at her chair a beat until Hitler quickly jumped up and pulled it out for her.

"Fräulein Dodd, it is so very nice to finally meet you. Ernst has told me the most wonderful things about you," Hitler said in his best, broken English.

"And he has told me the most wonderful things about you. Though, you are much more handsome than he described," she joked. Hitler shot a stare at Putzi that revealed to Martha the true demon inside. Everything else about him seemed normal almost unassuming, even his mustache didn't seem as ridiculous as it did in papers and magazines. But his eyes showed his true character, they were as fiery as hell itself. The ashen colored, swollen, bags underneath appeared to be the inferno's collateral damage.

Putzi shifted uncomfortably with mouth agape, and a defenseless puppy dog look on his face. Sensing she may have gotten one of her lovers in grave trouble, Martha laughed it off. "I'm only poking fun. He has only said the most respectful of things about you. You are his hero, and most of Germany's it seems."

This placated Hitler but he couldn't resist, "Most of?"

"Well, I don't think German Jews regard you in the same light but that's a whole different matter altogether." Then Martha asked a curious question, curious because no one ever initiated questions from him, except Eva, and those only in private. "Herr Hitler, what motivates you? Who are you, really?"

The men stood, about to protest what they believed to be presumptuous behavior. But Hitler motioned for them to sit back down. It was refreshing to speak with a beautiful and intelligent American woman. He answered in German and Putzi translated, "I am a German citizen, one who only wants to see his people live in peace and prosperity again. Before internationalism began to dilute all of Europe, Germany was a once a great, pure, and powerful kingdom. And I shall restore that. No matter the cost or the means, I shall make Germany great again. Just wait until you see what we have in store for the 1936 Olympic Games. Even your father will be impressed." He rose, "It has been a true pleasure *Fräulein*." He kissed her hand gently once again and left with his entourage in tow.

*   *   *

Mildred Fish-Harnack had pulled off a successful and dangerous mission at the SS barracks and now she wanted more. And her Communist comrades were happy to oblige. Harnack was becoming an asset to their cause. They liked the way she, as an American professor, could move in and out of situations without suspicion. Though brash and outspoken in private, she seemed quite adept at being unassuming in a crowd.

She arrived at the warehouse at 8:30pm and was quickly led to a secret room where Vladimir and Nikolas, met her.

"It is so very nice to see you, comrade," Nikolas, the bigger of the two bellowed and received her with an enthusiastic handshake. "Moscow has been very impressed by your devotion to the cause."

"I hate the Nazis and think Hitler is a degenerate junkie," Mildred offered unabashedly.

Nikolas laughed heartily. Vladimir, wiry and intense looking, never changed his expression, and never said a word. He simply sat and kept his eyes glued on Mildred. "We have a new mission for you, Comrade Harnack," Nikolas began. "It is of the utmost secrecy and will take some time to coordinate. You will be working with operatives from here and Moscow around the clock for the next year and a half."

"What about the university?" Not that Mildred wanted to teach anymore, but she couldn't just up and leave without questions being raised.

"Life will go on as normal. That's why you are the best suited for an assignment of such magnitude. Just go about your business in your usual way. But Comrade Harnack, do tone down your political rhetoric to your students and friends. There is no reason to draw unnecessary attention to yourself. These are dangerous times. You never know who is watching or listening."

"Well, what the hell boys, are you going to tell me what I'm doing, or just what I can't do while doing it?"

Nikolas smiled. "You are going to plant a bomb under Hitler's ass on Opening Day of the Berlin Olympic Games," he revealed. "And you are going to kill him, his whore, and whatever trash is sitting with them."

"The fucking motherlode," she beamed. "I'm going to personally send that menace to hell."

This got a grin from Vladimir; a look so macabre it even made the usually impervious Fish-Harnack recoil.

BRUNDAGE

The *USS New York* arrived into Hamburg shortly after nine in the morning, and Ritter von Halt and his men met Avery and Elizabeth Brundage as they disembarked the gangplank. Elizabeth was put in her own Mercedes Benz limousine so she could unwind privately after what she deemed, "a miserable trip, where most of my time was spent suffering retching seasickness." This gave her husband and von Halt the opportunity to talk business freely in the limo that followed her to Berlin. She would only find the whole conversation dreadfully boring, so she was more than happy to have a backseat to herself.

"Avery, has it really been two years since Los Angeles?" Von Halt began. But Brundage wanted nothing of the pleasantries. On board the ship, John Heartfield's photomontages were being distributed and shared with passengers like baseball trading cards, and they were the least bit flattering. Brundage pulled one out of his coat pocket. It was an Olympic inspired picture. However, in Heartfield's vision, German athletes used weapons and played deadly games of war.

"And that was one of the rather tame ones, Karl!" Brundage exclaimed then continued, "This does not help your cause. What am I supposed to think from this?"

Von Halt replied, "Calm down, Avery. The man is an anarchist. He is a two-bit artist trying to gain notoriety. His antics will wear
thin soon enough. And he is a coward to boot, who ran off to Prague with his tail between his legs. I promise you that this trip of yours will satisfy everyone's suspicions of evil-doings and conspiracies."

And von Halt and Osten would make sure every minute of his trip would be closely calculated and choreographed to hide just that.

In the grand ballroom of Hotel Adlon Kampenski, three banners hung from the rafters behind the main stage: on one side, the Nazi flag, on the other, the Stars and Stripes, between them the Olympic rings. Brundage smiled at its beauty and symmetry.

It was a gala event in honor of Avery's visit, and Osten and von Halt spared no expense. Von Halt knew all about Brundage's extravagant tastes and how he would swoon over all the pageantry, so he wanted to start the whole charade off with a bang. Black-tied, Aryan, young men served endless trays of caviar, champagne, and canapés. The buffet stations over-flowed with everything from wild game to white asparagus and desserts ranged from apple strudel to Bienenstich, with copious platters of fresh fruit and local cheeses. The guests were only the most important VIPs in Germany, which included Ambassador Dodd and his daughter Martha, and Bella Fromme and William Shirer, just to name a few.

The Nazis throw Avery Brundage a huge party in honor of his visit to Berlin to inspect construction and planning of the '36 Games. Right to left, GOC Members Karl Ritter von Halt and Theodor Lewald, Louis Lochner, Chief Editor at AP, Brundage, and Ambassador Dodd next to him.

Osten thought the addition of Fromme and Shirer and any other American reporter would be a dangerous invite, but Von Halt said it would be a grave mistake not to have them present. Brundage would see right through it and request an audience with them at some point anyway. At least at the gala, political debate would acquiesce to social mores and thus be more contained.

Diem knew he had to watch what he said to Brundage. Osten was like a hawk and had people all over the party listening in on conversations. But the inevitable elephant in the room came up as soon as Brundage laid eyes on his old friend.

"Is someone going to tell me what happened to Theodor? Or am I to guess?" Brundage seemed genuinely concerned, though he and Lewald had not always seen eye to eye. But before Diem could utter a word, a random female guest grabbed his arm and led him away.

"Oh Mr. Diem, you just have to tell me more of your Olympic heroics in Athens." She snatched him as if nothing out of the ordinary was occurring. Brundage smiled, thinking his friend was being a charmer to the pretty young lady, but Diem had no idea who the woman was. And she was not relinquishing her grip.

"Avery Brundage." Brundage whipped around. "My name is William Dodd; I am the US Ambassador to Germany. It's nice to meet you."

"And you sir as well. I feel like our paths have crossed many times over the last two years, though we've never met." This was a slight dig at Dodd because of his relationship with Jahncke and Mahoney. And Dodd immediately saw the comment for what it was.

"May a fellow Chicagoan who's been here a few years give you some words of advice."

"Please do," Brundage urged.

"Phaedrus once said, 'Things are not always what they seem; the first appearance deceives many; the intelligence of a few perceives what has been carefully hidden.' Remember that during your visit."

"These are friends of mine, Mr. Dodd. And the only people I must be suspicious about, are Americans conspiring behind my back."

"Behind your back? I thought we were being much more transparent than that. I'll have to tell Secretary Jahncke and the Judge to be much more aggressive in their nature."

Brundage shot him a look.

"You are out of your league, Brundage. Have fun being made a fool of," Dodd ended with and walked away defiantly.

But Avery was too full of wonder and good champagne to take heed from what he deemed such a 'disreputable pseudo-diplomat'. He worked his way over to William Shirer. But if Avery was looking for any positive spins on his trip, he wasn't going to get it from Shirer, another fellow Chicagoan.

"Avery, I'm not gonna sugarcoat it. This place is as mad as Alice's Wonderland."

Brundage looked over the elegant party as if he belonged. "Well, the view from this side of the looking glass doesn't seem so horrible." At that moment von Halt swooped in and whisked him away from the conversation. Shirer just shook his head, downed his champagne, and headed for the buffet.

"Come Avery, I want you to meet Leni Riefenstahl. She will be shooting the Games in their entirety. It's sure to be a cinematic tour de force. She's just plain genius." Von Halt gushed as he led his guest to the second-floor balcony where Leni was shooting down at the event.

"Fräulein Riefenstahl, this is our guest of honor. May I present Avery Brundage." Von Halt said proudly.

The two shook hands. And though Brundage was fit for his

age, Leni was not impressed. "I've heard so very much about you," she began in English. "So, this is the world's final word on whether my masterpiece is going to be shot?" She ended in German looking at a horrified von Halt. But Brundage, whose German at the time was not that strong, thought she said, 'He is a masterpiece, that must be put in shots of my film.' And Brundage beamed like an idiot.

"Let us move on, Avery, and let Fräulein Riefenstahl . . ." he glared at her with contempt, "continue on with her work."

"It was very nice meeting you. And just so you know, my left side is my good side," Brundage joked. Von Halt couldn't get him away quick enough. Brundage turned to von Halt as they walked away. "I think I'm going to retire, Karl. The champagne and the travel are catching up to me. The party was swell. And I can't wait to get started on the tour tomorrow. Let's meet at 8 a.m. in the lobby."

Von Halt smiled. The first part of his plan had worked. Brundage was drunk and satisfied.

*   *   *

The next morning, Brundage began his tour walking through the now nearly constructed Olympic Village with Carl Diem, Furstner and von Halt. Furstner gushed on and on about his design's superiority over the Los Angeles Games, and Brundage couldn't believe the attention to detail. The Nazi Captain had made the place a haven. He was skeptical of one thing, however.

"Do you really think it is a good idea to have the women staying here as well? The place is going to turn into a cesspool of lewd behavior."

"We can only trust the athletes will comport themselves appropriately." Diem responded.

"I guess we will have to. And your Jewish athletes are staying with all the others, correct? This is very important. The United States Olympic Committee and the Amateur Athletic Union expect the likes of Gretel Bergmann to be eating right next to Jesse Owens, who will be eating right next to Luz Long and so on. Understand?" Brundage challenged.

The Nazis that surrounded him assuaged him; some duplicitously, like Osten and von Halt, some half-heartedly, like Diem, and some, like Furstner, with an honest and proud naiveté. As the group continued their walk-through, Brundage became more at ease and less skeptical. He seemed to blend right in with the company surrounding him.

Later, at *Olympiastadion*, Diem, von Halt, and Brundage made their way to the top of the half-built arena. Brundage looked out over the surrounding Olympic construction in the distance, which was happening all over a revived Berlin. It was like Rome in its heyday, breathtaking in an epic way to Avery.

"It's too bad Theodor couldn't be here," Brundage began, and then turned to Diem. "What the hell happened to Lewald, Carl?"

Diem was just about to tell his friend the truth, but von Halt sensed it and cut in immediately. "The work finally got to him. He became overwhelmed and his performance began to slip." Diem turned beet-red, but von Halt continued, "He is still on the IOC and is working with us as a part-time consultant. He needed a break, Avery. Simple as that."

"I can understand that. I always thought he didn't have the stomach to make it to the finish line." Brundage added. Diem turned away in quiet disgust. And von Halt continued.

"Look around Avery. This is going to be the biggest and grandest spectacle the world has ever seen. And not only are we filming it for posterity, but certain events will also be telecast live through the television all around Germany!" He came close to Brundage and put his arm around his shoulder. "These will be a fair and all-inclusive Games my old friend. The Führer only wants to glorify the Olympic spirit. He and Goebbels want to show the world that Germany is a peaceful but strong nation again, that we are capable of being good neighbors and fantastic hosts. The cards are in your hands now, Avery. You must convince the AAU we are united in our approach. If you can take care of that, I will take care of Jahncke. I want him out of the IOC, and the sooner the better. If you can sway your vote, I assure you, I will sway mine. And you will take Jahncke's place on the IOC," von Halt promised boldly.

Brundage grinned from ear to ear. That's exactly what he wanted to hear. He shook von Halt's hand and promised him he would do whatever it took to persuade the United States to vote in his favor.

HITLER

It was February 26, 1935, and Hitler and Putzi waited impatiently inside the Führer's office at *Braunes Haus* in Munich for Goering and his men to arrive. They were thirty minutes late and the Führer shook his head in disapproval. "He is probably having a hard time getting out of his car, that fat piece of lard." He said to his trusted advisor, and then pulled out a glass pipe from his desk drawer.

"Ah, ah, *Mein Führer*," Putzi said and stopped him. "The blob approaches." Just then Goering and two of his Luftwaffe guards entered the room and saluted. Hitler was aghast.

Mein Got, Hermann! Did you eat one of your zoo buffaloes before coming over?"

Goering slapped his belly, "It's not all that bad; winter weight," he said as if that were truly a thing.

"Well, if you can fit behind my desk, sign the document and let's get this done." Hitler said. Though he appeared cavalier, this piece of paper would make the Luftwaffe the third powerful tier in Germany's arsenal. The Army and Navy were bigger than ever and now Hitler would rule the skies. More significantly, the document was also the final blow to the Versailles Treaty and that is what Hitler relished most. Germany would never have to live under such oppressive rules again. *"Schnell gros fettig,"* he implored the large man. "The sooner this is completed, the sooner we can announce to Britain and France their reign of terror is over."

Goering picked up his pace. And in just a few steps he began breathing hard and perspiring. "I'm moving as fast as I can." He grabbed the pen and signed his name on more than a few pages. "We will have the greatest Air Force in the world, yet again *Mein Führer.* In fact, we already do," he said with a big smile. The German airline *Lufthansa* had secretly been training pilots and building war aircraft for Goering over the last few years, and the stockpile was ample.

"Good," Hitler replied and shook his general's hand. "Because tomorrow I'm announcing this expansion of the Armed Forces and commencing a civilian draft."

Goering was surprised, "That's going to piss off half the world, I'd say."

Hitler smiled at the thought. *"Natürlich, genau das dachte ich auch."*

*   *   *

Hitler stayed in Munich and worked at *Braunes Haus* for three months. Then one fateful May night led to a decision that changed the course of his and Eva's lives. It was late by the time Hitler, Putzi, and another guard arrived back to the Führer's Munich apartment at 16 Prince Regent Square. For some reason it had taken Hitler all day to instruct his upper echelon on how to formulate a new law restricting Jews the right to serve in the Armed Forces. "How fucking hard is it to write on a fucking piece of paper the words that are coming directly out of my fucking mouth?!" He pleaded. It was the first step to the upcoming, and much more sweeping, Nuremberg Laws he was devising, and the last thing he needed was unnecessary bureaucracy.

As soon as the men entered the spacious but unusually dark living room, Hitler sensed he had walked into a situation. *"Poopsie?"* He called out and then drew his revolver. He motioned for the other two to do the same and scout the area. He walked into the ornate dining room and saw what he had feared, a mess. A fresh, home-cooked dinner had been served on the finest of china the Nazis could steal from the Jews, and then thrown about the room. Food and broken dishes were everywhere. Two candles in the middle of the table had burned to nubs. Hitler had forgotten about Eva once again. He had invited her to dinner days before, and only after, he had been forced to cancel twice previously.

"Oh, Eva." He said with a sense of dread.

"Mein Führer, here!" Putzi yelled out.

Hitler ran to the bedroom Putzi was standing in. On the bed, half naked, was a passed-out Eva with thick foam oozing slowly from her mouth. Next to her on the nightstand was a half empty bottle of barbiturates.

"Good God!" Hitler screamed. "Not again!" He remembered how she had tried it once before, early in their relationship in 1932. It was a cry for attention then, and an even bigger cry for it now. "Help me get her upright, Putzi." He pointed to the other man. "You, get me a bucket of some kind, and a basin of water." The guard ran out of sight to oblige.

It took a while, and a harried house call from one of Hitler's private physicians whom he promptly fired for providing Eva with such strong medication to begin with, but Eva finally came out of it. She looked at Hitler who was by her bedside, "You should have let me die."

"Nonsense."

"Why do you constantly ask for my time, then not show?! I can't take it anymore!" She began to get upset.

"Please relax and sleep, *meine Leibe*." He turned to Putzi, "Get me that doctor," he thought hard for the name, "Morell, Theodor Morell, the one who helped Heinrich Hoffman. I want him here by sunrise." Putzi didn't wait for another instruction. He was gone in a flash and on his way to fetch a man who would become one of the most influential people in the rest of Adolf and Eva's lives.

GOULD

Alan and Mary Gould entered Radio City Music Hall, the beautiful three-year-old theater in mid-town Manhattan and looked for the best seat, or Alan's version of a best seat anyway. Mary knew he only liked to sit in the back center during a movie, so she didn't even attempt to coerce him to go anywhere else. The film was *Living on Velvet*, a George Brent Warner Brothers release. The two had decided on that one because Mary liked musicals and Alan liked Brent, even though he preferred him in straight dramatic roles. The movie also had the beautiful Kay Francis, and that was quite all right with Gould as well, but he kept that part from Mary.

"There's an animated short beforehand. It's one of those funny *Merrie Melodies* cartoons, and this one is in color," she said, impressed.

Gould smiled, but before he could say a word, the lights went down, and the newsreels began. And one topic dominated the news: Germany's announced rearmament. Gould shook his head disgusted. All he could think of was Brundage and his so-called 'favorable' visit to Berlin. The images on screen were frightening; rows and rows of what seemed like millions of men marching in unison with their rifles on their shoulders, thousands of tanks, and jeeps, and flatbeds carrying large long-range weapons were paraded in front of rabid on-lookers. Swastikas were everywhere, on people's clothing and hanging on buildings. He could feel Mary glaring at him.

"And this is where you want to go and cover sports?!" She said with contempt. "You are out of your damned simple mind, Alan Gould."

"Okay honey," he tried to pacify her. "The cartoon is about to start," he leaned in and gave her a kiss and then grabbed her hand and held it on his lap. She peered at him with pursed lips and then turned to watch *I Haven't Got a Hat,* starring a new Warner Brothers' animated character, Porky Pig. It was a sensation, and the couple forgot all about the news and laughed for the next seven minutes straight.

The feature presentation couldn't hold a candle to the stuttering pig and Alan fell asleep thirty-seven minutes in. Mary called it a five-poke film. That's how she rated each movie they saw, the higher the number of times she had to stop Alan from snoring, the worse the film was. And he rarely slept through a good one. *He should've become a film critic,* she thought. It would've been safer.

After the movie they strolled along 6th Avenue toward Central Park. There was a beautiful spring snowfall and seeing that the City was fairly empty, the soft white blanket remained mostly untouched. Gould admired how Mary always looked her most attractive in her coats and winter hats. But he could barely get a smile out of her now, and she was being unusually quiet. He was too trepidatious to inquire why; he was certain it was about his Germany trip.

He splurged for a carriage ride through the park, which got

some warmth out of her. But as soon as they got going, she turned to him with tears in her eyes. "What I saw in those newsreels was an aggressive country on the prelude to war, Alan. I want you to think very strongly about your decision to go over there."

"Honey, honey," he took her hands in his, "I know you realize now this is huge. It's the biggest story sport has ever seen." He tried to make light, "I don't know if you've noticed but I'm a pretty big deal in this kind of reporting." She rolled her eyes and smirked as he continued, "and it would be glaring if I weren't there as the AP representative."

"Really? There are going to be thousands of you idiots from all around the world there. No one is going to miss my husband," she cuddled under his arm, "Except me. Hitler scares me to death, Alan. I can't help but think, what if something terrible happens? This man is capable now of anything. Not one country is willing to stop him. Why should he care if he kills a bunch of reporters?"

"He's not going to kill a bunch of reporters, baby."

"Okay, one then! Anyone who gets in his way seems to go by the wayside. You write something over there he doesn't like, and suddenly no one has seen or heard from you in weeks. Are you going to tell me with a straight face he isn't capable of that?!"

"Please calm down, Mary. You're gonna frighten the horse. I am not worried about my safety. I don't think you should be either. At the very least Brundage is friends with all the Nazis throwing this bash. Nothing is going to happen like that."

She looked at him hard, "You don't know that for sure. And it's still a year away. Hitler is only going to make things worse for everyone." She rested back under his arm discontented as the carriage continued uptown through the wintery wonderland.

*   *   *

Spring turned to summer in 1935 and pleas to boycott the

Berlin Olympics kept getting to the White House doors. President Roosevelt's wheelchair was positioned in its usual spot in the Oval Office near the couches in front of the fireplace. The family's Scottish terrier *Meggie* sat on a blanket draped across his lap and Louis Howe stood to his right. On this day, the President listened to top Jewish-American leaders state their cases on why America should not go to Berlin the following year to participate. It had become a weekly parade of opponents and Roosevelt grew tired of it all.

"Gentlemen, I hear your pleas. But later today I will be passing a Social Security Act that will guarantee every American will be taken care of in their old age. That's what I am concentrating on, stabilizing our infrastructure, and shaping the Nation's future. The Olympics just aren't my concern. Talk to the AAU in New York, their vote is coming up in December. Speak to Judge Mahoney, he is the man in charge over there."

"But we have spoken to the Judge, Mr. President. Our point is it shouldn't even have to come to a vote," a young Rabbi responded.

Roosevelt shook his head, "I'm sorry. I just can't help you boys."

The group left highly unsatisfied, but Roosevelt sighed in relief. "Get me a brandy please Louis," he asked Howe, who had one ready for him. "Sit down, I have a question for you."

His now frail confidante sat across from him and sipped on some tea. "What is it, Franklin?"

"What do you think of this whole hullaballoo regarding these damned Games?"

"Mr. President, I think it's a quagmire you need to stay far away from. Either way you're gonna piss too many people off, and you have an election coming up. Why risk it?"

"But what do *you* think, Louis?" the President prodded him.

Howe lit a cigarette to mull it over and after two puffs was hacking uncontrollably. Roosevelt looked at him concerned while he composed himself. "If politics were set aside, I wouldn't send one damned person. The last thing Americans need to be doing is spending time and money in Germany. But I'm hearing that the athletes, Jews and non-Jews alike, want to go and beat the Nazis, and that makes the decision even harder. But speaking strictly as your advisor, my advice is to leave it be." He began coughing again and grabbed a handkerchief from his jacket pocket. The President noticed thick blood and his heart sank.

"What am I gonna do without you, Louis?" he wondered aloud.

*   *   *

A month later Goebbels was suddenly wondering what he may have to do without the Americans. At the Reichskanzler office in Berlin, Goebbels was red-faced with anger. "Why would you announce these now?! This could doom the American vote!" Goebbels screamed at Hitler regarding the newly passed Nuremberg Laws that basically stripped German Jews of their remaining rights. "Why don't you ever consider the propaganda elements of your moves?" He threw up his hands, "Or the timing!" We had that idiot Brundage and the American press exactly where we wanted them!"

"This took years of hard work by a lot of good men, Joseph. Did you even read the Laws? It's a masterful declaration," Hitler responded.

Goebbels looked at him in disbelief. "Would it have killed you to let Germans marry Jews for five more goddamned months? Would it have been the end of *Germania* if a 44-year-old Aryan woman worked in a Jewish household until January?! Yes, I read the decree, it's wonderful." he said. "But Jahncke and the AAU are looking for any weapon to use against us to win that vote, and

- 206 -

you've just handed them a zeppelin of fucking dynamite!" Goebbels was shaking and lit a cigarette.

"Calm yourself Joseph. Remember, you hate them just as much as anyone."

"We need the Americans, Adolf." Goebbels pleaded. "There are no Olympics without them. Let me announce to the international press tomorrow that prosecution for these new crimes will not take place for another year. That may be our only hope."

"Ach! Fine! If you feel it necessary to calm those Jew Yorkers, be my guest." Hitler consented with bitter disdain. "You care too much what the Americans and other people think."

"Only when it's too our advantage, after that I'm as callous as you are, *Mein Führer*."

THE ATHLETES

It was September 1935, and football season was underway at James Madison High School in Brooklyn, NY. Marty Glickman got into his three-point stance behind the quarterback. The defense knew he was getting the ball, but it didn't matter. The quarterback took the snap and handed the ball to Marty. He hit the opening around the left end like a blur and the defensive backfield soon gave up on the play; they never had a chance to catch him.

His track coach approached the football coach on the sideline. "Do me a favor, coach--give him a rest after he's scored a couple of touchdowns, so he doesn't get injured, please?" the track coach implored.

"There's no stopping him," the football coach said. "He's a unique competitor . . . we have to let him play. You can take the lion out of the fight, but you can't take the fight out of the lion. He's playing football next season, too, and I can't wait."

"He has Olympic aspirations, Coach. Let's not mess that up." Marty's track coach reminded the other man.

The football coach just shrugged his shoulders and laughed, "You're gonna tell him he can't play?" At that moment Marty took a shovel pass around the right corner of the line and bolted 40 yards into the end zone without ever being touched. "Unstoppable," the football coach said in awe.

When Marty came back to the sidelines, he was mobbed by his teammates. At the water cooler, the track coach approached him.

"Great job, Marty. I think you've done enough for one day. Better save those legs for Berlin. I've asked your coach to take you out of the game."

Marty looked at him sideways while guzzling some water. "That's not up to you. Nobody takes me out of the game, but me. And I would never do that to my teammates."

The track coach knew there was no stopping him. As much as he wanted to protect Marty, he admired the kid. His attitude would suit him well in Berlin.

"Enjoy the show." Marty put his helmet back on and ran onto the field, ready for the next offensive series.

*　　*　　*

At that moment, in an indoor swimming pool, Eleanor Holm practiced her backstroke at an efficient and astonishing speed. Eleanor always coveted the spotlight, but what people didn't see was the serious nature of her training. A couple of unwitting women waded across her lane a little too slowly and Eleanor awkwardly swam into them. She screamed, "Outta my way!!" and splashed them before resuming her lap. The women, mortified, swam away quickly.

*　　*　　*

In the middle of Lake Washington just outside of Seattle, Bob Moch yelled out orders to his rowing team as the boat crew cruised into the foggy dusk. "L-G-B! L-G-B!" (Let's Go to Berlin), he roared. They had taken Coach Ulbrickson's words to heart since their disappointing season a year ago. They were rowing tightly, evident by their breath, visible as they exhaled in sync in the cold evening air.

*   *   *

On a Colorado farm, Glenn Morris prepared to begin a makeshift obstacle course that his father Edgar had prepared. There was a sledgehammer station with spikes lined up on railroad ties, a row of tires for high-stepping, and a rope tied to an old car for towing. Edgar yelled, "Go!" and Glenn grabbed the sledgehammer and began slamming spikes into the thick wood. Edgar smiled.

*   *   *

In Berlin, Dora Ratjen set the high bar on a set of pegs. Gretel Bergmann signaled her to raise it higher. Her teammates shook their heads as if to say, "No way." Gretel backed up, took her signature starting step and sprinted towards the bar. She leaped high and as she cleared her shoulders above the bar, her foot grazed it and knocked it off the pegs. Gretel's teammates laughed. "Set it up again," she said. Coach Waldmann took notice.

*   *   *

In the fencing training center in another part of Berlin, Helene Mayer finished off her practice opponent, and whipped off her mask. A coach waved the entire fencing team over to a table where a large box rested. The team walked over and formed a line. Helene approached the table and was handed a uniform, complete with a red armband sporting a black swastika. She stared at it, frozen, until a teammate nudged her aside.

*   *   *

On a practice track outside of the Berlin Olympic Stadium, Luz Long sprinted with gusto. He approached a line on the track and launched himself in the air, arms pumping. He landed in the sand and raised his fist. His coach smiled and nodded as an assistant signaled a measurement in the sand pit with a thumbs-up.

*   *   *

Jesse Owens trained on his own long jump track in America. At the sound of a whistle, he sprinted down the track and exploded into the air, landing in impressive fashion a long way from his launching point. He smiled at his coach, who pointed at the launch point. The coach shook his head pointing to a faulty over-stepping of the line. Jesse clapped his hands in frustration.

*   *   *

In a smoky boxing gym in Manhattan, Judge Mahoney sat watching his Olympic hopefuls. At the other end of the gym, Avery Brundage entered and immediately covered his nose, disgusted by the thick air and musky odor. Mahoney purposely sat at the opposite end of the entrance and grinned as Brundage walked over, dodging the young men who were shadowboxing and jumping rope.

"Is there a place I can shower after this meeting?" Avery asked.

"My wife will think I'm cheating on her with farm animals."

Mahoney laughed. Not *with* him, but *at* him. "Sorry you feel so above this scene. I love it. I really feel a need to know my athletes on a personal level. That's what this is all about after all, isn't that right? The athletes?"

Brundage inspected a place to sit and sat down in the bleachers next to Mahoney. "Don't make an ass out of yourself, Judge. You want to know how my trip to Berlin went. That's why we're here in this sweatshop. I'll tell you that my inspection in Berlin went perfectly fine. The Jewish facilities are just as good as any of the others Germany has to offer."

"Why not train together?" Mahoney asked. "It's a little transparent, don't you think?"

"It may seem so, but it's complicated. I'm not sure you'd understand. See, there are so-called fears of a Jewish Communist conspiracy. Ridiculous if you ask me, but the athletes won't be swayed by the current altercation."

Mahoney was appalled. "Avery, sending a team to Berlin gives credence to Nazi policies. You're a fool or such an anti-Semite that you've taken a blind eye!"

"It doesn't matter what you think, Judge," Brundage responded. "The vote will go in my favor, and there's nothing you can do about it. And don't try to change it if you know what's good for you." Brundage smiled and stood up with bravado. Mahoney immediately stood up and got right in his face.

"I won't be threatened, Brundage. Others might, but not me. And if you want to continue your threats, I'll drag your ass into that ring over there and beat the hell out of you with a good old-fashioned, Irish Catholic, Medal of Honor winning ass-kicking! Now get the hell out of my gym!"

Brundage backed away slowly and grinned again--secretly wishing the Judge would dare try to kick his ass--and turned and left the gym.

THE VOTE

It was a freezing December day outside the Commodore Hotel in New York City, but the bitter cold didn't keep away the various groups that were protesting Nazism and any US involvement in the Games. Inside, the AAU vote was about to take place. Outside, Jewish War Veterans of the United States, the Catholic War Veterans, the Anti-Nazi League, the Young Circle League, the Move-the-Olympics Committee and the American League against War and Fascism all had banners risen and they all chanted, "Down with Hitler, boycott Berlin!"

Since the Commodore was perched above Grand Central Terminal in the heart of New York City, it was attracting quite a crowd. They were mostly supportive, but there were pockets of onlookers who engaged in heated arguments about the bridging of sports and politics.

Emerging from the steps of Grand Central was Tony Accardo, dressed in his finest Canali suit. He struggled to pass through the mob, shoving a man to the side in frustration. He adjusted his fedora and made his way to the entrance of the Commodore.

Accardo walked through the lobby crowded with AAU officials and snaked his way towards the infamous Vice President of the Central AAU and Chairman of its National Finance Committee, Mr. Owen Van Camp.

"Mr. Van Camp, I hope you do the right thing today," he said.

Though the two men had never met, Owen knew immediately this was the man behind his attack. "I understand your tactics were performed on many of my Union members," the shy man began. "I don't think you have much to worry about, sir. Most of these folks are quiet family men. And want to keep it that way."

Accardo grinned, then without a goodbye, made his way to the conference room where Mahoney was preparing to speak.

The Judge took the stage in the packed room with much applause. He stood behind the podium and looked out over the seated members of the AAU and the press standing in the back and sides of the room. As the applause died down and the room fell silent, he felt a swell of American pride. "Free speech is one of the guiding principles of our great society," he began. "And this is one of those moments in our history where these principles must not only be exercised but fully understood as well. For there are now places in this world where freedom of speech and the freedom of the press," he pointed in their direction, "and the freedom to gather, are strictly forbidden. And Berlin is the main breeding ground for this contempt on these basic human rights! These Nuremberg Laws are a perfect example. The AAU must set an example for the rest of the world that we will not accept, we will not tolerate, nor will we participate in any Nazi associated activities. German citizens are being rounded up and imprisoned in work camps according to their religious, ethnic, and racial backgrounds. American officials abroad have, for the past two years, been updating me on the situation there and it has been getting progressively more hostile. Neither the AAU nor the AOC should ever appease this type of behavior!"

The room erupted with cheers, however, there were murmurs and some contentious shouting among the crowd.

Avery Brundage stood behind a curtain to the left of the stage and took Mahoney's last statement as a personal affront after his investigative trip to Berlin and the positive report he gave Mahoney himself. He couldn't wait to speak next.

Mahoney continued, "We should not place our athletes in such a precarious position. As a union it would be reckless, and as a nation it would be foolish. I ask the AAU to stand tall and vote in favor of boycotting the Berlin Games. We must send the proper message to our children, to our athletes, to our government in

Washington, and to that hysterical madman in Berlin. God Bless America!"

The crowd stood up and cheered wildly. Even the dissenters seemed to have been won over by Mahoney's tenacious rant. In that moment the possibility of a boycott was as real as the silly mustache on Hitler's face.

There was a brief intermission and reporters scurried into telephone booths. Others wrote feverishly in their notepads, collecting details for tomorrow's newspapers. Brundage didn't speak to anyone during this intermission. Even Margaret, never at a loss for words, chose not to disturb him as he paced backstage, knowing he would have to choose his words carefully if he had any chance of getting America to Berlin. He thought Mahoney had tried to be a salesman and did a bad job at that.

The crowd gathered to hear Brundage's final arguments. There was an excited murmur as people took their seats. Backstage, Margaret squeezed Avery's hand in support as he approached the podium. He looked out at his audience and had an immediate feeling of confidence. He took a sip of water and began.

"Gentlemen, the very foundation of the modern Olympic revival will be undermined if individual countries are allowed to restrict participation by reason of class, creed, or race. The Olympic Games belong to the athletes and not to the politicians. American athletes should not become involved in the present Jew-Nazi altercation." The room stirred. "Initially, I was torn between this decision. But I've recently returned from my trip to Berlin. I've inspected the facilities first-hand, and I can tell you; the Jewish athletes are being treated fairly. There is no exclusion of Jewish athletes, and in fact, they have embraced them. Mr. Mahoney, take a lesson from your President of the United States and don't punish our athletes because of political rhetoric! These Games should go on as planned!"

Many in the crowd applauded.

- 214 -

Avery fed off the applause. "Some of you are interfering with the Olympic doctrine of separating politics from these great Games. I saw nothing that would impede fair play at these Games, and nothing that would put our athletes in any danger. I say we go to Berlin! Go, and show the world this is not about politics, but about American pride!" The crowd stood on its feet, erupting with applause.

Brundage smiled and looked over at Mahoney, then left the podium. He shook hands with his supporters while Mahoney fumed silently off-stage. This signified the end of the debate and now it was time to vote. AAU members formed a line outside the voting room, and one by one, entered their vote in a secret ballot box.

Mahoney got in line and surveyed the room. There was an eerie silence among the AAU members. He couldn't tell if it meant that his speech took hold, or if Brundage had changed their minds. Or, if there was something else at play. Whatever the case, it was now in the hands of his AAU colleagues.

*   *   *

The next morning, the hungover writers and AAU members gathered in the auditorium to hear the results of the vote. An AAU spokesperson approached the podium. Avery Brundage looked relaxed as he sat next to Margaret. Judge Mahoney looked concerned.

"After careful deliberation by our voting body, I'm proud to say that the United States has voted to attend the Berlin Olympics by a margin of 56-52!" Brundage grabbed Margaret and kissed her, then quickly walked off the stage. He shook Tony Accardo's hand on the way out.

Judge Mahoney walked up to the podium and slammed his fist. The crowd that was about to leave took notice and all eyes were on the Judge. Alan Gould stood off to the side; curious as to what the Judge would say after the controversial verdict was now made public. Mahoney stood tall. "With great regret, I hereby resign as AAU President. I cannot, with good conscience, be party to our American Olympic Committee's decision to be included in these Games, when there are obvious social wrongdoings being carried out for the entire world to see. Contrary to Mr. Brundage's belief that sports, and politics should not mix, we have found that in this case it is an unfortunate inevitability. Mr. Brundage . . . I wish you good luck . . . and I hope your conscience is sound. Mine is."

Alan Gould watched from the crowd. While Brundage shook hands with his followers, Mahoney left the building alone.

It was a great victory for Avery Brundage, and a great defeat for the head of the American Athletic Union boss, Judge Jeremiah Mahoney. It would change amateur sports forever. Despite the protests amongst athletes, politicians, and civilians, Avery Brundage had won; America was heading to Berlin to compete in the Olympic Games.

*   *   *

At the Dodd residence in Berlin, Ambassador Dodd had just hung up the phone when his butler approached him and asked, "Is this true? Are the Americans really coming?"

Dodd nodded. "It appears so."

PART III

TAKEN FOR A RIDE

GOULD

Alan Gould prepared a footlocker and small valise for his stay in Germany to cover the Winter Olympics. Mary helped him pack for the cold Bavarian weather. She had finally come to peace with the fact that Alan must cover Germany's games. She was still extremely scared for him but surprised how he still saw no danger at all. He was about to enter, as he put it, 'a precarious arena of fiery political machinations and corruption, thinly veiled as a sporting event,' and he was foaming at the mouth to do it. This worried her. "Do not embarrass the Nazis directly in any way. Understood?"

"How can I promise that Mary? I'm a reporter."

"Yes, *my* reporter, my living and breathing reporter. And I'd like to keep it that way." She said in rapid-fire succession.

Gould walked up to her and held her closely, "I'll watch my ass. But if I see one slip up or concession made by Brundage to appease those morons, I'm gonna pounce on him."

"That doesn't make me feel any better, Alan. The whole thing really scares me. Can't you send Baker or Tank, at least to the Winter Games?"

"This is my story, baby. It's my big game. I wouldn't trust this with anyone else, it's too important. The *Times* is sending John, and they wouldn't be doing that if the Olympics weren't the biggest story of the year." He kissed her gently, "I'll be back in late February, but until then, we are alone . . ." he kissed her even more.

She stepped away, "Enough. Get your ass back here in one piece and we'll see about all that."

"Mary," he pleaded. "The Nazis are going to be so calculated and guarded. I'm sure every step has been carefully orchestrated." He once again began to kiss her, this time on her neck where she was most vulnerable. "And if something does befall me, I need to have the memory of my loving, beautiful, bride naked on top of me."

The neck kisses almost made her cave-in for a split second, but she gathered herself quickly, "You already have that memory stored," she said confidently. "And the wanting more will be good for you. It'll make you come home quicker," she said, then put her finger up to her temple to think. "And don't they say that athletes should feign away from sex before big games. This is a big game for you, honey. You said so yourself."

They continued to pack his things, but every time she looked his way, he gave her sad puppy dog eyes. She laughed, but never swayed.

*   *   *

Garmisch-Partenkirchen, Germany was the picture perfect snow covered Bavarian village hosting the IV Winter Olympic Games that February. And the turnout was good despite the negative press Hitler had amassed throughout the world since becoming *Führer*. Twenty-eight nations sent athletes, mostly from Europe, but from as far as Japan and Australia as well. And spectators came in droves to root for their favorite athletes and spend money at the local shops that had conveniently jacked up prices ninety percent just in time for their arrival. Gould and Kieran, and a large group of the international sports reporters sat in a cafe taking a break from the cold and snowy weather. They discussed how eerie the whole feel of the Games was with the constant presence of SS guards, and not only in the athletic venues. They were on every street corner and could be seen from every direction.

Gould also mentioned the fact that despite the GOC promising that Jewish athletes would compete, there was not one on any of the participating nation's squads. Kieran wondered if it was a harbinger of things to come in Berlin. Gould showed him a picture one of the AP photographers took of Karl Ritter von Halt snapping a Nazi salute at a medal ceremony. "The picture is being used in papers around the world," Gould gloated.

"He sticks out like a fat pimple on the tip of a teenager's nose." Kieran shook his head, "Boy, he isn't doing himself or the GOC any favors."

Just then a thunderous rumbling came from outside the cafe'. Reporters jumped out of their seats and flocked to the sidewalk. And what greeted Gould and Kieran and the rest of them, was a full-blown military exercise. German tanks with flanking troops paraded through the narrow, snow-covered cobblestone streets. The soldiers goose-stepped in perfect rhythm as their commanders peered out of Panzers like eagles atop their perches. The sound was deafening and every street sign and window in the village shook violently. Photographers began snapping pictures in wild fashion.

Kieran smiled at Gould, "Not doing himself any favors at all."

*　　　*　　　*

A week after the Winter Games ended, at the *Reichssportsführer* Office in Berlin, the usually mild-mannered President of the IOC, Henri Baillet-Latour, lit into Osten with a furious barrage. The military exercise during the Winter Games was a complete and utter nightmare, and it reflected in the media around the world. Forget any boycott of the Berlin Games; Latour now threatened to shut them down completely and move them to Barcelona, whose competing People's Olympiad being planned was now in danger of overshadowing the actual Olympics.

"This is your new reality now, *Reichssportsführer*! The Germans have gone back on their word and used the Winter Games as some sort of political platform. The IOC, I, will not stand being made to look like a fool!"

"*Messier* President, please. This is the fault of one man. It was a lack of communication. Nothing more." Osten blamed the Winter Games debacle all on von Halt (whose fault it truly was) and promised Berlin would be different because the more seasoned Carl Diem was heading the effort.

"And I took von Halt's side every time and now I look like an idiot in the press! I'm strongly considering siding with Jahncke and letting the 1936 Berlin Games go the way of the 1916 Berlin Games – cancelled!"

Osten could do nothing but sit and take it. Von Halt had put him in an incredibly awkward situation, not only with Latour and the IOC, but even worse, and with deadlier consequences, with Goebbels. If Latour decided to merge the Games with Barcelona, Goebbels would look for blood. And Osten was unwilling to die for von Halt's fuck-up.

"I will take care of this. Do not do anything hasty," he implored Latour.

Later that day Osten hosted Karl Ritter von Halt in his office. He poured him an *Asbach* and brushed off a seat for him across from his desk. He patted it and motioned for the younger man to sit. Von Halt was pleased with the reception; he felt he had shined while managing the Winter Games and appreciated Osten's response. That is until Osten began to speak.

"You have embarrassed the Third Reich beyond compare," Osten began as von Halt's face sank. "It was your responsibility to keep the Army away and you failed. A simple phone call or dispatch would have done the trick and now Latour is ready to back that fucking nuisance Jahncke!" He lifted a stack of newspapers and waved them in von Halt's face. "The AP in New York and the press all over the world are having a goddamned field day and now the Games may be moved to Barcelona!" Osten threw the papers in a rage and moved close to von Halt's face. "If we lose Berlin, Goebbels is going to want to know who and why. And I will not hesitate to let him know how recklessly you acted."

Von Halt jumped up to defend himself. "The Games were successful!"

Osten looked at him like he was nuts, "Jahncke and Latour are calling to relocate the Summer Games! How is that a success, you idiot?!"

Von Halt's face turned beet red. He knew he had to think of a plan, and it started with the IOC and getting rid of Jahncke once and for all.

HITLER

At the Reichskanzler (Reich Chancellery) in Berlin, Goebbels, Hitler, and Osten met to discuss the cleaning up of Berlin. Now that the Americans voted to attend the Games, the other countries that were also threatening to boycott would soon fall in line. Hitler was determined to show the world that Berlin was a cultured and sophisticated city, and Germany could host a dignified international event. But to impress, they needed to be prepared.

Goebbels, who had ordered Jews to paint Stars of David on their shop fronts when the Nazis took command of Germany, now ordered them washed clean. Hitler demanded the homeless and Gypsy populations around the city be rounded up and relocated to a makeshift camp just on the outskirts of town. The Marzahn Camp had been constructed over an old sewage plant, which had recently been deemed hazardous by Nazi scientists. It was also heavily walled to keep any occasional passersby or roaming member of the international press from seeing, or smelling, what was on the other side.

Hitler and Goebbels worked themselves into a frenzied state as they explored every alternative to rid Berlin of what they considered "undesirable looking" people or locations.

"Don't forget the train stations," Hitler said. "The amount of people using them will be significant. They don't need to see Roma, much less smell them."

"Consider it done," Goebbels said.

"And the newspaper kiosks. Can we fill them with international papers?"

"We've made arrangements for that as well," Goebbels replied.

While this went on, Osten mostly kept his mouth shut. He did not want to bring up his conversation with Latour or anything about the Winter Games unless Goebbels mentioned it. And luckily, he did not. But if Ritter von Halt couldn't convince the IOC to keep the Games in Berlin, and the People's Olympiad took center stage, Osten would have to face the unstable wrath of both these men.

Hitler unwittingly saved the day though when he announced that he was planning on supporting General Franco in the rising civil unrest in Spain. Any day now a full-blown civil war was expected to begin. "Germany can sharpen her military skills on foreign soil, and we will gain a great ally in the General," the Führer boasted. "Barcelona and Madrid are scrambling as we speak." Osten smiled a wide grin. With the outbreak of a Spanish Civil War, he knew The People's Olympiad in Barcelona was never going to happen.

*   *   *

Such abrupt changes were not limited to the sanitizing of Berlin or the political posturing of Hitler. They were also taking place within the International Olympic Committee.

Henri de Bailet Latour sat at his desk refusing to make eye contact with Ritter von Halt. Von Halt had called this "emergency meeting," and Latour had a feeling where this meeting was headed. Nonetheless, as per IOC constitution rules, he was required to assemble as many members as possible given such short notice. He purposely held the meeting at the Hotel Adlon Kempinski Berlin--a frequent stay for foreign dignitaries--as opposed to the Hotel Kaiserhof, which was the hotel of choice of the Nazis and sat across the street from the Nazis Office of Propaganda.

Ernst Lee Jahncke sat back in his chair suspiciously eyeing Von Halt, trying to figure out what the emergency was. Von Halt was leafing through his files until he found the document he was looking for.

The translators looked to Latour, who grabbed the microphone. "Welcome gentlemen. Representative von Halt of Germany has summoned us to this meeting. We have a quorum and can now begin. Mr. von Halt, you have the floor."

Von Halt began. "Thank you, Henri. And thank you, gentlemen, for attending on such short notice." The IOC members sat up in their seats. "Something has come to my attention . . . a letter written by the American committee member, Mr. Jahncke, to our president, Mr. Latour." He held up a document. "A curious letter, one which I would like to read to you now."

Jahncke interrupted, "And how did you get a hold of this letter?"

"That's of no consequence at this moment, Mr. Jahncke," von Halt replied. "What *is* of consequence are the contents of the letter. Perhaps you would like to read it aloud to our fellow members?"

"No. In fact, I don't think it should be read at all, as it was a private letter from me to Mr. Latour."

"This is a *public* office, Mr. Jahncke, and all affairs regarding this committee should be brought to attention, especially one of this nature," von Halt continued. "In the letter, after the usual pleasantries . . ." He searched for a section of the letter and began to read. "Here . . . Mr. Jahncke writes, 'Neither Americans nor the representatives of other countries can take part in the Games in Nazi Germany without at least acquiescing in the contempt of the Nazis for fair play and their sordid exploitation of the Games.'"

There were murmurs from members of the committee. Jahncke sat back in his chair and shook his head. Von Halt slammed the letter down on his desk. "How much more are we going to take from this man? Roosevelt himself thinks these Games should be played! The American public wants it! The rest of the world wants it! This man has used every opportunity to subvert this committee and try to divide us! I therefore motion for a vote to excuse Mr. Jahncke of his position!"

Latour rose from his seat. "I will not allow it! This is blasphemous!"

Von Halt ignored him and addressed the other members in the room. "A show of hands! We have a quorum for a vote. All those in favor of excusing Mr. Jahncke from representing the Americans in this committee raise your hands." A few members immediately raised their hands, and then others reluctantly did the same. Jahncke couldn't believe what he was seeing. "There you have it, Henri," von Halt beamed.

Latour was astounded. He looked to Jahncke, who slowly rose from his chair. "If I may, Mr. Latour?"

"Yes, please."

Jahncke glared at the members of the committee; some couldn't look him in the eye. "Where is your dignity? What happened to your love of sports? Sports that are not poisoned with Nazi doctrines, the kind these animals are trying to spread all over the world. What a fool I was for believing in the purity of sport. I see that it doesn't mean much to you people. Well, it still means something to me."

Von Halt stood up. "I think we've heard enough, Mr. Jahncke. Henri, we understand that America still needs to be represented. I would like to nominate Avery Brundage to take the place of Mr. Jahncke, if Mr. Brundage accepts, of course."

Latour rose, somewhat stunned. "By show of hands we will nominate Mr. Brundage to replace Mr. Jahncke." Enough hands rose for a positive nomination. "We'll let Mr. Brundage know at once. I'm certain he will accept, but we'll await his official word."

Jahncke gathered his things and stormed out of the room, beaming at Latour, who could do nothing to stop what had happened. The vote had been cast, and in a matter of minutes, Jahncke was out. It was the first and only time a committee member had been voted out of his position.

And Brundage's dream had come true. If he accepted the nomination, he would finally become a member of the International Olympic Committee.

*   *   *

Brundage and Margaret had gotten into their New York City office early in the morning to start compiling all the preliminary travel documents they would need for the American team to leave for Berlin. When the phone rang before 7:00 a.m., they looked at each other curiously.

"Hello, Avery Brundage's office," Margaret answered and then listened. "Yes, he is here, hold please." She gave the phone to Brundage, "It's Germany." He grabbed the phone.

"Hello."

Von Halt on the other end smiled like the devil himself. "Avery, old boy, sorry to bother you so early but I thought you'd like to know as soon as possible . . ." he proceeded to give him the whole account of his victory over Jahncke. "And if that's not exciting enough . . ."

"Yes, Karl, go on."

"You've just been elected to take his place. The committee is just waiting for your response to announce it to the press."

Brundage was numb. "I whole-heartedly accept. Thank you."

"You held up your end of the bargain and now so did I. Congratulations Avery. See you in a few weeks."

Brundage hung up the phone in a haze. "What the fuck happened?" Margaret inquired.

"I just got elected to the IOC," he said and broke a smile. "I need a moment alone," he told her and opened his door to let her out. She left; surprised he didn't want to share in the joy.

When she was gone, he walked over to his desk, sat down, and pulled out a bottle of his finest *eau de vie*. He poured himself a healthy glass, lit his best Cuban cigar, and leaned back with his feet on his desk. He had dreamed of this moment since first becoming an Olympian. Jim Thorpe may have upstaged him then, but now Brundage was at the very top of the American athletic scene while Thorpe was drunk and drooling in a gutter somewhere in the Midwest. He beamed at the thought and raised his glass, "Fuck you, Injun Joe," he said with a huge smile and then took a victory gulp. The only things left now before he could triumphantly enter Berlin were the American Olympic Trials. To him these were mere formalities at this point, but to the athletes competing, it was do or die time.

THE ATHLETES
The Olympic Trials

A few nights before their big race, Bob Moch and his seven teammates maneuvered their sturdy craft with deadly precision on the Hudson River between Hoboken, NJ and mid-town Manhattan. Moch liked to train his rowers at night, especially during a full moon. He implored them to use all their senses, to *feel* the water underneath them, hear the oars slicing through the dark water, and not rely solely on their vision. A full moon gave Moch just enough light to keep them safe. Even so, this night, Moch was a little on edge in such unfamiliar waters.

With the timing of one of his father's Swiss watches, he guided the group of Washington University scholastics upstream on the river. "Catch, press, swing . . . catch, press, swing . . ." and the team responded by grunting out their secret slogan "L-G-B! L-G-B!" Moch suddenly stopped and looked up at the moon, then down to the water. The rowers stopped as the boat continued slicing through the calm water. A hint of mist rose from the surface.

The team's Stroke Oar, Don Hume, broke the silence. "The river's real quiet tonight, eh Bob?"

"A little too quiet," Moch said. He looked up at the full moon and saw a wall of fast-moving clouds conspiring from the west.

From the back of the boat, Shorty Hunt yelled out, "What's it mean, Bobby?"

"Storm's coming. Let's bring it in." The team nodded and began maneuvering the boat back around, heading south to the dock.

*   *   *

Most of the Olympic Track and Field trials were held in New York City at Randall's Island Stadium, but the qualifying event for the Decathlon was held in a wide-open field in Milwaukee, Wisconsin. A lone American flag waved at one end of the barren field as spectators stood inside a roped-off viewing area.

Glenn Morris' father, Edgar, stood next to Judge Mahoney as they watched the long jump event. "Last jump. He needs to keep Clark off his back," Edgar said. Mahoney nodded in agreement.

Glenn Morris sprinted down the track for his final jump. He took a gargantuan leap, and the crowd roared, but the judges pointed to the launching area--Morris had been disqualified for jumping too late. Bob Clark lined up for his final jump and nailed it--setting a new Decathlon world record.

Mahoney patted Edgar on the back. "Not to worry. Glenn will kill him with his throws. Then, if he's clean on the hurdles, it's on to Berlin."

"The hurdles . . ." Edgar mused about the early days of Glenn's training, when it seemed that the hurdles were literally the one hurdle he needed to conquer.

Sure enough, Glenn Morris was unbeatable in his throwing events; he placed first in the shot put, javelin, and discus. All he had to do was place in the top three in the hurdles and there would be a cabin waiting for him on the *USS MANHATTAN*.

Glenn Morris lined up alongside Bob Clark, who was still in the hunt to make the Decathlon team. As he planted his feet, he noticed a gorgeous young lady next to the track, holding a pad and pen, wearing a patch that read "Milwaukee Press Corp." She was sharply dressed in a long skirt and button-down jacket. Glenn wasn't sure he'd ever seen a woman dressed so professionally.

BANG! went the gun and Glenn snapped to attention, blasting out of his position. He knew that all he had to do was stay "clean" and not knock over any hurdles. But like a true champion, he ignored any conservative pangs he might have felt and shifted his body into another gear, a gear nobody in this field could contend with. Glenn quickly gained a full five yards on the competition, and ran through the finish line with his arms raised high.

Mahoney smiled proudly and applauded his protégé. Edgar jumped and cheered for his son like never before. "Let's go!" Edgar said as he pulled Mahoney towards the finish line to greet Glenn. As they navigated through the crowd, a sign was held up at the judging tables. It read, "*Glenn Morris, 1st place, 7,875 points - World Record (not ratified)*".

"What does *not ratified* mean?" Edgar asked Mahoney.

"It has to be an international competition for it to stand in the record books." Mahoney said. "He'll just have to do it in Berlin, then." Edgar thought about that for a moment as they reached the winner's circle. It was hard to find Glenn amongst the crowd of trainers, reporters, and athletes. It was a bit overwhelming.

"Do you think he'll be okay in Berlin? You know, big city, crowds of people? He's never seen that kind of thing." Edgar wondered.

Mahoney tugged at Edgar's shirt and pointed to an area where photographers were snapping photos of Glenn--who happened to have his arm around the sharply dressed Milwaukee reporter, smiling, and posing with supreme confidence. "I think he'll be just fine."

"Ha - look at that! Let's go congratulate him," Edgar said.

Judge Mahoney shook Edgar's hand and said, "You go be with your son. My job is finished here."

Edgar looked into the older man's eyes with deep affection, "I can't thank you enough for all you've done, Judge. Glenn never would've gotten this far without you."

"Wish him luck in Berlin. I'll be reading all about him, I'm sure," Mahoney said. He fixed his hat and shook Edgar's hand for the last time. As the crowd formed to meet the man who would compete in the Decathlon in Berlin, Mahoney looked back with a bittersweet smile. He knew it was his last encounter with an amateur athlete. If he had failed to convince the country to boycott the Nazi Games, at least he had succeeded in convincing one young man that he could make a difference in his own life. He was proud of Glenn Morris.

*   *   *

The swimming and diving trials were held in an indoor facility in Astoria, New York. The diving competition was up first and in full swing. Katherine Rawls, the favorite, walked out onto the springboard for the final diving category--the 3-Meter Fancy Springboard. Having already cemented a place onboard the *USS MANHATTAN*, Rawls gracefully perfected her dive, which put her in first place.

Alan Gould watched from the bleachers and took notes as young Marjorie Gestring stretched and prepared for her dive. He noticed Rawls and Katherine Poynton-Hill say something to Gestring as she passed them on her way to the ladder. He made his way down to the coach's bench to have a better look at the young girl's dive.

Gestring took her place on the springboard. She took a deep breath and slowly let it out. She then smiled an impish grin, and suddenly sprung high in the air; twisting, turning, flipping, and landing almost perfectly. There was a slight gasp amongst the crowd who had been heavily rooting for the two favorites. Marjorie emerged from the bottom of the pool as the judges held up their scores. She was in second place! Only Rawls had a higher score, and she had beaten Poynton-Hill by a fraction of points. She was going to be an Olympian and she did underwater flips in celebration.

Gould smiled widely, but also took note of Rawls and Poynton-Hill, who looked very disappointed. Rawls consoled her friend. "Don't worry, you took first on the High Platform, and you'll have another shot at beating that little brat in Berlin!" Poynton-Hill half-smiled; she didn't like losing.

Marjorie hopped out of the pool and was toweling off as the two other women walked by her without a word. She just shrugged it off as she saw Gould approaching. "Congratulations, Marjorie. Do you know that you'll be the youngest Olympian in history?"

"I didn't know that," she replied.

"And do you know who was the youngest before you?"

"No."

"It was Rawls, back in '32."

"Did she win a Gold medal?"

"Silver."

"Good," she said defiantly. "Then I'm definitely winning Gold."

Gould smiled, impressed with her confidence. "What did they say to you before your last dive? Poynton-Hill--she said something to you on your way to the board. What was it?" Gould asked.

Gestring smiled. "She said, 'Don't slip.' I think she was genuinely concerned," the girl said wryly as she put her towel around her neck and began to walk off. "See you on the *USS Manhattan*, Mr. Gould."

Gould shook his head in disappointment at the thought of the two older women acting less mature than a 13-year-old girl. He began jotting down notes in his notepad as he walked towards the other end of the pool where the swimming trials were about to commence. The 100m backstroke trials were about to begin. Gould watched his friend Eleanor Holm enter the water and when he saw that her game face was on, he knew it was already over.

The gun echoed throughout the facility and Eleanor took an early lead, which she never relinquished. Gould watched as she pulled off her goggles, waiting for her competition to finish. She exited the pool and toweled off, not even looking at the scores. She knew she had made the team easily. Gould approached her from behind. "Eleanor."

She turned and saw that it was her friend. "Alan, hi!" She gave him a hug.

"I'm happy to see you'll be joining me on the voyage to Berlin."

"I can't wait. I've been dreaming about the trip for days," she said. "I'm more excited about the cruise than anything." She put on her jumpsuit and gathered her things.

"Are you where you want to be?" he asked.

"Athletically? Sure." she said nonchalantly.

"Things won't be so easy in Berlin, you know. I hope you're prepared."

"I'm prepared," she said confidently. "Let's have a few drinks as we cross the Atlantic," she insisted. "Make it a real soiree." She then gave Gould another big hug, "I'm so excited. I've gotta go run and catch up with Art. See you in a couple of days." Gould watched her go and rolled his eyes. Life was still all one big party to Eleanor.

*　　　*　　　*

At the rowing trials in Princeton, New Jersey, Bob Moch and his University of Washington rowing team were running late. As their truck barreled up to the docks, and Moch and his boys quickly grabbed their boat and ran to their position, the University of Pennsylvania coach dropped his head--he had hoped the Huskies from Washington wouldn't show up.

When the boats were all aligned and ready to go, Moch looked at Don Hume and Shorty Hunt with insatiable hunger. The teammates smiled and nodded. Coach Ulbrickson felt his team's confidence and glanced over at the Penn coach with a smile. The opposing coach looked back at him with a knowing defeat.

The starting gun blasted, and the boats steadily cut through the waters of Lake Carnegie. The University of Pennsylvania and the Navy teams took an early lead and were almost surprised by it. But they knew the Huskies would be coming for them. With only 700 meters to go, Moch roared a hellish command to his team. "L-G-B!!!" And the team responded, chanting back, "L-G-B!", swiftly gaining position, stroke after stroke, demoralizing the competition and winning the qualifying race with ease.

It was such an impressive victory that the American Olympic Committee officials broke tradition and decided that the whole

University of Washington team would not be broken up; they would be the team representing America in Berlin. Moch, Hume, and the men rejoiced and even got a smile out of old Coach Al Ulbrickson, who approached the team.

"What is this L-G-B bullshit? What's it stand for?" Ulbrickson asked. The team paused and naturally turned to Moch, who quickly responded.

"Let's Get Better. That's what you told us after the loss to California, right? 'You just have to get better'. So, we did."

"You did indeed," said their coach. The Huskies shared a knowing smile and looked forward to a well-deserved celebration that night.

*　　*　　*

At Randall's Island Stadium, on the banks of the East River, overlooking uptown Eastside Manhattan, the US Track and Field Olympic trials were entering their second day. Head Coach Lawson Robertson and new Assistant Coach Dean Cromwell watched over the events with sharp eyes. Four of the longer field events, including the decathlon, were being held elsewhere, but all the races, 5,000 meters and below were here. It was all up to the athletes now. Win, and you headed across town to the Westside, next stop Germany. If you lost, you pay your own way home, no matter how far away.

The African American athletes were shining the brightest. Jesse Owens, ARCHIE WILLIAMS, the 400m specialist, the 800m specialist John Woodruff, and sprinters Ralph Metcalfe and MACK ROBINSON, fared higher than expectations. Coach Robertson would field the largest contingent of African American athletes than all previous American Olympic teams combined.

On the whiter side of the color spectrum, Cromwell's USC athletes, Foy Draper, Louis Zamperini and Frank Wycoff all made the team, as did the standout Jewish sprinter from the University of Michigan, Sam Stoller. But there was one more spot to be filled, and that was what the mostly New York crowd came to see. Hometown Brooklyn high school favorite, 18-year-old Marty Glickman, was running for this last spot. It was the 100-meter dash, and all Marty had to do was place in the top 6 of all the runners in the final heats.

Glickman took his place at the starting line. As a freshman, he had shattered most of the New York City High School racing records and proceeded to break most of them every year leading to his just completed, and very successful, Senior year.

The starter put the runners on their mark and Glickman calmly took his place. Then came the call for set position. Glickman let the last of his butterflies fade away as he focused on the sound of 'go'. When the gunshot exploded, so did Glickman. He jumped out early. It was an insanely fast pace and it looked like Glickman could win the heat outright. Only a lightning bolt by Ralph Metcalfe got him at the end.

But Glickman's finishing time had put him in fifth place overall in the 100, which meant he had made the squad. He would join Stoller as the only Jews on the entire US Olympic Team, male or female. He looked up at his parents sitting in the front row. Romanian Jews who had emigrated after the Great War; they didn't quite understand Marty's passion for the sport nor where his speed even came from, but it didn't matter. They jumped up and down and cheered like everyone else in the stadium, and then cried for joy over his achievement.

So, the track team was in place, but Cromwell couldn't help himself after seeing the complete squad lining up for photos. "A few talented white boys, a pack of niggers and two kykes are how we're going to beat the Nazis? I don't think so. My boys stick out like sore thumbs surrounded by those monkeys and Shylocks," he complained to Robertson.

Robertson looked at him with absolute contempt, "Dean, these are America's best and I," he stressed that word heavily, "am their head coach. And I don't care one damned bit what they look like or what God they pray to. I care about bringing home Gold and then bringing them back in one piece. If you have a problem with that, or any of them, you can turn your ass around and head back to Los Angeles," Robertson barked, then turned and walked over to congratulate his team.

*   *   *

The night before the US Team embarked, Bob Moch lay back on his hotel bed at the Chelsea Hotel and stared at the ceiling. His excitement was overwhelming, but he would have to find a way to get some sleep. Music usually worked. He rose from the bed and as he reached to turn on the radio, there was a knock on the door. He walked over and opened it, and there in the doorway stood his father, Gaston.

"Father!" he exclaimed, and Gaston gave him a big hug. "What the heck are you doing here?"

"Hello, Robert! There was no time to send a letter. There's something I needed to tell you before you left for Berlin," Gaston said.

"Is it Mom? Is she okay?"

"Yes, she's perfectly fine." Gaston put his suitcase down and sat on the bed. "I'm exhausted. What a journey!" He took a deep breath as Moch anxiously waited to hear this important news. "You know where our family came from?"

"Yes, Switzerland." Moch said.

"Well, your mother and I never told you this. In fact, we never told anyone once we got to America."

"What is it? Please."

Gaston looked at him. "Your mother and I are Jewish. And you, too, are Jewish."

Moch stared in stunned silence, bewildered. "Why didn't you say anything?"

"I'm sorry. Your mother thought I should wait until you came back, but you understand why you had to know, don't you?"

"Yes, I understand, but . . . this is absolutely crazy." He paced around the hotel room. "Is that the reason you left Europe?"

"Not entirely, although the attitude towards Jews in Europe was not altogether kind, even in Switzerland. Things were changing all over. My parents had died along with your mother's. We wanted a new start, and we were not afraid of an adventure."

"Well, this is really shocking news. Not that it makes a difference to me, of course. But . . . what do I tell the team? Should I say anything?"

"That is entirely up to you," Gaston said.

"I have to say *something*," Moch debated.

"The reason we never told you was because we didn't know how people would react here in America, or if they'd react at all. After a while, we felt at home here, and didn't want that to change, so we just kept it a secret. I suggest you wait, and see how the water feels before diving in, if you understand."

Moch did understand, and he would wait before telling anyone. He walked into the bathroom and stood at the mirror. He didn't *feel* Jewish, whatever that was supposed to feel like. He was just surprised. And he was glad that he knew. He did feel something actually . . . he was proud. He thought he should tell his father that.

He walked back into the room, but Gaston was fast asleep, still in his clothes, splayed out on the only bed in the room. Moch covered him with a blanket and grabbed a pillow to find a spot on the floor. *So much for getting sleep tonight,* he thought, and flipped on the radio to find some music to soothe his nerves.

- 237 -

*   *   *

The next morning, July 15th, 1936, the *Husky Clipper*, all sixty-two-feet of her, rested on top of a New York Police Department truck as it made its way up 10th Avenue in Manhattan. The Police escort led the University of Washington rowing team and its prized rowboat through the streets of the city towards the Westside Piers. It was a most peculiar sight--the long, thin shell of a boat tied to the roof of a truck surrounded by police cars parting traffic with a couple of vans trailing closely behind, filled with young men who looked like they had never seen the light of day before. Pedestrians watched in wonder, gawking at the convoy. People peered out of windows and fire escapes above, smiling and waving. The team was in awe of the sights and sound of the Big Apple--most of them had never left Seattle before.

After a sleepless night, Bob Moch was tired and nervous, and he was preoccupied with his father's revelation about being Jewish. He wondered how the team would react. He would have to tell them when they got to Berlin. He would find the right moment, and hopefully it would further galvanize the team. A jolt from a pothole snapped him out of his head. As the police escort van turned a corner, he turned to Don Hume, who was also a little nervous but managed to enjoy the ride like the rest of the team. "You think we tied it down all right? What if the boat cracks?"

Shorty Hunt overheard him, slapped him on the back and said, "Relax, Moch, if anything happens to the *Clipper*, Uncle Sam will buy us a new one--he loves us!"

"He doesn't love these streets. There are potholes everywhere. Look at the--". Shorty gasped and grabbed Moch's head with both of his hands. As the police escort turned down 23rd Street, he slowly turned Moch's head to face the Westside Piers. "Holy crap," Moch said. The team was astonished--it was a true spectacle.

The Westside Piers were a mob scene as The American Olympic Team boarded the *USS Manhattan*. Huge crowds of supporters showed up to either join them or wish them a bon voyage. Movie cameras rolled and photographers from every outlet in the country flashed their cameras as the athletes arrived to walk the gangplank. Whistles on tugboats and ferries shrieked and sirens on fireboats wailed as they shot water into the air from their canons. Bi planes overhead, tipped to one side, circled the ship as photographers scrambled to snap aerial shots.

Marjorie Gestring and Eleanor Holm were especially popular targets for the cameras. Brundage took notice of Eleanor as he overlooked the arrivals from the ship's deck. He watched her as she worked the press with a charm and sexiness none of his other athletes possessed.

As Woodruff, Williams, and Owens got to the gangplank, reporters, including Gould, swarmed around them. As they were handed tiny American flags to wave to the crowd of well-wishers, a reporter asked the three runners what they thought of Hitler's treatment of Germany's Negros. Woodruff laughed. "We'll feel right at home," he said with a sheepish grin. The other two men laughed alongside him as they climbed aboard.

Gestring walked over to Katherine Rawls and Dorothy Poynton-Hill before boarding and thanked them for being such inspirations with their (not so) kind words every time they had met. "It was exactly the motivation I needed to make it here and steal Gold from the likes of the two of you," she said in a not-so-subtle teenage contempt, and then walked away without saying another word. The two older women were left standing in shame.

Moch and his boys, with the help of the police escort, parted the mob and drove right up to the gangplank. They hopped out of the vans, gently unhitched the *Husky Clipper*, hoisted her above their heads, and carried her up onto the ship. The crowd was cheering their every move.

When all the athletes, coaches, and press were aboard, the Olympic Flag was raised just below the American flag flying above the *USS Manhattan*. The crowds cheered and a spontaneous *God Bless America* broke out as the ship pulled away. Brundage, still overlooking the festivities from an upper balcony, clinked champagne glasses with some of the other Olympic officials. He was riding high until Gould walked by and had to ruin the mood.

"Congratulations on your appointment into the IOC. You must be very proud of yourself." Gould began with the utmost disgust in his tone and on his face. "I imagine it will be quite the challenge following in the footsteps of such an honest, humble, and . . ." He got close into Brundage to stress his next point, "such a patriotic man like Assistant Secretary Jahncke. I question whether you're up for the task." He was mortified that the IOC had dismissed Jahncke, and he wasn't going to ease off Brundage for one second regarding his new appointment.

"Are you calling me some sort of traitor? I'm all about Americans winning and being justly represented!" Brundage was shocked and truly offended. He had never once imagined himself unpatriotic. "I did my duty and got this team here. That's why I got elected to the IOC."

"You conspire with people who seem more than willing to lead this world into another war, and all because of their wounded pride and shameless prejudice. And all because of your high aspirations. It's not about the team to you, Avery. You didn't do any of this for them. You could give a fuck. And they are going to win despite you. It's just sad you're going to take all the credit." He ended with and continued working his way to John Kieran, who was also overlooking the reveling athletes.

"That seemed like a charming and intimate conversation." Kieran said with a wry smile.

Gould shook his head. "The world is run by shameless opportunists. It's a foul realization."

"And someone once promised the meek shall inherit the earth." Kieran quipped back.

Brundage looked over at the two reporters chatting. He knew Gould would be especially relentless throughout the Games, but *fuck them all*, he thought. He had indeed gotten his way. They were off to Germany. He had defeated Mahoney, helped get rid of Jahncke, and then gotten unanimously appointed to the IOC to fill his spot. He was now in complete control of every aspect of American amateur athletics. And he wasn't going to stop there. Avery was going to make sure the Americans played nice in Berlin. His goal was the Presidency of the IOC, and these Olympics were the next stepping-stone.

HITLER

Osten, aware the Americans were en route, called Goebbels to give him the good news. The Propaganda Minister was ecstatic and said to Osten, "Execute the next phase of the plan." Goebbels called Hitler with the good news. While the Führer was pleased, he did not like to be awakened in the middle of the night, and make it quite clear by slamming down the phone.

Somehow Avery Brundage had actually convinced his country to attend. Through all the international bad press and basic worldwide antipathy towards the Nazis over the past four years, Brundage had swayed his flock of sheep that all was perfectly normal. Osten took a sip of cognac and pondered his next insidious steps.

*   *   *

Across Berlin, shop owners began taking down anti-Jewish signs from their windows. Women washed away soap-drawn

Stars of David from storefronts of evicted Jewish businesses. Construction crews removed signs stating, "JEWS NOT WANTED" and similar slogans from primary traffic intersections. On every street corner there was a kiosk selling the rabidly anti-Jewish newspaper, "*Der Stürmer*" (The Stormtrooper). The newspapers in these kiosks were rapidly removed. (The paper was still published however, using racist slurs and caricatures to ridicule Jews in its special "Olympics" issue.)

Berlin was being transformed back into a perfect cosmopolitan capital of the world. But it wasn't just the cleaning up of building facades, Stars of David on windows, and racist publications; there was a human element to the great cleanup of Berlin.

In ReichsCentralburo, Berlin, dozens of armed SS Officers paraded through the doors of a great meeting hall with purpose. One by one, they descended a wide staircase and began lining up outside on the street, awaiting orders. The doors of the meeting hall slammed shut, revealing in bold letters, "REICH CENTRAL OFFICE FOR THE SUPPRESSION OF THE GYPSY NUISANCE."

Since the beginning of Reich's ascension to power in 1933, Dr. Robert Ritter, a child psychologist at the University of Tübingen, became the central figure in the study of Roma (Gypsies). His specialty was criminal biology--the idea that criminal behavior is genetically determined. In 1936, Ritter became the director of the Center for Research on Racial Hygiene and Demographic Biology in the Ministry of Health and began a racial study of Roma. At the conclusion of his study, Ritter declared that Roma were once Aryan people that originated in India. But mingling with lesser peoples during their long migration had corrupted them. Ritter estimated that some ninety percent of all Roma in Germany were of mixed blood and were consequently carriers of "degenerate" blood and criminal characteristics. Because they allegedly constituted a danger, Ritter recommended they be isolated in concentration camps and be forcibly sterilized.

In the early morning dawn on the outskirts of Eastern Berlin, a Gypsy encampment was beginning to stir. There were dozens of makeshift tents erected haphazardly. Alongside them were wooden wagons in various states of condition. A four-year-old boy exited his tent and walked towards a small ditch to pee. As he walked back, he saw a group of trucks heading towards the encampment. He began running, yelling to his parents. Gypsies began to stream out to see what the commotion was.

Police transport trucks descended on the encampment. SS guards barked orders and rounded up the inhabitants, separating the men from the women and children. They began escorting them onto the transport trucks at gunpoint. The young boy clung to his mother's dress in shock. As the trucks began to depart, a group of German citizens cheered on the SS in support. That morning, in and around the streets of Berlin, the rounding up of Roma was fully underway. A team of SS Police converged on a family of Roma hiding in a dark alley. They would soon no longer be homeless.

On another street nearby, the SS and a vicious guard dog were chasing a teenage Roma girl. She vaulted fences, ran through back alleys, and sprinted down a main street. An Aryan woman, who was witnessing the chase, tripped the young girl with her umbrella and yelled to the SS. The guards came running; the dog was the first to catch the girl.

In a rundown, abandoned tenement complex, SS guards raided a room. The father of the family inside briefly escaped and tried to shimmy down a drainpipe. One of the guards whacked his hand with a nightstick and the man fell twenty feet, shattering his legs.

*   *   *

On the outskirts of Berlin, in the borough of Marzahn, the smelly camp the Nazis had set up, was growing steadily. Truck after truck rolled into the camp. Men were separated from their families, but everyone who entered was ushered to medical tents for sterilization. There were hundreds of them. A young boy and his mother were shoved into a line. Beyond the medical tents, the boy saw a group of Roma men getting sick at gunpoint, vomiting into a pool of urine and feces.

*   *   *

The cleanup of Berlin had implications which were felt not only by the citizens of Berlin, but the German Olympic athletes as well. Gretel Bergmann returned to her room after an early dinner out with some of her fellow teammates. She had faced none of the angry anti-Semitism since making the German Olympic Team. She had to wonder if Berlin's recent transformation was just a smokescreen for Olympic tourists. Suddenly no Stars of David on shop fronts, all anti-Jewish posters stripped from street signs, and Jews could walk into any restaurant or shop and get served without harassment. It was either a two-week charade or maybe, just maybe, the Nazis were finally turning the corner on their prejudiced views.

She looked in the mirror and smiled. She was the odds-on favorite to win Gold in the high jump. And she was not going to let the opportunity pass her by the wayside. She stripped off her blouse, bra, and skirt and went towards the bathroom to freshen up before retiring.

But when Gretel opened the bathroom door, she was shocked to see Dora Ratjen peeing . . . standing up. Dora was just as shocked but was literally caught with his pants down. Ratjen was a MAN! Gretel could not believe her eyes and stumbled back out of the door. She grabbed her blouse and covered her breasts.

Heinrich "Dora" Ratjen waiting to compete in the High Jump at the 1936 Berlin Games.

"I can explain, Gretel."

*　　　*　　　*

Theodor Morell was a 50-year-old German physician who concentrated on skin and venereal diseases. He was an unassuming man who looked much older than his age. He had been a doctor on the front lines during the Great War and in 1920 at the tender age of thirty-four, started a practice of his own. Through his new wife's fortune, he had armed himself with the finest and the fanciest private office in the city and served only the wealthiest of patrons. You see, Morell also happened to be one of the biggest opportunists in all of Berlin. And in a city now teeming with them, he ruled the roost. He was known as "Dr. Feel

Good" to the celebrities of Berlin; his concoctions of painkillers had become widely popular, and he profited greatly from prescribing them.

He had recently become Hitler's personal physician after saving the life of Hitler's personal photographer, Heinrich Hoffmann, and helping Eva recover from her latest suicide attempt. When Morell then helped ease the Führer's on-going flatulence, which in turn cleared a skin rash on his leg, Hitler was convinced of the mad doctor's genius and hired him on the spot, firing all his other practitioners.

Although Morell was still making money from his financial interests in drug manufacturing companies in Hamburg and Budapest, he took a pay cut to be the Führer's personal doctor. He had always had a fascination with the military since his involvement in the Great War and couldn't pass up the opportunity to be embedded in its highest ranks. Morell desperately wanted to be part of the military, but since he held no official military rank, he was not issued any military uniform. So, he simply invented his own. He fastened gold buttons to the darkest gray suit jacket he could find and made up his own official medical medallion of intertwining snakes around the SS symbol (a member of which he was not a part of). Other members of the Nazi party often ridiculed him behind his back, not only because of his preposterous fake military uniform, but his obnoxious body odor and poor hygiene. Once, when confronted about Morell's crudeness by one of his entourage, Hitler responded, "I do not employ him for his fragrance, but to look after my health!"

Goering called him "the Reich Master of injections," and it wasn't a compliment. His list of drugs was vast and dangerously unfounded as proper prescription medicines went. Morell's preferred prescription always included a needle. Meth-amphetamines were usually thrown into the cocktails in some amount or another. The long list of "medications" included *bromide* (to counteract the stimulating effects of methamphetamine), *cocaine* and *adrenaline* (via eye drops), *oxycodone* (for intestinal spasms), *mutaflor* (bacteria cultured from human feces), *orchikrin* (an extract of bovine testosterone), and a wide variety of vitamins and caffeine extracts to ward off infections from all the injections. The list of drugs was voluminous, and Eva and Adolf couldn't get enough.

"Just give me the shot already, you little troll," Eva demanded of Morell in her bedroom as he prepared the syringe full of speed, heroin, and vitamin B as quickly as he could. Eva dropped her panties and lifted half of her skirt, exposing one of her buttocks. "Now, before I collapse from exhaustion."

As soon as the thick brown serum entered her body, she became limp. The good doctor helped her to the couch. "Here you go, Fräulein Braun."

"Okay, you can get the fuck out now."

He left the room on command, and she started to take off her clothes. She stumbled a bit walking to her closet while undressing, but regained composure and began to place different dresses in front of her as she looked hazily into her full-sized mirror. None of them made her happy and she tossed each of them with growing contempt. When Hitler entered the room, she immediately started whining, slurring, but whining, "I don't have one thing to wear at the Opening Ceremonies that doesn't make me look like a *Milchkuh*."

He recognized without a second glance, that she was impaired. "Has Morell been in here already?! What the fuck, Eva? You couldn't wait for me?"

She walked over to him laughing and began to rub her naked body on him. "Am I a *groß Milchkuh, schätzte*?"

"Stop being ridiculous," he snapped back. "Why would you start without me?" he pouted.

"Forget about that," she continued in her sexiest voice. "Let's get the glass table out, I feel a movement."

"Morell!" The Führer screamed out without hesitation, *"Komme uber schnell!"*

THE USS MANHATTAN

A cocktail party of grand proportion was being held in the ship's main dining room, a swank affair for the athletes hosted by the traveling press. The theme of course was red, white, and blue. The tables cloths and settings were all patriotic inspired and the servers wore little Uncle Sam hats, most cocked to one side of their head or another. Everyone was free to relax and let his or her hair down. Servers passed out appetizers and champagne and the bars could barely keep up with drink orders. Food was everywhere and seemingly bottomless. To many of the poorer athletes, the whole scene seemed like heaven.

Now that the ship was in international waters, Marjorie Gestring sipped from her first glass of champagne. She stared straight up at the much taller John Woodruff who was very impressed with the teenage phenom. "You like half mermaid or something?"

"You might have the biggest feet I've ever seen," she quipped back. "How can you even walk with those things, let alone run fast?"

He smiled, "That's no problem. Getting shoes that fit. That's the problem."

The Washington University crew team, now the US Olympic Crew Team, was happy to be out of their cramped staterooms in the basement of the *Manhattan*. Some began to get sick from the oppressive heat and uncomfortable sleeping arrangements, so the main dining room and adjoining outside deck were a welcome relief. The food and drink were also more than welcome. Joe Rantz and Don Hume consumed shrimp cocktails like two starving seagulls. Shorty Hunt and James McMillin sat on deck chairs drinking red wine and discussing what was tastier, the Au jus or Bearnaise sauce for the roast. It was surreal to Bob Moch, who knew most of his teammates had never seen such a spread in their lives. He certainly hadn't and he was taking full advantage of the situation. Moch didn't know what a canapé was, but he sure thought they were delicious.

In another part of the room the men's 4x100 relay team was debating with the women's 4x100 relay. Both were heavy favorites to win Gold in their respective events but who would win by more was the question. Glickman was confident his men's team would prevail, but speedster HELEN STEPHENS was having none of it. "Ain't a chance in hell that happens. I will personally beat all four of your times and that alone would give us the edge."

Jesse Owens, overhearing Stephens' boast laughed out loud at Glickman, Draper, Stoller, and Wycoff, the four runners Robertson chose to run in the relay. "She's right. Without me, you guys will barely win the race at all," he joked, but not without a trace of disappointment. Jesse wanted four Gold medals. No athlete had ever done that before in Olympic history and the relay was the only way for that to happen.

Stephens, from Fulton, Missouri, and nicknamed the "Fulton Flash" matched his wit. "Don't be so cocky, Buckeye," she pointed to herself, "this filly would beat your ass one on one. Which would mean, I'M the fastest person on earth." It took a moment for Jesse to react.

"You've been hitting the champagne a little too hard, girl."

Archie Williams and Ralph Metcalfe were scoping out the female athletes as they picked off every appetizer tray that passed them. They loved being treated like kings. Metcalfe, who had won Silver and Bronze in Los Angeles, and was Owens' chief rival in the 100m these Games, did not receive any of this treatment in 1932. "We were served grub just above dog food level. Brundage didn't give two shits how we were treated at home."

"I'm sure if the press hadn't sponsored this, we'd be getting gruel." Williams remarked. He wasn't a Brundage fan and saw right through his and Dean Cromwell's false facades. They were bona-fide racists in his eyes, and he had seen it firsthand with Cromwell whenever Williams' UC Berkley met USC in competitions. And Cromwell didn't need much prompting for his real self to emerge.

Cromwell, more than tipsy, walked over to Louis Zamperini as the young athlete grabbed another champagne, "Feeling good Louis?"

"Yeah, why?" he asked with a mix of curiosity and contempt. He did not like his USC coach at all.

"I'll bet you're real excited to see that Jew-broad girlfriend of yours, huh?"

Zamperini smiled, "Your ability to motivate your athletes never ceases to amaze me, Coach. It's quite the magic touch," he said sarcastically and then walked away. Cromwell just grinned.

On the deck just outside the dining room Coach Robertson and Mack Robinson spoke about Mack's younger brother Jackie, a rising star in California amateur athletics. "He can hit a BB with a twig, Coach. Never seen anyone that can play ball like him. And he just won a junior championship in the Pacific Coast Negro Tennis Tournament."

"Sounds more talented than even you, Mack," the coach joked.

Robinson shook his head disappointed, "He is, damned kid. And he is just as nice as he is talented. I should hate him," he joked.

Just behind them, doing drunken one-armed pushups for the photographers, Glenn Morris awed the men with his brute strength. He also showed his drinking prowess as he sipped a beer with the unused hand every rep. All of this was done with a big smile and in perfect rhythm, as if practiced and performed hundreds of times.

Everyone at the party was engaged and having a great time, but none more than Miss Eleanor Holm. She looked beautiful and sexy in a long, slim, black dress slit on one side from hip to ankle, and she was holding court with the press, including Gould and Kieran. Between swigs of champagne and drags of her cigarette, she belted out *Someone to Watch Over Me* while George Gershwin himself accompanied her on piano. Gershwin was transfixed and couldn't hide his amazement with the talented and beautiful athlete's rendition. His smile reached from ear to ear.

Eleanor directed much of the song towards Gould, who turned beet-red when she playfully and flirtatiously toyed with his bow tie during her performance. Kieran jokingly patted Gould's forehead with a wet bar napkin, eliciting laughs from the crowd and further embarrassing him.

But across the room on the balcony over-looking the dining room, Brundage wasn't laughing. He watched on with a burning desire that consumed him. He wanted Eleanor very badly and felt his advances a couple of years before must have been too subtle. He turned to Margaret, "I want to see Holm in my stateroom in ten minutes."

"Why?" she asked incredulously. "And why in your stateroom?"

"None of your fucking business. Just do as I say."

Margaret looked at him with an anger she didn't even know she possessed. When he turned away without another word, she threw her drink to the ground in disgust, and dutifully made her way toward the piano.

*   *   *

Brundage sat with an almost eerie calm. He wasn't sure how he was going to have sex with Holm, but it was going to happen one way or another. And it was going to happen now whether he had to force the issue or not.

When Margaret knocked on the door, Brundage coolly let the two women in and promptly excused his assistant. "I think I should stay, Avery. I'm not sure it's safe in here if I leave," Margaret said.

Brundage looked at her with fire in his eyes, "Get the fuck out or you are heading back to New York the minute we dock in Germany!" Holm was confused. A little drunk and very confused.

"What is happening? Why was I dragged in here by your whore, Mr. Brundage?"

Margaret looked at Holm and scowled. "You just signed your own death sentence, bitch." She looked at Brundage, "Do your bidding, Beelzebub." She then turned and slammed the door behind her as she left.

Holm turned towards Brundage. "That's a pretty big word for her."

"Your behavior has been very inappropriate so far this trip. You are not comporting yourself in a very Olympian manner, Ms. Holm."

"It's actually Mrs. Jarrett," she reminded him.

Brundage grinned. He knew she had been far from chaste in her wedding vows. Holm was not the good-wife sort of material and had already been spotted on the ship a few early mornings leaving other men's cabins. He continued, "But as a newly appointed member of the IOC I can look the other way, if certain arrangements can be made."

Holm knew right away where this was going. She also figured she could've been a little nicer to Margaret, so she could've walked out with her. "Mr. Brundage I will work on my behavior aboard this ship. I don't think any other arrangements need to be made."

"On the contrary," Brundage insisted. "The damage has been done and there is only one way for you to rectify it." He went in for the kill with his eyes wide and his zipper already halfway down. The minute he grabbed her, however, Holm sprang into action. Brundage had forgotten she was a young elite athlete, much faster than he, and his crotch paid for it. She kneed him so hard between the legs; he dropped to the floor like a toppled Goliath. His eyes rolled to the back of his head, and he couldn't move nor speak. But she could.

"Mr. Brundage, what, on God's green earth, would make you imagine that I would even remotely consider sexual relations with you?" She dragged him by what little hair he had left over to the mirror then propped his head up violently so both their faces were showing in the reflection. "Look at you, then look at me. Look at YOU, and then look at ME. Enough said." She threw his head back to the floor. "Don't ever touch me again. I'm going back to the party, where even with all that man sweat flying around, things are safer there than in here."

"Get back to your cabin," Brundage squeaked, "Or it'll be the end of you!"

She pointed towards a champagne bottle, "You might want to empty that ice bucket you got over there down your pants, Brundage. It will reduce swelling," she said as she sauntered out the door and back to the party.

GRETEL

At three o'clock in the morning on a crystal-clear night, a lone military jeep pulled up to the entrance of the living quarters of the women's Olympic Team. The *Sportsführer*, Hans von Tschammer und Osten, exited the jeep in his leather duster and walked up the steps to the main entrance. Inside, he approached a desk where a guard was sleeping on the job. Osten regarded him with disgust and marched down the hallway, not caring that his boots echoed loudly with each step.

Osten liked surprising young people with important news in this manner--half asleep and off-guard. It was a tactic that fared him well on the front lines during the Great War. Stealthy raids in the middle of the night built up his reputation as a brave leader despite his well-known, charmed upbringing. He liked to picture his unsuspecting victims asleep as he crawled through the mud in the quiet of night. The halls of the women's dorm were deadly quiet on this night.

Knock, knock.

Dora Ratjen woke up, startled. "Who is that?!" Gretel was wide-awake in her top bunk, still reeling from her awkward encounter with Dora in the bathroom. In her heart she thought they were coming to get him. *HIM! Did anyone else see Dora like that? Did anyone else know?*

Gretel climbed down from her perch. "Coming." Dora covered herself with blankets as Gretel opened the door. Osten stood there with a wry smile.

"May I come in, Fräulein?"

"Of course, Herr Osten," Gretel said and ushered him inside the room.

Dora sat at the side of her bed. "Good evening, Herr Osten. Good *morning*, rather."

"Good morning to both of you . . . ladies," Osten said as he sauntered in, silently noting how the room had become their home; pictures and drawings on the desk, notes and reminders scribbled on note paper. He picked up an empty chocolate wrapper from a chair and tossed it into a trashcan. "Too much chocolate can keep you up at night, you know."

"We were fast asleep," Gretel said as she sat beside Dora who was nervously watching Osten's every movement.

"Well, I hope I didn't interrupt any pleasant dreams, but I have some important news that couldn't wait until sunrise," he said. Dora shifted uneasily. Gretel just stared at him. Osten continued. "I have the unfortunate duty to inform you, Ms. Bergmann, that you will not be performing at the Olympic Games."

"What?!" Dora exclaimed. Gretel didn't flinch.

"Miss Bergmann will be able to stay in the Village and even dine with the rest of the team, but participation is not an option. You can watch the competition with the other spectators. Dora, you will take Gretel's place on the team's depth chart."

Dora stood up from her bed. "Excuse me, Herr Osten, but this is crazy. We're so close . . . and Gretel, well, she's our best shot at Gold---"

Osten addressed Gretel, feigning pity, but deep inside he loathed her, and all Jews like her. He had a burning desire to tell her what he really thought. "I understand how shocking this must be for you."

"Not shocking at all, to be honest," Gretel said. Osten was stunned but hid his reaction well. "And what reason may I ask will be given for my sudden scratch?"

"I guess that is a valid question. You will tell everyone you have a hamstring injury." He walked up to her and spoke right into her face. "I expect you to continue to represent your home country admirably and do the very best you can to behave."

Gretel smiled at Osten with such a calm murderous look it scared him for a moment. "I guess we shall see about that," she said. And then walked out of the room, slamming the door behind her, and leaving Osten dumbfounded. He still needed her and if she didn't go along with the plan, it would be a disaster. He would have to keep a close eye on her.

"Gretel!" Dora called after her.

"*Miss* Ratjen," he said, "you are looking more and more like a woman every day. Keep it up--the American reporters are getting suspicious of the athletes in our program. Let's keep your pants on and your secret to yourself, okay?"

Dora nodded. "Yes, Herr Osten. I'm just having a hard time understanding the change of plans. It's so sudden."

"Germany cannot be humiliated by letting a Jew win a Gold medal. That's all you need to understand," Osten said as he left the room. Dora sat back down, holding her head in her hands, wishing that what had just happened was only a bad dream.

Gretel stood alone on the empty practice field. It was still pitch black out except for the few stars illuminating the scene. She took a deep breath. All the work she had put in the last year here, all the training, all the sweat, and there would be nothing to show for it. She realized her supposed participation in the Games was simply a ploy to get the other countries to Berlin, and they had all taken the bait. She felt so used. She hadn't lied to Osten, though she really wasn't surprised. She was more amazed it took the big brute this long to bring the hammer down.

She walked to the middle of the field and lay down, staring right into those stars. She began to cry. If only her father had listened to her years before, the whole family would be in England far away from all this insanity. And she would be competing as a British National. But now Gretel was forced to put on a brave face for all the world's athletes, and she wasn't sure she could keep her mouth shut. She imagined walking right over to IOC President Latour or the American Olympic president Avery Brundage and telling them everything. This would embarrass Osten to no end. Yes, she would find the right time to tell, at least Brundage, the truth. Surely, as an American, he would be a man of compassion and wouldn't accept this type of injustice.

DODD

On a stormy afternoon late in July, William Dodd sat at a desk in his study drafting a letter. As he signed his name at the bottom of the page, he suddenly grabbed his stomach and fell to one knee on the floor. The desk chair fell, and the papers scattered across the floor. Mattie heard the commotion and rushed into the study.

"Bill! C'mon, let's sit down." She helped him back into his chair and said, "Drink the tea I brought you. Doctor's orders." She handed him a cup of tea that was now cold. "I'll make you a fresh cup."

"Thank you, dear. No more tea--if I have another sip, you might be sleeping on a waterbed tonight." She smiled and rubbed his belly.

"I'll be upstairs if you need anything," she said.

"Thank you," he said. She left the room and Dodd began collecting his papers, ordering them neatly on his desk.

Bill Jr. walked in, coat and umbrella in hand. He noticed the papers all over the floor. "Hey Dad, everything okay?"

Dodd looked up and nodded to his son. "Fine. Just fine." He sat back down. Bill Jr. removed his coat and picked up a few pages of his father's letter.

"What's this?" he asked.

"It's a letter to Secretary of State Hull. My old friend Cordell might be the only sane man left in Washington." He looked to Bill Jr. who was engaged in the pages he picked up off the floor.

"Dad . . . you can't send this."

"The hell I can't."

Bill Jr. read from the pages, ". . . *Hitler's domestic economic policies, rearmament, and Rhineland initiatives have consolidated his support to the point that he could count on the support of the German people for a declaration of war, in any measure he might undertake.*" Bill Jr. looked at his father and said, "What makes you think he'll actually read this letter? He's ignored you in the past."

"Because he wants to form a United Nations. He just proposed it to Congress. If there's anyone in Washington who might be concerned with world peace, I think it's him."

Bill Jr. laid down the pages and sighed. "You still thinking about resigning?"

"Now more than ever."

"Do us all a favor, okay? Before you resign, stand tall at the Games. Be a leader. Let your presence be known. Then let's take a long vacation."

"That sounds great, actually." He gathered the pages and handed them to Bill, Jr. "Send the letter to Hull."

In the staircase leading to the second floor, Mattie had secretly listened in to the conversation between her husband and son. One man filled with youthful optimism: the other, her husband, growing skeptical of the situation in general. Two men wanting only the best for their family and for those lives around them they could impact. *It may take an army*, she thought.

When the conversation ended, she quickly and quietly made her way up the staircase. Passing by Martha's room, she saw her daughter putting her makeup on, dressed in her finest clothes. She paused at the doorway and gazed at Martha, and for a moment it reminded her of herself as a young girl back in North Carolina getting ready for Sunday mass--minus the fishnet stockings.

"Going out again?" she asked, startling Martha.

"Maybe."

"Who is it today? Rudy? Putzi? Or that pilot . . . What's his name?"

"It's none of your concern," Martha said defiantly.

Mattie stomped over to Martha's desk where she sat. "Oh, it most definitely is my concern. We're not safe here, Martha. *You're* not safe sleeping around with all these Nazis. It's giving your father ulcers."

"How dare you? He was the one who made us come here!

Don't blame me for that."

"I'm not blaming you. I just want you to be safe. And I want to know where you're going and who you're going out with at all times."

"Fine. I'll tell *you* when you tell *me* where you're sneaking off to all the time holding secret conversations with Mildred." Martha resumed applying her lipstick. Mattie slowly walked out of the room and went downstairs. She put on her coat and hat, grabbed an umbrella, and looked back at William still working in his study. She quietly exited the house.

Outside, the air was cool, and she took a deep breath. There was hardly a soul walking around in the inclement weather, but she still felt surrounded by a thousand eyes watching her. She turned a corner and looked back to see if anyone had been following her. Feeling a shred safer, she hurried down the street avoiding puddles, careful not to get her feet too wet.

She held her umbrella low, hiding her face as she climbed the steps to Mildred's front door. She checked her surroundings then knocked. After a long moment she heard a series of locks being unlatched. When Mildred opened the door, Mattie shot out, "Where the hell have you been?!"

"I've been so busy at work," Mildred said.

"You haven't *been* to work!" Mattie replied. Mildred immediately shushed her with a finger to her lips and ushered her inside. She quickly shut the door and fastened the series of locks. Mattie was frozen. Mildred grabbed her by the hand and led her to the mantle over the fireplace. She pointed to a picture frame, then to her ear.

What? Mattie mouthed. Mildred flipped over the picture frame and pointed to a tiny metal device that had been taped to the back.

"What's that?" asked Mattie.

"They're listening," Mildred whispered.

"Are you sure?"

Mildred walked her over to a chair in an adjacent room and forced her to the ground, pointing under the chair. Mattie, on her hands and knees, reached underneath the chair and eventually found another metal listening device. She grabbed Mildred and pulled her to a corner of the room, mouthing, *What are you going to do?*

Mildred used her best sign language and mimed carrying a suitcase. She walked across the room and put the imaginary suitcase under a couch and wound up an invisible timer. Mattie was confused until Mildred backed away from the couch and put her finger in her ears, then mimicked an explosion with her arms. She then mimicked running away, turned to Mattie, and took a bow.

Are you crazy!! Mattie mouthed. Mildred mimed for her to 'zip her lip shut'. Mattie responded by tracing a finger across her throat and mouthing, *They'll kill you.*

*   *   *

A black limousine splashed down Prinz-Albrecht Street not far from the Gestapo headquarters. In the back seat Goebbels was sipping cognac. Putzi sat across from him reading a pamphlet entitled "*Native Nazis--Stomping Out the Olympic Spirit.*"

Goebbels finished his cognac. "We found those pamphlets at Lichtenrade Station."

"That's on the new Berlin-Dresden high-speed line," Putzi noted.

"The midway point, if that's of any significance," Goebbels said. "The bomb was hidden inside a cigar box. A fucking cigar box!" He threw his glass aside. "It was found by a construction worker. A good man using his God-given hands to help to rebuild this country."

"That's a long way from Berlin," Putzi said.

Goebbels erupted, "Anywhere in the homeland is too close to Berlin! I thought when we got rid of the Brown Shirts this sort of behavior was over."

"You can drown a rat but sometimes it's fleas jump away and hide." Putzi put down the pamphlet. "We have informants underground. We'll kill each flea one by one."

"Good. I want you to keep your eyes, and *ears*, wide open."

*   *   *

Mildred walked hurriedly down the dimly lit street, checked a piece of paper with an address written on it, and turned around see if anyone was following her. Down the street, about fifty meters away, a man in a black hat stood on the corner smoking a cigarette. She felt a chill then did what she was supposed to do; walk past the entrance, continue around the block, and see if the stranger followed her. She did just that, and when she arrived back at the basement entrance, the man was gone.

She quickly ran down a flight of steps made of stone with iron fencing lining each side. When she made it to the entrance, the smoking man emerged from a dark corner. Mildred gasped and froze, thinking she would be arrested and tortured, maybe even killed. Instead, the man offered his arm and said, "Well done. Come this way." He led her through an archway and into the basement of what seemed to be an old housing complex, empty except for a few stray dogs minding their own business.

Mildred was shaking; less nervous than anxious. The stakes had been raised after her successful bombing of an SS army barracks back in November of 1934. Back then she was told that her next mission would be "planting a bomb underneath Hitler's ass" at the Opening Ceremonies of the Olympics which were starting next month. Mildred had been preparing for this mission for two years. She had done everything the Communists had asked of her. Mainly, keep a low profile and stay vigilant. She had done that but somehow someone managed to plant two listening devices in her apartment. As she followed the smoking man down a corridor, she wondered if she should mention the bugs.

She followed the man through a thick door and into a meeting room where two other men stood around a table. She instantly recognized one of them--the steely-eyed Vladimir; the man of few words but many glares.

"Vladimir!" she said.

"Welcome back," Vladmir said without emotion.

"Is Nikolas here?" she asked. Vladimir looked at her and shook his head 'no'.

The other man, a short, stout man with glasses, addressed her. "I am Leon. Welcome. My comrades have told me of your bravery and devotion to our cause. For that we are grateful."

"It's been two years," she said. "Why has it taken so long? I've been ready all this time--"

Vladimir spoke up. "This is a more serious, and much more dangerous mission."

Leon patted Vladimir on the back, approving his participation. "That is precisely why we've waited. Nobody suspects you."

Mildred pictured the listening bugs on her mantle and under her living room chair and decided right there that it would be wise not to mention them. "The last time we met I was told I would be attending the Olympics. I've seen the posters everywhere. Very exciting." Mildred smiled confidently.

"Yes. In fact, you'll be at the Opening Ceremonies."

Mildred, Leon, and Vladimir spent the next two hours in the underground meeting room going over the plans. She was given papers with a fake identity; VIP passes to the Opening Ceremonies, and a new passport. She was fitted for a wig and a new coat.

There were maps and schematics of the stadium. "One of our

comrades helped to build this place," Leon said. They showed her exactly where Hitler was to be seated, and how she would find her way directly under his box by counting the sections above her as she made her way through the bowels of the stadium. They knew where the checkpoints and security stations were going to be and how many men were supposed to be on duty. Mildred was impressed; her Communist friends had been doing their homework.

Then Leon produced a package wrapped in cloth. He unfolded it to reveal a sleek, black handgun. "The TT-30," he said.

"It's a Tula-Tokarev, the best." Vladimir said, admiring the gun.

"Do you know how to use one?" Leon asked.

"No, but I am not only a good teacher, but a good student as well."

They took her to a soundproof room where she fired rounds into a makeshift target area. Vladimir was the gun expert. He showed her everything she needed to know about the weapon. After that, they took her to another room where a black suitcase rested on a table. It was the explosive device that was to be used in the stadium bombing. It was bigger than the device used in the SS barracks bombing; she hoped she could carry it without drawing attention to herself.

"It's not much heavier," Leon insisted. "Here." He closed the suitcase and handed it to Mildred. She paced around the room feeling a bit more confident. "As before, you won't have to worry about detonating it. You will arm the device before leaving your apartment. Once you secure it in position, you will walk to the café we showed you, and make the phone call." Leon handed her a piece of paper with a number written on it. "And then we make history."

Mildred nodded with a smile; she had never been surer of herself in her whole life.

LENI

"More dolly tracks on the straightaway. I want to be able to move along the whole final stretch like I am one of the runners!" Leni yelled to the army of Hitler Youth assisting her. She was setting up Olympiastadion for the finest and most inclusive coverage of any sporting event ever filmed. And it wasn't going to end with just the stadium. She was outfitting the aquatic center with underwater fixed cameras, as well as having scuba-diving handheld cameramen sitting at the bottom of the pool or swimming upside down below the swimmers as they raced. A fixed camera would also be manned at the frontside of the pool as divers started their races. It was revolutionary coverage.

"Fraulein Riefenstahl, we will need two more handheld cameras for the field events. Is this something Herr Goebbels will acquiesce into purchasing?" her assistant Ertl inquired.

"If I tell him he must, he will. What are your thoughts?"

"I'd like to be able to have one on the action and another on the athletes warming up and following their competitors. I think we can get some good dramatic cutaways or at least have the option."

"Done. Excellent idea." Leni didn't need much of a reason to spend the Nazi coffer. Money was no object or hindrance to her when it came to *Olympia*. She had already gone over budget and the Games hadn't even begun yet. Goebbels, however, was getting quite perturbed and tried in vain to put a cork in it once already. But she just went over his head and pled to the *Führer* directly. And Hitler never said no to Leni Riefenstahl, much to Goebbels chagrin.

While Leni and Ertl spoke on the field, Carl Diem and Karl Ritter von Halt sat in the stands and went over every nuance of the Opening Ceremonies. Von Halt was a sweaty bundle of nerves and Diem found it difficult to carry on a conversation with him.

"Karl, you are losing your mind. Everything is planned down to the very second the torchbearer enters downtown Berlin. We have examined all possible situations ad nauseam."

Von Halt jumped off his bleacher seat, "This is my life we are weighing here! If anything fails, I will be to blame."

"These are my Games, Karl," Diem reminded him. "If anything goes wrong, I am to blame! So, take it easy and stop shitting yourself! If Hitler and Goebbels wanted you dead, they would've done it after Garmisch-Partenkirchen." He implored the sniveling man, "If you can't execute a simple conversation without first falling apart, then maybe you should step down. Otherwise get a hold of yourself!" Diem had had it with the Nazis and their games of fear and paranoia. He just wanted this spectacle to begin and end as soon as heavenly possible.

*   *   *

Hauptmann Wolfgang Furstner was beside himself with excitement. He was leading his boss, *Sportsführer* Hans von Tschammer und Osten around the grounds of the Olympic Village, and now he was going to show him his latest accomplishment. They walked past the dormitories down a tree-lined path.

"This better be good, Wolfgang. I'm expected back at the *Sportsreich* for a meeting with Goebbels at noon." Osten said.

"You won't be disappointed," Furstner beamed. He had been keeping it a secret until all the preparations were complete. They rounded a bend, and it was revealed: an enormous man-made lake with a dock for paddleboats and an area covered in sand for sunbathers. *The way the morning sun shined on the water was perfect,* Furstner thought. Osten was stunned.

"See that?" Furstner pointed to the far edge of the lake. "Waterfowl brought in from the Berlin Zoo!"

Osten looked at him. "Ducks and geese? That's what you came to show me?"

"Oh, it's much more than that --"

"Furstner, I came here to let you know that you are to be relieved of your duties here." Furstner was stunned, dumfounded. "Your efforts notwithstanding, I have demoted you to 'Local Vice Commander'. Effective immediately."

"What?! Wait, sir, this is absurd. I have built this place from nothing! The village they built in Los Angeles looks like an outhouse compared to what I've built! You can't do this!"

"It's the law, Wolfgang. That's all."

"But I've given my life to this country. I've got the medals to prove it!" Furstner protested.

"Your grandfather--"

"My grandfather was a devout Christian!"

"After he converted, I'm afraid."

Furstner walked to the edge of lake. "I can remove this lake. The birds, everything. We can turn it into--"

"It's not about the lake, Wolfgang." He walked next to Furstner. "Listen, there's going to be a banquet to honor your successor, Werner von Gilsa. I expect you to be there."

"Von Gilsa?!" Furstner exclaimed. "That animal?!" Furstner was stunned not only by the name of the man who would replace him, but also by the audacity of being invited to the banquet honoring his replacement. "I won't do it, Osten. You can call me Local Vice Commander, whatever that means, but I won't let someone else take credit for the years of blood and sweat I've poured into the creation of this village!"

Osten stepped back and suddenly two Nazi guards approached them, each brandishing a pistol. Furstner sighed and looked at Osten, who turned his back and walked off without a word other than muttering to himself, *"Mischling."*

Furstner stood silently for a moment, then said, "You can put your toys away. I'll gather my things."

*   *   *

Helene Mayer drove her foil directly into the heart of her sparring partner. For a moment, Helene wished the foil were a real sword so she could split her pathetic opponent in two.

"Get rid of her!" Helene roared to her coach as she threw open her mask. Her coach, whose face was buried in a clipboard, turned to a group of female fencers who were working on their form in front of a large mirror. They were all aware of what would happen next--one of them would get chosen to spar with Helene and get thoroughly humiliated.

The coach pointed to the largest female of the group. "You, *Fräulein*, you're next." The fencer took a deep breath and donned her mask. She walked over to the center of the room where Helene waited impatiently.

At the entrance of the facility, Dora Ratjen, in a white sweat suit, stood leaning against a wall quietly watching the practice session. Dora was in awe of Helene's athleticism; graceful and quick, powerful yet precise in her moves, agile and balanced like a cat. Dora always understood the athletic part of fencing, and now she was witnessing the artistry. Helene was simply great. *So is Gretel* she thought.

On the padded center of room Helene goaded her large opponent into engaging, but the woman was tentative. Finally, Helene faked left and right and stunned her opponent with a quick stab to the chest. Another victory. She walked over to the mirrored practice area and the other fencers dispersed. She tossed her mask aside and turned to her coach. "I'm wasting time. Find me a worthy sparring partner. In the meantime, I guess I'll have to fight myself," she said, striking a pose in front of the mirror with perfect form. The coach sighed and followed the other women to a

- 267 -

different part of the gym.

Dora seized the opportunity and walked over to Helene as she sparred with herself in the mirror. Helene acknowledged Dora but kept practicing.

"Pretty soon you'll be facing some real competition," Dora said.

"Did someone invite you here to interrupt my training?" Helene shot back, not taking her eyes away from the mirror.

"Why are you still on this team when Gretel has been removed?"

Helene stopped dead and turned to Dora; her foil pointed at Dora's chest. "Because I'm the greatest fencer in Germany and the best the world has ever seen."

"It's not because you are the 'token Jew' then?"

"I'm not a Jew," Helene said, returning to her place in front of the mirror, looking at herself standing side by side next to Dora.

"Your father is a Jew," Dora said.

"My father is dead."

"Then what are you?" Dora asked.

"A woman who is going to win another Gold medal for her fatherland," she said. "What exactly are you?"

*   *   *

Later that day, Hauptmann Wolfgang Furstner sat on a bench with a box of his belongings on the banks of the lake he had built at the Olympic Village campus. *It was positioned precisely for moments like this,* he thought. Sunset drew near, casting its light through the trees onto the subtle waves of the lake. He envisioned athletes from around the world, convening after a long day of competition, enjoying the camaraderie in this setting that shielded them from the outside world, if only for a few weeks. Maybe they would never appreciate such peacefulness, but Furstner was soaking in every moment of its serenity.

It was quiet except for the occasional hammering in the distance; final preparations that were no longer of his concern. The hammering sounded a bit like gunfire, he mused, and his thoughts turned to the piece of metal in his hands. It was the Iron Cross of the First Class, given to him for bravery during the Great War as a Captain of the Wehrmacht.

From his breast pocket he pulled out a folded note. He opened it and stared at the words.

Hauptmann Wolfgang Furstner, is hereby awarded the Iron Cross of the First Class for his bravery and heroism during the Great War. For his dedication to service, devotion to his countrymen, and the sacrifices made by his flesh . . .

The commendation continued but Furstner had read enough. *He did sacrifice his flesh,* he thought, as he pulled a revolver from his waistband. He looked out over the lake, raised the gun to his forehead and pulled the trigger. The geese and ducks from the Berlin Zoo scattered into the air as the gunshot echoed across the lake and the Iron Cross dropped from the palm of his hand into the dirt.

USS MANHATTAN

It was dawn over the Atlantic as Sam Stoller and Marty Glickman ran laps around the perimeter of the ship. They smiled as early bird reporters took pictures, but the two never broke stride. They were by far the proudest American athletes on the team, and they were ready to provide the ultimate "fuck you" to the ultimate super-villain. Gould watched from a deck chair sipping coffee. He could only wonder how the two young men must've felt.

"Not too much pressure on you guys, huh?" Gould joked during a break in their training.

"I don't feel pressure. From an athletic standpoint, we are by far the better team," Stoller said stretching his calves.

"It's just we are the cherry on top of the sundae. And I can't wait to see Hitler choke on that when we get the Gold medal," Glickman added.

"So, it's personal for you, Marty?" Gould pressed.

"Anyone here should take it personally. We don't want to just beat the Nazis; we want to embarrass them." Glickman said with righteous indignation.

"Just beating them is fine with me," Stoller said.

"Well not me. Hitler is going to remember my name," Glickman promised Gould. Seconds later the two athletes continued their running routine.

After a moment, Kieran joined Gould and stood beside him. He sipped his tea and looked hard at his friend. "Let's take a morning stroll around the deck."

"That sounds fine indeed," Gould said while rising from his chair. He grabbed his coffee, and they began to walk.

Kieran knew how close Gould was with Eleanor Holm Jarrett and knew whatever he was about to tell him may hurt his feelings, but he also knew it would prompt Gould to get to the real story. "So, Eleanor was a very busy bee last night after the party," Kieran began, as Gould snapped to attention. "After being led out of the party by Brundage's secretary and returning thirty minutes later full of piss and vinegar, she proceeded to drink heavily for about an hour before escaping on her own."

"And of course, you followed her?" Gould added.

"Being the professional I am, of course I did."

"And where did she sneak off to, John?"

"Charles MacArthur's suite, and she didn't leave until this morning." Kieran dropped the bomb and Gould dropped his jaw.

"Goddammit," Gould said exasperated. "This girl just doesn't know when to stop. Are you going to report it? And does anyone else know about it?"

"No and no. I was the only creep who caught wind and waited there all night. I'll leave this one for you. But I want full details off the record!"

*   *   *

Later that day Gould visited Holm in her stateroom on the Second-class deck where most of the female athletes were staying. He implored her to stay away from other men at least while she was in the spotlight. "Don't be so damned cavalier, Eleanor! The boat is swarming with press, and you go and spend the night with Helen Hayes' boyfriend?! What kind of Hollywood career do you think that will get you?!" Gould was hot, but what she told him next mortified him.

She divulged the whole story of Brundage and his attack. And didn't shy away from her more violent aspects. She began to cry. She knew this probably meant the end and she needed no more proof than the horror she read in Gould's face. "I'm the victim here, Alan!" she demanded.

Gould could do nothing but sit in a stupor. Though he knew she was the victim, she didn't look it; not a scratch on her. And because she went back to the party, then drank, then ended up in another man's bedroom, no one would believe Eleanor to be anything but a black widow who preys on middle-aged men. Gould knew she had put herself in quite the no-win situation. "Why did you have to hit him? Why couldn't you have just avoided him and run out and gotten someone? Me, anyone!"

"You're taking his side?" Eleanor asked even though she knew better.

"I would never do that. He is an animal. I know this to be true. And for you to accuse me of that hurts deeply." He rose from his chair, "Let me leave you with a few choice words of advice, Mrs.

Jarrett. Keep yourself scarce the next few days and just hope and pray this whole thing blows over. Maybe, just maybe, Brundage will be too embarrassed to say a word. But don't count on it." Gould finished, then walked out without saying goodbye.

*   *   *

A story below them, Bob Moch had his own problems. He walked down the cramped and humid hall of the Third-Class deck to the sounds of his rowing team vomiting from their staterooms. "What the hell is going on?!" he yelled.

Shorty Hunt burst from his room. "Seasickness. We got it bad," he said.

"Who does?"

"Damn near everyone except me and a few others. I grew up working on my Pa's ferry, so it don't bother me none. I think Hume's got it the worst."

"Where is he?" Moch asked.

"End of the hall."

Moch went down to where Hume was bunking with John White. He knocked once and entered the room. The two men were wrapped in blankets and looked like hell. "You guys seasick?"

"More than that," Hume said. "We just got back from the infirmary--we both got fevers."

"Okay. I want you to stay in your rooms. You need anything you let me know," Moch said. "We don't need to get the whole team sick."

Just then, Shorty Hunt barged in. "They're having casino night upstairs. Anyone in?" John White threw a pillow at him and grabbed a nearby bucket and proceeded to vomit. "I guess that's a 'no'. See you later!" Hunt said and left the room.

Moch leaned into Don Hume at his bedside. "You gonna be, okay?"

"If I die just throw me overboard," Hume said.

"Okay, but you know we can't win without you," Moch joked while thinking there couldn't be any truer statement.

*   *   *

Upstairs, Brundage's beautiful and spacious First-class stateroom dwarfed the accommodations of the athletes. But Avery could hardly move himself five feet from the bed to an office chair. The pain of Eleanor's kick was still lingering and all he wanted to do was groan and stay as still as possible in a fetal position. Paperwork piled up on his desk, mostly consisting of the documents the athletes needed to disembark in Germany.

He had been humiliated, and now he was angry, in excruciating pain, and angry. He had never been refused in such a manner, and to top it off, he was physically assaulted by a woman. *What arrogance*, he thought. With every sway of the ship, his balls ached; a reminder of Eleanor that further enraged him. He could barely concentrate on the tedious work that was staring at him.

Margaret was more than happy to help. She typed away with a big grin on her face that got wider with every one of Avery's groans. She knew he had not only failed to sleep with Eleanor but had paid quite the price. Though she could give a rat's ass about Eleanor personally, Margaret sure did appreciate the woman's athletic prowess.

*   *   *

Another type of athletic prowess was on display on the ship's bow. Glenn Morris hung half his body off the *Manhattan* and performed almost upside-down sit-ups. Reporters couldn't get enough. The 'big, thick, half-witted cowboy' was a hit with the press, and he knew how to work it. He had them eating out of his oversized hands, and was poised to become the talk of Berlin.

Two of the darlings of the previous Summer Games, Rawls and Poynton-Hill sunbathed not far from Morris' antics. The Atlantic sun was beaming down and mixed with the coolness of the ocean spray, it was a blissful setting for the two divers.

"Why white people suddenly want to look like black people?" Jesse Owens asked as he and Ralph Metcalfe sat nearby the two women.

"Black?! God forbid," Rawls joked.

"Tan is all the rage now, Buckeye," Poynton-Hill added. "One day we are all gonna be one color anyway. Plus, we don't want to be pasty white when we get to the Olympic Village. The American women need to represent. There's gonna be a lot of exotic women there."

"I can't wait to see the black female athletes from South Africa. I bet they are beautiful," Metcalfe said innocently.

Rawls looked at him confused, "You do know all the South African athletes are white, right?"

Metcalfe looked at the diver like she had just told him his dog died. But she was correct. South Africa had never allowed any black Africans to represent them. Apartheid was strong there and would soon become strict law. He and Jesse just looked at each other defeated.

"Where does it fucking end, man?" Metcalfe pondered aloud

PART IV

LET THE GAMES BEGIN

THE ARRIVAL

It was the morning of July 24, 1936, and a loud, piercing air horn blasted from the *USS Manhattan*. Eleanor Holm almost fell out of her bed. Hung over from another late night of partying and carousing, she crawled to her nightstand and checked a desk clock--she had overslept again. She took a deep breath and stretched. The drunken nights and deep slumbers had stiffened her neck. Then, from the porthole in her stateroom, she heard distant cheers and music . . . and seagulls. She ran to the porthole and peered out. The ship was about to dock in Hamburg to a waiting crowd of thousands.

Eleanor quickly grabbed her suitcase from a closet and tossed it on her bed. She tore off her silk nightgown and caught herself standing in front of the mirror completely naked. Her journey had been like a dream; such a strange and unique experience like no other time in her life. She stood and reflected for a minute; the long trip flashed in her mind in a matter of seconds. She tried to feel a sense of pride, but the feeling never came.

The sounds of the cheering crowd grew louder. She walked to the porthole naked and peered out once more. The crowd was growing larger, but the ship was moving so slowly, it seemed as if it was idling in the bay and the dock was moving towards it. Eleanor looked down at the Elbe River, anxious to get back into the one place she always felt most comfortable--the water.

At the port, the gangplank was lowered, and the Americans were welcomed in grand fashion; balloons and streamers fluttered in the wind, confetti rained down from all directions, and a brass horn band did their best American jazz interpretation. A huge banner hung above the entrance to the port. It read 'Welcome to Germany' with a large red Nazi flag on one side and an American flag on the other.

Spectators lined a roped-off area, which led to a row of buses queued up to take the American team to the Olympic Village. Jesse Owens and Ralph Metcalfe, followed by Glickman and Zamperini and the rest of the US Men's Team were herded through the chaotic parade of reporters and photographers toward the buses. Moch and his team hoisted the *Husky Clipper* over their heads and pushed through the throng of people. The women, led by the young, confident Marjorie Gestring were in awe of the welcoming party.

Already on a bus, Eleanor Holm stared out the window from her seat in the back row. The boisterous and excited group of athletes began boarding. She shifted her seat to accommodate a fellow athlete, and then stared back out the window at the *USS Manhattan*. She swore she could see the porthole of her stateroom. This prompted a strange sensation that she had left something behind. She couldn't put her finger on what, but the feeling would not leave her.

Outside, surveying the operation of the athletes boarding their buses, Margaret stood nearby with a clipboard, checking off boxes. Everything seemed to be in order. Just then, Ritter von Halt approached them. "Avery, my friend! You're finally here," he said. "For a minute I thought you turned around and went back to America." They shook hands.

"You know that would never happen!" Avery was beaming.

"Let me be the first German to congratulate you on your International Olympic Committee membership. It's been too long."

"Thank you. I look forward to working with you," Avery replied.

"Then let's get this thing started!" Von Halt said and gestured to a waiting black stretch limousine adorned with little Nazi flags. Brundage smiled as he and Margaret followed von Halt into the lavish vehicle.

*   *   *

A bird's eye view of the main boulevard in The Olympic Village revealed a bustling thoroughfare of people. The finest athletes from around the globe teemed in and out of view; others gathered in groups, meeting for the first time, and others helped themselves to the copious amounts of German food and drink being served from vendors manning their carts.

A camera attached to a tall crane boomed down just above the crowds. Leni Riefenstahl sat in a chair next to the camera and directed the shot. Ertl and two assistants maneuvered the crane.

"Swing me to the right and slightly forward, Ertl!" Leni screamed down at them.

Glickman and Stoller were speaking to a few of the Czechoslovakian Jewish athletes. The Czechs showed them some flyers featuring photomontages from John Heartfield who had indeed fled Germany and landed in Prague. The two Americans were shocked at the audacity of the satire. The flyer had Nazi athletes competing in Olympic Games that were all war related, and racist and violent at that.

Riefenstahl quickly panned the camera away. She then caught Jesse Owens speaking with his German rival in the long jump, Luz Long. The two seemed to discuss their sport with animated enthusiasm. This pleased Leni very much. She planned on paying close attention to their event while shooting the Games.

Close to Owens was John Woodruff who towered over a group of Chinese athletes. Woodruff had never seen a real-life full-blooded Asian prior to this. He was from Connellsville, Penn., the heartland of coal, coke, and steel production. Not many Asians around those parts. And most of the Chinese athletes had never seen an African American, let alone a 6' 4" one. Both sides marveled at each other.

Leni then began roaming the crowd with her camera and

stopped dead on an American Adonis who was staring right back up at her. He had a grin that conveyed definite animalistic intentions. Leni's heart stopped. She had never seen such a perfect specimen of a man. She zoomed in for a close-up and when Glenn Morris licked his lips provocatively, she gasped audibly. He smiled, threw her a kiss, and was out of sight in an instant.

"You okay up there, Fräulein Riefenstahl?" Ertl asked, concerned.

"I'm fine!" She yelled down at the men. She had, however, just experienced the miracle lightning bolt of love at first sight, and she felt both woozy and nauseous, but she was fine.

Beyond Leni's frame, Louis Zamperini searched and found the German female dorms. He was looking for Mayer but none of the other athletes or coaches he asked seemed to know where she was. He then approached an odd-looking athlete he could've easily mistaken as a young man.

"Excuse me . . . Fräulein?" He began, not too sure how to address the person. "I'm looking for Helene Mayer," he said loudly in complete English.

Dora Ratjen looked at him blankly. She didn't speak a word of English. She understood he said something about Mayer but everything else was indecipherable. She stood there and just stared back at him. After a few seconds of very uncomfortable silence, Louis gave up and slowly backed away with a grin and a nod.

Men and women from the German track team surrounded Archie Williams and led him to a table outside a small biergarten that had been setup off the main thoroughfare. They also had never been this close to an African American and Williams was sculptured, good-looking, and gregarious. The Germans couldn't get enough. They seated him at the front of the table and ordered copious amounts of black beer, pretzels, and schnitzel sandwiches. Williams was floored at the hospitality. He had never in his life experienced white people being so friendly to him, and for it to come from the Nazis! This is not what he was told to expect. What he quickly started to realize though, was that these young people weren't much different than he was. They were student athletes who wanted to succeed but have a good time doing it. Politics wasn't really their concern, especially now that the Games were days away. So, Archie Williams, a black American from a very poor area of Oakland, dropped all his preconceptions and partied with a table of happy and non-judgmental white folks and all on Hitler's tab.

Eleanor Holm, on the other hand, wasn't so happy and walked with her swim coach through the crowd. She had been summoned to the American Olympic Committee offices. And she knew it wasn't going to be pretty.

"I'm excusing you from the Games, Ms. Holm, because of your behavior aboard the *Manhattan*. Here are your papers to return to Hamburg and board the next ship home." Brundage coldly dropped the documents in front of her on his desk. Holm's coach was shocked.

"What are you doing, Avery? She's the favorite in her race," the coach shot back.

"Nevertheless, you will not be participating, Ms. Holm," he responded.

Holm smiled, which took Brundage by surprise. "I must have gotten you pretty good, huh Brundage? My behavior was nothing compared to your attempted rape."

"WHAT?" her coach asked defiantly.

Brundage ignored her and kept addressing Holm, "Well, you have your story and I have mine. But I also have power and you don't, so what I say goes. You're out."

Eleanor approached Brundage with an intense hatred and he immediately cowered. She laughed at him. "You are the most pathetic man I've ever had the misfortune to come across, Avery.

And yet, knowing how badly you want me gives me the ultimate satisfaction. I'm not going anywhere. You can remove me from the team but I'm not going anywhere."

"You are not welcome to stay in the American facility, so I'm not sure what you think you are going to do for lodging."

Again, she smiled and again Brundage became uncomfortable. "I've never had a problem finding a place to rest my head, Avery. But you can rest assured you are going to have to deal with me." She faked kneeing him, which sent him to the floor by reflex. She laughed as she grabbed her papers and her coach and walked out his office door.

*   *   *

Later that day Eleanor sat on Gould's bed in his hotel room and cried her eyes out. Gould was livid at Brundage but knew there was not much he could do. With the way she had acted on the ship, any report he would submit of abuse by Brundage would smear Eleanor just as much, and probably end her marriage. It was a very unfortunate conundrum. Gould knew he was powerless to change Brundage's mind, but he did have an idea.

"You will stay in Berlin and work for me. You can report on all the aquatic events. Having an actual athlete as a reporter might be a good thing. You can see things from a different perspective. I'm not sure that has ever been done before actually," he pondered. "Anyway, how's that sound?"

Eleanor jumped up into Gould's arms, "That would be swell, Alan! That really sounds like a great opportunity. And Brundage can't say a thing?"

"I'll push AP press credentials through for you today and we will put you up here at the hotel. Brundage can't stop the free press, Eleanor. He can try to obfuscate it, but he isn't going to stop it." He looked at her hard. "It's going to be work though. And I expect you to be professional and do your job in that manner."

"I promise," she said with absolute honesty.

*   *   *

The sky was crystal clear on the night before the Opening Ceremonies and the streets surrounding the stadium were deadly quiet. Jesse Owens crept past sleeping guards in a booth and entered *Olympiastadion.* He wanted to see the arena unencumbered by the noise of the parades, the rituals and fanfare that would accompany the team's arrival for the Opening Ceremonies. Under the stars in the crisp air, he looked around in awe at the sheer size of the arena. Then he imagined himself running around the track. He slowly fell into a focused trance.

"How'd you get in here?!" A voice boomed from an upper level. Jesse gasped and looked around until he saw a figure sitting in the stands. It was Coach Robertson, who laughed at Jesse's reaction. "What are you doing here?" Robertson asked.

"Butterflies kept me up."

"Me too," Robertson replied. He walked down from the stands and climbed over the railing to enter the field.

"Never had the butterflies like this before," Jesse said.

"That means you care. I'd be worried if you *didn't* have butterflies," Robertson said, laughing.

Jesse looked around the stadium. "Didn't think it would be this big."

"Now you know," the coach said, and put his arm around Jesse. "How about we both get some rest before this whole thing gets started." They both stood for a last look at the vast arena and the bright stars, then walked silently towards the entrance.

THE OPENING CEREMONIES

On the morning of the Opening Ceremonies, August 1, 1936, there was a buzz throughout the halls of the Reichskanzler, but it was quiet inside Hitler's office. He stood solemnly as two male valets dressed him in his full military uniform. They tightened his tie, which complimented his newly pressed shirt, placed his jacket on, and pinned on his Iron Cross. All he could think about, however, was the choreography Goebbels had laid out for him once he entered the stadium. Walk here, then there, then this way to a different location; address this person, then that one, and take great care not to offend the Americans, or Japanese, or the Italians. *Fuck the Italians*, he thought. *Fuck them all, but especially the Italians.* Hitler felt the way they flip-flopped sides in the Great War was disgraceful. They weren't to be trusted. Even though Mussolini was his closest ally, Hitler didn't really trust him. Hitler would have to bite right through his tongue, as not to offend the Guinea buffoons he would be forced to address at the stadium. He would need Morrell to calm his demeanor. Only the good doctor could prescribe the right medication that would help him through the day without a meltdown.

And what a day it would be. Berlin, the capital of Germany, *his* Germany, in all its glory for the world to see. Everything had come together as planned. As he looked in the mirror, he was glad he let Goebbels convince him to host an Olympic Games. It was the perfect opportunity to celebrate the virtues of their reborn state while showing off their physical prowess--perfectly aligned with their ideology of youth, fitness, and strength.

The two valets finished dressing him and stepped back from the wall-sized mirror. Hitler couldn't suppress his smile at the thought of his German athletes completely dominating their opponents from all over the world.

In a different room, Eva was preparing for her big moment. She looked at herself in her full-length mirror as her trusted maids dressed her in a traditional German *dirndl*. She had fasted for a week to fit into the size she wanted to be for the ceremony and her body looked fabulous. This was the day she would finally be revealed as the First Lady of Germany.

"Eleanor Roosevelt doesn't have shit on me," she said aloud wearing nothing but high stockings and lace underwear. She then turned to one of her maids, "Maybe one of you should get Doctor Morrell. I need to settle my butterflies."

*   *   *

On a bus that was headed to *Olympiastadion*, it was standing room only in the center aisle. Mildred was wedged between two tall, fat German teenagers. The bus was packed to the hilt, and *it smelled like sausage,* she thought, trying to keep her nose away from the armpit of the teenager. She clutched her bag like a swaddled infant. It was the bag that held the bomb. She wondered what would happen if it accidentally detonated at this moment. Burning flesh flying in all directions; arms, legs, heads falling from the sky in front of pedestrians screaming in the streets . . .

"*Flatowallee Straße!*" a voice bellowed from the front of the bus, snapping her out of the daydream. She was jostled about as the crowd exited the bus and poured out onto *Flatowallee*. The street led to the entrance of the Stadium and people were lining up by the thousands. Mildred stepped off the bus and weaved her way through the crowd and found a side street where she stopped to catch her breath. She put the bag down, pulled out a piece of paper from her coat and read an address. She scanned the area for street signs then took a deep breath and continued down the side street passing others who were headed for the stadium.

Inside a dark apartment building, Mildred climbed a set of stairs. She could hear the commotion outside as she made her way down a corridor. She pulled out a key and opened the door to a small, tidy room with no windows. She placed her bag on the bed and opened it. Inside was the bomb--the bomb that would send Hitler and his cronies to meet their makers. She studied the device and tried to remember what do to next. *Right, arm the bomb.* She flipped one switch, then another. The bomb clicked and whirred and made a low, faint humming sound. She closed her bag and unfolded a blueprint of the stadium. As she studied the map, she caught a glimpse of herself in the mirror and realized she had been smiling the whole time.

*   *   *

Back at the Reichskanzler, Dr. Morrell carefully concocted a potion befitting of his employers' pending event. He mixed a little of this, a dash of that, and as always, a spoonful of heroin to finish off the cocktail. He then filled the slightly brownish liquid in an eyedropper, sealed it, and headed toward the *Führer*'s bedroom where Hitler and Eva waited, none too patiently.

"What the fuck takes you so long, Herr Morrell?" Hitler snapped.

"Trust me, *Mein Führer*. It takes time to make magic happen." He said with a grin and then tilted Eva's head back and prepared her for the drops. "Open up and don't blink or move your head right away. Let the liquid envelope your whole eye and seep into your brain. Believe me, the two of you will feel nothing but joy today." He drugged them both and waited the few seconds he knew it would take to kick into effect.

"*Wunderbar* Doctor," Eva slurred. "You are truly a magician."

"In a half hour you both will be smiling, entering the stadium in glorious fashion, and not having a worry in the world," the good doctor assured them.

"Will I be able to carry on a damned conversation though?"

Hitler wondered.

*   *   *

A few hours later down on *Flatowallee Straße*, German citizens stood shoulder-to-shoulder, one hundred deep, waving little Nazi flags in the air, chanting and cheering. Nazi soldiers, neatly uniformed, stood on every street corner. Towering over the throng of Germans were government buildings covered with humungous banners bearing swastikas. It was a sea of red, white, and black.

The most excited people among them were the young and the middle-aged. There were very few elderlies, and those who were there participated with less enthusiasm. But this wasn't their Germany. This was the new Germany.

Suddenly, the crowd started to notice something down the street. Children squeezed through their parents' legs to get a better look. It was a wave of outstretched necks and people jostling to get a better position. Some were pointing as the cheering got louder, more excited. And then it came.

A blond-haired, blue-eyed young man adorned in a modified Greek toga, complete with a crown made of twigs and fig leaves, jogged steadily through the streets of Berlin carrying a ceremonial torch. The flames rose and fell with each step of the runner. As he ran past the adoring crowd, they cheered him on, yelling epithets for their beloved Germany. The runner endowed every embodiment of the Aryan race--a perfect specimen of the Third Reich.

Some of the crowd stood out more than others. They were not waving Nazi flags or cheering or chanting. They were Germany's Jews who had come to see the spectacle, but there was a serious tone about them. They were less interested in the runner than they were with the nationalistic tone of the crowd that surrounded them. As the chanting grew more fevered, they disappeared away from the masses.

The largest crowds were assembled near the entrance of the Romanesque *Olympiastadion*. It was a colossal construct decorated with flags of every participating country, although the Nazi flags were, by far, the largest and flew the highest. This was a crowning achievement for the increasingly wealthy German government. An enormous zeppelin flew overhead, bearing a large swastika on its tail.

As the torch-wielding runner made his way past the spectators and into the entrance of the stadium, Mildred watched as she stood in line with other ticket holders at one of the entrance gates. She checked her watch, not wanting to be late, then realized she had plenty of time. The Opening Ceremonies would last hours; more than enough time to plant the bomb.

She handed her ticket to an older gentleman wearing a uniform. He was about to punch the ticket but paused and looked at her. *I'm alone. What woman attends an event like this without an escort?* She thought. Maybe she should've entered with Mattie, but no, she had done what she was instructed to do. Better to leave her friend out of it; she probably knew too much already.

"All alone, *Fraulein*?" The gentleman asked.

"No. I'm surrounded by my friends as you can see." Mildred winked at the man, and he smiled back.

"Very well. Enjoy." He punched Mildred's ticket, and she walked through the gate.

As the crowd navigated towards their various sections, she thought it was a good idea to blend in with them and check to see if she had been followed. She stopped at a water fountain and gulped for what seemed like minutes. Her nerves left her parched, and she wondered if the athletes felt this way before a race, a dive, or some other main event.

Satisfied that she was not being followed, she focused her attention to her memory of the blueprints she studied with

Vladimir and Leon. The entrance of the stadium faced east. That meant Hitler would be seated one section below the press boxes, mid-field along the southern length of the arena. She scanned the area and saw the corridor that led underneath the seating sections. Vladimir said there wouldn't be anyone guarding it. "All of the guards will be escorting Herr Hitler as he makes his way into the stadium. That's where they think the most danger will be. You should be free to go where you please," Vladimir said.

The German Olympic Team enters the stadium at the Opening Ceremonies of the XI Olympiad in Berlin, Germany.

He was wrong. Two armed guards stood by the open canal that led beneath the stands. Mildred didn't see any way around them. She started to feel her nerves rising. She wondered if she looked nervous. *Stop being paranoid,* she told herself. Then, she heard a commotion coming from the entrance; some cheering, and shouting, accompanied by drums and trumpets blaring. An excited father and son turned and started walking towards the noise. "Herr Hitler must be coming! Let's go see!" The father shouted and grabbed his son's hand. Mildred looked back at the entrance to the corridor--the guards had left. She knew this was her chance and she took it, walking towards the open canal without hesitation, clutching her bag tightly. She had made it inside the guts of the immense complex.

At the far entrance of the stadium, Hitler and Goebbels, Diem, von Halt, Osten and Latour, and a few of Hitler's main generals and bodyguards got in position to enter the festivities. Eva Braun, accompanied by two young German girls dressed in Bavarian outfits, was forced to walk twenty feet behind the men. Eva was crushed. Hitler had no intention of introducing her to the German people. To make matters worse, Goebbels had convinced the Führer to send Eva to Berchtesgaden for the remainder of the Games.

"The Führer cannot be encumbered by any outside disturbances during these next two weeks," he demanded.

"You can try to hide me all you want, but I'll always be with him," she said to Goebbels.

Goebbels smiled and said, "Of course you will." He would make sure that Eva was ushered straight out of Hitler's private box once he gave his opening speech. She would not even be able to stay and attend the first day's athletic events.

When the time came for the group to enter the field, Hitler walked forward with great pride. The crowd went insane as their beloved leader strode toward a young girl walking toward him carrying flowers. He smiled as 100,000 plus people chanted 'Heil Hitler'. When the young girl got to him, she began to lift her arm to give him a Nazi salute. But Hitler would have none of that. He stopped her in mid motion. Somehow, he felt embarrassed by this, whether it was the drugs or just plain modesty, he couldn't stomach seeing it. He leaned down, and accepted the flowers and a brief hug and then continued his way to his seat with Goebbels close behind him.

Brundage was already at his seat waiting for his German friends in Hitler's box. He felt so proud this day had finally arrived and he had personally guided the US team here over such adversity. When the entourage finally arrived, Brundage shook the hands of Osten, von Halt, Latour, and Carl Diem. Von Halt then introduced him to Hitler and an extremely unimpressed Goebbels. But Brundage didn't notice the Propaganda Minister's disgust; he was meeting the greatest leader of the times. Hitler was to Brundage a modern-day Caesar, a leader who had guided his country from the brink of devastation to a modern, thriving, and global powerhouse. He shivered at the man's mere presence.

"Not too shabby, huh Avery?" Von Halt noticed his friend's starry eyes.

"Not too shabby at all," Brundage replied looking around the stadium and up at the Hindenburg floating overhead.

Down on the field, the famous composer Richard Strauss raised his hands and cued up the Berlin Philharmonic Orchestra and a chorus of one thousand singers all dressed in white. They commenced with Strauss' *Olympische Hymne*, written especially for these Games. It was Theodor Lewald who convinced the IOC to allow Germany its own Olympic anthem for the Berlin Games, as the hymn played in Los Angeles in 1932 was supposed to be the official Olympic anthem for all time. The music filled the stadium and every German spectator beamed with pride. Carl Diem looked over at the row where the International Olympic Committee members sat and found Theodor Lewald staring blankly at the floor, emotionless. Carl thought it was odd and made a mental note to seek out Theodor after the event. In the meantime, Carl would enjoy the pageantry. The "parade of nations" had begun.

The Greek team entered first, commemorating the birthplace of the original Olympics. They all saluted Hitler with their arms outstretched as they passed his box in the center of the stadium. He proudly returned the salute. The teams followed in alphabetical order, each donning a unique uniform; *Afghanistan, Argentina, Australia, Austria, Belgium* . . .

From a tunnel near the entrance to the field, the American team watched as each country's athletes gave the Nazi salute to Hitler. In another show of subservience, the flag bearers at the head of each team lowered their flags in deference to Germany. The Americans couldn't believe it.

Egypt, Finland, France . . .

Leni Riefenstahl leaned on Ertl's shoulder, watching intensely. His camera's motor spun relentlessly, capturing everything in a wide shot from their position in the stands. The cheering crowd, the music, the flags, the *Hindenburg* flying overhead - it was all coming together for Leni. She raised her binoculars to inspect various camera positions around the stadium. Her team was shooting every detail of the ceremony.

Poland, Sweden, Switzerland . . .

Next it was the United States' turn. As they passed Hitler's box, the athletes did not give him the Nazi salute. Instead, they held their hands over their hearts with flagrant disobedience. Hitler's eyes narrowed as he tried to maintain a dignified posture. What made things worse for him was that the American flag was not lowered--instead it was raised proudly, even a little bit higher than when they entered the stadium. Hitler turned with a forced, menacing smile at Brundage, who quickly turned away and nudged von Halt. "Army regulations," Brundage said, fumbling to hide his embarrassment. Von Halt gestured as if to say, *drop it.* The crowd's cheers lowered into hushed tones and murmurs at the American's show of defiance. Jesse Owens, Glickman, Gestring, Glenn Morris, Zamperini and 379 other proud American athletes stood tall as they honored their country.

Finally, the German team entered the stadium last as the host of the Games, and the crowd resumed cheering wildly as they saluted their Führer. After all of the fifty-three nations settled into their places in the center of the stadium, Strauss conducted his orchestra, and they held a single, sustained note. The crowd stood in anticipation.

A bell rang and the orchestra launched into its Olympic Hymn as the torch-wielding runner burst through the opening gates and entered the arena. The one hundred thousand spectators erupted in applause. He circled the track towards the far end of the stadium and climbed a canopy of stairs to a giant raised cylinder, which was the Olympic torch. He reached up and tipped his torch into it to ignite it, sending the crowd into a frenzy. In unison, they gave the Nazi salute with a hearty "*Heil Hitler.*"

At a podium near Hitler's box, Carl Diem walked to the microphone to address the crowd. "Ladies and gentlemen, as Secretary General of the Organizing Committee of these games, I am proud to introduce an athlete to recite the Olympic oath. The 1932 Olympic Gold medalist in Weightlifting, your very own . . . Rudolf Ismayr!" The crowd went berserk as the blond, hulking champion took center stage. It was the first time in Olympic history for an athlete to recite the oath.

"We swear . . . we will take part in the Olympic Games in a spirit of chivalry, for the honor of our country and for the glory of sport." Ismayr gave the Heil Hitler salute and waved to the crowd. Carl shook his hand and walked to the podium.

"And now, please rise and welcome the Chancellor of Germany, Adolf Hitler."

It was now Hitler's moment to open the Games. And though he was a man of many words most of the time, on this occasion he would keep it short and sweet. Morrell's eye drops had left him somewhat skittish, so he didn't want to chance sounding moronic.

"I proclaim the Olympic Games of Berlin, celebrating the

Eleventh Olympiad of the modern era, to be open!" He said into the microphones and newsreel cameras, as well as cameras from the new communication medium, television, which would be broadcasting the Games to specific locations in and around Berlin and other cities in Germany. Hitler's speech was concise but to the point. The crowd was thunderous, and Hitler smiled and waved before taking his front row seat.

The sounds of Hitler's speech echoed throughout the stadium. To Mildred, it sounded like she was underwater. She had carefully and inconspicuously walked to the end of the stadium underneath the stands. The bowels of the construct were surprisingly empty. Only once, a maintenance crew passed her and nodded politely. Counting the seating sections above her, she walked back, exactly halfway to where Hitler should be sitting. When she felt the vibrations of his booming voice, she knew she was in the right place.

She checked her surroundings once more to make sure she was alone. *Stay calm.* She opened her bag and carefully cradled the explosive device. Remembering the blueprints, she reached above her head and felt for a shelf-like trough that supposedly ran along each row of seating. She found it, not as wide as she expected, but wide enough to seat the bomb. She placed it ever so gently and held it for a moment, feeling its vibrations.

As she lifted her hands and closed her bag, she felt a presence. A shadow of footprints. She slowly looked up and her heart stopped beating. A large man stood before her, smiling.

It was Putzi.

Outside, Strauss' *Olympische Hymne* rose to a crescendo as the Olympic flag was raised at the top of the stadium. On cue, rows and rows of wooden boxes released 25,000 pigeons into the air. The crowd gasped in awe at the majestic sight as the birds flew in a tight circle above the center of the stadium. To put an exclamation mark on the ceremony, a large canon fired into the sky with a thunderous BOOM!

On the ground, the athletes all looked up at the spectacle. Zamperini searched the rows of athletes, and then caught the eye of Helene Mayer as she stood with her fellow German teammates. They smiled at each other soaking in the wonderful moment--that was until Helene suddenly looked down at her uniform. Something had hit her in the chest. Then, all around him, Zamperini noticed the pattering sounds of wet droppings coming from above. It started small, then athletes started wiping their arms and shoulders frantically, looking up at the sky. The pigeons, frightened by the canon blast, were shitting uncontrollably all over them. Female athletes covered their heads as white blobs smeared their hair and uniforms. Some ran under their country's flags for cover. A cymbal player in the orchestra looked up and was greeted by a flying turd to the face. Zamperini looked around and all he could do was laugh. He looked at Glenn Morris, who was also laughing as he wiped his head clean. Jesse Owens stood still, shaking his head in disbelief, as a literal shitstorm rained down on them.

It lasted but a moment in time and went unnoticed to von Halt, Osten, Brundage, Carl Diem, and the thousands of Germans in the stands. Hitler folded his arms and beamed with pride.

The Opening Ceremony was a colossal success.

DAY 1
August 2, 1936

With the pageantry, and bird shit, of the Opening Ceremonies cleared, the first day of competition had finally arrived. Radio reporters from around the world gathered in the sprawling press box for the first day of the XI Olympiad. There were notebooks and typewriters everywhere, telephones, a water cooler, and a giant coffee machine in the back of the room. Almost everyone was smoking; cigarette and cigar smoke billowed out of the press box into the open air facing the field. In one corner, an argument broke out between the Egyptian and Polish reporters. In another, the French reporters stacked their cigarettes and matchboxes in preparation. Off to the side, the Japanese reporters were stretching and doing calisthenics.

Gould turned to Kieran. "I should've brought my track shoes."

"You should have." Kieran lifted his leg and planted his foot on the desk. He *was* wearing track shoes.

"Good Lord, man!" Gould said, laughing.

"I think we can take 'em," Kieran replied confidently.

Gould looked around the room, smiling. He had covered big events over the years, but never anything like this. What was most unusual were the TV cameras stationed on the level above them in the radio booth. German reporters were addressing their audience live in front of the cameras.

"We are gazing upon the future of sports, my good friend," Kieran prognosticated.

Gould smirked, "God help us all. It'll become a carnival."

"Pen and paper will become as obsolete as dinosaurs and the Weimar Republic," Kieran quipped back. "That camera is going to lead to the eventual destruction of mankind as we know it."

"Just imagine what Herr Goebbels and his kind will be able to do with it," Gould added.

*   *   *

Hitler sat in his booth surrounded by Goebbels, Osten, von Halt, Diem, Latour and Goering, who, squeezed into his tight uniform, was sweating profusely. They watched the action on the field, in particular the women's javelin and the men's shotput. Both were being dominated by the Germans.

"Why is Fräulein Riefenstahl focusing solely on the 100-meter heats? How much footage of that American monkey Owens could she possibly need?" Goebbels noticed.

Brundage, also in the box and sitting next to von Halt, overheard the Propaganda Minister's statement and chuckled, "That monkey sure can run though, Herr Goebbels." Hitler and Goebbels both gave him a belittling sneer.

On the field, the 4 x 100 relay team of Marty Glickman, Sam Stoller, Foy Draper, and Frank Wyckoff watched Jesse Owens prepare for his first 100m heat. Jesse was wearing a hooded sweatshirt and was stretching his neck and bouncing on his toes.

"He looks like a prizefighter in that robe," Draper said.

"He looks a bit nervous to me," Stoller responded.

"He's never raced in front of a crowd like this. Neither have we. It's normal to have some butterflies," Marty said.

Wyckoff laughed. "Three strides in, those butterflies will disappear. Watch."

Jesse and the other competitors took to their starting spots. The gun went off and the sprinters exploded from their blocks. Sure enough, after a few lightning quick strides, Jesse separated from the pack. The race was over well before he crossed the finish line. Like the rest of those in attendance, the relay team was amazed by

Owen's speed and power.

Stoller turned to Glickman and said, "You think you could take him, Marty?"

"I don't know, I really don't. But I'd love to get out there and give it a shot," Marty said, shaking his head.

Foy Draper chimed in. "Don't even dream about it--did you see what I just saw? He's gonna sweep every event."

"Yeah, but can he handle a baton?" Sam Stoller said, mimicking the relay maneuver. "The 'four-by' is when we'll get to show our stuff." They all nodded in agreement, then Foy and Marty slapped hands with Sam. When they dispersed, Marty looked out onto the track like a hungry lion waiting to pounce on its prey.

Across the field, Riefenstahl was ecstatic. The finals of the 100m were shaping up to be exactly what she had hoped. Owens' next race would be against the German champion, Borchmeyer. Leni knew any event that pitted Germany against America would captivate audiences on both sides of the Atlantic. She scoured the field in search of her next position, but Ertl would take care of that within minutes.

For a man who didn't really care too much about sport, nor ever participate as a youth, Ertl was having the time of his life shooting the event. Action was happening all around him and he couldn't get enough. He found himself beginning to root for certain athletes, like the American Helen Stephens, who was as tall as the goddess *Rindr* but ran like *Baduhenna* in battle, and the German Hans Woellke, who could heave a heavy metal ball like a thunderbolt from the hand of *Thor*. He didn't know anything about either athlete or their varied disciplines, but somehow now he wanted to, and on top of that his heart raced when he watched them. *What was this feeling,* he wondered? This was usually only a sensation he experienced when reading about Nordic or German gods at war. Could it be he was becoming a sports fanatic? Is this what his friends felt when they were watching Dortmund play

Fußball? Ertl was all giddy. He quickly summoned Leni and began setting up his camera to capture the final of the men's shot-put competition.

*   *   *

While the shotput final was gearing up, the Men's High Jump was well underway across the field. Gretel and Dora, wearing special lanyards that gave them field credentials, stood behind the German team, and studied the techniques of the American high jumpers. Cornelius "Corny" Johnson was leading and was clearly the best athlete of the competition.

"The way he lifts off the ground is so graceful for a man, don't you think?" Gretel said.

"Graceful . . . like a woman, you mean?" Dora responded. "Anyone can be graceful, Gretel."

"This is true," Gretel said, and put her arm around Dora.

"Come, on Gustav!!" Dora suddenly bellowed as the German competitor, Gustav Weinkötz nervously prepared for his final jump. Gretel and Dora clenched their fists, hopeful, as Gustav began. He loped forward, lifted off, and at the height of his jump, his right foot caught the bar, knocking it completely off its hinges. He was disqualified. A collective groan filled the air of the stadium. Dora took notice of the crowd's reaction. The Americans had swept the Men's High Jump with "Corny" Johnson leading the way.

Watching from his box, Hitler turned to Goebbels, "What the hell is going on? Did we supply them with lead track shoes?"

"Cornelius Johnson . . . another monkey. They're used to climbing trees, jumping from limb to limb," Goebbels said. "Our athletes are strong, powerful! Never mind this nonsense. Watch what happens in a real event!"

Hitler nodded, hopeful that his German athletes would put on

- 298 -

a show as the shotput finals were taking place. Woellke didn't disappoint the Führer as he heaved the iron sphere in record-breaking fashion, taking Gold. His teammate, Gerhard Stöck took Bronze. Hitler beamed with pride. Goebbels, Osten, von Halt, Diem, Latour, and Goering all congratulated themselves. Even Avery Brundage was celebrating. After all, now he was part of the International Olympic Committee. He was one of them.

It was a fine ending to Day 1 of the Games. There was cheering, singing, and chanting from the crowd. The athletes had put on a fine display and Germany won the most medals of any country, despite the Americans winning the High Jump. And Leni and Ertl captured it all.

*   *   *

Later that afternoon, Carl Diem walked down the street towards Theodor Lewald's place wondering what was wrong with his old friend after witnessing his behavior at the Opening Ceremony. Theodor was largely responsible for its planning and execution, and it all resulted in a spectacular event, exceeding expectations by all accounts. But Theodor acted as if it meant nothing.

He rang the doorbell, and it was Theodor's wife Elisabeth who answered. Without a word, she opened the door and motioned for Carl to enter. At the kitchen table he found Theodor sipping a glass of schnapps.

"Theodor. I was wondering where you've been. Room for two?" Carl asked, sitting himself down at the table. He grabbed the bottle and helped himself to a glass of the sweet liqueur. "I didn't see you today, and after seeing you yesterday I thought you'd gone ill. Are you okay?"

"I'm fine."

"Wasn't it magnificent!? Strauss and his orchestra were the

highlight, I'd say."

"Ceremony, Carl. It was all a ceremony. A big show, that's all it was. Like everything else around here. A big show."

"You were a big part of that show, Theodor. You still are part of everything. You're still an official member of the IOC."

"I'm an advisor, that's all. It's your show now . . . until it's not."

"What do you mean?" Carl asked.

"Because right now I'm only a member of the IOC because technically only two of my four grandparents are Jews. How long do you think you 'white Jews' have?"

"White Jew? That's what they're calling me now? Because I'm married to a Jew?"

"That's right," Theodor said.

Carl stood up and slugged down his schnapps. "I have a duty, Theodor, and so do you. I'm going to fulfill that civic duty with pride, and I wish you would do the same. The law says that I'm a German citizen and nothing less." He walked out of the kitchen and headed for the door. "Hope to see you there tomorrow."

"Laws change quickly around here, Carl. Remember that." Theodor called out as Elisabeth showed Carl to the door. Neither of them said another word.

DAY 2
August 3, 1936

Though the big event of the day, the Men's 100m Final, would happen a little later, the women of the 100m took the stage with their opening heats just after the men concluded their 100m semis. It was Helen Stephens' time to put up or shut up. She had talked a big game on the *Manhattan* and with 100,000 people in the stands watching, and both the Men's and Women's American Track Team making sure she backed up her words, including Owens who had just won his semi-final, Helen needed to start strong. She did just that. She took a big lead as soon as the gun blasted and never gave it up. 'The Fulton Flash' decimated her opponents with the closest runner finishing almost a full second behind. Helen entered the semis later that day as the favorite to make the finals. Her streak was still intact. She had never in her life lost a race. Never.

Up in the stands not far from the field, Martha Dodd watched in admiration as Helen stomped the rest of the pack. The other runners seemed to run in slow motion compared to Helen. Martha thought the woman was half gazelle the way she ran so gracefully but with such speed. She would have to meet this Missouri phenom. She turned to her brother, Bill who was munching on hard pretzels. "What's next?"

"Let me check." He leafed through his program. "Whatever it is, I gotta split right afterwards. I gotta meet Dad at *Poststadion*." He found the list of the day's events, "Oh, good! Next up, we will learn if Jesse Owens wins his first Gold," Bill said excitedly. "Keep your eye on the Führer." They looked over at Hitler's Box where he and all his stooges sat, including Brundage. "If Borchmeyer doesn't win, place, or show, the little troll may put him out of his misery and shoot him," he joked.

*   *   *

The length of the track was cleared for the Men's Final of the 100m. Hitler sat next to Goebbels and Goering in his box, and they settled in to watch one of the most renowned events of the Games. The winner would not only win Gold but be deemed "the fastest man alive." The drama would take place right in front of them and Hitler was jittery with excitement.

In the front row of the stands, Leni and Ertl were stationed in a perfect position to capture the race. Ertl checked his focus and his tripod mount, making sure everything was completely in order. He gave Leni the thumbs up. She nodded and looked up towards Hitler's box and through her binoculars saw that her team was in place to capture his reaction to the race.

On the track, the runners walked to their places. Jesse Owens looked over at Ralph Metcalfe and Frank Wykoff and the three of them shared a confident nod. Jesse calmly walked to his place at the row of starting blocks. He glanced at the German speedster, Erich Borchmeyer, who smiled at him then waved to the adoring crowd. Jesse would look at nobody else until he crossed the finish line.

He planted his feet into the chunks of wood, one after the other, his belly full of butterflies. It reminded him of what his Ohio State coach Larry Snyder used to say. "Let those butterflies be like the engine of a car that rumbles before that light turns green--don't be completely still."

With the six runners in place, Jesse looked up at the length of track with a singular focus. The starter's gun blasted, and the runners exploded from their blocks. Borchmeyer had the lead for about a half a second before Jesse took over, quickly distancing himself from the field.

Leni glanced up at Hitler's box and the surrounding crowd and was ecstatic. Ertl kept his camera trained on Jesse. In the press box, Gould and Kieran stood up from their seats to get a better glimpse at the greatness unfolding before their eyes. Hitler rocked back and forth in his seat, urging on the German sprinter. But it was no use--Jesse Owens' speed and grace, his power and rhythm, put him ahead of the competition by a wide margin. He won easily, setting a world record that would not be broken for an astounding twenty years. The press box erupted in cheers as Gould and Kieran jumped up and down, arms raised.

Martha and Bill jumped up and down with the thousands of others in the stands. They waved small American flags and hugged any other American fan that was close by them.

Jesse wound down into a slow jog and turned around to find that his teammate and friend, Ralph Metcalfe, had come in a close second place to capture the Silver medal. They laughed and hugged. The German sprinter, Borchmeyer, had come in a disappointing fifth place and hung his head. Against his better judgment, the defeated runner looked up in the direction of the Führer at the very moment he turned to Goebbels, "I thought you said Borchmeyer was favored to win?!" Hitler screamed, "He looked like he was running through wet cement!"

*   *   *

A few hours later, it was time for John Woodruff to run his 800m semifinal. And Marjorie Gestring was in the stands to watch. She had asked Eleanor Holm to join her, as she did not feel comfortable going to the big stadium by herself. She had also taken a particular liking to both Eleanor and Woodruff. They were both, 'real gassers' as she put it to her mom in a letter home.

Eleanor was more than happy to chaperone. It was a nice break from covering the Games for the AP, which she performed dutifully and without incident thus far, much to the relief of Gould. "Woodruff looks like a tower compared to the rest of them," she said to Gestring as the runners took position.

"I am so nervous for him," Gestring said. "I just want him to make the Final. His last heat wasn't that spectacular."

"He did what he had to do. He was conserving himself for this one." Eleanor said with a knowing smile.

"I hope so," Gestring replied anxiously and looked down toward the track.

*   *   *

John Woodruff got into place and thought of nothing but making that final. He also wanted to make a bit of a statement to the favorites; Canadian runner, Phil Edwards, and the Italian, Mario Lanzi, whose semis followed his. Those runners had snubbed him in the locker room when John approached them to wish them good luck.

The starter shot his revolver and Woodruff never even saw his competition after that. He won by a full two seconds. It would be the largest margin of victory in any of the semis and Edwards and Lanzi took notice, especially after they barely made the Finals, coming in third and second respectively in their own semis that followed Woodruff's.

Gestring was relieved and recognized Eleanor had called it. She smiled at the older athlete's knowledge. "I told you so," Eleanor joked. "Now let's go grab a drink and some popcorn. You think they make popcorn in Germany?"

"Let's go check," the popcorn loving teen said excitedly, "But I want to be back for the Women's 100m semis if we can," Gestring said. "I want to see if Helen Stephens keeps rolling."

It was once again Stephens' time to compete. She had a quick nap in the woman's locker room in the hour and a half break between races, and that was enough to feel refreshed. In her semi, she was facing one of the other two favorites to win the final, German Käthe Krauß. This would be the most difficult competitor Helen would ever face up to now.

The crowd was all behind Krauß, except for the patch of Americans surrounding Gestring, Eleanor, and Martha. As the runners took their places, Stephens took a deep breath. She had never thought of her competition before, but she knew this was going to be a mad dash, and as she stared ahead at the finish line, her blood began to boil, and her heart began to race. The gun went off and Helen was right, the German was neck and neck with her the whole way. The stadium jumped to their feet as the runners ran stride for stride toward the tape.

Helen bore down and gave it that extra push. She crossed the finish line a scant .04 seconds ahead of Krauß. Once again, the American contingency in the stands had reason to wave their flags and hug each other. And once again, Stephens had won a race. Though it was closer than it should have been in her eyes, and she would see the German again in the final the next day, her unbeaten streak had remained intact.

*   *   *

Later that day, Bill had made his way to his father. They sat in Berlin's *Poststadion*, along with 8,998 rabid *Fußball* fans and watched the highly contested Round One soccer match between Italy and the US. Italy, the favorite to win it all, had just taken a 1-0 lead 58 minutes in, but the US team was keeping up a relentless offensive barrage. Dodd had always loved the sport and wished it would catch on more in the States. "It's a healthy sport for the kids; lots of running, not a lot of contact, teaches teamwork," he had always preached to the administration in Chicago. But the University, and President Robert Maynard Hutchins, didn't see the benefit, and Dodd's pleas, like his many over the past few years to the current US Administration about the these very Games, fell on deaf ears.

"Peru looks to be Italy's strongest competition, Pop. Maybe we should hold a lunch for them," Bill suggested. He pointed down toward a few rows near the field, "There's Miguel Dasso, head of the Peruvian Olympic Committee. Go ask him if he and the team and coaches would like to join us. It'll be nice to host an event. It's been years."

Dodd agreed. It had been too long. Maybe this Olympics could turn his sense of impending doom around and finally bring unadulterated joy to his Berlin life, even if it was for only three weeks. Dodd went down and approached the Peruvian Ambassador, who was overjoyed at the invitation. This put a big smile on Dodd's face.

But no sooner had that grin flashed, than a gratuitous and flagrant double foul by Italian midfielder Achille Piccini put two US forwards on the ground writhing in pain. Worse, some Italian players grabbed German referee Carl Weingartner around his waist, held his arms at his side, and covered his mouth so he couldn't issue Piccini a red card, which would've meant his immediate dismissal. Play went on and the mostly Italian crowd went wild. Dodd just shook his head and looked up at Bill, who stood in shock at the non-call.

*   *   *

Later that night, after all the competition of the day had ended, it seemed like every athlete from every country packed the spacious Dining Hall of Nations, and it quickly became *the* place to be. Riefenstahl and Ertl roamed the scene with small 8mm cameras in hand. Ertl captured Owens wearing his Gold medal while laughing it up with Helen Stephens. Owens walked up close to the camera, grabbed his medal with one hand and put up one finger on the other, "this is only the first," he mouthed.

Before Leni could shoot even one minute of film, Glenn Morris once again populated her lens. This time however, Morris was right in front of her. She looked up from her camera and stared Morris up and down.

"You like what you see, *Fräulein?*" Morris asked flirtatiously.

"At least what I can see from the outside," Leni flirted back in her own stolid way.

"You are gonna see a lot more of me Ms. Riefenstahl. I assure you that. And I'm gonna see everything of you."

Leni smiled, "You are pretty cock sure, as you Americans say."

"Oh, that's one thing I'm definitely sure of," he responded proudly. "My name is . . ."

"Glenn Morris, from *Dakota,*" she said in her best cowboy imitation. "I know who you are."

Morris smiled, "I like that."

Near the Eastern European food section, Stoller and Glickman were carrying on a conversation with two Hungarian Jews from their water polo team, goalkeeper György Brody and field player Miklos Sárkány.

"The Regency goes along with Hitler and his crazy politics?" Glickman asked in shock.

"It's either go along with it or be invaded and be forced to go along with it. Either way, we will lose, and we Jews will die. Miklos Horthy does not care about our plight. He will make a deal with whomever will keep him alive at that moment." Brody said in broken English.

"We do not have an ocean to separate us from our enemies.

And our neighbors, especially Austria, are going to crumble any day now to the Germans," Sárkány added in even worse English.

Stoller couldn't fathom it. He had rarely, if ever, encountered anti-Semitism in his life. He didn't doubt its existence, but he had never come face to face with it growing up in Ohio or attending the University of Michigan. And to think, now Jews all over Europe feared their very own survival. It was just too much for him to consider.

"We just need a place of our own. I mean, fuck, if no one else wants Jews around, let's find a place, settle down and tell the rest of the world to go fuck themselves," Glickman said with beer glass raised. The three other men couldn't help but smile and toast in agreement.

Marjorie Gestring sat with her best new pal, John Woodruff. He had taken just as much a shine to her on the voyage over as she to him. He would be competing in his Final the next day and Gestring, whose competitions didn't begin for a week, would be right at the finish line to watch Woodruff cross.

"Are you nervous, John?"

"Nah, but I do have to watch out for the Italian and the Canadian. They are experienced and the favorites and will pull out all the stops to win." He looked down at the girl, "I gotta be craftier. You know what I mean?"

"Sure do." Suddenly she noticed Rawls and Poynton-Hill coming their way, "Ah geez. What's this all about?"

"John, would you please excuse us for a moment?" Hill asked.

Woodruff looked at Gestring, who motioned it was okay.

"I'll grab us a few pretzels, Marjorie," he said and looked at the other two women with piercing eyes as he walked past them. They looked down in embarrassment as he left.

"For what do I owe this honor?" Gestring began.

"Marjorie, we've both been major bitches to you, and we think its counterproductive to our cause," Rawls started.

"Really? Is this an actual apology I'm getting right now?" Gestring asked, shocked.

"Yes, kid. We've been assholes, and we figure all any of us want to do is win. Beat the Nazis and grab Gold. But the three of us together, we can do something better. So, we propose a pact." Hill said.

"A pact? Go on," Gestring was listening.

Rawls laid it out. They would work as a team. Practice together, push each other, make each other better, and then sweep the event. Rawls and Hill both admitted that they underestimated Gestring in the beginning and that she truly was just as capable of winning the Gold as any of the three. They unanimously agreed that they did not need the distraction of being each other's enemy when the enemy was out there.

"Okay, I'm in. But if you two are grifting me, may you both end your first dives like breaching whales," Gestring hexed them.

The two women and one teen put their right hands in front of each other and on top of each other and swore to dominate their sport.

It had been almost two years since Zamperini had seen Helene Mayer and he was anxious to catch up with his dear friend. They sat outside the Hall overlooking the lake on the same bench Fürstner had shot himself. It seemed that no time had passed at all since they had laid eyes on each other. Mayer was looking in top shape to Louis, and he to her. They had always had affection towards each other while at USC, but he had hoped to take it a step further while in Berlin.

"I really missed you, Helene. College just wasn't the same after you left."

"Oh Louis, you're so cheesy." She smiled, "You're cute, but cheesy. I must admit I missed you too, though," she looked into his eyes.

He put his hand on her lap and she held it, "I hope we can see each other properly these next few weeks," he said with a sexual overtone Helene didn't overlook.

"Well, we have a few problems," she said. He looked at her inquisitively and she continued. "One, there is a curfew, two, I can't have boys in my dorm, and three, you can't have girls in yours. But I'm hoping we can work around that somehow."

He smiled. "I'll dress up as a girl and sneak in if I have to."

She laughed. "Let's hope it doesn't come to that."

Back inside the Hall, Dora Ratjen couldn't stop laughing from nerves. Ralph Metcalfe, with his new Silver Medal around his neck, was flirting hard with her. She had never expected this! And she didn't know whether to be horrified or aroused. Neither boy nor girl had *ever* hit on her in her entire life. She also didn't understand a thing he was saying, but she certainly recognized he was flirting. The second the speedy runner grabbed her hand to hold it though, she spotted Gretel across the room and took off towards her. Metcalfe looked around embarrassed, noticed no one had seen her run away, and then walked off, head held high like nothing happened. When he got to Foy Draper, he assured the fellow runner Ratjen would be his by the end of competition. But Draper had seen Ratjen run away and just shook his head and laughed.

Archie Williams, whose 400m heats were still days away, had never in his life heard anyone speak French. Like the friendly Germans he ate and drank with when they first got to the Village, a French person was equally as foreign. And though he may have never heard the language before, he sure did like hearing it when he met French sprinter Marguerite Perrou at one of the long tables. She was beautiful, twenty-one years old, and very receptive to Williams. He really couldn't believe his experience so far. He had heard Berlin was the stuff of nightmares, but this was just the opposite. Metcalfe, who had also won a Silver in the 100m at the Los Angeles Games, had told him that L.A. was the real nightmare. 'The ambiance Brundage had created at that Village was all wrong,' Metcalfe had said. 'It was hot, dry, uncomfortable and had no women!' This place, Williams thought, was shaping up to be a paradise in comparison to what Metcalfe described.

"Maybe you would like to take me on a stroll around the lake?" Marguerite suggested innocently in her best broken English.

Paradise, Williams thought. *And it just keeps on getting better.*

Moch and his boys joined in the festivities as well. They sat and drank beers with the Women's Czech gymnastics team. It was a perfect match; 8 of them and 8 of the boys. There were technically nine of the guys, but Donald Hume was still sick as a dog and lay shivering under blankets in his bed. Language was not a problem for the group. Of course, none of the young men and women understood what each other was saying, but they all understood each other's motives perfectly well. The Dining Hall of Nations had become a huge meat market, a Sexual League of Nations, and the boys from Seattle and the girls from Prague were up to the task of global partnership.

As the party raged, Dora and Gretel sat near the lake and looked at the swans. They giggled at Metcalfe's attempts at wooing Dora. Gretel invited Dora to dinner with her family at her father, Max's, favorite restaurant in Berlin, which had suddenly began serving Jews again. Gretel's family had been forced to come into the city to watch the Games. It was Osten's way of perpetuating the illusion that everything was normal. Dora was pleased, nonetheless, and accepted the invitation for later in the week before the high jump event began.

Gretel had pretty much kept to herself since arriving at the Village. She felt angry and oddly out of place. Other countries had Jewish athletes and she shouldn't have felt uncomfortable, but she was a world record holder that was being forced to sit out. And whenever she was introduced to athletes who recognized her name and plight, they pitied her. She could not believe that the

American, Avery Brundage, whose whole argument to the American people was based on Gretel's participation, had not said a word, or filed a formal complaint.

The problem was Brundage didn't know yet . . . but he was just about to learn.

*   *   *

Diem, von Halt, and Brundage shared cocktails in the lobby bar of the Hotel Adlon Kempinski while discussing the way the Games had unfolded so far. All agreed it was quite the show and couldn't be going better. Brundage was looking forward to more American victories. He knew Owens' victory ate at von Halt's craw, so he tried to assuage the situation in his best condescending manner.

"At least you will grab Gold in woman's high jump, gentlemen. No one can touch Bergmann," he said with a grin. The other two men looked at each other hesitantly. "What?" Brundage asked naively.

"There has been an update on that. I neglected to tell you when you first arrived, then it just slipped my mind," von Halt began.

"What did, Karl?" Brundage asked more pointedly.

"Bergmann is out. She injured her thigh. She's been replaced by Dora Ratjen," von Halt informed him.

Brundage sat, mouth agape. The other men waited uncomfortably for his response, and it took more than a beat. Brundage couldn't help but feel duped. Bergmann was never going to be able to compete. He became flushed and teetered on verbally exploding on the two men, but he silently regained composure. "A thigh injury, huh?" He finally muttered through gritted teeth.

"Simple as that," von Halt said matter-of-factly. "Right, Carl?"

Diem looked at von Halt, and then Brundage, who looked back

at Diem mortified, "Simple as that," Diem said in disgust.

*   *   *

In an undisclosed location somewhere in Berlin, Mildred sat tightly blindfolded with a pounding headache. She was enveloped in complete darkness shortly after she was shoved violently into a jeep just outside *Olympiastadion*. Putzi had then led her through a corridor of some kind, and she could smell the damp, cold air. She knew she was underground, but where? A door opened and the smell of sweat, body odor, and cigar smoke hit her like a punch to the face. She was thrown into a chair and the large man accompanying her then began tying up her arms and legs. *Futile*, she had thought, and chuckled at considering trying to escape. Putzi never said a word. She heard him walk a short distance away and sit at what was probably a desk. Then she heard metal scraping against a rock, or stone. Scraping? Or sharpening?

Her wrists were chafed and sore from the rope that bound her. After about thirty minutes of trying to make small talk with her captor, the door opened. Someone walked in. She felt a knife cutting her blindfold and when it dropped, the light in the room blinded her at first. When her eyes began to adjust to the light, a man's face was staring directly into hers, only a foot away. As focus returned, she saw that she was staring into the face of Adolf Hitler.

He studied her for a moment. She felt powerless and could not look away. Finally, he backed away, turned to Putzi, and said, "This is the American?" Putzi nodded. Mildred turned to her right and saw another figure tied to a chair, not moving. It was so bloody she could barely make out any features, but it was a man. Dead. She sensed it was Vladimir. On the floor in the corner of the room she saw a bloody mess curled up in a heap. *Probably Leon*, she thought.

- 313 -

Hitler leaned on the desk as Putzi continued to sharpen his knife. He pulled a small, glass pipe from his jacket and lit it, inhaling deeply, and then exhaling. Mildred didn't recognize the scent. Hitler looked at Putzi.

"What does she know?" Hitler said.

"She likes to talk but says nothing." Putzi said.

Hitler took another drag while staring at Putzi. "I'm growing tired of hearing you say that." He exhaled. "If you can't make yourself useful, I'll find someone who will."

"I'll make her talk, then send her to *Sachsenhausen*."

"No . . . *Toten*." Hitler said, and Putzi knew exactly what that meant. Hitler walked out of the room without another look or another word. Like a ghost, he was gone, and Mildred was once again alone with the large man and two dead corpses.

Putzi smiled demonically and said, "It's time." He walked towards Mildred, knife in hand, and her heart sank. She thought of her best friend Mattie, wishing she could just see her smiling face one last time.

DAY 3
August 4, 1936

Olympiastadion was host to a flourish of activity on Day 3 of the Games. By 3:30 in the afternoon Jesse Owens had already shattered the Olympic record in winning his first heat in the 200m, and then followed that by matching the same time in his Quarterfinal. His closest competition going into the next day's Semis and Finals was going to be his teammate and friend, Mack Robinson, whose fastest time in his own heat was a mere .01 second behind Jesse's Olympic record.

Either happening concurrently or just after the 200m heats, the 400m hurdles semis, and the women's discus trials and finals all took place, as well as the long lump elimination stage, which Owens also breezed through. Leni, Ertl and their minions covered every event from warmups to finals and Leni couldn't have been happier with the competition. It was thrilling and the crowds in the stands made for lively cinema. She checked her watch and saw it was nearing 4pm. She grabbed Ertl and reminded him to relocate to the starting line of one of the biggest events of the day; the final of the women's 100m, the race to finally determine who was the fastest woman on the planet.

Martha and Mattie were in the stands ready for the showdown. Mattie turned to her daughter. "I can't believe Mildred. She told me yesterday morning she'd be here by noon."

"Don't fret about Mildred. She's a big girl," Martha responded. "Let's watch Helen! Putzi and I met her at a club in Berlin last night after he finally got off work. She's a real gas!"

On the track Helen Stephens calmly walked to the starting line. As she set herself up at the starting blocks, she nodded to the current record holder, Stanisława Walasiewicz of Poland. "Let's have a ball, Stella!" she said, receiving a confused blank stare back from the Pole. She then turned to Krauß, "See you on the other side, Cathy!" The German runner was not impressed and scoffed.

When the race began, Helen steamed ahead to grab an early lead. She stayed two full body lengths ahead of her competition. The mostly German crowd in the stands cheered Krauß on, but the German was running a distant third. Martha and Mattie cheered furiously with the surrounding American fans, and as soon as Helen crossed the finish line first, Martha ran down the steps flashing her badge to a security guard. She hopped over the fence and ran to Helen, who was still catching her breath. When she was done receiving congratulations from her coach and teammates, Martha approached her.

"Helen, that was spectacular! You must come out with me and Putzi tonight. We'll show you all the best places!" Martha said.

"I'm in! But right now, I'm being told I must go backstage to meet Hitler so he can personally congratulate me." Helen said with a playfully fearful face.

"I've met him. He's a pussycat." She assured the runner. "We will pick you up in front of the Bell Tower at 7pm, okay?"

"I'll be there," Helen said as she was ushered away to the stadium depths.

She was escorted to a private dressing room where Hitler, Goebbels, and Brundage waited. "Ah, Ms. Stephens," Brundage began. "That was quite an impressive win for the good old US of A." She nodded with a half grin. "I'd like to introduce you to our hosts for the next two weeks who insisted on congratulating you in person. This is Herr Goebbels . . ." The menacing Propaganda Minister forced a smile. "And this is Herr Hitler. I'm sure you are familiar with him."

Hitler smiled and shot up a Nazi salute. Helen, without missing a beat walked right up to him and gave him a good old fashioned Missouri handshake. Brundage and Goebbels recoiled, but Hitler laughed. "This one has moxie," the Führer smiled. "You are quite the specimen." He walked around her, looked her over, and then grabbed a handful of her buttocks. "Oh yes, quite the specimen." Helen was shocked and in any other circumstance would have given the man a severe beat down, but she just stared right at Brundage with mounting contempt. It made the US Olympic President flush with embarrassment. "You should come to Berchtesgaden and summer with me and Eva. You would like it." Hitler finished.

"I appreciate the offer, but I enjoy the simple plains and corn fields of Missouri," she said, and then with only an uncomfortable 'Goodbye' and awkward smile, she walked right out of the room. It took her a second to compose herself in the hallway before she ran back to the field to follow the competition.

Up in the stands, Mattie looked around the stadium nervously as if Mildred would miraculously appear. She tried to push away dreaded thoughts, knowing full well what could happen to Mildred if she wasn't careful. *Mildred was always careful,* she thought, *but never late.* Martha noticed her mother's anxiety, "Come on, Mom. Let's watch the final of the 800m. Forget about Mildred. She's fine!"

*   *   *

When the runners for the 800m final were called to begin their warmups, Woodruff was sitting in the middle of the field having just watched fellow American Glenn Hardin take Gold in the 400m hurdles. He took off his jacket and stretched. He began remembering the time when he was a wiry ten-year-old in Connellsville, Pennsylvania walking down a dirt road alongside a wooded area near town.

His younger self stared up ahead at the local steel mill where a

- 317 -

tall smokestack spewed steam into the air. He was going to meet his father who would soon be finished with his Friday shift. He was carrying a stack of books tied together with a strip of cloth and was swinging it back and forth whistling a Gospel tune he had remembered from church. His mother Sarah made sure she took him and his sister to church every Sunday morning. The hymns were the only thing he remembered each week, but by Friday he would start to forget the tunes so he whistled loudly thinking it would help him remember. He was whistling so loudly that by the time he heard the pick-up truck, it was almost upon him. It was a beat up old red heap that squeaked to a stop.

A short, muscular teenager hopped out of the passenger seat and the driver, a lanky red-headed kid, jumped out of the truck holding a bottle of whiskey.

"Where you goin', boy?" the short one said. John kept walking but the teenagers quickly blocked his path.

The lanky one grabbed his books and said, "What you doing with all these? I didn't know niggers could read."

"I bet there's just pictures in them," said the short one and they laughed. John started to walk again, and the teenagers walked beside him looking at his books. "Check this out. 'Winnie the Pooh'!"

"I bet you can't read the words. You just look at the pictures, right?" John steamed inside. Yes, he could read, and routinely impressed his teachers with his reading acumen. The lanky red head tossed the book aside and they stepped in front of him to block his path again. "You want a ride? We can give you a ride if you want." John was frozen, trying to stay calm. Overhead, he saw a sparrow whizzing past them.

"Yeah, why don't you get in the truck, so we don't have to throw you in," the short one said. John thought for a second, then suddenly dashed around them and sprinted down the dirt road as fast as he could. They gave chase and he veered off the dirt road and disappeared into the woods. He knew the woods well and he thought his only hope was to outrun them. As a black boy in a Pennsylvania steel mining town, it wasn't the first time he had to outrun danger. It made him think of his grandparents. He was one generation removed from Virginia slaves who ran from their owners and escaped to the north. He loved when his father proudly told the story of how they managed to flee their captors. *They were faster . . . and smarter.*

So, he ran and ran, through the woods until he made it to a clearing at the edge of the steel mill. He was faster, and just so his pursuers would think he disappeared, he stopped, turned, looped around, and backtracked. He ran right past them, quietly avoiding their view all the way back to the dirt road. They never heard nor saw him. When he arrived back at the road, he let the air out of their truck tires and nonchalantly met up with his father.

When the starter's gun shot into the air to begin the 800m final, Woodruff was snapped back to his current situation. In the pack, he stood at least five inches taller than all the others. American fans had no problem recognizing their runner. The race was not a sprint, but not a marathon either. Phil Edwards, the five-time Olympic medalist from Canada, jumped into the lead position and established a very, very slow pace. John followed him and soon the other runners surrounded Woodruff. He was boxed in, especially by the Italian runner Mario Lanzi, and seemingly on purpose.

In the stands, representatives from Italy's sports administration could hardly contain themselves. They stood next to Hitler and shouted, "Lanzi!" as loud as they could. The Italian delegates irritated Hitler and slightly embarrassed him with their antics, but they were his special guests; the things he had to put up with ever since Mussolini joined him in his support of Francisco Franco's Nationalist forces in the Spanish Civil War were trying, at best.

Hitler was also cheering on the Italian because no German

runner qualified for the final heat. Rudolf Harbig, Germany's favorite to win, had developed a gastrointestinal infection day's prior, and came in at a disappointing sixth place in his first heat. (After breaking the world record years later, Harbig would join the Nazi Party and become one of von Halt's favorite tools of propaganda.)

Alan Gould stood next to Jesse Owens and Archie Williams on the field. Owens noticed what was happening to Woodruff. "He's gotta get out of there! Make a move, John!"

Archie replied, "He can't force his way out--if he does, he could be disqualified."

"It's Lanzi and Edwards. Look at them--they're working together," Owens concluded.

"They know they can't keep up with him. It's their only chance," Archie said. Gould made a note in his pad and then all three of them ran to the final turn to get a better look at the action.

Gestring and Eleanor were on the sidelines, and they too noticed the predicament the Canadian and Italian runners had put Woodruff in, and they were steaming. "Bastards!" yelled Gestring as the pack passed in front of them.

On the track, John Woodruff was getting frustrated, and about halfway through the race, he did something that would become legendary in the annals of track and field forever.

He stopped running.

Nobody could believe it. A hush fell over the crowd. Owens grabbed Archie, who threw his hands in the air and yelled, "No!"

John simply had had enough. He slowed to a complete halt, stepping his way to the third lane as everyone else maneuvered around him. All alone, with a clear view ahead of him, he started the race--*again*. He gathered every ounce of strength left inside him and took off back for the pack. Within seconds, he not only reached them but then flew past them and into first place. Lanzi and Edwards were stunned. During the final stretch, the crowd of

100,000 was cheering wildly as Lanzi inched his way back into first place. It was neck and neck from there.

The Italian delegates were jumping up and down like lunatics, further embarrassing Hitler. But with less than five meters to go, John Woodruff willed himself past Lanzi to steal the Gold. The crowd erupted. Owens and Archie Williams hugged and hollered. Amidst the bedlam, Gould wrote in his pad, 'We've just witnessed the most daring move ever seen on a track.'

The Italians slumped into their chairs, utterly speechless. Hitler backed away from them and Osten leaned in. "Should I call Morrell for some sedatives?"

Hitler shook his head, "No, don't bother. I don't even care. Luz Long should easily win Gold, so the day won't be a complete waste."

Osten quickly responded, "The day has already been a success, *Mein Führer*. Gisela Mauermayer has already won Gold in the discus! We've assembled a fine team by all measures." Hitler nodded affirmatively and looked out over the arena, soaking in the spectacle.

On the field, Archie and Gould were still in awe of Woodruff's victory. Jesse Owens, however, gathered his belongings and his thoughts, and suddenly became very serious. "Gotta fly."

Gould took notice, "Good luck, Jesse." Owens slapped hands with Archie and made his way to the sand pit where the long jump final would take place. Gould ran back up to the press box, anxious to get a full view of the event.

On the track, John Woodruff was on his knees, crying and pointing up to the sky giving thanks to God. He wished his father were alive to witness the feat of his proud legacy. *Faster . . . and smarter.*

When he returned to the sidelines, Marjorie Gestring was there to greet him as promised, with as big a bear hug as a little girl could give a conquering giant.

*   *   *

Back on the field, Leni and Ertl ran to reset their position for the long jump. If that event shaped up to be anything like what she just covered in Woodruff's win, Leni's day would be a cinematic gold mine. As Ertl put the camera on its tripod, Leni surveyed Owens and Long and the rest of the jumpers stretching and mentally preparing. She pitied Long. He was the favorite, and one of the Nazi's poster boys for these Games, but if he were to lose, she could just imagine the humiliation the Nazis would impose on him.

"We are hanging out tonight," an assertive male voice declared from behind her.

Leni spun around and there was Morris once again at her side. "For a big strong man, you sure are good at sneaking up on people," she said. "And you are positive I will accept?"

He leaned in close to her face and whispered in her ear. "Cock sure." He pointed toward beyond the stadium at the Bell Tower, "Let's meet there at 7pm."

She bit her bottom lip and gave a crooked smile, "Okay Dakota, we're on."

Gould and Kieran took their seats in the press box, and then noticed that everyone else was standing in anticipation of the finals. There was a buzz, not only in the seats around them, but all throughout the stadium, and Gould could feel it. Even amongst the most hardcore German spectators, the American phenom was intoxicating. Gould put his pad down and his pen away, not wanting to miss a moment of the event. Kieran did the same.

On the track, Jesse Owens remembered another piece of his old coach Larry Snyder's advice; never change your warm-up routine, whether at the practice track at Ohio State University, or in front of 100,000 onlookers rooting against you. So, he didn't change a thing. First, a light jog, then a quick stretch, then a faster trot, followed by a deeper stretch. He nodded to his rival, Luz Long, who was amid his own pre-jump routine. They had developed a very close relationship during the run-up to this event, spending time eating dinners at the Village and talking as much about the political situation in their respective countries as they did about jumping, training techniques, and of course, the abundance of beautiful women they were surrounded by. He appreciated Luz's openness and wished him well.

Jesse's final preparation was a test run on the actual track. Usually, it was a half-speed trial run to feel the surface of the track pressed against his feet, the feel of the sand upon landing. Deep focus. But with his adrenaline bubbling inside, this trial run was more like three-quarters speed. He ran effortlessly down the track, concentrating on his form, and landed in the pit, completely satisfied and ready to go.

Suddenly, an official ran onto the sand pit and took a measurement then signaled to the sideline judges. The crowd cheered and flags were raised. Jesse abruptly looked around and was confused by the all the activity. The judges raised their cards showing a measly 5.5-meter score. He looked back at the other athletes and saw Luz Long with his arms outstretched as if to say, "What are you doing?" It was then he realized that the judges had counted his trial run as his first official attempt!

"Wait, wait, wait!" he shouted. Coach Lawson Robertson went berserk, gyrating like a madman as he ran toward the judge's bench, screaming. Jesse looked up to the sky and realized that he was so focused on his preparation that he never heard his name announced or that the competition was even officially underway. He hadn't even taken off his tracksuit!

In the press box, Gould and Kieran couldn't believe it. "How could they count that? He wasn't even trying!" Kieran shouted.

"He's so fast he must have fooled them. That, or something

else," Gould said, sharing a disappointed look with Kieran, hoping something more nefarious was not at play.

Jesse walked back to where the other athletes stood. Most of them avoided eye contact with him and whispered some sort of comical barb to one another. Luz, mid-stretch, shook his head and said, "Forget it." Jesse sighed and walked away from the group to gather his thoughts. When he heard the crowd cheer, he turned to see that the Japanese standout, Naoto Tajima, had completed his first jump, setting the bar at 7.1 meters.

In the stands, Hitler, von Halt, Osten, Goebbels, Carl Diem, Goering, and many of the other *Sportsreich* members, as well as Avery Brundage and IOC President Latour, stood and cheered as Luz Long made an impressive jump of his own, challenging for the lead.

Jesse listened for his name to be called this time and patiently took his position for the second of his attempts. He raced down the track and hurled himself into the air, landing well past Tajima's mark. Before the official could step onto the sand to take the measurement, the starter raised his arms, signaling a foul. He had crossed the line on his takeoff, rendering his attempt fruitless. Lawson and the other coaches clapped their hands with encouragement. Jesse walked to a clearing in the grass, alone, knowing he had wasted a jump.

Leni Riefenstahl saw a great opportunity and directed Ertl to focus his camera on the American. What happened next proved to be an even greater opportunity--Luz Long approached Jesse and sat next to him in the grass.

"What's eating you?" he said, proud of his English slang. Jesse smiled.

"What's eating *at* you, I think you mean," Jesse said. "Nerves, I guess."

"You know, you've been doing that all week," Luz said.

"What's that?"

"Your last step is too close to the line. You've fouled on half your practice runs. I've been watching," he said. Luz hesitated for a minute, remembering how much he hated when his father drilled him about his own takeoffs.

Olympic Long Jumpers Luz Long of Germany and Jesse Owens of the US share an infamous moment together during their event.

The interaction also didn't go unnoticed from Hitler's box. Avery turned to Latour and grimaced, both waiting to see how the Führer would react. He was not at all happy. "What's he doing?" Hitler screamed at von Halt, who wasn't too pleased himself.

"The same thing he's been doing all week. I'll have to have a talk with him," von Halt responded. Avery watched and wished the tryst on the field would end immediately. It was getting embarrassing.

Luz said to Jesse, "Give yourself an extra step for safety and you'll beat us all by a meter. Without that distraction you can put all your focus into the jump." Jesse nodded at Luz affirmatively. Behind her lens, Leni smiled at the camaraderie. To everyone else, it was an oddity to see an American black man and a blond-haired, blue-eyed Aryan specimen together, their heads mere inches apart with a familiar comfort.

In the press box, Gould and Kieran also took notice. "Only one jump left," Kieran said.

"All it takes is one." Gould replied. "If he comes close to his world record, he'll win it."

Jesse rose to his feet and did a last-minute stretch. As his name was called, he casually lined up for his final attempt. He took a deep breath and drew an imaginary line a foot before the launching strip. He began his sprint and quickly reached top speed. With a clean takeoff behind him, he exploded into the air, feeling like he could jump clear out of the stadium. The crowd was in awe and even his fellow competitors were astounded. Tajima didn't even watch the landing--he knew he had been beaten.

A cloud of sand blasted into the air with a thump, and Jesse knew it was a good one. He leaped up and felt a wave of relief wash over him. He left the pit, closed his eyes, and bent over to catch his breath. Luz Long lined up for his last jump. Jesse watched and rooted for Luz, who completed his own successful attempt, just beating Tajima's mark to take Silver. He walked over to Luz, and the two competitors from opposite ends of the racial and sociological spectrum, embraced in front of what seemed like the whole world.

Hitler slammed his fists into his thighs. The impressive display of athleticism was overshadowed by what was now happening. Goebbels turned to Hitler and said, "Long better be careful. He might catch a disease."

Von Halt was also perturbed. "Very careful."

"I'm not watching any more today! The *schwarzes* should never be able to participate in any more Games ever again! Primitive jungle creatures," Hitler was heard mumbling as he stormed away from his seat, utterly annoyed. Latour and Carl Diem shrugged. Avery didn't like to see Hitler so aggravated, but what could he do? He got the Americans to the Games. What happened on the field was out of his control. Still, it bothered him.

In the press box, Gould and Kieran watched every detail of the events and were still clapping. "Remarkable," Gould said. He and Kieran knew there was only one thing to do. They picked up their pads and began to write.

Later that day at the medal ceremony, Jesse, Luz, and the Bronze medal winner Tajima took their places at the podium. As the American National Anthem blared, Jesse proudly put his hand over his heart. Behind him, Luz Long gave the Nazi salute and Tajima stood tall. To each of them the day was a complete victory, and for future generations, Long and Owens became a triumph of sportsmanship that superseded any medal worn around a competitor's neck.

It was an image that would forever define the 1936 Berlin Olympics and Leni Riefenstahl was there to capture the moment.

*   *   *

The day's competitions had ended, but the night had just begun. Putzi and Martha waited at the entrance of the Bell Tower for Helen. When she arrived, she had wanted to tell Martha first off Hitler's advances earlier, but she wouldn't dare say a word in front of the Führer's personal henchman. It would have to wait for a convenient moment the two ladies could step away from festivities and powder their noses. Before they hopped into Putzi's BMW Roadster however, the group ran into Glenn Morris and Leni heading into the Tower.

"Giving him a private tour, Frau Riefenstahl?" Putzi inquired.

"Go about your own business, neanderthal," she said to him in German.

Putzi grimaced. He so wanted to shoot the overbearing bitch right on the spot, but knew if he did, his boss would cut his balls off, so he politely opened the door for Helen and Martha, who were oblivious, and let them in the car. He turned to Leni and answered her back in German, "Have a delightful night with your own neanderthal, bitch." He said with a smile, got in his car, and screeched away.

Glenn just smiled politely, not understanding a word. Leni then led him up into the Olympic Bell Tower. He kept asking as they climbed the stairs the 253 feet up if she was okay. She laughed. He didn't realize she had made her mark in mountain films, and this was a mere stroll in a meadow. When they got to the top, the view was breathtaking. They could see right into the stadium, and beyond that the forest and then the twinkling lights of downtown Berlin. They stood silent for a moment and looked out into the shimmering night.

"Perfect. The setting couldn't be more perfect," she said and then turned to look into his eyes. "Perfect."

He immediately grabbed her and began tearing off her clothing. She reciprocated like an attacking lioness and tore his shirt in two as they kissed wildly. He picked her up and rammed her back against the stone wall as she wrapped her legs around him. Within seconds they were fucking like out-of-control animals. She tore at his flesh with her nails, as he penetrated deeply into her with every violent thrust.

They were totally lost in the moment and forgot they were in a very public place. Two tourists, a middle-aged Japanese couple, who had trudged all the way up the Tower before closing time, had gotten more of a view than they bargained for. They stopped dead in their tracks at the top of the stairs and watched in mild states of shock and arousal as Leni and Glenn just kept at it, changing positions, and howling into the night.

DAY 4
August 5, 1936

Brundage had asked for a private appointment with Osten's office that morning to clear some bad air. He felt the Bergmann affair should have been dealt with differently and voiced his opinion to the man he felt most responsible. "I'm not sure what bothers me more--the fact that Bergmann was pulled off the team, or the timing of it."

"Knowing you, I'd guess the timing of it," Osten said.

"Let's just say it was slightly less than tactful," Avery said.

Osten didn't even try to hide his contempt for the American's disapproval. "I care little what another country's representative has to say about my team. Worry about what you yourself can control, Mr. Brundage."

"I'm not just the American Olympic President anymore, Herr Osten, I am now a sitting member of the IOC," Brundage threatened.

"Then bring your grievances to them. Complain to old man Latour and see how far that gets you," Osten said, losing his patience. "My team is performing very successfully so far. No one can prove we haven't put our very best competitors out there, so stop complaining about fair play. When did you grow a conscience?"

"This has nothing to do with my conscience," Avery responded. "I convinced the AAU to come here because you assured me this wouldn't happen. And I believed you."

"You are acting like that self-righteous ass, Jahncke. It's a little too late for regrets, Herr Brundage." He threw his hands up in the air, "For God's sake, we have a German Jew in an event later this morning. And she's the favorite to win! What more do you want?"

"Helene Mayer has always professed to being Methodist. So that part of your argument falls flat," Brundage reminded him.

"In our records she is a Jew. And she is competing, so bring your petty grievances to someone who will want to listen." Osten rang a bell on his desk. Two Nazi soldiers rushed in and waited patiently to escort Brundage out of the building. He glared at Osten the whole way out.

Suddenly, the hallways of the *Sportsreich* offices seemed to lose a little of their luster. Since becoming a member of the *International* Olympic Committee, Avery expected to have a little more say when it came to such matters. He had every right to express his opinion on *any* team competing in these Games. *This is my job now, isn't it?* he thought, as he was escorted down a staircase towards the exit. He also wondered why he was being followed by a personal escort as he left the building, as if he needed to be watched like some kind of secret agent.

*   *   *

Later that morning, in the *Haus Des Deutschen Sports*, just northeast of *Olympiastadion,* and not far from Osten's office, Leni and Ertl finished tweaking some stage lights. This was the venue specifically built for all the fencing events. Leni was not pleased to see that an enormous television camera was planted in one of her camera positions.

"Who put this thing here? It must be moved behind me," she said to no one in particular, but loud enough that a producer ran over.

"I'm sorry, Fraulein Riefenstahl, but I am unable to move it," the producer stammered.

"By the authority given to me by the Führer himself, I can place

- 330 -

my camera anywhere that I wish," she said. "And I would like it to be here, instead of this . . . monolith."

"You don't understand, I am physically *unable* to move it," he said, and pressed his weight against the tube-attached behemoth. It didn't budge. Leni grunted and stormed off. She would have to work around it.

Around them, the arena slowly filled up with spectators, all looking to witness the final of the Women's Fencing (foil) and hometown hero and former Gold medalist Helene Mayer's return to Olympic glory.

When Mayer was called to the piste for her first semi-final, Riefenstahl was flabbergasted at what she saw. She leaned into Ertl's ear. "Start rolling on Mayer right away and slowly push in about waist high. Don't lose the damned armband." Helene Mayer was boldly wearing a Nazi armband around her left bicep, and she waved to the crowd enthusiastically. They roared back at her in approval. "Unbelievable," Leni expressed.

Ertl reminded her the two of them were just as bad because they were willing employees for the Nazis. "We are making a fortune off of them and filming what may be an even bigger piece of propaganda than *Triumph of the Will*."

"Millions of people make a lot of money working for folks they despise and disrespect every single day all over the world. We are no different than that. But I wouldn't be caught dead wearing their accoutrements. And for Mayer to do it – let's hope it isn't willingly."

Ertl wasn't about to argue with Leni. His response was to push in even tighter on the swastika on Mayer's armband.

*   *   *

In a nearby biergarten, one of the only public places in Berlin you could watch the Games on the television, Gould, Kieran and other reporters discussed the drama of Day 3 and if it were truly possible Owens could win his third Gold in the 200-meter. Ever the wit and master of coining phrases, Kieran was effusive about the American runner. "He's so damned fast, he leaves a dark streak behind him. That's it, he's the 'dark streak from Ohio State'." Reporters booed and threw napkins at him.

"Just a shade racist possibly, Jon?" Gould proposed.

That wasn't the esteemed *New York Times* reporter's intention by any means. He was thinking Owens was faster than his own shadow or the black smoke an engine leaves in its wake. He soundly rejected any criticism to the contrary and penned the term. It would be a moniker that would stick with Owens the rest of his career.

"Holy shit. Everyone, get your asses over here right now!" One of the reporters yelled from in front of the television. Twenty eager reporters smelling blood jumped over themselves and ran to the screen. It was the women's fencing medal ceremony and they watched in shock as Helene Mayer gave the Nazi salute and wore a swastika armband as she received her Silver Medal. She had lost the Gold to the Jewish Hungarian Ilona Elek-Schacherer in the final bout, and the cameras couldn't hide the twinge of disappointment on her face, but she stood proudly for her country none-the-less.

"I'm completely at a loss for words. I don't know whether to feel pity or shame for the girl," Kieran confessed. "Alan, help me here."

Gould was equally as confused; All three women on the podium were Jewish with the Austrian Preis getting Bronze. Mayer must have recognized this. "There is no way she is doing this on her own. Right? This is the same Helene Mayer who was forced by this same government to leave her home a few years ago because she was a Jew, right?" He looked hard into the screen at Mayer's behavior, "Right?"

      *   *   *

Inside *Olympiastadion*, Mack Robinson was lining up next to Jesse Owens for the 200m final. He couldn't help but notice how relaxed Jesse was. He had already taken Gold in the 100m and the long jump and was beaming with confidence. To Mack, it looked like Jesse stood a foot taller than his 5' 9" frame. Losing his father before he could remember, he looked up to Jesse, not only as a father figure but as a friend and mentor. Now he would race against him for Gold. He knew he had a chance; in his own heat days earlier, he was only .01 seconds behind Jesse's time. But this race was about so much more. Mack's family was extremely poor; his mother raised him and his siblings while working hard hours in various manual labor jobs in Cairo, Georgia before moving the family to Pasadena, California where he eventually earned a scholarship at Pasadena Junior College. He had to fight the feeling of just being grateful to have made the team if he was going to be .01 seconds faster than Jesse.

Just outside the track, Archie Williams stood next to Marguerite Perrou behind a fence. Archie was excited to see Jesse go for Gold again, but noticed that something was distracting Marguerite. "One thing I learned when running against Jesse . . . you're not going to win every race."

"I didn't even qualify!" she said and slumped against the fence.

"Hey, you made it to the fight. And you fought, right? Look at me." Marguerite looked up at him. "If you gave it your best shot, and I know you did, then you didn't fail because that's the only thing you had control over."

She thought about it for a moment, then smiled and said, "It makes me happy when you say things like that."

"Then let's be happy we're here, right now, in this place . . . about to watch something special."

When the starter's gun sounded, Jesse exploded off the line and grabbed an early lead. Mack was side by side with the Dutchman, Tinus Osendarp, but squeezed every ounce of energy within himself to try to catch Jesse. Rounding the last turn, he and Jesse separated themselves from Osendarp as well as the rest of the pack. He was right on Jesse's heels and finished only .4 seconds behind him. As they wound down, he and Jesse hugged and laughed.

Mack seemed more excited that Jesse had won another Gold medal than he was for himself. "You did it, brother! Another Gold!"

Jesse grabbed Mack's' head and turned him towards the judge's bench. "Look!"

Mack looked at the times displayed by the judges and realized that not only had he won the Silver medal, but he and Jesse had both just broken the world record. Jesse slapped him on the back and said, "We both did it! I felt you on my heels the whole time. You were pushing me."

When Mack finally caught his breath, he thought of his mother and his siblings back home, especially his younger brother Jackie Robinson, who he knew would be so proud.

Nearby, Leni and Ertl were cheering, not just for the athletes, but because they had captured 'Gold' once again through the lens. Leni would make sure to be front and center for the medal ceremony where Jesse Owens would receive his third Gold medal and was already an international sensation. But before that, she wanted to capture other athletes who were making headlines, especially the Frenchman Robert Charpentier who was dominating the cycling events. She dashed over to the event in a private car, and her crew stationed themselves at the finish line at the Avus Motor Road and saw Charpentier win easily. The French would go on to win five Gold medals in cycling events. Leni wondered why the French and Americans seemed to have a stranglehold on the "speed" sports, namely cycling and running, while the Germans seemed to dominate events highlighting feats of strength.

While the wiry thin athletes who moved like the wind impressed her, she was proud of her German countrymen who were proving to the world that Germany was a strong nation, fit and powerful. She had seen Josef Manger win Gold for Germany in weightlifting and they fared very well in Greco-Roman Wrestling. *Glenn Morris would make a good German*, she thought, and began daydreaming until Ertl broke her spell. "What the hell is canoeing, anyway?" He asked, as they were escorted to the Langer See, a lake on the outskirts of Berlin.

"It's a new event. We'll burn one roll of film and get back to catch field hockey. I heard the Indian team is unstoppable. They've never been scored on. I've been told that we must see Dhyan Chand play and find out why they nicknamed the Indian team 'Magic'."

"No doubt it's because they're Muslim. I hear they like to dabble in the dark arts." Ertl said. Leni thought his reaction was odd, but turned her attention to the crowd surrounding the lake as they approached the canoeing venue.

After shooting a roll of film, she and Ertl returned to Berlin to film the men's field hockey event and saw exactly why India had been so dominant. Dhyan Chand came as advertised; a 'magician' with his stick, not to mention his blinding quickness. *They would easily win Gold*, she thought.

After that, they rushed back to *Olympiastadion* to film the 200m medal ceremony. Jesse Owens proudly donned his third Gold medal, but it was the Silver medalist, Mack Robinson, that caught her eye. Up on the podium, she saw a tear well up in Mack's eye when he put his hand over his heart and was reminded of a story about him. Apparently, Mack had recovered from a heart problem while still competing in college. If no one else knew the significance of the moment, she knew it and saw it. She made sure Ertl's camera was rolling.

The last event of the day, the pole vault, was next, but the sun was dipping fast which meant the light was fading quickly. Ertl kept checking his watch until Leni assured him, "Stop worrying. The low light and contrast will work in our favor. The long shadows will accentuate the height of the vaults. Work with what you have!" Ertl nodded with a silent appreciation. Not only was the master right once again, but she was teaching him the craft like nobody had ever done before.

The pole vault was quickly becoming the most dramatic competition of the Games so far, and it turned into one of the most dramatic stories in Olympic history.

Heading into the final, 25 athletes from 16 different nations had qualified. The field was wide open and that included three Americans, Bill Graber and NCAA title holders Bill Sefton and Earle Meadows, The Heavenly Twins, as they had been dubbed. They were all from USC, which made Coach Cromwell beam with pride. But that field also included two talented young Japanese athletes Shuhei Nishida and Sueo Oe. And all five went at it during the final round.

Nishida and Oe took the lead over Sefton after the sixth height change with Meadows close behind. But on the seventh, at 4.35 meters and on his second attempt, Meadows flew like an eagle and cleared the bar. It was majestic. No other vaulter came close. And Leni captured it like no one ever had before her by stationing her camera underneath the bar near the landing pad.

Second place was a tie between Nishida and Oe, who just nudged out the two Americans. The Olympic judges declared they must resume the competition to break the stalemate. But neither athlete wanted to shame the other and refused to continue. The judges then forced the Japanese team to decide the outcome. After some time, Nishida was chosen for the Silver for clearing

4.25m a jump before Oe.

In a show of ultimate camaraderie and respect, the two athletes, after returning home from Berlin, cut their two medals in half and fused them together, each man receiving half Silver and half Bronze. The fusion became known in Japanese and Olympic lore as "The Medals of Friendship."

*　　　*　　　*

Dodd and his family returned home from the day's sporting events and collapsed in the living room. Putzi accompanied Martha but kept quiet as usual when around the family. Mattie, pouring herself a scotch, began to voice her concern about Mildred's disappearance. She was emphatic something must have happened and pleaded with Putzi to help find out whatever he could about the situation.

"Herr Hanfstaengl, it is very uncommon for my friend not to call on me like this," she said and took a big swig. "She is very outspoken but harmless. If you know anything or can find out anything at all, for God's sake please let me know. If she is in harm's way you must help to return her safely."

Putzi nodded respectfully, "I cannot promise an outcome, but I will do my best to inquire, Mrs. Dodd," he lied, straight-faced to her and her family.

Martha took Putzi's hand and led him to the backyard, and away from her family, Putzi once again expressed his true love to Martha.

"Martha, I've been in love with you for three years now. You are my one and only love. I want you to feel the same about me. Only me."

She laughed like she had so many times before, "Why must you be so dramatic, Putzi darling? I am with you right now. Enjoy the moment." The problem was he knew she was enjoying many of these moments with other men and more intimate moments at that.

"I can't stand the thought of you with other men!"

"What other men? Rudy is out and who else is there?" He paused to think, and then she continued, "Relax, Putzi. For the time being, I'm all yours." He seemed content but it was a bald-faced lie. Martha had begun sleeping with Boris Vingradov, intelligence officer for the NKVD, who was now in Berlin posing as a press attaché. The NKVD had become the premiere spy department in the Kremlin and Vingradov was one of their best players. He had recently persuaded Martha to begin spying on Putzi to gain vital information on Hitler and the Nazis. And this was the only reason Martha continued to see Putzi. She felt no remorse at all gaining info from the weak-minded assassin when he was in a post coital haze. And now that she was spying on him, the sex was better than ever. *It was a win-win situation for everyone,* she thought.

*　　*　　*

That same night in downtown Berlin, Brundage, von Halt, and Diem smoked cigars and drank cognac at the popular *Club Palais* while they listened to a sultry young cabaret singer do her best Marlene Dietrich. From behind them and seemingly out of nowhere, John Kieran approached the men and asked the Germans if they could give an update on Gretel Bergmann's injury. They began to trip over their words.

"What do you say you two walk with me to the bar so I can buy you another round of cognacs? It'll give you a few minutes to get your stories straight," Kieran proposed. The German men could do nothing but oblige which left Brundage all alone, for about a second. Gould swept in and sat right next to Avery before he could grasp what was happening.

"Feeling like a fool yet, Mr. Brundage?"

"Fuck off, Gould. Unless you have questions pertaining to competition, I've got nothing to say."

Gould shook his head, "Must be frustrating finding out you have no control and really never did."

"I control my team and problems within it, like Holm. She was sent home because she broke the rules."

Gould let out a hearty laugh, "You can't bullshit me, Avery. I'm the American press. We always know the real story. Oh, and just a follow up on that, Eleanor is in Berlin working for the AP as a reporter." Brundage shot him an angry look. "I hired her as soon as she became available. She's covering special interest stories during the Games," Gould continued, "I think she'll be perfect."

Brundage slugged down his drink, slammed down his glass, and left without another word.

After Gould and Kieran left the club and said their goodnights, Gould could not get the thought of Gretel Bergmann out of his head. He wanted to hear the truth straight from the poor girl's mouth. There was no way the Nazis would agree to a sit-down interview with her, that was for sure, but he had a plan.

"Get dressed. We are going on an adventure." Gould said to Eleanor, as she answered the door to her hotel room in some very small pajamas.

"I'm interviewing Gestring at six in the morning, Alan," she protested.

"A reporter's job is a twenty-four-hour cycle. Get your shit together and I'll meet you in the lobby in five minutes."

The intrepid Gould mapped out his plan to Holm as they walked to the Olympic Village. Holm, who had access to all the women's facilities through her AP credentials, would go and find Bergmann in the women's dormitories and bring her to a waiting Gould. "I'll be sitting on a bench at the lake."

"Jesus, you're gonna get us in trouble. That's the last thing I need," Holm exclaimed. But Gould was determined.

Holm easily made her way past a female security guard and wound through the halls of the dorms. Each door was marked with the first initial and last name of the two or three (or four!) women residing in the room. The building was very quiet and creepy as hell, but Holm kept reading name after name until she got to D. Ratjen and G. Bergmann. She knocked on the door very quietly and Gretel answered. "I'm sorry for the intrusion, Ms. Bergmann. My name is Eleanor Holm."

"I know who you are. Why are you here?" Gretel was completely baffled.

"I can explain everything, but you have to come with me. I'll fill you in on the way."

Gretel looked around to see if anyone was watching, "This is very dangerous, Ms. Holm. Curfew is in a few minutes."

"I don't like it any more than you do, but . . . get dressed. My boss is not gonna take no for an answer."

The two women then very quietly and methodically made their way back to the security guard. Holm promised to have Bergmann back in less than fifteen minutes. The older woman looked at them both suspiciously, but at the same time both Gretel and Eleanor smiled widely and innocently at her. She let them pass without any further questions. The two women then kept up a good pace and made their way to the lake.

Gould was sitting on the same bench that Furstner had shot himself. In the daytime you could still see bloodstains, but Gould was unaware as he saw the two women approach. "Ms. Bergmann, it's very nice to meet you. My name is Alan Gould. I am the sports editor of the Associated Press in America."

"Yes, I am familiar with your work, Mr. Gould. I am not sure I should be talking to the American press, however."

"Why?" Gould asked, completely confounded. "You're one of the athletes, and a world record holder, that can't compete because of an injury. And you were one of the main reasons why the US Team came to the Games--that's news in America, Ms. Bergmann."

Gretel looked around nervously. "Did you come to ask me if I'm really injured?" She thought very hard how to express her next intention in proper English. "You don't understand, Mr. Gould. I can't comment on that. And even if I did, if you were to mention that we even spoke, that would mean grave trouble for me. I appreciate your concern, but please do not let this conversation go any further than the three of us." She turned to Holm. "I think you have a good idea of what I am going through. It's helpless." Holm nodded in agreement. "Now, I must get back before curfew begins. I do thank you both for at least trying to get to the truth." And with that, the lanky high jumper shook both their hands and escaped back to her dorm room.

"I hope to hell you aren't gonna print a word of that," Holm pleaded.

"I'm not. But that story epitomizes the whole Games, Eleanor. And the world will never know until it's too late." Gould replied as the two of them began walking back to their hotel.

As soon as Gould and Holm walked into their lobby, Osten and two Nazi guards met them. "Mr. Gould, good evening, and Ms. Holm, what a nice surprise." Gould and Holm knew right away their whole conversation with Bergmann had been watched.

"Is this about our interview with Ms. Bergmann earlier, Herr Osten?"

"How perceptive. You know you could have scheduled a proper interview through the press department," Osten informed them.

"Why would I do that? And it doesn't really matter anyway; she confirmed her thigh injury. You have nothing to worry about, Osten. It's a non-story." Osten was pleased with this answer and bid them both a quick farewell.

He thought of Mary's last words back in New York. *Be careful.*

In his room, he sat down at his desk and began writing a telegram that he would wire back to the States in the morning.

Dearest Mary. Hope you and the kids are well. Sending hugs and kisses to you all. Buy yourself a dress for the Pulitzer award ceremony! The Games are as exciting as I had hoped, and rest assured, the only drama being played is on the field. The one thing that could improve Berlin is having you in it. Missing you terribly. Love, Alan

At least that last part was true, he thought. He peered out the window at the quiet Berlin streets, and wondered what other games were being played behind closed doors in this city. He made sure to check the locks on his door and went to bed, eager to rest up for the next day's drama, on the field and off.

DAY 5
August 6, 1936

Early the next morning, Gestring was out taking dives at *Olympiapark Schwimmstadion* before most of the athletes were even awake. There was one athlete however, who watched on from the stands. Eleanor Holm had taken on her new role as AP correspondent very seriously. Concentrating on the favorites in each aquatic event, she examined their roads to Berlin, their strengths and weaknesses, their performances in world competition, and their national trials. Through her diligent work, and the down time spent with the young diver the previous few days, Eleanor established that Gestring indeed was the most compelling story of the pool. For starters, at thirteen she was the youngest ever Olympian, but she was also the humblest athlete Holm had ever met. And everyone in Berlin had fallen in love with her, athletes, and fans alike. When she and her coach walked anywhere in the streets of the city, they were mobbed by reporters, and German girls and boys. Holm had been met with similar fanfare in LA before medaling, a much more innocent time in her life, she reflected. She saw many similarities in her younger self and this young phenom, the drive for perfection and insatiable thirst for victory, to be exact.

"You look good out there, Marjorie. Nailed every one of them as far as I could see," Holm said as Gestring sat down for a chat, still shivering from the pool. "I'd like to ask you a few questions on a professional level. Is that okay, Marjorie?"

"Of course," the girl smiled back at her.

"I heard you and Rawls and Hill have made peace. Care to comment?"

"We came to an understanding," the young girl said and left it at that. Holm nodded and accepted the answer for what it was.

"Outside of your teammates, who do you fear the most?"

"The three Germans, Jensch-Jordan especially. She's a European champion and an all-around beast," Gestring said and then changed the tone. "Ms. Holm . . ."

"Eleanor, please."

The girl smiled. "Eleanor, I never got a chance to tell you this before now, but I'm truly sorry what happened to you. I think it was a crumby thing Mr. Brundage did."

Holm was taken aback. "Thanks Marjorie, that's very sweet. I thought it was pretty crumby too."

"My mom always says 'a woman, no matter what her age, should be the master of her own destiny. And the only man that she should ever answer to is her daddy'."

At that moment Holm could've cried. She hadn't thought about her own parents in months.

*　　*　　*

At the regatta course on the Langer See in Grünau, the eight young men from Washington took some practice. They had gone out about an hour after Gestring began diving at the swimming stadium; Moch once again asking his troops to get up early and start working. The morning water was calm, but the temperature was already steaming. Most of the guys were fine, but Don Hume still felt sick as a dog and the heat was making him weaker and getting him nauseous.

Moch's calls were fruitless as the men could not get any proper speed going. Hume was literally pulling up the rear. After a few futile attempts, Moch had them relax and rhythmically row at a moderate pace; that was until the Italians floated by and urged them on for a drag race. The boys pressed Moch to accept. He looked at Hume, who was slightly green, and wondered if it were the right thing to do. Hume, however, glanced back at Moch with no hesitation; he was a go. Moch turned to the Italian coxswain, Cesare Milani, and screamed, "Il tre, amico!" Milani smiled back and began counting out loud.

"*Uno . . . due . . . tres!*" The Italian boat jerked to a start. The American Team, who had been slowly gliding, began to pick up speed rapidly. The two boats were even, and though the race was just for fun, neither wanted to lose. Moch and Milani looked at each other, then ahead, and then back at one another, non-verbally choosing a distance pole about 500 meters away as the finish line. That's when the two men began to urge their team on in earnest.

The Italians were grunting, and the Americans were sweating, and Hume was turning a darker shade of green, all while keeping up a strong pace. Milani screamed encouragement and expletives in Italian. Moch screamed similar words in English. As the two boats approached the designated finish line, it was too close to call, and neither coxswain would accept victory nor defeat. They both instead grinned widely at each other and bade farewell until the next time their paths crossed.

*   *   *

Later that morning in *Olympiastadion*, actual competition continued, beginning with Archie Williams' first attempt at the 400m. Just before entering the track, Marguerite wished him good luck with as big a French kiss that an actual French woman could deliver. Williams strode to the line, feeling like he was Don Juan of Oakland, California. *This fine ass black man is not going to lose his heat*, he assured himself. And out of the eight heats held that morning, his being the seventh, his 47.8 seconds was the best of the day. He would have to wait another twenty-four hours for his semifinals and final, but beside Glenn Morris, Williams, at that moment, was the most confident athlete in Berlin. And he owed it all to his beautiful French muse.

The rest of that day in the stadium Leni had her crew cover the entire men's javelin and triple jump competitions, the men's 110m and the women's 80m hurdles, semis and finals, and the men's 1500m final. The medals were evenly distributed across the global board including a victory for Germany in the javelin final, which appeared from Leni's lens to make Hitler "wild-eyed and ecstatic." The triple jump was a near Japanese sweep. New Zealand won what would be their only medal of the Games, a Gold in the men's 1500m. An Italian and German placed first and second respectively in the 80m hurdles women's Final. And in the last event of the day, the 110m men's hurdles, a blond, blue-eyed kid from the University of Georgia, Forrest Towns, the only Georgia athlete that had ever been chosen to an Olympic Games, came .01 seconds away from tying the World and Olympic record he had just set in the semis, and blew away his competition to win Gold.

Once again, the athletes had helped shape *Olympia* into the impending epic Leni imagined it could be. She helped Ertl wrap up their gear after the last medal ceremony and headed for the exit. "Want to grab a *bier* with me, Leni? We can look at some dailies," Ertl asked in much need of the beverage.

"I've got urgent plans to attend to this evening. Let me know how the coverage looks. Make notes." Leni urged. Ertl looked at her, disappointed. He didn't really want to work, and especially not alone. "Don't look like such a puppy dog, Hans. Grab a few biere and view your masterful work. But take copious notes," she demanded. Ertl's head dropped in exasperation.

*   *   *

That evening, in a government building not far from the *Sportsreich* offices, a single window on the top floor was illuminated. Inside, in a sparse office, Hitler sat in a chair in the corner of the room while Goebbels was pacing back and forth. Putzi sat at a desk with his legs crossed, coolly sucking on a cigar. "The American spy won't be a bother anymore," he said confidently. "I cut off her fingers, one by one. Then her toes. Real ugly pair of feet--smelled awful, too." He laughed.

Goebbels and Hitler looked at each other, un-amused. "That's wonderful, but what did she say about the conspirators?" Goebbels asked.

"The one she called Vladimir was behind the bombing of an SS camp back in '34," Putzi said.

"Vladimir is not his real name," Goebbels said.

"I didn't know that." Putzi said.

Hitler shifted in his chair uncomfortably. "There's a lot you don't know. Stop jerking off that cigar and tell us what you *do* know!" he demanded and slammed his fist against the chair.

Putzi exhaled a long cloud of smoke, unsurprised by Hitler's impatience. He was used to it. "Like I said, she won't be a bother anymore."

Goebbels walked up to Putzi. "What about her relationship with the Dodd's? I understand she is close friends with Mrs. Dodd."

"*Was*," Putzi corrected him.

Hitler stood up. "And what about the daughter? Martha? You seem to know her well."

"What about her?" Putzi asked.

Goebbels cocked his head. "I hear she's fucked her way through half the men in Berlin. She'd probably fuck me if I asked her." He laughed and drew a cackle out of Hitler. Putzi angrily snuffed out his cigar in an ashtray in such a way that made Goebbels suddenly stop laughing. "You've fallen for the American, I see."

"Martha Dodd is innocent. She knows nothing." Putzi remarked.

"Seems that nobody knows anything around here. I'll tell you something that *we* know," Goebbels said, motioning to Hitler. "Martha Dodd is in contact with Boris Vingradov, a key intelligence officer for the NKVD."

"Nonsense."

Goebbels produced a photo of Martha and Vingradov drinking coffee at a café. Putzi stared at it, his jealousy beginning to boil. "Have you been compromised, Putzi?" Goebbels asked, looking back at Hitler.

Putzi stared at the two men and had about enough. "How can you ask me that?" He thought he was walking into a congratulatory meeting. Instead, it turned into an interrogation. He had seen it before with others like him. One minute, a prized and vital tool for the Nazis, the next, just a greasy screw in the machine.

"I have work to do," he said, and walked out of the room thinking only of Martha and what else he didn't know about her.

Goebbels and Hitler watched him go without saying a word. When he was gone and out of earshot, Hitler stood next to Goebbels and said, "Send him off to where he can put his knife to better use. Against the rebels . . . in Spain."

*   *   *

With another day of competition over, the athletes' village commissary was becoming the place to be during evening hours. Earlier in the week the tension was high and there was trepidation between rival athletes. Now, while many still had not competed, the atmosphere was much looser. Athletes of every shape, size, color, and creed shared common goals and aspirations. It was hard to tell the winners from the losers in this place. Jesse Owens and Mack Robinson were sharing stories at a table surrounded by Luz Long and his German teammates. They listened to Jesse's every word (poorly translated by Luz) and Mack's face would be sore the next day from the permanent smile on his face.

"Long John" Woodruff was hanging out with a group of Australian runners while Archie Williams didn't leave Marguerite's side, nor she his. The two Japanese Pole Vaulters, Nashida and Oe were trying their best to communicate with the American Equestrians, and they laughed at each other's odd dialects. Marty Glickman was sitting with Sam Stoller and Foy Draper. They were making fast friends with the Indian field hockey team and their phenom, Dhyan Chand. Glenn Morris was walking on his hands to impress anyone who was watching, and Metcalfe was still spying on Dora Ratjen from across the room, desperately trying to make eye contact.

Bob Moch and his rowing team though, sat alone at a table. They felt a bit like outcasts since they were being housed in a police precinct outside of the Olympic Village. But it didn't take long before their friends from the women's Czech gymnastics team joined them, bringing the new hot American board game that had just reached Prague, *Monopoly,* and a special bowl of hot garlic soup, *Česnečka,* they coerced the commissary chef to make for Don Hume. The sick stroker was able to manage a smile. Everyone was in a joyous mood . . . everyone except Louis Zamperini.

Through the throng of athletes, Zamperini walked with purpose. In the back corner of the hall, he spotted Helene Mayer talking with her German fencing teammates and approached her.

"Helene. Can we talk?"

Mayer handed her glass of wine to one of her teammates and they walked to a quiet area away from the others. "What are you doing here?" she asked. "Aren't you running tomorrow?"

"I wanted to see you. I saw what you did." he said with more than a hint of disappointment.

"I won a medal." She replied defiantly.

"You know what I mean. A swastika? On your arm? You saluted the Nazis--"

"Stop it, Louis. It doesn't mean anything to me. And it shouldn't bother anyone else." She sighed, clearly uncomfortable.

"You don't think it's going to bother every single Jew in the world? You're the only one on the German team."

"It's just a label. They put the armband on me. What was I supposed to do? Rip it off and start quoting the Torah in front of all those cameras? What would you have done?"

Zamperini shrugged. "I would try to think of all the others out there watching."

"You say that now, but you have no idea the pressure I'm under." They stood in silence for a moment. Zamperini put his arm on Helene's shoulder, and she briskly shoved his hand aside.

"And I thought you came here to congratulate me," she said, and turned her back to him to rejoin her teammates, leaving him alone. As he walked away, he looked over the gathering of athletes from around the globe, some whose homelands the Nazis had already had a profoundly negative effect on, and wondered if Helene's actions meant anything to them.

*   *   *

Much later that night at Leni's apartment, she and Glenn Morris lay naked in her spacious bed. She was in the prime of her womanhood but hadn't had a physical relationship in over five years, and never quite like this one. She couldn't believe it, but she was falling in love with this ridiculously brutish lout who could barely spell his own name. She turned over toward him and stared at his face while he slept. It was still that of a little boy and he seemed to have such a childish naive way about him. He also appeared to have a huge heart and any man who spoke so highly of his own father, was essentially a good man. She smiled, rolled back over, and he wrapped one of his arms around her. She was very satisfied and fell asleep immediately.

The moment Leni repositioned herself; Morris awoke but didn't make a sound or movement. He just wanted to take in the moment. A beautiful, successful, and incredibly sensual woman was wrapped in his arms. She had turned out to be much more than one of his mere conquests. He was falling in love with this crazy, high-strung artist whose name he could barely pronounce. But it all just felt so natural. He was the most content he had ever been before in his life, and he began to doze off. The next morning, the young man from Simla, Colorado, who had overcome his own personal demons to get to this moment, would begin his quest for Decathlon Gold.

DAY 6
August 7, 1936

Olympiastadion was buzzing with activity. There was a full schedule of events and Hitler was in attendance and in good spirits. Morell had injected him with 'an exciting new concoction' of drugs; a few dashes of liquid cocaine, a healthy portion of methamphetamine, and a swirl of Grade A morphine as to add 'a clean calming agent to the mix' in the good doctor's own words. It was a blend that would've killed a horse, but the Führer was unfazed other than a permanent grin.

The usual crowd surrounded him in his booth and the Germans were especially pleased. They were ahead in the medal tally by a far and wide margin and boasted such. But Brundage wanted to make sure they didn't overlook one thing, "You may be winning elsewhere, but you couldn't prove it in this venue. My men and women are dominating," he said with a smile.

"Your darkies are dominating," Goebbels interjected. "Let's make no mistake about that. If you had full-bred humans competing instead of jungle beasts it would be a different story."

"That may be your belief, Herr Goebbels, but with all due respect, three American white men lead in the Decathlon. And isn't the winner of that usually dubbed 'The World's Greatest Athlete'?" Latour chimed in, to everyone's surprise. Goebbels looked at the IOC President in shock and huffed. Latour had been very muted during these Games so far, but had secretly concluded that these would be his last. And since finding peace with that decision, he wasn't going to remain passive anymore.

On the field, Leni covered the first day's events of the Decathlon with incredible fervor. She was personally invested now, and by God, to everyone's shock, Morris was near the top. In fact, he was in a close second behind teammate Bob Clark with fellow American Jack Parker right behind them. If Morris were to win the 400m discipline, he and Clark would be in a dead heat going into the finals the next day.

When the gun went off, Morris and Clark jumped out to a lead neither would surrender. And it was nose-to-nose the whole way around the track. Each runner took a slight lead but never for more than a split second. When they entered the stretch run, they ran even further away from the rest of the field, but still not away from each other. It was in the final twenty-five meters that Morris kicked it into a gear that only his father and Judge Mahoney had known he was capable. He beat Clark by a healthy sixth of a second. Parker came in twelfth but was still poised to medal the next day.

Morris ran right over to Leni after his win. She was over-joyed in her own stoic way and leaned into the sweaty athlete's ear. "My whole body is at your disposal this evening," she promised him, and then grabbed Ertl and a camera and ran toward the starting line of the 5000m final. Morris stood motionless with his mouth agape and slightly watering. No woman had ever spoken to him like that, and the bulge in his shorts showed it. He quickly sat down on the field until the moment passed.

*   *   *

One of the longer races in the Games, the 5000m, is a beast. It is too long to sustain a sprint but too short to jog, therefore the pace seesaws constantly. It is a grueling test of high endurance and mental acuity. On this race day, Louis Zamperini had neither. He was dead last going into the final lap and his body ached. He had never fully recovered from his heat three days before, nor the thought of Mayer's indifference to the swastika and Nazi salute.

- 353 -

He thought of his parents and his brother and how he was glad they were being spared this pitiful performance. But as he approached the flag signifying the final lap, he saw Glickman and Stoller and Archie Williams cheering furiously for him from the sidelines despite his position.

Zamperini was instantly inspired and like the Phoenix, he rose from the ashes. He shook off his pain and took off running at a pace no one had ever witnessed. He began passing opponents by bunches and at the stretch run, he had overcome seven men. Though he couldn't catch the leaders and medal, he raced for a top ten finish. With one last surge at the end, he held off the Dane and Norwegian to secure the eighth spot, missing out on seventh by a mere .10 of a second. It was a miraculous last lap. Louis Zamperini had run it in 56 seconds. No 5000m runner had ever accomplished that after already running 4600 meters. The crowd went insane, and not over any of the top three finishers. Zamperini's mad dash had spun the spectators into a real frenzy. They were chanting his name and calling for a victory lap. Glickman, Stoller, and Williams looked around the packed stadium in wonderment. The eighth place finisher had stolen the show.

Hitler was incredibly impressed and stood the whole final lap. He had never seen such a brave athletic attempt. He turned to Brundage and smiled, "You will get me a reception with that gentleman later this evening. Bring him to *Reichssportsführer* Osten's office at 7pm. This boy deserves a personal accolade from me." Brundage answered without hesitation.

"Your wish is my command, *Mein Führer*," he replied with a smile. Latour scowled at Brundage and leaned into his ear.

"YOUR *Führer*?" Latour challenged. "Watch out, Avery, you may get mistaken for one of them."

In the press box, Gould and Kieran were also awed. "That was hands down the most ridiculous ending I've ever seen," Gould said.

"Could you imagine if he would've medaled? The whole crowd would've stormed the field," Kieran joked and then turned his binoculars back toward the track. "Let's see if Williams can run one lap with as much enthusiasm."

*   *   *

It was the moment for Archie Williams to shine. Since the 1936 season had begun, Williams had taken the 400m and made it his own. He had broken the world record while capturing the NCAA championship in the spring with a tremendous time of 46.1. He had never even broken 49.0 seconds before in a race! He then followed that with a 47.0 and a victory at the Olympic Trials. In these Games so far, he had won his heat, his quarterfinal, and his semifinal, lowering his time each race. Williams was feeling blessed, but he also knew his opponents were going after him, and no one more so than his own African American teammate, "the Westwood Whirlwind" James LuValle.

LuValle was a Southern Californian by way of San Antonio, Texas. He was the fastest kid in his elementary school and would sneak onto the nearby High School track and beat their runners as well. And LuValle was whip smart. He had just paid his own way through UCLA and graduated Phi Beta Kappa in chemistry two months before the Games. He was a very wily runner and Williams had to pay close attention.

The other runner he had to keep in mind was the European Champion, Britain's Godfrey Brown. Brown was the anchor of Britain's highly touted men's 4x400m relay and the man had guile. He would always save his best for the best. He never let an opponent see the true Godfrey Brown until a Final, and then all they usually saw was his back.

The runners took their places. "On your mark," the announcer bellowed through a bullhorn. Williams thought of nothing. He wanted his physical instincts to take over his whole body.

"Get set," the announcer continued. The runners took positions. Williams only focused on one sound.

BANG, the gun echoed, and the three favorites exploded off the blocks. This was their race to win and none of the other runners put up even the slightest challenge. Brown took an early lead off the first turn with Williams recovering quickly. LuValle was only a step behind the other two at the half, and it was a blistering 23-second pace. The crowd jumped to its feet and American and British flags waved wildly. Around the final turn all three men were running even, until Brown seemed to make his move heading into the stretch. Williams just kept his head down and ran faster, and faster, and faster. He met Brown's challenge, and the two men were now head-to-head with 100 meters to go. LuValle was right behind them, but he wasn't catching the other two. Brown and Williams traded the lead three times in that short distance, each runner pushing himself to the limit.

At the finish line, with *Olympiastadion* the loudest it had been all Games, Archie Williams ended his miracle year with Olympic Gold. He beat the Brit by two tenths of a second. LuValle got the Bronze, losing the Silver by a tenth of a second to Brown. It was one of the closest and most exciting races of these, or any Olympic Games, and the fans appreciated every bit of every single second.

When Archie found Marguerite waiting for him on the sidelines, she was shedding tears. Williams thought how lucky he was to have found a woman that would literally cry over his accomplishments. And though she was overjoyed by his win, she was crying because of what she had to tell him. She would be leaving back to Bordeaux on a train the next morning. Her father had taken gravely ill, and she would not even be able to compete in the 4x100m relay starting the next day. And if having to leave Williams wasn't bad enough, Perrou's departure would mean the

French Team would have to forfeit their position in the 4x100m, as the FOC did not carry enough female sprinters.

Archie was floored. All the joy of capturing Gold was quickly wiped away, and his own tears of joy turned to despair. At the very least, the star-crossed lovers had expected one more week before having to say goodbye. "My heart is literally breaking. We shall never see each other again, Archie," Marguerite expressed between sobs.

"Why would you think that?" He said, trying to console her.

"Whether we would like to admit it or not, there is going to be a war. And most certainly France is going to be involved. I'm not sure what the future holds, but I'm positive it holds this." She touched his face lightly, "Mon amour. You are quite fabulous in every way. You've touched me like no other person I've ever met."

"And you, me, *mon petite chatte*." He said in his best French, and then held her hands in his. "After my medal ceremony, let's go out in the city and enjoy our last day and night together. No more of this gloomy behavior. What do you say?" She smiled resolutely between tear drops.

"I say, *Oui!*"

*   *   *

Dodd and his Fußball fanatical son, Bill, welcomed the Peruvian Olympic officials into a circular pavilion in the center of *Haus Vaterland*, a sprawling steel building with a copper dome that stood 35 meters tall. The complex also housed the largest cinema in all of Berlin. Dodd thought it was appropriate to host a luncheon there for the South American delegates. Peru had just launched its film business with a successful and unique brand of cinema. The country was feeding off an intense arrival of foreigners due to the rubber boom and was being exposed to new technologies and customs, and the movie industry was one of the more popular.

There was a long table crowded with plates of *spätzle, bratwurst* and *Bratkartoffeln* (boiled potatoes), *Leberkäs* (pork), and *maultaschen* (lamb disguised in pasta dough) for those pretending they didn't eat meat. The Peruvians were gracious and proud to be welcomed to the world stage by the Americans. Dodd and Bill approached POC President, Miguel Dasso, who was gorging on a plate of food. He quickly wiped his mouth with a napkin and shook their hands.

In quite good English he said, "Sorry--I like to eat when I'm nervous. I'm not sure what it is I'm eating, but I like it. Thank you again for having us." He introduced the Dodd's to the star of the *futbol* team, Jorge Alcalde, and they shared well wishes and pleasantries. After Mattie said a brief hello and flew off like a social butterfly, Dasso grabbed another plate of food from the table.

"Not sure why you're nervous. Your team has a great chance to win tomorrow," Bill said.

"That's not why I'm nervous. Tell me, Ambassador Dodd, should I be as trusting of European athletics as some of our fellow competitors?" Dasso asked.

"What do you mean?" Dodd queried.

"In Peru, our sports are rooted in faith, not politics. There are a lot of uniforms in these stadiums. And I don't mean *futbol* uniforms." Dasso said as he munched on his bratwurst. "It's quite unnerving."

Bill tried to appease the Peruvian, "If it's any consolation, it's not just during the Olympics. Their presence is a norm all over Germany."

"As American Ambassador, doesn't this concern you?" asked the man of Dodd. "It is a police state, and all the soldiers appear ready to shoot at any moment. It gives me a very bad feeling."

"Don't worry too much, Mr. Dasso." Bill said confidently. "I'm sure the Nazis are going to play very nicely while hosting the Games. The last thing they want is an international incident." The senior Dodd wished he could be as certain, but kept his feelings to himself.

*   *   *

At the *Zur Letzten Instanz*, Max Bergmann sat at the head of a table sipping beer next to his son Ernst, who was now eighteen years old and fully grown into his athletic body. His sister Hannah, now fourteen years old, sat next to him. She, too, had an athletic appearance despite a layer of baby fat that was clinging to survive. Paula, at the other end, looked at her family in appreciation while enjoying a glass of Riesling.

The restaurant was always one of Max's favorites to come to when he was on business in Berlin. It was a three-story town house situated in a medieval building and it was a perfect place for a great German meal on the spur of the moment. Everyone from Napoléon to Charlie Chaplin had been doing that very thing since 1621, it was Germany's oldest eating establishment, and 315 years later the place had kept its charm.

Hannah asked, "Why are they still friends? If I was kicked off the team, I wouldn't stay friends with any of them."

"She didn't get kicked off the team. She's injured," Ernst reminded her.

"Oh, right."

Max grunted, and this time took a gulp of his pilsner. Paula grimaced; her husband had taken the news of Gretel's so-called injury very badly. "So much time practicing and preparing, her whole life and half mine," he was constantly grousing. She too felt bad about the whole situation, but she also knew her eldest daughter had in mind to leave Germany as soon as the Games

- 359 -

ended, and that is what Max resented most. He had lost his daughter, like every father will at one point, but never under such extreme circumstances. Her husband was having a hard time accepting this.

Gretel and Dora entered, and Max stood and hugged her before she could say hello. "It's so great to see you, *Liebchen*," he said, and introduced himself to Dora. After Ernst, Hannah and Paula exchanged hugs and greetings; they sat back down and prepared for the meal.

Ernst looked at Dora with a confused look on his face. After years of crushing on Gretel's cute teammates as a boy, he was anticipating meeting one of them and maybe even developing a relationship now that he was a man. Not this time. This girl was almost as manly as he was.

The family ordered, and Max caught Paula's eye. He couldn't get over the fact that his daughter Gretel, the best in the world, was relegated to being a spectator while this oddly masculine friend of hers, "Dora", would be competing for an Olympic medal. Paula looked back at him, and her eyes pleaded for restraint. Hannah was oblivious to the tension in the room.

"Did you get to meet Jesse Owens? I heard he runs faster than the wind. Is that true?" Hannah asked.

"Fastest man I've ever seen. Nobody can catch him." Gretel said. Hannah smiled in wonder.

"It seems Germany is doing very well, overall," Paula said.

"We're doing great. Dominant, I'd say. I don't know how many medals we've won, but it's a lot," Gretel said, stealing a glance at Max. "Dora's going to add to that medal count in a couple of days. I think Gold is in her future." Everyone smiled except for Max.

"So, who's better between you two?" Ernst asked.

Dora interjected immediately. "Your sister is the best in the world," she said. "I wouldn't stand a chance against her."

Gretel noticed her father's agitation. She then braced for what she was about to say next. "I guess I'll have to wait until the World Championships in America next year."

"You're going to America?!" Hannah said excitedly.

"Yes. As soon as this is over," Gretel replied.

Max slammed his fist on the table. "Still talking about going to America? I don't believe it."

"Max, please." Paula urged, and looked around the restaurant to make sure no one noticed.

"Where would you like me to go?" Gretel asked calmly.

"You should be competing right here in Germany. This is a farce!" Max said.

"Dad, geez, she's hurt," Ernst said, stuffing his mouth with bread. Max shook his head, and the table went silent. Dora shifted uncomfortably.

Paula quickly changed the subject. "It'll be fine. You go to America and prepare for the next Olympics. I hear it's going to be in Tokyo. That'll be exciting."

"I want to go to Tokyo. Can I come with you?" Hannah asked.

"Of course, you can. Maybe we'll be teammates," Gretel said.

The conversation resumed to politeness. Dora was clearly uncomfortable, but Gretel was fine. The situation was clear to her after being shunned by her country, exiled to England, then invited back to compete for her homeland, only to be shunned again. She wasn't happy to leave her family, but she had plans, and they didn't include Germany.

Max stewed silently. His thoughts were in the present. This wasn't what he had dreamed for his daughter. And not what he had dreamed for his family. Anything about the current situation in Germany wasn't what he had imagined.

After dinner, they took a walk back to the hotel Osten had reserved for them during their Olympic stay. Gretel sang with her siblings and Dora tried to keep up with the music, but was a terrible singer. Paula held her husband's hand. "We are together now, Max. Enjoy these precious moments while we still have them." He looked at her and his eyes were filled with tears. He had been thinking that very thing.

They said their goodbyes in the hotel lobby. Hannah and Ernst wished Dora good luck. She politely thanked them and thanked Paula and Max for the wonderful dinner. After hugs and goodbyes, Max pulled Gretel aside. "You're not really hurt, are you?" he asked.

"Just my pride," Gretel said and gave half a smile. "I'll get over it." Max hugged her tight and then watched them leave. Paula put her arm around him and led him to the elevator. He turned and took one more look at Gretel before she disappeared.

*   *   *

Hitler walked through the hallways of the *Reichssportsführer* Office with urgency. He was excited to meet the American runner, Louis Zamperini. He was enthralled by the young man's final lap of the 5000m. The Führer had no Olympic medal to give him, only genuine congratulations. And a question.

Inside the office, Avery Brundage, Goebbels, Osten, and Zamperini were waiting. They all stood when Hitler entered and immediately saluted, even Brundage. But not Zamperini, who looked at the AOC President like he had gone mad; standing at attention with his arm stretched out like he was one of the Nazis. Hitler couldn't have cared less and shook Zamperini's hand with genuine enthusiasm. The American runner couldn't believe he was standing face to face with Hitler.

"I watched your race, Mr. Zamperini," Hitler said. "Very impressive, indeed!"

"Thank you, sir," Zamperini said. "I didn't win, though."

"Never mind that. It was a finish like I've never seen. I had to meet you to find out what possesses a man to rise above others in a time of desperation." Hitler said, anxious for an answer.

"It's hard to say--" Zamperini said.

"Can you teach it?" Hitler asked. Zamperini looked at him quizzically. Brundage, Goebbels, and Osten were equally curious.

"What I'm asking is; how would you like to stay in Berlin after the Games to coach our runners? " Hitler asked and the others nodded agreeably.

Zamperini laughed, but he knew Hitler was serious. "I'm flattered."

Avery interjected. "We'll take that into consideration, Herr Führer." He turned to Zamperini. "Won't we?"

"Yes, of course," Zamperini said, completely stunned by this whole encounter.

Hitler smiled. "Excellent." He turned to the others. "We could use some good coaching, eh? These Americans are running all over us." Everyone laughed politely. "And, Mr. Zamperini, should you accept my offer, I'll personally see to it that you are taken care of. I take very good care of all my people."

                    *   *   *

Somewhere high in the skies over the Swiss Alps, the drone of a *Heinkel He-70,* a newly built reconnaissance airplane, roared in Putzi's ears as he sat strapped behind the pilot. In the seat next to him was an operative named Otto, whom Putzi had never met before. The two of them had parachutes strapped to their backs. The mission was handed down from the Führer himself: the two of them would drop into Spain, rendezvous with a German undercover unit near the village of Alquezar and await further transport to the town of Zaragoza. They were sent to assassinate a Spanish Republican Army officer who was routinely executing captured Nationalist rebel forces by way of feeding them to pigs. Putzi would make sure the pigs were hungry when he secured his target.

He looked out the window at the darkness below and thought about Martha and the photo that Goebbels had shown him. They told him that Martha had been lying to him since the day they met, but he didn't believe it. He decided that he would confront her about it when he returned. He also decided that he wouldn't waste any time in making this a short mission.

He regained focus on the task at hand and turned to his companion. "She moves fast for a big plane." Without eliciting a response from Otto, he looked behind him towards the cargo bay and noticed it was empty. Usually, a recon plane this big was filled with military supplies or bags of mail. Probably the reason the large plane was cruising so fast. "I hope we'll slow down for the jump," he said. Again, no response.

They suddenly encountered a flash of turbulence and Putzi concluded that they were entering the airspace over the Swiss Alps. As he took a deep breath to calm his nerves, the pilot slowed down the speed of the plane. Otto stood up from his seat and opened the door behind Putzi. The sound was deafening, and the freezing air filled the plane.

"Get ready to jump!" Otto shouted.

"We're not even close to the drop point!" Putzi shouted back. With that, Otto reached into his coat and pulled out a Luger. He pointed it at Putzi's head.

"You jump now." Otto said.

Putzi immediately realized what was happening; the interrogation from Hitler and Goebbels, the sudden mission, the new operative standing above him, that goddamned Mildred woman! He thought of attacking Otto, but the pistol was aimed right at his temple and Otto looked like he was no stranger to using it. He slowly unbuckled his seat belt and made sure his chute was fastened tight. "You don't have to do this," he said, not expecting a response. He didn't get one, other than Otto motioning to the door with the gun.

Putzi stood at the edge and looked down at the vast darkness of the mountain range. Before he could jump, Otto kicked him in the back, and he was thrust out of the plane and into the freezing air. It took him about a thousand feet to stabilize his fall. The sound of the plane's engine quickly dimmed to silence as the cold air filled his lungs. After descending another minute above the treacherous landscape of the Alps, he pulled his chute, and it suddenly became quiet. He was alone in the black night, floating down into the unknown.

Now, aside from the bitter cold, it was almost serene. While he was floating, his mind was racing like rapids. He tried to understand how he wound up 10,000 feet above Switzerland. How fast things had changed. A week ago, he was smoking cigars and sipping cognac with the Führer; laughing, and telling stories, lounging in front of fireplaces, or sitting in fancy dining halls eating delicious meals with men who would one day rule the world. He was Hitler's muscle and he loved it, even the killing. But he had seen how fast Hitler had changed, especially since meeting that mad doctor of his, and how the country had changed and how people sometimes disappeared overnight. He just didn't think it would happen to him.

It was then he realized he would never see any of that, or Martha, again.

*   *   *

The servants at the *Reichskanzler* heard loud moaning and heavy breathing coming from the Führer's bedroom well before dawn the next morning. Eva had demanded a return to Berlin and this time Hitler couldn't stop her. He knew she was furious about how her situation went down at the Opening Ceremonies. Ever since being led to Berchtesgaden, she had sent him disturbing wires and letters threatening another suicide attempt. This scared the hell out of Adolf. If she tried it again, a third time, and succeeded during the Olympics Games no less, Hitler would be embarrassed internationally. He had no recourse but to have his *Poopsie* back for a visit and appease her fragile ego.

There was a trail of undergarments along the carpet in the bedroom; panties, suspenders, bra, shoes, an undershirt, all lay strewn in a line . . . then a syringe, a pill bottle, and a bloody tissue followed. On the bed Hitler, eyes glazed and sweat dripping from his forehead, was dressed in full military uniform and fucking Eva with a baton. Eva was in another world, writhing and groaning on all fours, and Hitler seemed to be enjoying the exercise completely. Maybe having Eva around wasn't so terrible, he started to think.

It was a violent, beautiful, surreal reunion, and Hitler felt himself getting aroused. He unzipped his pants and penetrated Eva, who was shocked to feel her lover inside her. She smiled widely, and just when both were about to reach a climax, Blondi jumped on the bed and began barking.

"Sei still, du dummer Hund! Steig aus dem bette!" Hitler shouted over and over. But Blondi thought he was playing and barked louder, then he started springing up and down on the bed. *"Steig aus dem bette, du kleine Scheiße!"* Hitler screamed at the top of his lungs.

Eva began laughing. Somehow, she really did miss the chaos.

DAY 7
August 8, 1936

At the Hertha BSC Platz, the Soccer Quarter Final between Peru and Austria, was about to begin. Players on both sides warmed up and stretched on the field. It was a foregone conclusion the two teams would meet after the draws were initially announced, and the match quickly became one of the more anticipated events of the Games. One of the two powerhouses of European Fußball was playing against THE powerhouse of South America, and Hitler was right there to cheer for his hometown team. Latour, Diem, and von Halt sat with him, and the two Germans assuaged the especially agitated Führer that Austria was the favorite. "From what I have seen so far during the Games, Austria is playing much better Fußball than the Peruvians right now," Diem commented.

"The match is a shoo-in for your boys, *Mein Führer!*" von Halt added baselessly. Diem wouldn't have gone that far, and looked at von Halt with disapproval.

Closer to the field, FIFA officials, all clad in dark suits with their emblem emblazoned on their jacket pockets, sat ready to act if called upon. And not far from them, Dodd, William, Martha, Miguel Dasso, and a large Peruvian contingent convened.

The pro-Peruvian crowd was wild and vocal. Their cheers of *"Arribe Peru!"* could be heard for miles as they prepared for the ball to be put into play. And when play did begin, they only got louder. But it was Austria that would strike first, 23 minutes in with sure-footed Walter Werginz putting one past Peru's keeper, Juan Valdivieso.

"What did I tell you?!" Von Halt shouted to Hitler, who smiled and applauded for the Austrians.

The crowd noise waned a bit and Dasso shifted uncomfortably in his seat. Fourteen minutes later Austria would once again beat Valdivieso with Steinmatz hitting a beauty in the upper right corner of the net. The Peruvian goalkeeper screamed at Norwegian referee, Thoralf Kristiansen, that the striker was offside and Peruvian coach, Alberto Denegri, saw the same. He was furious and let Kristiansen know it. Dasso looked at Dodd with great concern as the referee called it off and let play continue. It was a curious "non-call" and Dodd hoped this wouldn't be the beginning of a very bad day.

The score remained the same at the half, and Martha excused herself to take care of some unfinished business. "I'll be back before the second half begins," she told her brother and walked up towards the Führer's seats. He saw her approaching and recognized her immediately.

"Fräulein Dodd, a pleasure to make your acquaintance once again," Hitler said.

"Yes, I'm sure," she said with a subtle display of arrogance that wasn't lost on Latour. "Herr Hitler, I haven't seen my friend Putzi in a few days, and I was curious if you may have?"

Von Halt shot up from his seat, "Who is this woman who questions the Führer?!"

Hitler looked up at von Halt with a rage so strong, von Halt sat down immediately and never said another word. He then turned back to Martha, "My dear young lady, Herr Hanfstaengl has been temporarily reassigned. Unfortunately, neither one of us will be graced with his presence anytime in the foreseeable future."

"It must have been so sudden. He would have surely said goodbye to me otherwise," she said with believable innocence and concern.

"I cannot speak of things I do not know. I can only say his expertise was needed elsewhere. It's been a pleasure Fräulein

Dodd," Hitler said with a grin.

Martha smiled back at him, "Until next time, Herr Hitler," she responded, and then made her way back to her seat. She had found out what she wanted. Russian intelligence had reported Putzi had been dropped somewhere over Spain the night before, and Martha had confirmed it. She began to contemplate the past four years she had just spent with Putzi . . . *Oh well, at least they didn't kill the big sap outright,* Martha quickly concluded without giving it a second thought. She bought a pretzel and rushed back to her seat to watch the second half of the match.

The second half began as the first half ended, as neither team could score. Then the Austrians began to play defensively, and this gave the famous Peruvian, Rodillo Negro, time to create opportunities. At the 75th minute, Peru, and their big three of Alcalde, Villenueva, and Fernandez began their comeback. Alcalde scored with a lightning bolt from the top center of the penalty box beating two Austrians with some very balletic footwork. Six minutes later, superstar and Peruvian soccer god Villenueva, scored his third goal of the Games to tie it up. It was a breakaway and Austrian keeper, Eduard Kainberger, had no chance. Villenueva slipped one past his right side while Kainberger had guessed left. The score was tied, and Dasso and the Peruvian fans were ecstatic.

Hitler, however, was furious. He screamed at von Halt and Diem, "A shoo-in, huh? Rectify the situation, *jetzt sofort!*" Diem looked back at him, horrified at the suggestion, but von Halt jumped to action. Latour was more than curious and grabbed him on his way.

"How exactly do you plan on 'rectifying' anything, Messier von Halt?"

"None of your business old man," he shot back and made his way quickly to the FIFA officials.

This was indeed the beginning of what Dodd had feared, a

very bad day. And he knew it as soon as he saw von Halt run up to the group of well-dressed FIFA officials at the perimeter of the field.

*   *   *

At *Olympiastadion*, Marty Glickman waited on the track with an open hand as Sam Stoller sprinted towards him. Foy Draper and Frank Wyckoff stood nearby, loosening up and stretching. The four men were practicing for the 4x100m relay, and they were determined to be completely prepared, practicing the passing of the baton again and again, making sure there was not a single wasted movement during each transition. They were the favorites coming into this event, but they still practiced relentlessly. Stoller was first, Glickman second, Foy Draper third. Frank Wyckoff would be the anchor. Everything was planned and in order; they would leave nothing to chance.

From the press box, Gould watched them practice and admired how in sync they were. "They've been at it all day," he said to Kieran.

"All week, you mean." Kieran said and brought a sheet of paper scribbled with notes over to Gould. He was trying to figure out the standings of the decathlon. The final event--the 1500m was about to take place. "I can't figure this out. They changed the rules again." The scoring tables had been adjusted since the 1934 AAU Championships, which Bob Clark had won convincingly.

Gould studied the paper for a minute and said, "If we all finish in the top fifteen, it'll be a Decathlon medal sweep." With a good showing in the 1500m, Glenn Morris, Bob Clark, and Jack Parker would all win a medal, but it was Morris and Clark who were fighting for Gold.

On the track, Glenn Morris shook hands with Clark and Parker and readied himself for the final event. He was having the time of his life and was brimming with confidence. He looked up into the stands in search of his father. He finally spotted Edgar holding a little American flag with his arms raised and they locked eyes for a moment. He then looked around for Leni, who was in the center of the field with Ertl, adjusting her camera angles in preparation for the event. *She wants a show? I'll give her a show,* he thought.

The race started slowly with Clark setting the pace. The talented pole-vaulter from Finland, Aulis Reinikka, also took a share of the lead. About halfway through, Glenn Morris made his move. He maneuvered to the outside of Clark who tried in vain to keep up with him. Glenn knew he was spent. Reinikka took a commanding lead and Morris was a close second. Jack Parker was on his heels for a moment, and then faded into the distance. Now it was he and Reinikka. Glenn found that extra gear, like the powerful pick-up trucks he used to race down the back roads of Colorado. As he sped towards the finish line, only a meter behind the Finnish runner, he caught a glimpse of Leni--*was she cheering for him?*

Morris crossed the finish line and looked up to the sky. Reinikka may have won the race, but Morris, by coming in second, had enough points to win the Gold medal. It was an unlikely victory. Clark came in seventh, and Parker fifteenth. With this finish, they had swept all three medals in the decathlon. The three Americans rejoiced on the track. Through the gang of runners, Glenn saw Leni in the center of the field, cheering for him in her white suit. He was so turned on and full of adrenaline, that what he did next would go down as one of the most daring and unabashed display of jubilation anyone had ever seen.

Roaring like a lion, he ran over to Leni and upon meeting her, ripped open her blouse and kissed her naked breasts! She was stunned for a moment, then cradled his head and kissed him. The crowd went berserk. In the stands, Edgar put his face in his hands and shook his head, laughing uncontrollably. Ertl almost fell and had to steady himself on his tripod.

US athletes (L-R) Bob Clark, Glenn Morris, and Jack Parker sweep the Decathlon at the Berlin Games, with Morris taking Gold.

Osten, sitting in Hitler's box, along with Goebbels and Brundage, was flabbergasted at the public display of affection. Brundage gasped, his mouth agape, and they all turned to witness the exhibition playing out in front of the 100,000 spectators. Goebbels was frozen and couldn't quite make sense of it all. Hitler just giggled.

In the press box Gould and Kieran cheered. "That's the way a decathlon winner should be received!" Kieran said. Gould laughed and turned to the crowd of reporters.

"If I ever win a Pulitzer, I hope it comes with a beautiful woman's breast to kiss!" He exclaimed, and the group whooped and hollered in agreement.

*   *   *

Back at *Hertha BSC Platz*, the *futbol* match was still tied and went to extra time. Peru could smell blood; Austria looked tired and worn down from the physicality of their opponent, and they were not nearly as sharp. Within minutes, Peru grabbed a lead--or so they thought. Kristiansen called off the goal because of a mysterious foul on a Peruvian fullback that only he saw near mid-field. Because the ball wasn't anywhere near mid-field, no one else of consequence was watching there, therefore, no one knew any better. The score remained at 2-2. Minutes later it happened again. Peru scored, and this time an apparent offside negated the goal. Coach Denegri threw his hands up in frustration and screamed at Kristiansen once again, *"Ese es choro! Hacienda trampa culo!"* he screamed.

Dodd's stomach began to flare up; he knew this was not going to play out well. "Señor Dasso, are you sure you want to remain here?"

Dasso looked at him amazed, "How can I leave? I must see with mine own eyes the depth of this fallacy."

"You can't deny every score for God's sake!" William Dodd screamed towards the FIFA officials.

But again, they did. For the third time in the first 15 minutes of extra time, referee Kristiansen called off a Peruvian goal. This time the crowd wasn't having any of it; Peruvian fans began storming the field and they wanted the Norwegian referee's head. Those who made it onto the field were quickly and violently tackled by security guards. Everyone in the stadium was on their feet, some cheering on the Peruvian fans; others aghast at what was happening. Hitler was screaming, "Arrest them!"

The Austrian players formed a line, ready to protect themselves, their coaches, and the referees. The entire Peruvian team was as angry as their fans, and there was some pushing and shoving back and forth with their Austrian opponents. It took ten minutes for order to be restored and the game to continue, but ultimately, it would be a costly indiscretion.

As soon as the game restarted, however, Peru scored a breakaway with Villenueva once again. And once again, Kainberger went left while the Peruvian striker went right. Before anyone celebrated, they looked to the referee for any sign of a foul. It was a solid goal that could not be nullified. Peru had a 3-2 lead. Dasso shook his fists towards Hitler in defiance.

Two minutes later, another undeniable goal zipped by Kainberger, this time by Fernandez, the great 'Lolo' as he was nicknamed back in South America, and it was his sixth of the Games. It was 4-2 and the Austrians were deflated. When the horn blasted ending the match, despite an astounding three goals during extra time disallowed, the South Americans prevailed.

Hitler was angrier than at any time he could remember. He leaned into von Halt. "What the hell kind of behavior did I just witness?! Is this how they play Fußball in South America?! Von Halt, you *will* rectify this, or it will be the last Fußball match you ever see!" He stomped out of the stadium. Goering dutifully followed.

Things began to quickly unravel from there. Thinking quickly, and desperately, Von Halt raced down to the Austrians and their Head Coach, the Scotsman James Hogan. Von Halt commanded Hogan to demand from IOC officials a rematch on the grounds that the Peruvian players manhandled them, and that spectators, one holding a revolver, had swarmed down on the field.

"A revolver? How would you know that? I'm not sure what I just witnessed Mr. von Halt, but that whole game was a farce! I'd rather get routed fair and square than watch what just happened," the broad Scotsman exclaimed. Von Halt did not care about his opinion.

"You have about two seconds to comply," von Halt said.

"Or what?" the much bigger man said, moving closer to von

Halt. "Do whatever you want, von Halt, but I'm not saying a damned word." Von Halt stepped back in fear. He pursed his lips and then ran to where the FIFA and Olympic officials had gathered near mid-field with Kristiansen while awaiting further instruction. Diem did not join them. He had left the stadium right after Hitler did. He wanted no part of what he knew was coming next, and also knew whatever he argued would be in vain. Latour accompanied Diem on his way out. He, too, felt powerless and wanted out of this charade.

"Austria demands a rematch on account of the Peruvian pitch invasion," von Halt began. "The game should have been discontinued and nullified right then and there," he yelled at Kristiansen.

"Jesus Christ von Halt, do you blame the folks?!" Kristiansen protested. "I'm surprised the fans didn't kill me."

"That's not an excuse. Is it gentlemen?" Von Halt looked hard at the other men. "It's settled." He and the others then made their way to the Peruvian coaches and officials. Dasso had joined them on the field at this point and stood next to Coach Denegri. When the IOC announced its intentions, Dasso immediately filed a formal protest.

"I am on the IOC as well, Mr. von Halt." Dasso began. "And I seem to remember you promising fair play here. Now I believe the esteemed Mr. Jahncke was right all along!"

"Your protest is noted. We will hear your arguments at 5pm tonight at the Reichssportsfuhrer's office. I will have a car take you from here," von Halt said, and hurried off to the exits.

The Peruvian crowd was now at a near riot, and Nazi soldiers had to hold them off the field at gunpoint. Dasso stared at the FIFA officials who had stood there and said nothing the whole match. "You should be ashamed of yourselves. You are no better than they are."

Outside the stadium, a Mercedes limousine picked up Coach

Denegri, Dasso, and Ambassador Dodd, who felt compelled to travel with the Peruvians and speak on their behalf if necessary. Their limo took off right behind three others filled with von Halt and his group. Five minutes into the drive however, the first three cars went one way, and the Dodd/Peruvian limo went the other.

"Excuse me, driver." Dodd interrupted. "Which way are you going?"

"I'm sorry sir. I lost concentration for a moment. We will be back on direction right away, Ambassador."

But that is not what happened. The car drove right up to, and behind, an impromptu German parade, which surrounded them and stopped them dead in their tracks. Hundreds of Olympic tourists and German citizens flocked to the middle of the streets as a large *oompa* band began to march and play. German women in native garb hopped on a makeshift float that sprung up behind the limo. It was a masterful piece of orchestrated choreography that rivaled only the great Busby Berkley, and von Halt had pulled it off in a matter of minutes. The three unfortunate men, stuck in the sole automobile in the middle of all this sudden revelry, would not make their meeting by 5pm.

The Peruvian defense, never being heard, the present IOC members, minus Latour of course, and the FIFA heads, had no choice but to side with the Austrians. A rematch was scheduled August 10 with no spectators allowed. The thousands of Peruvian soccer fans who had travelled to Berlin to specifically follow their team, would not be invited back.

*   *   *

Later that evening, in the press room at the Olympic Village, a jam-packed press conference was underway. Dasso and Denegri, with their team right behind them, announced to a large group of reporters, including Gould, Holm, and Kieran, that Peru would not go along with a rematch. A collective gasp came from the Spanish speaking press.

"We've no faith in European athletics. We have come here and found a bunch of merchants." Dasso exclaimed. "The complete Peruvian Olympic delegation is pulling out of the rest of the Games in protest. Colombia has joined us in solidarity. And our neighbors in fair play, Argentina, Chile, Mexico, and Uruguay express their outrage." The whole group then walked out of the room, and out of the Olympic Games.

As reporters scrambled to their typewriters, Holm looked at Gould with disgust, "I'm surprised it took this long for something to happen."

"Now I'm sorry I missed the match. The decathlon was apparently tame compared to this doozy. And that even had naked boobs!" Kieran cracked with a half-smile.

Dodd, who was sitting on the other side of Gould, had had enough. His time in all this madness must come to an end. "I'm done here, Alan," he turned, and told the respected reporter. Gould looked into the tired man's eyes as he continued. "It's only going to get much worse. And no diplomacy in the world is going to stop it. It's an aggressive and incurable cancer that's going to spread to every vital organ on this continent."

Alan Gould knew no truer words could have been spoken. He put his hand on the man's shoulder, "I'm sorry Mr. Ambassador. You've performed more than admirably, and under the most insane conditions any country could ask of a citizen and his family. You should be proud."

William Dodd, at that moment, was not feeling proud. He was feeling empty, drained of every possible emotion.

*   *   *

Outside his home, William Dodd exited a taxi and watched it

drive away. He took a good, long look at his house, and then solemnly walked up to the front door. Inside, he took off his coat and hung up his hat. From the kitchen, he heard his family cleaning up after a dinner, which he also missed. Bill was describing the soccer match to Martha and Mattie.

". . . then it was mayhem. Everyone ran onto the field." The sound of washing forks, knives, and dinner plates suddenly stopped when they heard Dodd shuffle down the hall. Bill called out, "How'd the meeting go, Dad?"

Dodd slowly walked past the kitchen without a word, not even acknowledging his family's presence. Mattie watched him walk past and said, "I saved you some dinner." The three of them looked at each other and Mattie shook her head as if to say, "Leave him be."

Dodd carried his briefcase into his study, placed it on his desk, and sat near the newly installed rotary telephone. He looked up a number from a directory on his desk, picked up the receiver and dialed. "Long distance, please . . . The United States." He stared at the device while being patched from one operator to another, and it occurred to him how easy it would be for someone to listen in to his calls. It didn't matter now. Besides, it seemed that the Germans already knew his every move.

He gathered his thoughts until the transmission finally reached the United States. "State Department, Washington."

A young woman answered, "Hello, Secretary of State's office."

"Cordell Hull, please. This is William Dodd."

"Right away, Mr. Dodd. Please hold."

Dodd waited for a moment, then Hull got on the phone. "William, my friend, how are you? And how are the Games? I hear they are going very well."

"Hello, Cordell. Good to hear you, too. The Games? They're a goddamn disgrace. But I'm not calling to discuss the Games. I'm calling to officially announce my resignation." He heard Hull's familiar sigh. But this wasn't another threat. "I need you to inform Mr. Roosevelt and his cabinet first thing tomorrow."

"William--"

"I've had enough, Cordell. It's over. I can't do it anymore. And for those who are listening in to this telephone call, you can spread the word to your German heads of state that this 'irresponsible scandalmonger' will be out of your hair forever." There was an immediate silence. Dodd never took his old friend for a fool, but he wondered if it was the first time it occurred to Hull that their correspondence over the years had been bathroom-reading material for German spies.

As Dodd spoke to the Secretary of State halfway across the globe, Mattie stood at the doorway listening. Whatever happened earlier that day had tipped the scales. Over the years, she had watched him write countless letters to Senators and statesmen back home about the fascist dictatorship that was seducing this beautiful country. The family's nightly conversations, once fueled by eager optimism, had turned to frustrating futility for her husband, which, no matter how much he denied it, took a massive toll on his health. The three years they had spent in Berlin seemed like ten, and it also took a toll on their family. Even so, she was proud of her husband, and knew that whatever was fracturing this country could never breach their marriage.

Dodd hung up the phone and sat back in his chair. He looked at Mattie and asked, "You ready to go home?" She walked over and hugged him.

Bill came in the room asking, "What was the ruling? Peru won the match, right?"

Dodd, still holding Mattie, looked at his son with a content smile and said, "I never made it to the meeting." He told Bill and Mattie about the FIFA ruling to replay the match, and the press conference, where the South Americans withdrew from the Games in solidarity. Then he told them about the limo ride that was conveniently detoured. He had dealt with the baffling ignorance of his contemporaries, the fruitless appeals to his government, and the degrading insults, but being trapped like an animal in a cage was too much to endure. He refused to be intimidated. Bill agreed that they needed to get out of Berlin before it became impossible to escape.

Upstairs, Martha had her ear pressed against the floor vent, and had been listening to the conversation the whole time. Anger grew inside her until it boiled over, and she ran downstairs to confront them.

"You can all run away back to America, but I'm not going anywhere!" she said. Her audacity didn't shock anyone.

Bill shot back, "What are you going to do here?"

"I'm going to fight," she said. "There are people here who need my help and I'm going to help them any way I can."

Bill let out a laugh. "The Communist Party, you mean?"

"Quiet!" Dodd bellowed in a way that was immediately understood by the family that the walls may have ears. "They'll be no more talk of this! We're leaving Berlin, so make whatever arrangements you need."

"Never!" Martha cried and stormed out of the room. Dodd watched her go, and it occurred to him that his own ideologies had filtered down to his daughter. But while he was tired and sick, she was young and virile, and as passionate as he might have been at twenty-six-years old.

The family sat in silence for a moment, until Mattie and Bill left him alone in his study. He reflected on the many hours he had spent there, truly believing his efforts were not in vain. He had courageously tried to make a difference, but realized that out in the world, and inside his home, there were just some things he could not control.

*   *   *

Inside the American offices, on the grounds of the Olympic Village, Avery Brundage peered through the blinds and watched athletes from all over the world walking to and from the commissary and dormitories. He remembered how things were so different when he competed in the 1912 Olympics and how proud he was to be involved in its growth. As an IOC member, he expected to have the power to make sure that it continued to evolve.

Ritter von Halt sat at a desk smoking his pipe looking over the results of the day's competition. "Hmmm . . ." Brundage turned from the window. "Your Negroes have been exceptional on the track. Without them you wouldn't have half your medals."

"They have been remarkable," Brundage responded.

"Remarkable indeed. However, it is quite embarrassing to the Führer," von Halt said. "But what can we do?"

"Not much, I'm afraid," Brundage said.

Von Halt took a puff on his pipe and looked at Brundage. "The 4x100 relay is tomorrow. The Führer can accept another win by the darkies, but do you think it's necessary to further humiliate him by having your Jewish runners win Gold alongside them?"

"They haven't won yet," Avery said.

"I know that, but just in case they do, let Jesse Owens and the other Negro take the place of the two Jews," von Halt said.

Avery stared at him blankly as von Halt's words sank in. "You're asking me to remove two Jewish runners from the relay team the night before the race?"

"I'm not asking," von Halt said, and they stared at each other for a moment.

Brundage turned his back and paced to the other end of the room. "After what happened today between Austria and Peru, that farce of a ruling in front of the whole world--"

"The ruling was validated by FIFA and the IOC."

"The South Americans are leaving the Games!" Brundage yelled. "You've asserted your will on the outcome of a major Olympic event. Don't deny that. Now you're telling me to remove two Jews off the team so the Führer can sleep better at night?"

"Don't be so dramatic, Avery. It's just a race."

"I brought you the United States. I brought you these Games!" Avery said defiantly.

"And now you're a member of the International Olympic Committee. Isn't that what you wanted?"

"Yes, but not like this," Brundage said.

"Tomorrow's race could have a significant outcome on your future in the IOC. You don't want to wind up like your former colleague, Mr. Jahncke, do you?" von Halt asked. "It's your problem, Avery. Solve it." He walked out of the room, leaving Brundage alone.

When von Halt was gone, Avery looked at the papers on the desk that detailed the day's results. He crumpled it up into a ball and threw it in the trash. After years of service, loyalty, and commitment, it had come to this. He had always believed in his heart that he had done right by his athletes and his country, even in the face of stiff opposition. He thought of Judge Mahoney, wherever he was, and actually envied him for a fleeting moment. He was being used in an unfathomable way, and it cut a piece of his heart out thinking of how he was going to ask Coach Robertson and Coach Cromwell to remove their Jewish athletes from the team, hours before they were to compete.

He paced alone in the room for a while, trying to convince himself that von Halt was right . . . maybe it was just a race. He took a deep breath and gathered his resolve. No . . . he wouldn't ask his two coaches. He would tell them. He was the one in charge, and though Cromwell would follow him blindly, Robertson certainly would not. Brundage smiled; maybe von Halt had done him a favor. This could be the ruling that finally got rid of his old track coach. *And,* Brundage thought, *who would really care in the long run?* History never remembered the non-competitors. The names Glickman and Stoller wouldn't mean a hill of beans two weeks after the Games. He walked over to his desk with assurance and pressed down the intercom, "Margaret, get me Robertson and Cromwell. ASAP."

*   *   *

On the street outside of Brundage's office, Gould waited patiently on a bench as trolley after trolley passed by. He stealthily followed Robertson and Cromwell to Brundage's office after they abruptly left the relay team in the middle of their training session. He glanced up at the light coming from Brundage's office and wondered what the impromptu meeting was about.

When Robertson and Cromwell finally emerged, Gould approached them. "Hello, gentlemen." Cromwell rolled his eyes angrily, but Robertson had a sullen, withdrawn look on his face. "May I ask the reason for the sudden meeting up there?"

"None of your business, Gould!" Cromwell snorted.

Robertson turned to Cromwell and said, "Shut up and get the hell out of here! I'll see you tomorrow. Call the boys for the meeting." Cromwell looked at Gould, spat on the ground, and stormed off in a huff without another word.

"We decided to make a change in our lineup for the 4x100 meters. Glickman and Stoller are out. Owens and Metcalf are in," Robertson said, avoiding eye contact with Gould.

"Why the last-minute change?" Gould baited.

"We have reason to believe that certain teams are also making last-minute changes. They're going to unleash their secret weapons on us, so we had to respond accordingly."

"Sounds terrifying," Gould said, facetiously. "Can I quote you on this for tomorrow's papers in the US?"

Robertson paused, then looked back at Brundage's office, and begrudgingly said, "Go ahead."

DAY 8
August 9, 1936

In November of 1918, a horse-drawn carriage rushed through the countryside on the outskirts of Bremen, Germany. The shipbuilding city lay in northwest Germany on the banks of the Weser River, which connected to the North Sea. Being a manufacturing city populated with working-class citizens and geographically favorable, it became an important city to the military. Thus, the landscape was completely ravaged by The Great War. The carriage passed destroyed tanks and fallen trees amidst modest homes, and finally stopped at a cottage at the end of a graveled path. A midwife jumped out of the carriage and ran into the cottage clutching a medical kit.

Inside the house, a nervous Heinrich Ratjen paced outside a bedroom door. Screaming bellowed behind it. The midwife barreled up the staircase, jostled Heinrich aside, and ran into the room. The man resumed pacing, feeling completely useless while his wife screamed bloody murder inside the small room.

Then it abruptly stopped. There was silence. Heinrich slowly walked towards the door, hoping for the best, fearing the worst. Then, he heard the most glorious sound – the crying of his first child. He bent over and wept.

The midwife popped her head out of the door. "Heini, it's a boy!" she cried. Heinrich smiled and wiped the tears of joy from his eyes. He walked away from the door and laughed. "A boy," he said, and waves of thoughts went through his mind. What would he become? Would he work in the factories of Bremen like so many of his friends? Would he take over the bar that Heinrich owned and managed? He pulled a long cigar from his breast pocket and made his way down the staircase to smoke it.

When he got to the bottom, he proudly lit the cigar and took a big puff. Just as he blew a thick cloud of smoke into the air, the midwife yelled from above. "Wait – it may be a girl after all!" The cigar fell from Heinrich's hand, and he stood there staring, bewildered.

"May?"

Dora had heard the story from her father many times over the years. And as she grew up, her own confusion rose about her gender. She had the body parts of a boy, sort of, but the affectations, feelings, and mindset of a girl. But on this day, as she competed in the Finals of the Woman's High Jump, the confused child was never so sure of herself.

Gretel Bergmann watched the Final from the sidelines. She was in awe. She had never competed in front of such a large audience, and feelings of anger and betrayal crept into her. She knew she could've taken Gold in front of her hometown crowd. She had been reduced to a cheerleader and though she was openly rooting for Dora, things should've played out very differently.

Ratjen, on the other hand, was strongly and surprisingly contending for Gold or Silver going into the final jump. Csak from Hungary, Odam from Great Britain, and Ratjen's teammate, Elfriede Kaun were also fighting for a medal. When Ratjen spotted Gretel, she quickly left the field and ran over to her. "Thanks for coming. And thank you so much for everything the past year," Ratjen said, and hugged her roommate. "I want you to know that whatever happens next, you are my hero, Gretel Bergmann, and that you will always be in my thoughts for as long as I live."

"That's a funny thing to say, Dora. You should be concentrating on your jump. You are on the verge of winning a medal, and it could be Gold!" Gretel said, excited for her friend.

"I don't need to concentrate. I know exactly what I must do." Ratjen exclaimed, and gave Gretel one last hug before running back to the field. "I love you very much dear friend." Gretel watched curiously as Ratjen returned to the competition.

The bar was set at 1.60 meters. Odam was the first to clear, and did so by a hair. Csak followed, easily clearing the bar and then pumping her fist when she sprang back up off the sand. Like the American runners Stoller and Glickman, Csak was proud of her heritage and wanted to show the Nazis what a 21-year-old Hungarian Jewish girl could accomplish. Elfriede followed that with a strong jump of her own.

It was Ratjen's turn next. She was as focused on this jump as any she had ever attempted. At that moment, Dora Ratjen, the mentally abused and sexually confused eighteen-year-old, understood more than any other athlete in Berlin, the gravity and scope of these Games, and the precarious leap she was about to take. She looked over at Gretel, who had her hands together in what seemed like a prayer. After all her friend had been through, she was still there for her teammates. Ratjen took a deep breath and began her approach towards the bar. Her line was perfect, twelve strides at a 35-degree angle, and then a strong liftoff. In mid-air, she knew she was going to clear easily, but that was not what she had intended. As her body flew over the bar, Ratjen moved her hand down and gently tapped the bar, sending it crashing down. The whole stadium gasped in unison. It was just apparent enough she had done it on purpose.

Goebbels, sitting with Osten in Hitler's box, was furious. "Arrest that woman. I want an immediate investigation!" Goebbels yelled at the Sportsführer.

"Into what, Reich Minister, your own duplicity?" Osten reminded Goebbels in his ear. "If it weren't for the Bergmann girl getting in Ratjen's mind, we would've succeeded. Let her go to America. Get her out of our hair already." He pleaded. "I'll force Ratjen back in line," he promised.

Goebbels could do nothing but comply. He knew he had put

himself in a corner. He had needed Bergmann to get the US to the Games and now she had come back and bit him in his ass. "You should've never put them in the same room then," he snapped back, unwilling to take full responsibility.

"That was your idea as well, Joseph," Osten reminded him. "And look what good ANY of this did us. A fucking Jew is going to win anyway!" He grumbled, as Csak became the only competitor to clear 1.62 winning the event in the process. He and Goebbels threw their hands up in disgrace. And to make matters worse, the spunky Hungarian ran in front of their box and saluted them with two firmly raised middle fingers and a spit of disgust; a gesture that did not go unnoticed by the two Nazis. "At least our Jew would've acted accordingly," Osten said, thoroughly offended.

In all the madness of the final jumps, Ratjen had vanished. Gretel scanned the field, but her friend was nowhere in sight. Her eyes welled with tears. It was the most touching display of camaraderie Gretel had ever witnessed, and she would never get the chance to tell Dora how much she appreciated it.

Fearing her life, Ratjen had disappeared unnoticed, into the bowels of the stadium, and then out one of the entrances dressed in men's clothing. Remaining loyal up to that very moment, these two friends, who encountered the most dangerous and sinister of odds to get to these Games, would never see each other again.

*   *   *

As Ratjen was making her escape through the underground hallways of the stadium, Coach Robertson, Assistant Coach Cromwell, and seven American runners, Owens, Metcalfe, Draper, Wycoff, Stoller, Glickman, and Robinson, held a meeting in one of the clubhouses. Stoller and Glickman were juiced. The day had finally arrived for them to compete. And there was no doubt in their minds they were going to win.

"Boys, this is a tough decision," Robertson began, and rubbed his temples. "We feel the Dutch and Germans have been holding back their best runners this week while practicing for the 4x100. There has been talk of secret weapons. So, just to make sure," his voice trembled, "we are replacing Glickman and Stoller with Owens and Metcalfe." He looked up at the young men and could barely hide his emotion.

A horrible hush came over the room. Marty Glickman and Sam Stoller were blind-sided and at first, speechless. Metcalfe broke the tension, "Why me, Coach? I don't need to run that. I got my medal, and hell with the Silver I won in LA, that gives me two. Let's spread the wealth."

"Shut up, nigger. You'll do as we say!" Cromwell lashed out to a shocked Metcalfe. Robertson immediately rocketed out of his seat and stood over his assistant.

"Get out! Right now, and don't dare say another word or by God I'm gonna kick your ass right here," he threatened Cromwell. The assistant coach turned beet red, and knowing damned well even his own athletes wouldn't stop Robertson, he left in a hurry. The head coach sat back down and regained his composure. "I'm sorry gentlemen, I know this must come as a shock. But . . ." he began to get emotional, "It is out of my hands. Ralph, Jesse, you're in."

Glickman shot up, "There are no secret weapons. That's all bullshit," the quickly maturing young man began. "How convenient that Sam and I are the only Jews on the whole American team and we're the ones replaced. We earned our chance to be here!"

"I agree Marty." Robertson said. "But I have my orders. You're 18 years old and have two, probably three Olympics left to look forward to. And with Cromwell taking over as coach, well . . ." He looked at Draper and Wycoff, "at the very least, he creates champions," he conceded.

Stoller stood and spoke. Sam was not much of a public speaker and most of the time was very timid. "Cromwell lied to my face when we got here and told me I was running. I would've left this place the minute I arrived if I had even the slightest inkling this would've happened." He became quite grave, "I don't blame you, Coach. I thank you for it. I've been so blind, so sheltered. For the first time in my life my eyes are truly open." This cut Robertson to the core. He himself had never possessed one ounce of racism or anti-Semitism. He dropped his head, crushed by the young man's comments.

"Come on, Coach," Wycoff pleaded. "Owens and Metcalfe haven't ever practiced with us. And no relay team ever waits to bring out a ringer the day of the race. You know that."

"Our chances are much better with the guys we've been working with all month," Draper added.

But there was someone in the room who remained conspicuously quiet. Owens had secretly wanted a fourth Gold, a feat no Olympian had ever achieved in one Games. He had told a few reporters how badly he wanted the opportunity but knew this was the only way it could be possible, so he never broached the subject with Coach Robertson. But now that it was within his grasp, without any machinations of his own, he just sat there, mouth closed, and watched how the whole thing played out.

"I understand all your objections, but we have to compete with whom the AOC feels are its best, and that's Owens, Metcalfe, Draper, and Wycoff. Suit up and get out there and start practicing." Robertson said, defeated.

Stoller was shaking, he was so upset. "You mean with what the AOC feels is its less Jewish athletes. Shame on you, Robertson, and shame on Brundage as well!"

Glickman had the last word. "Jews from all around the world have been winning medals since Day One of these Games. A

Jewish girl just won the fucking High Jump for Christ's sake! How are we any different?!" He screamed at the top of his lungs, "Whose Nazi cock is Brundage sucking?!" This sent shivers down everyone's spines. Glickman tried to control his rage, "The whole thing sickens me." He seethed and then stormed out of the room.

Coach Robertson knew this would be the last time he would ever address Olympic athletes, and he so wished it could have been under better circumstances. He had given his whole adult life to the American Olympic cause, as player and coach, but this, he recognized, is how he would be remembered. It didn't matter that he and his teams had always performed well above expectations; with this one roster change his legacy would be forever re-written, tarnished. He began to wipe tears from his eyes as the runners slowly filed out of the clubhouse.

The eventual Gold-winning 4x100 relay team: (L-R) Jesse Owens, Ralph Metcalf, Foy Draper, and Frank Wyckoff.

At race time, Glickman and Stoller, in their USA sweatshirts, sat with Gould and Kieran and what seemed like a thousand reporters in the press box. Stoller had persuaded Glickman to stay at the stadium and root for the team. Draper and Wycoff were still competing and there was no reason not to cheer them on. Glickman wasn't keen on the idea but did feel loyal to his former teammates, so he agreed, but would not go on the field. Gould was more than happy to have them sit with him as his guests. And as the two young men watched the heats end, and the final about to begin, neither was surprised to learn there were no secret weapons on the Dutch or the German teams.

The Final was ultimately anti-climactic. The Americans won by almost a full two seconds over the Italians and the Germans and in World Record time. In fact, they had beaten their own World Record they had set a few hours before during the first heat. Glickman, Stoller and the reporters cheered. Gould and Kieran watched the two dismissed runners celebrate with genuine regard. "What sportsmanship." Gould said to Kieran.

"I'm not so sure I would have handled it with such class," Kieran admitted.

On the field, the four runners embraced. Wycoff had won his third Olympic 4x100 in a row, Metcalfe finally got his Gold, Draper won his first (and ultimately only) medal, and Jesse Owens cemented his place in athletic glory with his fourth Gold of these Games.

The American track and field team had performed brilliantly at *Olympiastadion*. And with the men's AND women's 4x100 victories, the last track and field events of the Games, they had established their true dominance.

They would now become mere spectators, as the XI Olympiad turned its attention to equestrian disciplines, gymnastic mats, and more importantly for the Americans, the aquatic events.

DAY 11
August 12, 1936

ATTN: AP OFFICES NEW YORK CITY

DATELINE: AUG 11, 1936

DAY 9 AND 10 OF THE BERLIN GAMES . . . US MEN HAVE MEDIOCRE SHOWING IN FIRST TWO DAYS OF BOXING COMPETITIONS. FLYWEIGHT, LOUIS LAURIE AND BANTAMWEIGHT, JACK WILSON FARED MUCH BETTER THAN THEIR TEAMMATES, MAKING IT THROUGH TO NEXT ROUNDS WITH EASE. GERMAN BOXERS LOOK STRONG ACROSS THE BOARD.

SOCCER COMPETITION CONTINUED WITH ITALY VS. NORWAY SEMIFINAL AND THE SCHEDULED REPLAY OF PERU VS AUSTRIA, IN WHICH PERU FORFEITS IN PROTEST. AUSTRIA WILL GO ON TO PLAY POLAND AUGUST 11 IN THE SECOND SEMI-FINAL.

MUCH ACTION AT OLYMPIC SWIM STADIUM AS THE MEN'S COMPETITION BEGAN. RIE MASTENBROEK OF HOLLAND WINS ONLY FEMALE RACE OF DAY TAKING GOLD IN THE 100M FREESTYLE FINAL.

MEN'S FENCING, FIELD HOCKEY, AND HANDBALL CONTINUED WITH NO GREAT AMERICAN SUCCESSES.

WOMEN'S SWIM AND DIVING TO BE FURTHER DISPATCHED BY AP CORRESPONDENT ELEANOR HOLM.

10:37PM CEST: ALAN GOULD

*   *   *

The next day, Gould, Kieran, and a swarm of other reporters, took their lunch at a popular Bierhalle near Olympic Park. Gould and Kieran had spent their morning watching the first few rounds of the equestrian jumping events, and felt lunch should have a bit more excitement.

The talk was mostly about the upcoming 3m springboard event later at the *Schwimmstadion*. Reporters were putting friendly bets on their choices to win, and though Rawls was the favorite, Gestring was bringing in the most dough.

"My money is on the 'little dolphin' in an upset. Oh, I like that one." Kieran said and jotted down his new nickname.

"It's better than 'Dark Streak'. I'll give you that." Gould added without hesitation, bringing the room to a collective belly laugh. Gould would attend the diving competition as a spectator. He was counting on Holm to do most of the heavy lifting at the women's pool events. He was impressed with how she had comported herself the last eleven days. She had really taken on her AP responsibilities with gusto, but he knew the next couple of days at the pool were going to be bittersweet for his young friend.

*   *   *

Eleanor sat by herself in the stands at Schwimmstadion as the semi-finals of the women's 100m backstroke ended, and the venue prepared for the highly anticipated 3m springboard diving finals. She had been forced to watch what would have been her main competition, Nida Senff and Rie Mastenbroek, both from Holland, win their semis and move on to the finals the next day. Mastenbroek was the world record holder, and Eleanor had held the Olympic record before Senff had broken it the day before. But Holm knew she could beat them both, and like Gretel Bergmann at the High Jump finals, she stewed while watching the competition.

The stadium began to fill to capacity for the compulsory part of the diving event. All the University of Washington crew showed up, including Don Hume, who still couldn't shake his flu. The Men's and Women's US track team arrived in full force as well. And front and center of that group was John Woodruff, who came to see his new best friend win Gold. In fact, most of the 15,000 people there were rooting for Gestring. But Rawls and Poynton-Hill had other ideas. Though the three divers had made a pact, each wanted to win. And while the field included three top Germans and two excellent Japanese divers, it became apparent quite quickly, that this was going to be an All-American civil war.

The compulsories were made up of three pre-selected dives; the straight run forward somersault, the standing backward header with pike, and the difficult straight running isander half gainer. Each of these dives must be completed perfectly in full, or points were shed for every minute mistake. The Americans made no gaffes, and by the end of the first round, all three were fighting for the top spots and by a wide margin. The three Germans performed adequately at best, and the Japanese divers even below that. The crowd was buzzing for the final three facultative dives. It was up to the athletes to wow the crowd, and more importantly, the judges, on these dives the woman had chosen themselves. Neither Rawls, nor Poynton-Hill, nor Gestring, knew what the other would bring. Though they had been practicing together all week, they kept it restricted to compulsory dives. These women weren't giving anything away to each other.

First up was Poynton-Hill. This was Hill's third Olympics; she had won Silver in the 3m at Amsterdam and a Gold in LA in the 10m. Her 10m final here in Berlin, in which she was favored, was the following day, but winning the 3m was always her Holy Grail and she planned on doing it here. She calmly approached the edge of the platform. She looked down at the water and then out to the crowd before putting her hand to her sides. She had chosen a forward one and a half somersault pike for her first dive, and she executed it with perfection. She entered the water with a slight bend that created a bit of a splash, but otherwise she nailed it. The judges had her now at the top.

It was Katherine Rawls turn. "The Minnow", as she was nicknamed, was an aquatic force. She was equally adept at the swimming competitions and was asked that day to fill in as one of the four swimmers of the 4x100m freestyle. The 3m though, was her favorite, and after getting Silver in LA, she wanted Gold badly. She approached the end of the platform and thought only of her dive, a reverse two and a half somersault tuck. She leapt into the air and performed her moves with strength and agility, entering the water with minimal splash. She knew right away she had done well, and the crowd and judges responded accordingly. She had momentarily taken over the lead, but now it was Gestring's turn.

The slight blonde turned her back to the water when she arrived at the end of the platform. Her dive was the back one and a half somersault tuck. She flipped off the platform and spun gracefully through the air, coiled into a tight ball, and outstretched her arms and legs just before entering the water. It was as if nothing at all had penetrated the pool. The dive was flawlessly executed, and Gestring was back in the lead.

The spectators were all abuzz, and Woodruff was as nervous as if he was about to run a race. He fidgeted and rocked back and forth. Archie Williams, sitting next to him, just laughed at him when the two made eye contact.

"Just be quiet, you," Woodruff snapped back. "I've never seen diving before. It's very nerve wracking."

"Oh, is that it?" Williams joked back. "You should be rooting for all three of them."

"Peeshaw." Woodruff waved him off. "Marjorie may be the most talented kid I've ever met," he said, and continued to rock.

Bob Moch had never watched competitive diving, either. None

of the rowers had, but they were just as vested as any of the crowd. Bob turned to Hume, who, despite looking like crap, was on the edge of his seat. "Fucking crazy, right?"

"I gotta admit, I had no idea I'd be so into it." Hume responded with his arms holding his belly, whose pain would not subside.

At the pool's edge, Holm was furiously writing notes as the swimmers prepared for the second round. The Americans actually had a chance to sweep, and Eleanor was completely into the drama of it all. She had never given two shits about diving, but she had to admit at that moment, that it was pretty damned thrilling.

The second round of facultative dives went pretty much like the first round, and the positions remained the same. The crowd was now hushed in anticipation as the third, and final round, of this American battle began.

Poynton-Hill again started things off, and this time she chose a back dive half twist in a straight position. She performed it beautifully and shot back to the top. The crowd went wild, and the American athletes in the stands roared.

Rawls was now ready to take her shot at Gold. She was about to pull out all the stops. She jumped into the air and executed a reverse one and a half somersault with two twists. It was a difficult dive, and when she entered the water with minimal splash, she knew her scores were going to be high. They were, and she regained the lead. The best Hill could do now was another Silver. The last jump of the competition, and the Gold medal, hinged on Marjorie Gestring. And if she wanted to upset Rawls, she had to perfect.

When she climbed the ladder and stepped upon the platform, the crowd was as loud as it had been the whole day. When she approached the edge and suddenly performed a handstand, the crowd immediately hushed. Gestring had chosen an arm stand back double-somersault tuck, with half twist thrown in for good measure. It was the most difficult dive chosen from all the competitors. Hill and Rawls held hands, and Rawls could hardly watch. Gestring seemed to stay in the armstand position for an eternity, and it made Woodruff want to puke from anticipation.

When Gestring took off cleanly, she immediately began her moves. She flew through the open-air, tumbling, turning, and twisting like the finest gymnast. Every move was tight and fast, and she entered the pool again, completely vertical. It was perfect. The stadium went nuts, and Hill and Rawls knew she had won before the judges even put up their scores. They ran over to the edge of the pool and greeted Gestring as she jumped out. She had a huge smile on her face, and the two women hugged her with genuine excitement. The three women had done what they set out to do; they swept the competition.

The US Women's Diving team, L-R, Katherine Rawls, Marjorie Gestring, Dorothy Poynton-Hill

Woodruff was elated and didn't hide it. As soon as Gestring hit the water, he sprang out of his seat and cheered. He wasn't alone; everyone in *Schwimmstadion* was standing and screaming. Even

Don Hume forgot his belly pain and overall achiness and jumped up and down like a schoolboy. Woodruff ran down to the sidelines and grabbed Marjorie as she was giving an interview to Holm. He lifted the girl high in the air and the crowd, which wasn't leaving, went crazy. Gestring was overjoyed. The little dolphin from the small town of Hillsborough, California, literally felt on top of the world.

DAY 12
August 13, 1936

In the town of Potsdam, Germany, just outside of Berlin, the sprawling movie studio called *Studio Babelsberg*, was Leni's home away from home. Complete with sound stages and outdoor lots, the industrial complex was turning into the central hub of the filmmaking community. It was before dawn, and all the studios were dark, except for a dim flickering of light coming from an editing room window, where Leni Riefenstahl was reviewing footage of the Games.

Strands of film were wrapped around her neck as she fed the movieola--a film viewing machine that was motor-controlled by foot pedals. It was a loud, obnoxious machine that sounded like machine gun fire as the celluloid rattled through the optical gate. Behind her in the studio, was an editing assistant sitting at a desk who was cataloguing the massive amounts of footage into a ledger.

Leni gazed into the viewer intensely, stopping occasionally to jot down some notes, until her foot suddenly lifted off the pedal to stop the motor. She was watching the dailies from Day 8, specifically the 4x100 meter relay. The shot racked focus and settled on Jesse Owens digging his feet into the starting blocks. She was instantly reminded of what Glenn Morris told her last night, after another one of their passionate and sweaty encounters. Glenn said that Marty Glickman and Sam Stoller, the only two Jews on the American track team, were suddenly replaced by Owens and Metcalf. Then she thought of the conversation she had with Ertl about their employment by the Nazis, and noticed that Ertl's camera was supremely focused on Jesse Owens. *Making a*

- 400 -

statement, Ertl?

She was interrupted by a knock on the door and a tall blonde woman, Claire, clumsily entered the studio carrying large movie posters. Leni unwrapped her neck with the strands of film and hung them in a film bin. She greeted Claire as old friends do, and helped her spread out the posters on the desk. They were samples of different fonts and sizes over various backgrounds to be used as title designs. Some said *"Berlin 1936"*, *"The XI Games"* and *"Olympia"*, and as Leni studied the options, something caught Claire's eye on the edge of the desk. It was a handwritten letter in black ink that looked like a child had scribbled all over it. She picked it up.

"Who wrote this?!" Claire exclaimed. Leni quickly snatched the letters from Claire and blushed.

"A friend of mine. And it's none of your business," she said, playfully. Claire stood with outstretched arms, silently demanding to see the letter. Leni knew that Claire wouldn't give up, so she surrendered and handed her the note.

Claire started reading, squinting her eyes, trying to make sense of the words, when finally, she said, "Oooh" and sat down in a chair smiling at Leni. She continued to read, struggling to decipher the handwriting. "Oh my!" she said, and Leni finally grabbed the letter from her and folded it up.

"You've read enough," she said, still blushing.

"Who is this friend of yours? A gorilla from the Berlin Zoo? My three-year-old writes more legibly. Although, I have to say, he doesn't mince words." Claire said with a sly grin.

"He's *my* gorilla," Leni said.

"I'll never eat off of your dining room table ever again."

"Very funny."

"Seriously, Leni, you can tell a lot about a person by the way they write. My guess, is that this individual was raised on a farm-- by farmers. It really doesn't suit you."

Leni put the letter in her pocket and tried to will herself to change the topic. She turned to the various title designs displayed on the desk and said, "I like this one," pointing to the poster that read, "*Olympia*". Claire separated it from the others and began pontificating about its merits, and the way the font meant this and that. All Leni could think about was Glenn Morris, and how much she loved him, despite what anyone thought of his handwriting.

Later that night, Leni and Glenn walked along an esplanade that overlooked the Spree River, which ran through the heart of Berlin. They held hands and stopped to gaze over the city. Glenn held her by the waist and moved in to kiss her.

"Stop," she said.

"What's the matter?" Glenn asked.

"The Games will be over soon. And you'll have to go back to America," she said, nestling her head into Glenn's chest.

"You can come with me. You'll love America. We'll go to California, and you can make films there," he said excitedly. "We'll take over the town!"

Leni let go and brushed past him, looking down at the river. "I can't leave Berlin. You know that." Glenn stood beside her and held her again. "But I could use a strong leading man here in Germany," she said, smiling.

Glenn flexed his muscles and struck a pose. "Never! Hollywood beckons!" She laughed and they kissed again.

"What are we going to do?" she asked, and they looked at each other, seriously, deeply.

After a minute of silence, Glenn said, "Let's go home." They walked hand in hand down the esplanade, slow and deliberate, trying to make the most of the time they had left together. Leni never thought anything like this would ever happen to her. There were romances, and a fling or two over the years, but this was different. She was deeply in love under the most unusual of circumstances. An American man, of all things. It didn't matter to her at all. He made her laugh and feel totally alive and free in a place that was increasingly becoming stifling and bound by rules and regulations.

Glenn was thinking the same thing, interrupted by flashes of their sexual romps, one of which was about to take place. But Leni was no shameless cornpone from Colorado. She was smart, sexy, funny, and intelligent. She opened his eyes to a world beyond anything he ever imagined. He loved everything about this woman, and thought he would never meet anyone like her ever again.

*   *   *

At the Hotel Adlon Kampenski, Hitler, Eva, and all the German officials including Carl Diem, who had made himself very scarce since the debacle at Hertha BSC Platz, attended a cocktail party sponsored by the German newspaper *Der Sturmer*. It was the night before the final day of competition. Germany had fared better than any other country, and the Nazi rag was quick to exploit it.

Brundage, who was also in attendance with many of the American reporters, wasn't feeling that bad himself. His team had fared well overall, second only to the host country in the medal count, and Avery walked around with a healthy strut. He noticed that a crowd of international reporters had congregated near one of the bars and seemed to be enjoying themselves collectively. He made his way to them, and his confidence, and demeanor, quickly dissipated as the crowd parted to reveal Eleanor Holm holding center court. And as she entertained the swelling group of journalists, Avery caught her eye. She didn't miss a beat; she subtly shot him the finger as she continued her story. He took the hint and quickly got the hell away from there.

But that only led him to Gould and Kieran, who intercepted him as he fled Holm. They were nice enough to have an extra glass of champagne for him as they led him to a cocktail table.

"Well Avery, this was quite the spectacle, wasn't it?" Kieran began. Avery was very intimidated by the respected columnist and thought hard before answering. He knew that his question was not complimentary.

"I believe the American team performed at the highest of levels," he said, and left it at that.

"Do you believe these were a fair Games?" Gould asked.

Again, Brundage took an extra second to gather his thoughts, "As humanly possible."

"Really?" Kieran asked, surprised. "Tell that to the Peruvians."

"I wasn't at that game, so I can't speak with any authority about how that transpired," he retorted.

"Do you believe all the athletes got a fair shake?" Gould shot back.

"Get to the point, Alan," Avery said.

"Let me rephrase that. Do you believe every athlete that could've participated, did?"

"I can't speak for the other countries, but the American team--" he suddenly thought of Stoller and Glickman, "well, I'm not sure." It was the first crack in Brundage's armor Gould had seen, and he jumped on it.

"Avery, as an IOC member, you are going to have to raise your standards. This whole charade was deplorable. And the IOC stood by and did nothing. No one ever checked on Gretel Bergmann's injury. You certainly didn't, did you?"

"I looked into the matter."

"And did nothing!" Gould shot back.

"I did what I could!"

"She was the one damned leg you had to stand on at the vote to come here, Avery!" Gould reminded him.

"You two sit behind your typewriters, thinking you know everything that goes on behind closed doors, because of a tip here or there, or an 'anonymous source' overheard from your bar stools, but you don't know anything about what I do or the people I'm dealing with!" Avery yelled in a hushed tone.

The three men paused, not wanting to make a scene. "Do you still think it was worth coming here?" Kieran asked, a little more calmly than his friend.

"Yes, I do. Our team performed at the highest of levels, so let's leave it at that," Brundage reiterated. "Now, if you will excuse me." He left the conversation abruptly, knowing the two reporters had gotten the best of him.

But on his way out the door, Holm got in his face. "One day, you micro-penised fuckwad, everyone is gonna know what happened here, and what happened between you and me. And it ain't gonna be pretty for you, Herr Brundage." Once again, she faked kneeing him, and once again Brundage recoiled. She walked away laughing. "Have a nice life, shithead."

DAY 13
August 14, 1936

At Schwimmstadion, Holm watched on as the finals of the Woman's Backstroke took place. And as expected, the two Dutch women, Senff and Mastenbroek earned Gold and Silver. But in a surprise, twenty-year-old Uxbridge, Mass. native Alice Bridges came in a close third, only two tenths of a second behind Mastenbroek. This brought some joy to Holm, but she only imagined what could have been.

She had decided in the last few days of competition to quit swimming all together and go back to Hollywood. Brundage had taken all the joy out of competing, and Holm wanted one more shot at stardom while she was still young and beautiful. She had also decided she didn't need her husband's permission. If Art didn't like her choice, he could stay in New York. She was very introspective and a little melancholy about it all. She had spent most of her life in the pool, and at one shining moment she was the very best of all the best in the world. She smiled. *At least she had that.*

*   *   *

The banks of Langer See, an offshoot of the river Dahme, flowed through the town of Grunau, a suburb of Berlin. Over 75,000 spectators flooded the town and lined the banks of the river. The final leg of the men's rowing competition was about to take place. Flags from the six final competing countries, The United States, Italy, Germany, Great Britain, Hungary, and Switzerland, stood tall in the wind near the starting line.

At the finish line, rows of bleachers were constructed to seat dignitaries and officials. Nazi banners surrounded the grounds. Hitler, Goebbels, and Goering took their seats, supremely confident that they would continue their dominance. Germany had won Gold in six of eight rowing competitions leading up to this finale, the eight-man final event. Osten and von Halt sat next to Latour right behind the Führer, and Brundage was also there with Margaret; the two of them surrounded by Nazi officials in full uniform.

Leni, with Glenn by her side and Ertl manning the camera, was in a perfect position to capture the finish. They were stationed on a buoy in the middle of the river. She had her crew install lighting balloons that were tied to other buoys nearby. Ertl performed last-minute preparations on his camera and gave her a thumbs up. Other cameras were stationed along the Langer See, ready and waiting for the race to begin. Leni loved the cinematic nature of the boats slicing through the water and the graceful timing of the rowing teams.

Suddenly, something caught her eye: her lighting balloon filled with helium must have sprung a leak and was starting to descend into the river. She was warned about her helium lighting balloons malfunctioning but did it anyway. Ertl reached out to the buoy to try and grab the line holding the balloon, and he slipped and fell into the water. The crowd laughed, but Leni was in a panic. Ertl's head emerged from the water and Glenn helped him back on top of the buoy. Dripping wet, he went back to his camera position and said, "We'll just have to do without it. I'm ready."

In the stands, Alan Gould sat next to Kieran, pens and pads at their side. He looked around for Eleanor, who should have been arriving soon. She had been covering the backstroke finals, and Gould thought that maybe it was wrong to have asked her to cover the event, that she probably would have won easily, had she not been kicked off the team. Eleanor finally arrived and sat next to him without saying a word.

"How'd it go?" Gould asked.

"Alice Bridges won a bronze."

"Thanks for covering."

"No Alan, thank you," Eleanor said. They nodded and smiled. Gould could only imagine what she was thinking, but it seemed that she had found some peace in all of this.

Down closer to the water's edge, members of the US Team stood in groups, mingling with athletes from other countries. They all wore the respective colors of their teams, ready to witness one of the final events of the Games. There was a relaxed camaraderie among them, along with some good-natured ribbing and teasing, and even a side wager or two. John Woodruff sat on a grassy bank next to Marjorie Gestring. Marty Glickman and Sam Stoller leaned against a railing near the finish line, proudly wearing their track sweatshirts, despite what had transpired just days earlier. Foy Draper and Frank Wycoff stood beside them; the former relay team united.

Louis Zamperini sat by himself and occasionally glanced over at Mayer, who was mingling with her German fencing teammates. She completely ignored him.

Jesse Owens, newly crowned four-time Gold medalist, arrived in a taxi with Ralph Metcalfe, Mack Robinson, and Archie Williams. Every athlete and spectator in attendance stood up and started cheering when they saw him. Jesse immediately spotted Luz Long, who was with his German track teammates, and the group walked over to greet them.

Luz said, "I almost expected to see you in that boat going for a fifth Gold."

"I would if they'd let me," Jesse said.

"Jesse and water don't mix," Metcalfe said. "But he'd probably win Gold anyway."

"Sorry to eat your bubble, but this is our race," Luz said

confidently.

"You mean 'burst' your bubble," Jesse corrected him once again. "Don't underestimate our team, Luz. They may be college boys, but they're a tight group." The two men and their respective teammates continued to joke and brag, until they heard a horn wail in the direction of the starting line.

Bob Moch sat pensively on the edge of the dock. He desperately wanted to tell his team that he was Jewish. It was all he could think about, especially after witnessing the events that had taken place these last two weeks. But he kept it to himself to protect them. What if Brundage had found out? Would he have been replaced at the last minute, the way Marty Glickman and Sam Stoller had been? What if the German Olympic officials found out? Would they be sabotaged like the Peruvian soccer team? He decided that it would be his secret until this was all over. Right now, it was go-time.

Moch studied the ripples on the water then looked up at the waving flags, carefully interpreting the wind speed and gusting tendencies. *Ideal conditions*, he thought. Everything seemed just right, but something was very wrong. Don Hume, the 'stroke' of the crew, responsible for setting the pace for the seven oarsmen rowing behind him, had his head down and his eyes closed. His breathing was labored throughout their entire warm-up. Moch had never seen his good friend so listless before a big race. Hume had been sick for two weeks straight, and his fever didn't wane at all. Moch wondered how he would get through the tremendous physical punishment that awaited.

Shorty Hunt, sitting behind Hume, said, "You're not gonna puke in this boat, are you?"

Hume slowly raised his head, and the team took notice, anxiously waiting to hear what he had to say. He took a deep breath and said, "I'm only gonna puke if I have to hear that goddamn German anthem one more time. Let's win this thing."

The team howled and Moch patted him on the back.

They untied the boat and sculled out to the starting line where the other teams were positioned. Moch nodded towards the Italian coxswain, Cesare Milani, who smiled and nodded back. There was a mutual respect between them since their hard-fought practice run days earlier. Moch then caught the eye of the German coxswain and gave a nod. There was no response. The Italians and the Germans were the two teams to beat. He would have to keep a keen eye on them during the race. He turned to his team and said, "Gentlemen, today we row the best we know how, and we *will* get there."

From that point, everything went wrong.

The horn bellowed and the race was on. Notoriously slow starters, the college team from Washington fell behind instantly. They were completely out of sync, and Moch yelled his orders louder than ever, urging them to focus. "Push! Pull!" he screamed, as the Germans and Italians fought for the lead.

About halfway through the 2000m race, the Americans were still dragging along. Moch thought, *my God, we've come all the way from Seattle just to end like this. It can't happen.* Just then, Don Hume's eyes lit up. With about 800 meters to go, he found something within and began rowing with authority. His teammates responded to Hume's emerging strength and the boat started to really fly. They overtook Great Britain but were still a full boat length behind the Germans and Italians. The crowd chanted *"Deutch-land! Deutch-land!"* as the finish line closed in.

Moch, Hume, Shorty Hunt, and the team, were screaming with every row, and with each thrust got closer and closer to the Italians. Then, the resolve from countless hours of practice kicked in. The training in Washington, the nights on the Hudson, and the grueling trials, all led to this moment. Their oars ripped through the waters with powerful synchronicity and with 300 meters to go, they were tied with the Italians. Germany was right there.

In the stands, Hitler couldn't believe what he was witnessing. Everyone was on their feet cheering wildly. Brundage and Margaret were chanting "U.S.A." with the other American spectators. The athletes were all jumping up and down, yelling and rooting for their teams. It was destined to be a finish for the ages.

During the final sprint, Moch and his boys unleashed every ounce of strength within themselves. Twenty strokes left, ten, five . . . and they crossed the finish line with a vigorous final stroke. They all collapsed in a collective heap and Hume finally puked over the side of the boat. They didn't know if they had won at that moment, and as they lay on their backs catching their breath, they heard over the loudspeaker, "U.S.A.-- 6:25:4 . . . Italy--6:26.0 . . . Germany – 6:26.4," and the team erupted in celebration. They had beaten the Italians by six-tenths of a second, a mere two feet, and the Germans by exactly one second. They hugged and hollered and waved to the crowd on the shore.

Hitler, astonished, turned to von Halt and whispered something in his ear. Latour noticed, and leaned into Hitler. "Nothing you can do about it this time!" Latour said, referring to the Peru vs. Austria debacle. Hitler and von Halt looked away in silence.

The other American athletes who had witnessed the unlikely victory were jumping up and down, embracing each other in celebration. Jesse and his track team, Marjorie and the divers, Eleanor, and Gould . . . it was a monumental closing event, and the underdogs were victorious. Even the other country's athletes couldn't help but get caught up in the excitement, applauding the heroic effort of all the competitors.

After regrouping on the boat, the team paddled over to the docks where they received the victors' laurel wreaths. Bob Moch put his arm around Don Hume. It was the most emotional moment of his life. The college team from Seattle had won the

Gold medal. It was the biggest upset of the Games, and their legacy would live on in the hearts of every American athlete to come.

The US Team (at top), beats the Italian and German teams by a nose to win the Gold.

CLOSING CEREMONIES
August 16, 1936

A full moon hung low in the night sky as people filtered into *Olympiastadion* for the last time. Officials and dignitaries from every country, athletes of all colors and creeds, spectators, coaches, janitors, vendors, and finally the press, came together in the giant arena like a potluck stew of humanity. As Gould entered the press box, he could feel the bittersweet emotions in the air. Nobody wanted it to end, but knew it needed to.

One by one, each country marched around the track, lit only by a giant spotlight from above Hitler's box. Leni wanted to float lighting balloons, but after the rowing final was almost interrupted (and Ertl almost drowned), her request was denied. She stood above Ertl on the edge of the track and couldn't help but laugh. He looked back at her, confused, and then dutifully went back to filming the parade.

The athletes waved to the crowd, smiling like never before, and they were hailed with standing ovations and chants. As each country's team passed Hitler's box, they lowered their flags to honor the Führer; all except the American team. When they passed, their flag remained standing tall. They didn't even look his way. Hitler expected that, even though he desperately wanted the Americans to pay their respects. *Ungrateful vermin*, he thought. He glanced at Avery Brundage, who, by his surprise, looked back at him with a thin smile. Osten and von Halt, Goebbels, Diem, and the rest of the Nazi officials, all looked tired and worn and maybe a bit relieved that this chapter was coming to an end. They could relax for one night, at least. But for them, another much bigger, and global, production would soon be underway.

The Olympic flame that stood at the top of the arena was dying out and the white flag with its colored rings was lowered to half-mast. Flags from each country stood side by side in order of total medals won; the Nazi flag waved right next to the American flag. Latour walked to the podium to address the athletes.

"We are gathered here again this evening, in this wonderful country, after fifteen unforgettable days. The Olympic Games are a celebration of humanity, and together we have experienced many strong emotions. We have shared the joy of dreams fulfilled. We have been moved by both tears of elation and tears of defeat. We have witnessed extraordinary acts of courage, and exceptional determination by athletes who refused to give up. Thank you to the people of Germany, for your generous hospitality, your warmth, and this unique celebration of sport. In four years' time, we will meet again in Tokyo, Japan. Until then, farewell, and thank you."

Gould shook hands with Kieran and the other reporters and took a seat behind his typewriter. He looked around the stadium at the spectacle. The athletes were all lined up in neat rows. The stands were jam-packed, shoulder-to-shoulder. The smell of torches hung in the air. He took a breath and began to write . . .

> As these Games come to a close, I wonder
> what's to become of these athletes who
> left their hearts on the track and field . . .

Luz Long raced through the mud surrounded by machine gun fire. It was 1943 in Sicily, Italy, and he was separated from his unit. His long jumping skills came in handy during the war, leaping over streams and craters left by mortar rounds. And dead bodies. Dodging enemy fire, he leaped over a small hill only to find himself suddenly surrounded by enemy troops. He was riddled with bullets and died instantly.

Carl Ludwing "Luz" Long would posthumously receive the PIERRE de COUBERTIN medal for sportsmanship for the way he treated Jesse Owens during the Olympics. He and Jesse continued their friendship by writing letters to each other until the Nazi invasion of Poland in 1939.

At Ohio State University, Jesse Owens, donned in a cap and gown, stood at a podium speaking at an all-black college commencement. The star-struck crowd stared in awe at the man who crushed Hitler's myth of Aryan supremacy.

James Cleveland "Jesse" Owens would go on to become an American icon and leader of the African American fight for equality throughout the rest of his life. His four Olympic Gold medals and numerous world records would stand for decades, ranking him as one of the greatest athletes who ever lived. After Luz Long perished in the war, he continued correspondence with Luz's son, enduring a friendship that lasted until his death.

Phoenix, AZ, 1980. Marty Glickman was late for a funeral. He sprinted up the steps of the church and thrust open the door to see Jesse Owens' body laid out on the altar. The crowd turned to face Marty, who slid into a pew in the back row. Jesse's track teammates, including Archie Williams, Long John Woodruff, Ralph Metcalfe, and Mack Robinson, urged Marty to come forward and join them on the altar to honor Jesse. He was the only white teammate from the '36 Games who made the trip to Jesse's funeral.

Martin Irving "Marty" Glickman had four children with his high school sweetheart Marjorie. He became the first TV announcer for the NBA and had a long, illustrious career as a sports broadcaster. He was the voice of the NY Giants, Jets, and Knicks, coining his trademark call,

"Swish!" He returned to Berlin Olympic Stadium in 1986 to honor Jesse's achievements. When he entered the Olympic Stadium, "suddenly a wave of rage overwhelmed me. Being there, reliving those moments, caused an eruption which had been gnawing at me for so long and which I thought I had expunged years ago." Marty died in 2001 as a decorated Marine for his service in WWII, having never come to peace with his removal from the 4x100 relay team.

Gould continued . . .
> The camaraderie between these young
> participants has transcended race,
> color, creed, and gender . . .

Dora Ratjen sat on a train traveling from Vienna to Cologne. He wore a flowered dress, tall-heeled shoes, and tried to shield his face with a hat adorned with daisies. A conductor walked by and paused when he reached Dora's seat. He peered at him to get a closer look, then nodded and went on his way. Moments later, the conductor returned; this time leading a police officer to Dora's seat. He was arrested on the spot.

Heinrich "Dora" Ratjen would be revealed to be a man dressed in women's clothing. He would be sent to an asylum for treatment. Upon his release he would be lost in obscurity for many years tending his family's bar in rural Germany; a job he held until his death in 2008. He never spoke to the hawking press that hounded him for the last twenty years of his life.

Gretel Bergmann was finally in America, competing in an international track competition. She took her place at the starting line and sprinted forward. She effortlessly cleared the bar, landing as softly as she had done in her father's backyard as a child.

Gretel Lambert Bergmann emigrated to the United States in 1937 and continued her athletic dominance in the high jump. The field she trained on as a child in Laupheim, Germany became the Gretel Bergmann Track and Field Facility. Gretel would travel there for the grand opening in 1999. It would be the first trip home since 1937, and her last.

Gould continued . . .
> The heroism they have displayed is
> matched only by the greatest of
> warriors.

Archie Williams paced back and forth in front of a group of pilots on the tarmac of an airfield. Young black pilots stood at attention. A row of B-17 bombers loomed behind them.

When he came home from the Olympics, someone asked Archie how the Nazis treated him. He said, "I only saw a bunch of nice German people... and I didn't have to ride in the back of the bus over there." During World War II, Archibald Franklin "Archie" Williams became an instructor for the African American Tuskegee Airmen and in his words, "returned to the Olympics--in the Pacific."

John Woodruff was in the middle of a three-on-three basketball game with inner-city kids in a gymnasium somewhere in New York City. He towered over the excited kids and looked for an opening to pass the ball.

John Youie "Long John" Woodruff became an officer in the Army and served in WWII and Korea. After his service he would become a mainstay in coaching youth athletes in the New York/New Jersey area. In 1937, John set a world record in an 800m race in Dallas, Tex., but it was rescinded because the track was measured "six feet too short." John planted an oak tree seed in Connellsville, Penn., that had been given as a gift to all the departing athletes in 1936. To this day, the tree stands at a towering 80 feet. Woodruff died in 2007 at his home in Arizona.

Marjorie Gestring stood atop a "1938 US Nationals" podium, adorned in a 1st Place ribbon and medal. Consistent with her team-first ideals initiated by Dorothy Poynton-Hill and Katherine Rawls in Berlin, she put her arms around her two runners-up and smiled for the cameras.

Marjorie Gestring, aka "The Little Dolphin," held the national title of every major springboard event from 1937 to 1939. In 1940, after the cancellation of the Tokyo Olympics, the US Olympic Committee awarded her a Gold medal in lieu of the games taking place, unanimously agreeing that Marjorie would have won Gold anyway.

Dorothy Poynton-Hill retired from competitive diving after the games. She opened her own aquatic club in Los Angeles, and was featured in many product endorsements, namely Camel cigarettes.

In 1937, Katherine Rawls became a National Champion in four different swimming events. By 1938, she held eighteen different national swimming records. In WWII, she became a pilot and helped form the Women's Auxiliary Ferrying Squadron in 1942, transporting military cargo by air as part of the US war effort.

Louis Zamperini spoke at a podium in front of a large group of people. A cross hung on a wall behind him.

Louis Silvie Zamperini enlisted in the US Air Force at the start of the World War II. He was shot down and lasted 47 days adrift in the Pacific where he was taken prisoner by the Japanese and treated savagely until the end of the war. He returned to California to a hero's welcome. He married and became a Christian evangelist and inspirational speaker.

Foy Draper gained control of his bomber as enemy fighters swarmed all around him, pounding his aircraft with bullets. His plane disappeared into a thick cloud of black smoke from the heavy shelling of anti-aircraft guns.

Foy Draper and his crewmen never returned from the Battle of Kassarine Pass over Tunisia in 1943.

Gould continued . . .
> And though the road may be rocky
> in the future, the decision to
> compete in these Olympic Games
> for their countries, and the
> sacrifices they made, will ring
> forever not only in their lifetimes,
> but in the collective consciences
> of all people.

Helene Mayer, at an exhibition in the United States, thrust her foil directly into the heart of her competitor. She ripped off her mask after taking the final point in the match.

Helene Julie Mayer returned to the US and continued to compete, and win, in fencing tournaments up until 1946. In 1952, she returned to Germany, married, settled, and died of breast cancer two months shy of her 43rd birthday.

Mack Robinson proudly put on his 1936 Olympic track warm-up jacket in front of a mirror and smiled. He exited his home in darkness.

While his brother Jackie Robinson would make baseball history in the coming years, Matthew MacKenzie "Mack" Robinson brought his 200-meter Silver medal back to his home in Pasadena, CA, where the only job he could find was as a street sweeper during pre-dawn hours. He angered the residents there by wearing his Olympic jacket on every shift.

Bob Moch sat on a swing with his wife watching their thirteen grandchildren play in the pool in his backyard.

Bob Moch and his "Boys in the Boat" all lived very long lives. Their unlikely victory over the Germans is considered one of the greatest athletic achievements of the 20th century.

Glenn Morris proudly wore a loincloth as he walked onto a movie set. The director called him over to rehearse the stunt scene that was about to take place.

After his love affair with Leni Riefenstahl, Glenn Edgar Morris returned to the US and tried to become a movie star. He played Tarzan in his one and only film role. Bad reviews led to him dropping the career. Eleanor Holm co-starred with him in "Tarzan's Revenge" where Glenn was seriously injured during a stunt sequence.

Eleanor Holm swam under the spotlights of an outdoor nightclub theater, pausing occasionally to dry off and drink champagne backstage.

After "Tarzan's Revenge" was released, Eleanor Holm appeared in four films as herself. She married the impresario Billy Rose and did 39 shows a week at Rose's "Aquacade" co-featured with Johnny Weissmuller. In 1954, her sensational divorce trial was deemed "The War of the Roses". Years later she married an oil-drilling executive and in 1966 was inducted into the International Swimming Hall of Fame.

She died at the age of 91 in Miami, FL, still holding her grudge against Avery Brundage.

At 101 years old, Leni Riefenstahl, in full SCUBA gear, was 40-feet underwater filming aquatic life for her documentary *"Impressionen Unter Wasser."*

Leni Riefenstahl is regarded as one of the most influential filmmakers in cinema history. Her film OLYMPIA, the detailed chronology of the 1936 Olympics, is considered a landmark motion picture. Legions of filmmakers would mimic her techniques in sports photography for decades to come. In 1939, shortly after the invasion of Poland, she joined the German troops and documented the takeover of a small town. There, after a group of Polish citizens staged an uprising, Nazi soldiers executed them one by one until Leni tried to stop them. She was threatened at gunpoint not to interfere. It was the last film she made for the Nazis. She was later arrested while hitchhiking outside of Berlin, and never completely shed her associations with the Nazi Party.

On her deathbed, she professed her undying love for Glenn Morris. The two lovers would mutually express their regret for not fulfilling the enchanting relationship they shared in Berlin.

Gould writes . . .
> They triumphed over the underlying,
> dark political mood surrounding
> these Games, and at times tried
> to pervade them.

At Hitler's vacation house in the Bavarian Alps, Joseph Goebbels presented him with a ledger. They shook hands and opened the book on a table. It was filled with pages and pages of notes and figures, *reichsmarks* in the tens of thousands listed beside each heading such as "tickets," "concessions," and "sponsors." All things considered, they were more than pleased with the way the Games unfolded. Hitler looked out over the mountains and smiled. The resources they accumulated during the Games would travel straight to the Nazi War Machine.

In 1945, as the Russian Red Army surrounded Berlin, Hitler would aid Eva Braun in her third, and final, suicide attempt. Huddled together in a basement bunker in Berlin, only forty hours after getting married in a civil ceremony, Eva bit into a cyanide capsule and Hitler blew his brains out with a pistol. When discovered, their corpses were burned.

The following day, Joseph Goebbels and his wife committed suicide after poisoning their six children with cyanide.

In the center of *Olympiastadion*, Carl Diem addressed a rally of thousands of teenage Hitler Youth in Berlin, 1945. He exhorted them to defend the capital to the death. As the Red Army closed in, they did exactly that.

After the war, Carl Diem avoided persecution despite his long association with the Nazi Party, maintaining that his duty was strictly devoted to "sport" and not politics. He assimilated into the mainstream of the newly democratic Federal Republic of Germany and became the Director of the Berlin University Physical Education Department.

Theodor Lewald continued his advisory role as a member of the IOC under intense pressure to leave. He officially resigned in 1938. Many of his innovations, including the torch relay, remain a staple of Olympic ceremonies to this day. He died of pneumonia in 1947 in Berlin.

In March of 1943, Hans von Tschammer und Osten took his last breath on his deathbed in Berlin. He also died from pneumonia, penniless despite his years of service. A Nazi to the very end, he never saw

Germany lose World War II.

Von Halt sat in a wooden booth in a smoky room at the Nuremberg hearings in 1945, beads of sweat pouring down the back of his suit as he listened to evidence mounting against him.

Karl Ritter von Halt succeeded Osten as Sportsfuhrer in 1943 and would lead a 1945 uprising of German war veterans against Russia. He would be caught and spend the next five years in prison in the former concentration camp of Buchenwald. The Nuremberg trials found him not guilty of being a Nazi – Avery Brundage's testimony of his innocence being the deciding factor in their decision. Despite his exoneration, in 2006 the residents of the old Olympic town of Garmisch-Partenkirchen, protested to rename a Fußball stadium named after him. He died in Munich in 1964.

Putzi walked with a group of American officials through the halls of the White House. They entered FDR's office, and he handed the President a dossier.

After surviving his "jump" into the Alps, Ernst "Putzi" Hanfstaengl wormed his way to London, where he was discovered and imprisoned after the outbreak of WWII. He was moved to a prison camp in Canada before he was turned over to the U.S. where he worked on Roosevelt's "S-Project". He provided information on over 400 Nazi leaders, including 68 pages on Hitler alone, giving details of the Führer's private life. In 1944, he was handed back to the British, who repatriated him to Germany after the war. He never saw Martha Dodd again. He died in Munich in 1975.

At his country home in Round Hill, Virginia, William Dodd sat on the back porch writing the last chapter of his book, "*The Old South: Struggles for Democracy.*" His wife Mattie looked over and smiled, happy to finally be back home.

After leaving his State Department post, William Dodd traveled on a speaking tour of the US and Canada, warning against the dangers posed by Germany, Italy, and Japan. He predicted German aggression against Austria, Poland, and Czechoslovakia. While his cautions went unheeded during his tenure in Berlin, at the Nuremburg Trials in 1946, Dodd's words were finally recognized when his diaries were used as evidence against numerous high-ranking Nazis. He died in peace in 1940.

After leaving Berlin, Bill Dodd, Jr. became a political activist and raised money on behalf of the homeless children who suffered during the Spanish Civil War. In the 1940's he became the target of a congressional crusade against communist sympathizers and was deprived of his position and salary. He lived out the rest of his life as a Macy's Department Store clerk.

Martha Dodd remained "close friends" with those in high circles, Nazis and spies of the Soviet Union NKVD. She engaged in espionage during WWII right through the Cold War. In 1956, when she was subpoenaed to testify in several espionage cases, she fled to Prague via Mexico with her adopted son. In the 1970's, she tried to negotiate her return to live in the United States. Her request was denied.

Avery Brundage sat alone in a hotel room in Munich during the Olympics in 1972. On the television, a masked terrorist held an Israeli athlete at gunpoint.

Avery Brundage became the President of the International Olympic Committee in 1952 and held the position for twenty years. Brundage was the sole word on continuing the Games after the horrible events that occurred to the Israeli team at the Munich Olympics in 1972, once again proving his nonchalant attitude towards the fortunes of the Jewish people. Brundage retired from the IOC later that year. In a hospital in Garmisch-Partenkirchen in 1975, Avery Brundage succumbed to heart failure at the age of 87. He died in the arms of his wife, a German princess who was 37 years old. He left his entire fortune to her and nothing to his two children.

Gould concludes . . .

> It is in this reporter's opinion,
> the heated debate whether to
> participate in these Games, was
> made moot by the athlete's behavior
> to rise above. A wise woman once
> told me 'no matter how much passion
> fans have for their sport, a
> knockout, a home run, a touchdown,
> is not comparable to famine, loss
> of life, and unemployment.' This is
> true, but the Games of the XI Olympiad
> will be remembered as the most
> important sporting event in history.

Alan Gould watched his children playing in the living room of his home in Elmira, New York. His wife Mary snuggled next to him on the couch. On the television was John Kieran's *"Kaleidoscope,"* a highly popular syndicated TV show.

Alan Gould and Mary remained married for 46 years until her death in 1966. He became the Executive Editor of the Associated Press soon after the Olympic Games. In January of 1944 he was sent to England to cover the Allied invasion of Europe. He remained with the organization until 1963 and under Gould's tenure the organization won 14 Pulitzer Prizes – none of them came with a beautiful woman's breasts to kiss.

The authors' extensive research of this topic spans over twenty-five years. Since 1996, they have studied every facet of the 1936 Olympic Games, acquiring insight from books, newspaper articles, documentaries and feature films, interviews, and museums. Some of these include:

Books:

- *Triumph – The Untold Story of Jesse Owens and Hitler's Olympics* – Jeremy Schaap
- *Unbroken* – Laura Hillenbrand
- *The Boys in the Boat* - Daniel James Brown
- *In the Garden of Beasts* – Erik Larson
- *The Games of 1936* – Stan Cohen

Documentaries:

- *Hitler's Pawns*
- *Glickman*

Films:

- *Olympia* – Leni Reifenstahl
- *Triumph of the Will* - Leni Reifenstahl
- *Berlin '36*

Other:

- National Holocaust Museum
- National Archives
- UCLA Library of Television
- NY Times archives
- Associated Press archives
- Footage Farm – Eleanor Holm interview

Photo Credits
(All Used by Permission)

(Page numbers may slightly vary. Ebook pages will be approximate if displayed in your e-reader like a traditional trade book.)